THE GRAPHIC NOVEL
William Shakespeare

QUICK TEXT VERSION

Script Adaptation: John McDonald
Pencils: Neill Cameron
Inks: Bambos
Coloring: Jason Cardy & Kat Nicholson
Lettering: Nigel Dobbyn

American English Adaptation: Keith Howell
Design & Layout: Jo Wheeler & Greg Powell
Publishing Assistant: Joanna Watts
Additional Information: Karen Wenborn

Editor in Chief: Clive Bryant

Henry V: The Graphic Novel
Quick Text Version

William Shakespeare

First US Edition

Published by: Classical Comics Ltd
Copyright ©2008 Classical Comics Ltd.

All enquiries should be addressed to:
Classical Comics Ltd.
PO Box 7280
Litchborough
Towcester
NN12 9AR
United Kingdom

Email: info@classicalcomics.com
Web: www.classicalcomics.com

ISBN: 978-1-906332-43-3

Printed by SURE Print & Design
using biodegradable vegetable inks on environmentally friendly paper.
This material can be disposed of by recycling,
incineration for energy recovery, composting and biodegradation.

The rights of John McDonald, Neill Cameron, Bambos, Jason Cardy,
Kat Nicholson and Nigel Dobbyn to be identified as the Artists of this work have been
asserted in accordance with the Copyright, Designs and Patents Act 1988 sections 77 and 78.

Contents

Dramatis Personæ

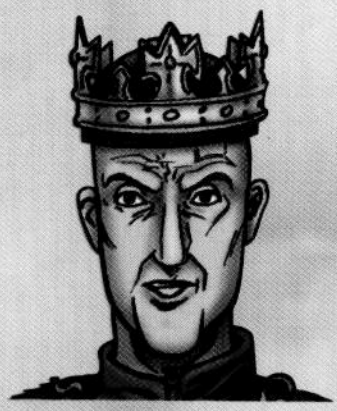

King Henry the Fifth
King of England

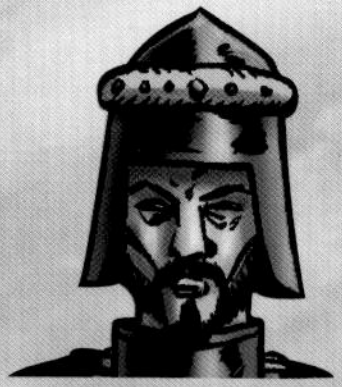

Duke Of Gloucester
Brother to the King

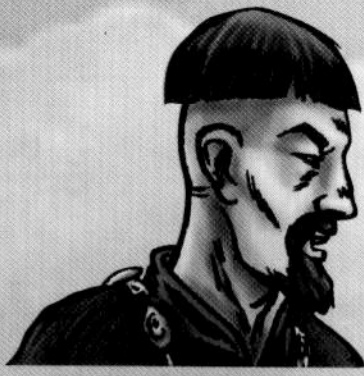

Duke Of Bedford
Brother to the King

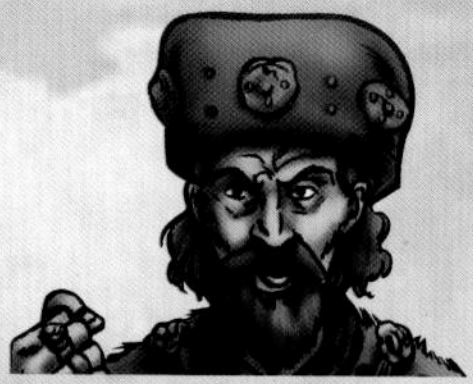

Duke Of Exeter
Uncle to the King

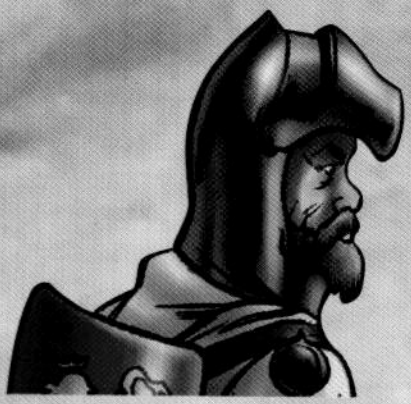

Duke Of York
Cousin to the King

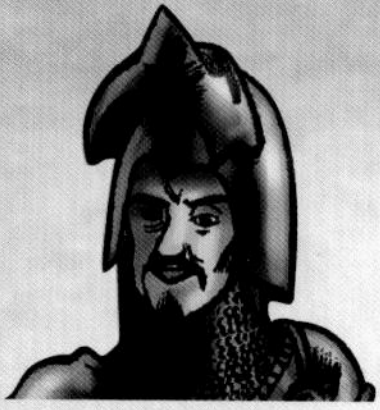

Earl Of Salisbury

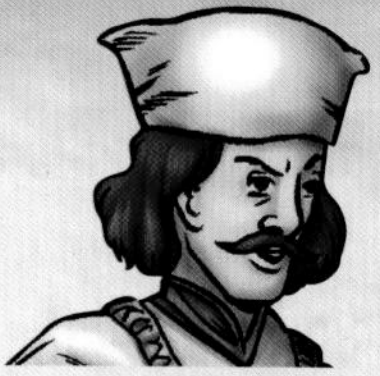

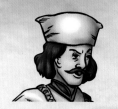

Earl Of Westmoreland

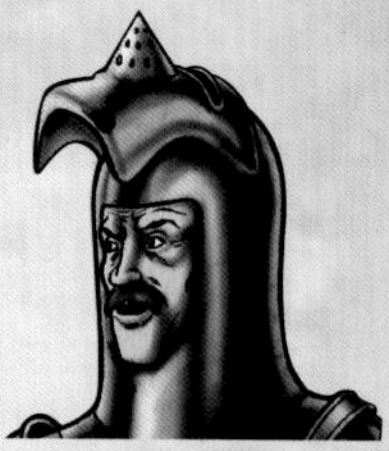

Earl Of Warwick

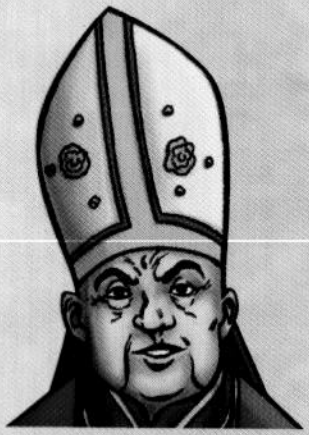

Archbishop Of Canterbury

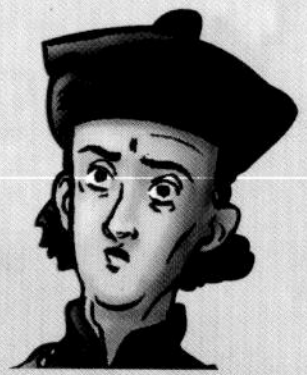

Bishop Of Ely

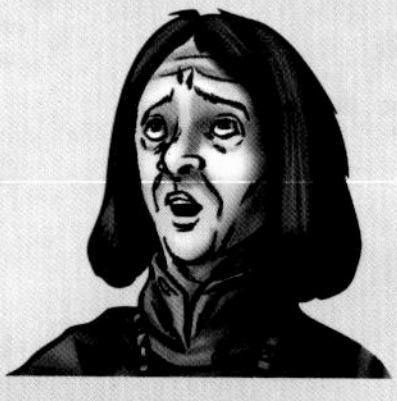

Earl Of Cambridge
Conspirator

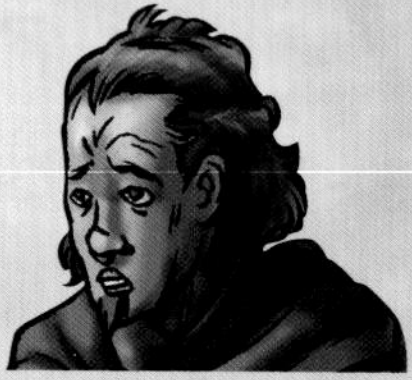

Henry, Lord Scroop of Masham
Conspirator

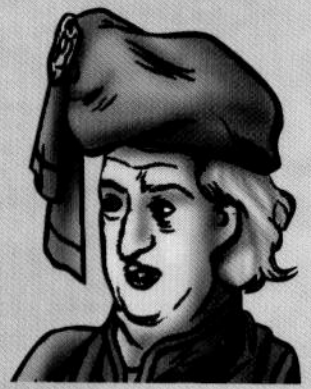

Sir Thomas Grey
Conspirator

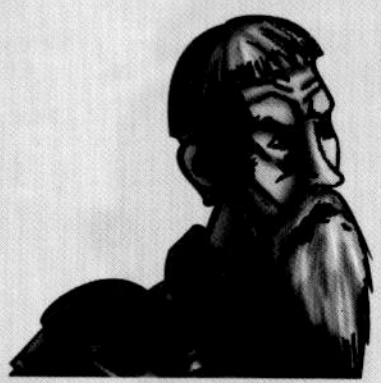

Sir Thomas Erpingham
Officer in King Henry's army

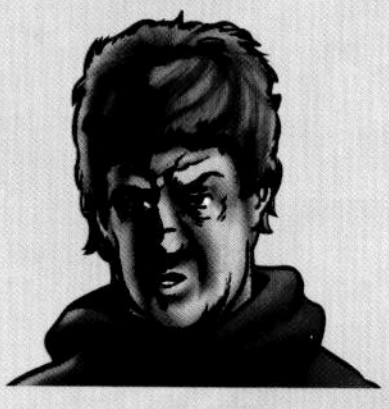

Captain Gower
Officer in King Henry's army

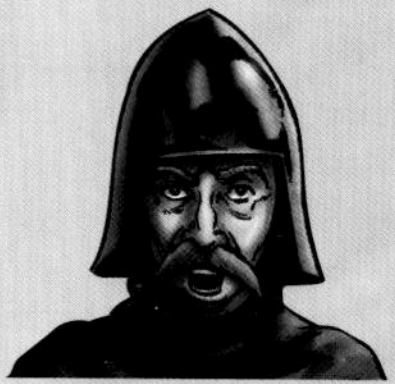

Captain Fluellen
Officer in King Henry's army

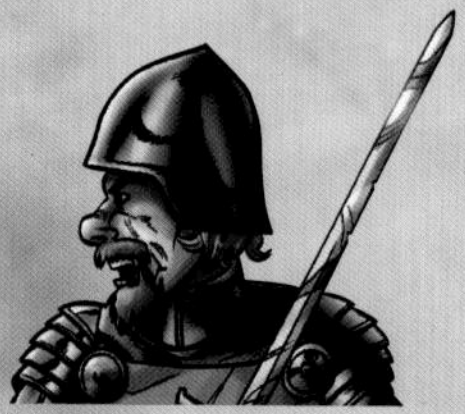

Captain Macmorris
Officer in King Henry's army

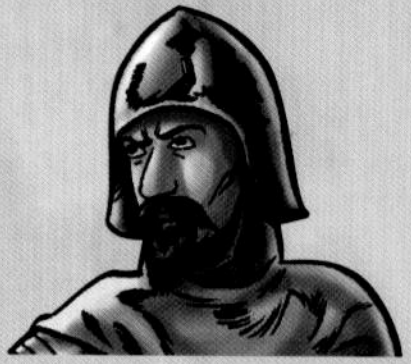

Captain Jamy
Officer in King Henry's army

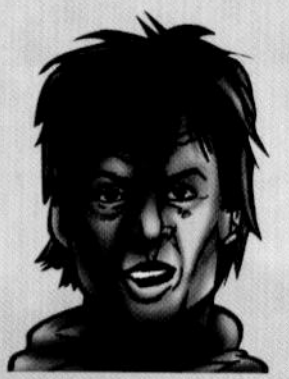

John Bates
Soldier in King Henry's army

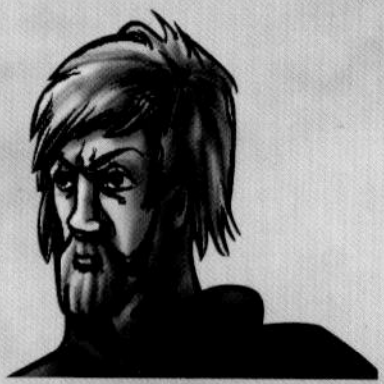

Alexander Court
Soldier in King Henry's army

Dramatis Personæ

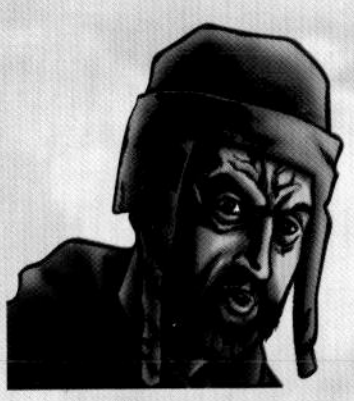

Michael Williams
Soldier in King Henry's army

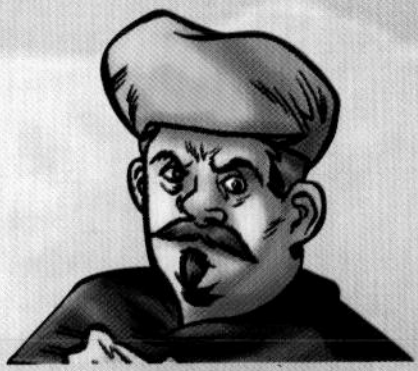

Pistol
Soldier in King Henry's army

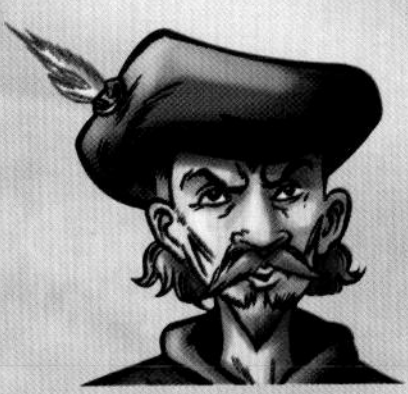

Nym
Soldier in King Henry's army

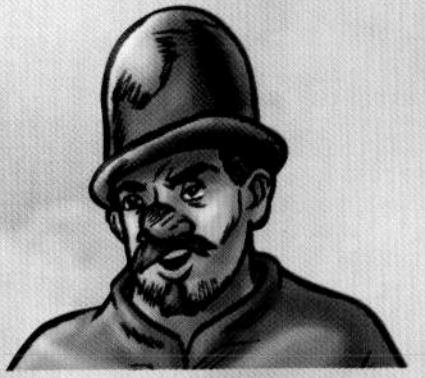

Bardolph
Soldier in King Henry's army

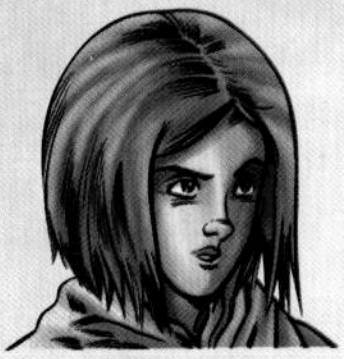

Boy
Servant

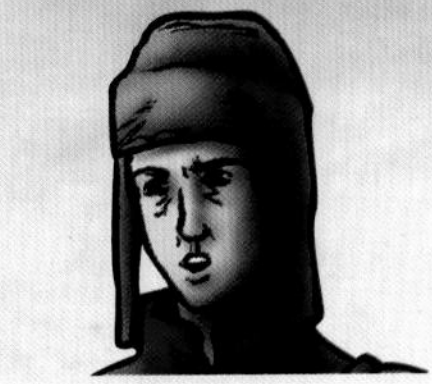

A Herald

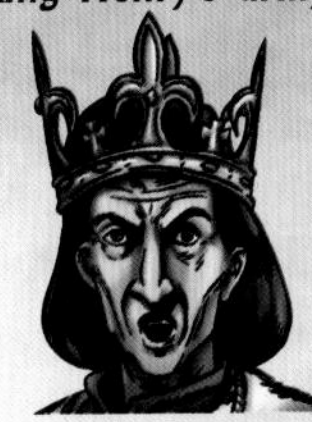

Charles the Sixth
King of France

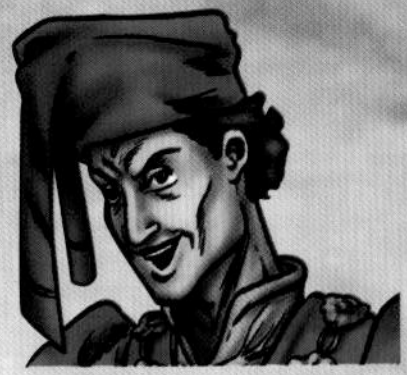

Lewis
The Dauphin

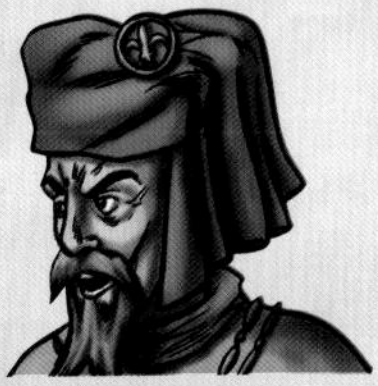

Duke Of Bourbon
French Duke

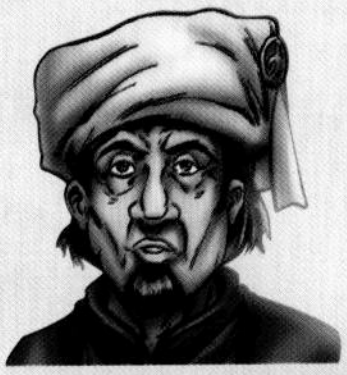

Duke Of Burgundy
French Duke

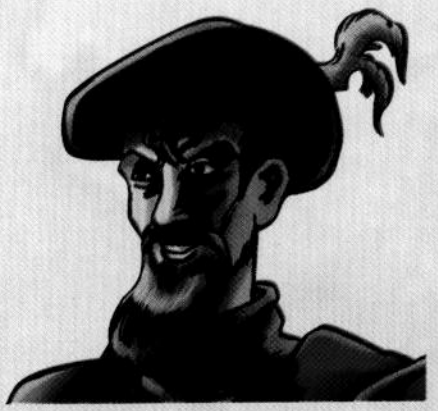

Duke Of Orleans
French Duke

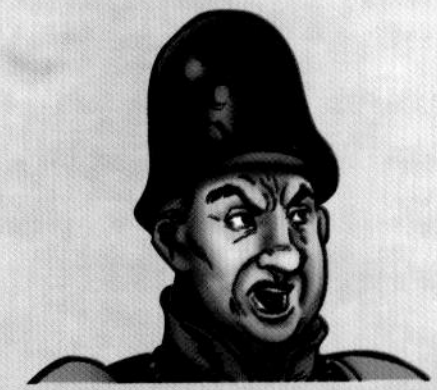

The Constable of France

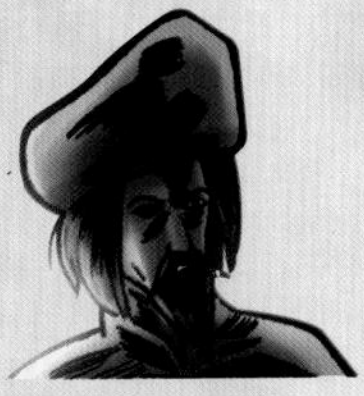

Lord Rambures
French Lord

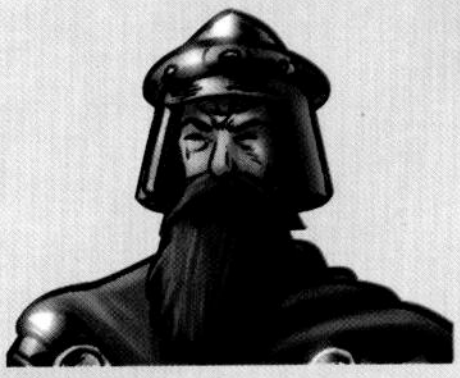

Lord Grandpré
French Lord

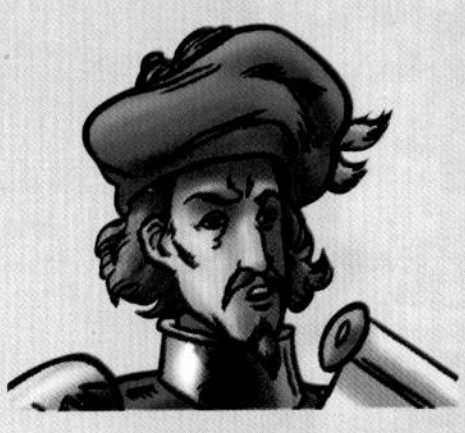

Montjoy
French Herald

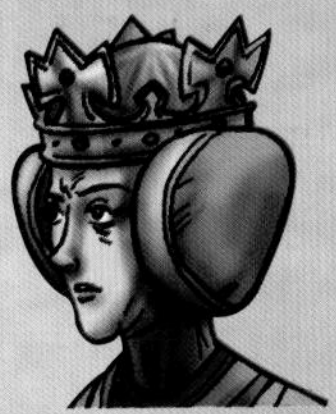

Queen Isabel
Queen of France

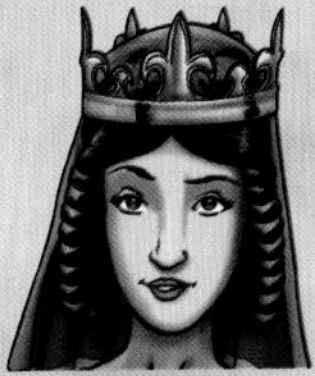

Katherine
Daughter to Charles and Isabel

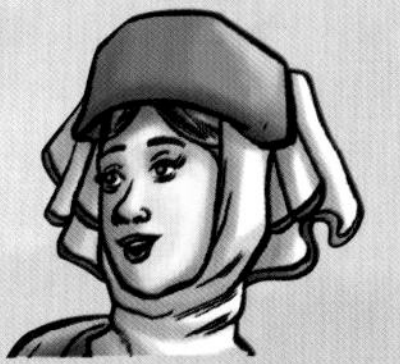

Alice
A lady attending on Katherine

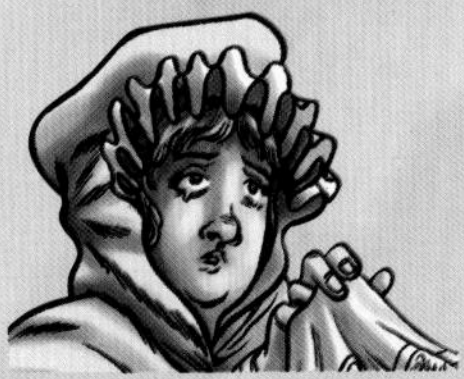

Hostess of a tavern
Formerly Mistress Quickly

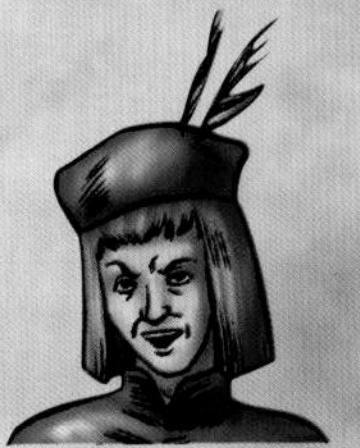

Chorus

Henry V

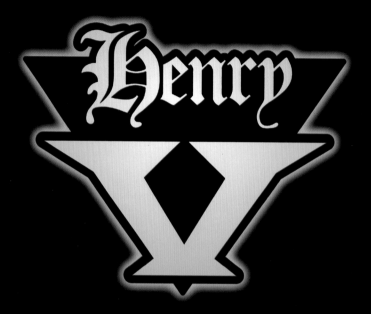

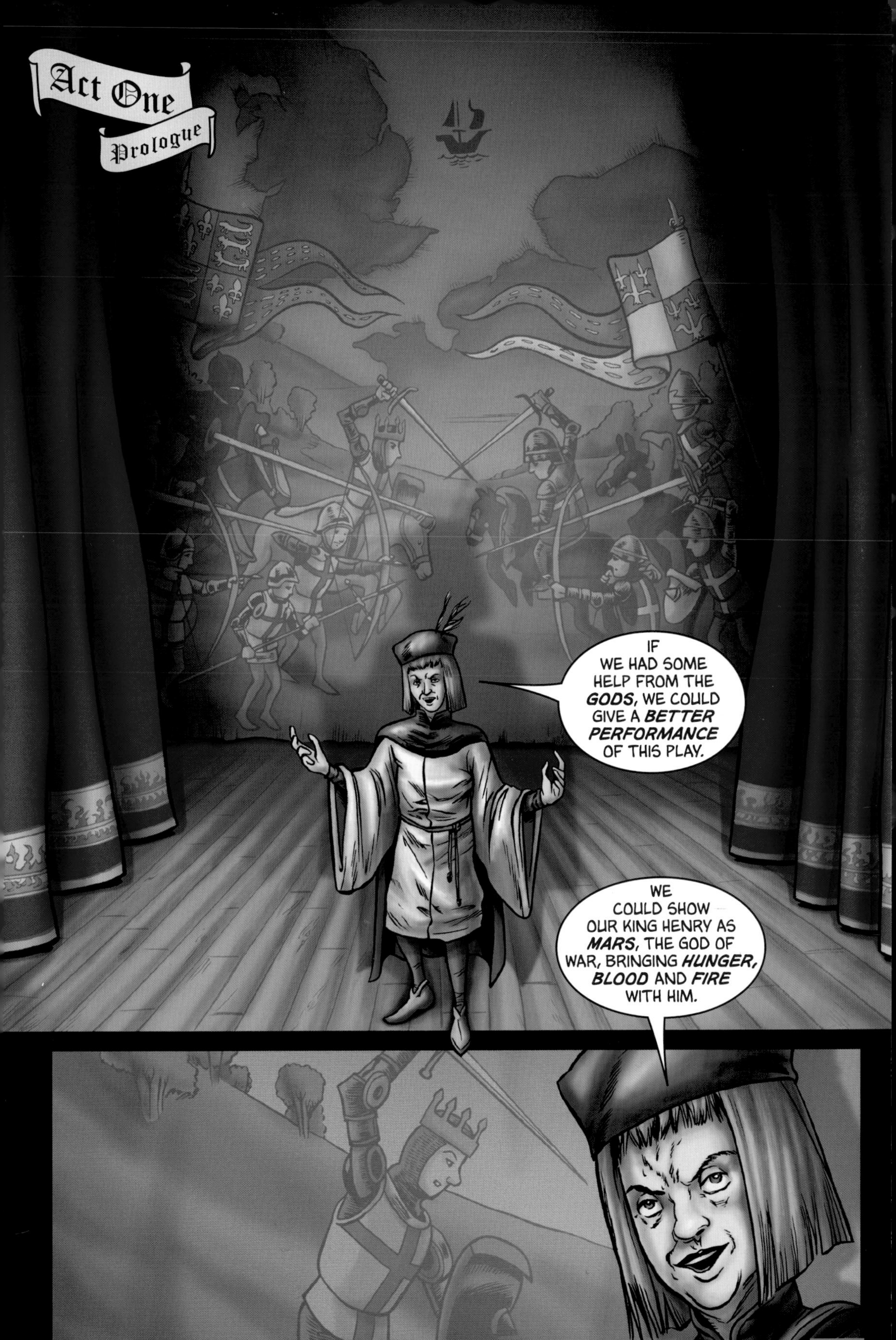
Act One
Prologue
IF WE HAD SOME HELP FROM THE GODS, WE COULD GIVE A BETTER PERFORMANCE OF THIS PLAY.
WE COULD SHOW OUR KING HENRY AS MARS, THE GOD OF WAR, BRINGING HUNGER, BLOOD AND FIRE WITH HIM.

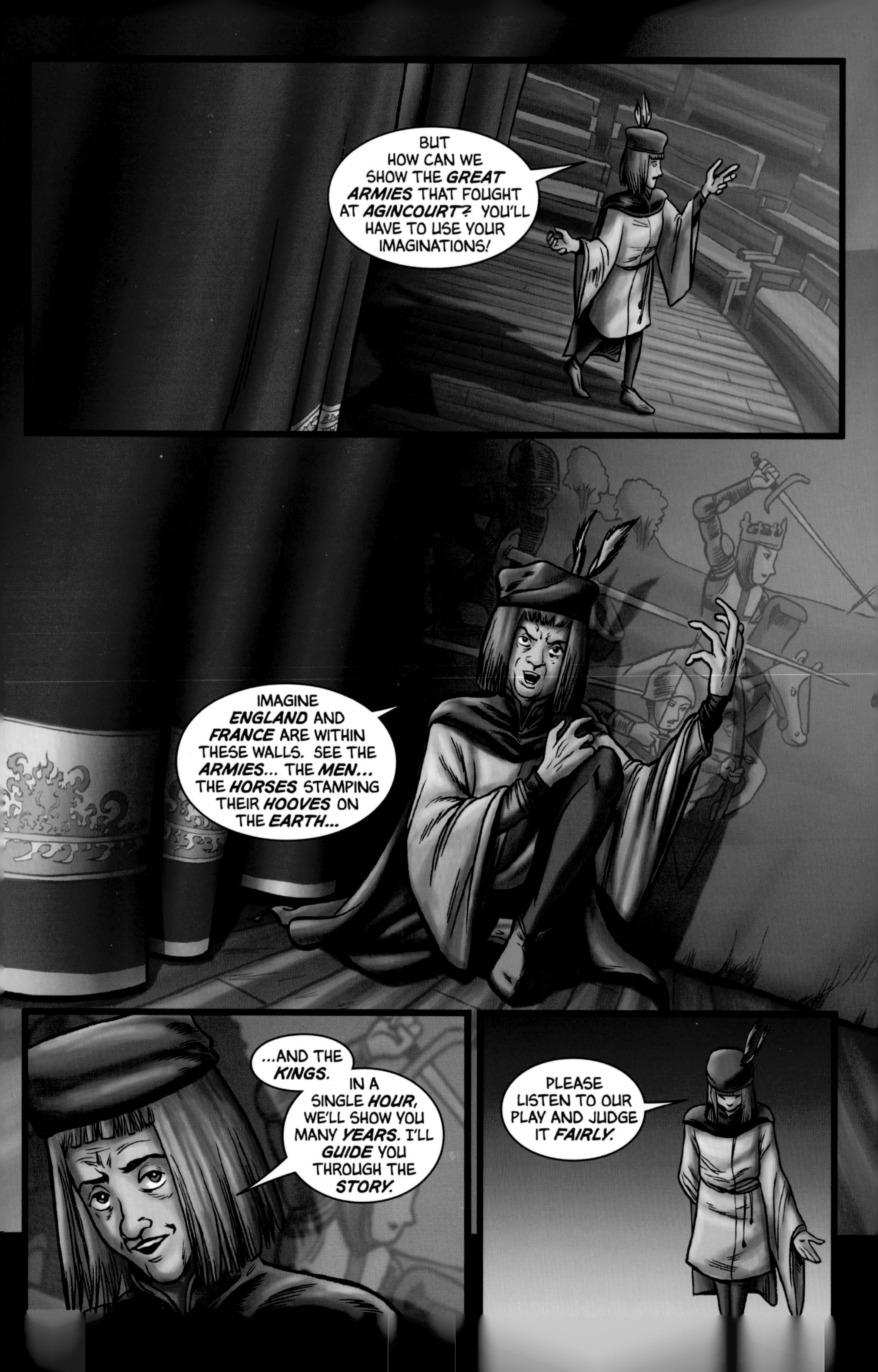
BUT HOW CAN WE SHOW THE GREAT ARMIES THAT FOUGHT AT AGINCOURT? YOU'LL HAVE TO USE YOUR IMAGINATIONS!
IMAGINE ENGLAND AND FRANCE ARE WITHIN THESE WALLS. SEE THE ARMIES... THE MEN... THE HORSES STAMPING THEIR HOOVES ON THE EARTH...
...AND THE KINGS.
IN A SINGLE HOUR, WE'LL SHOW YOU MANY YEARS. I'LL GUIDE YOU THROUGH THE STORY.
PLEASE LISTEN TO OUR PLAY AND JUDGE IT FAIRLY.

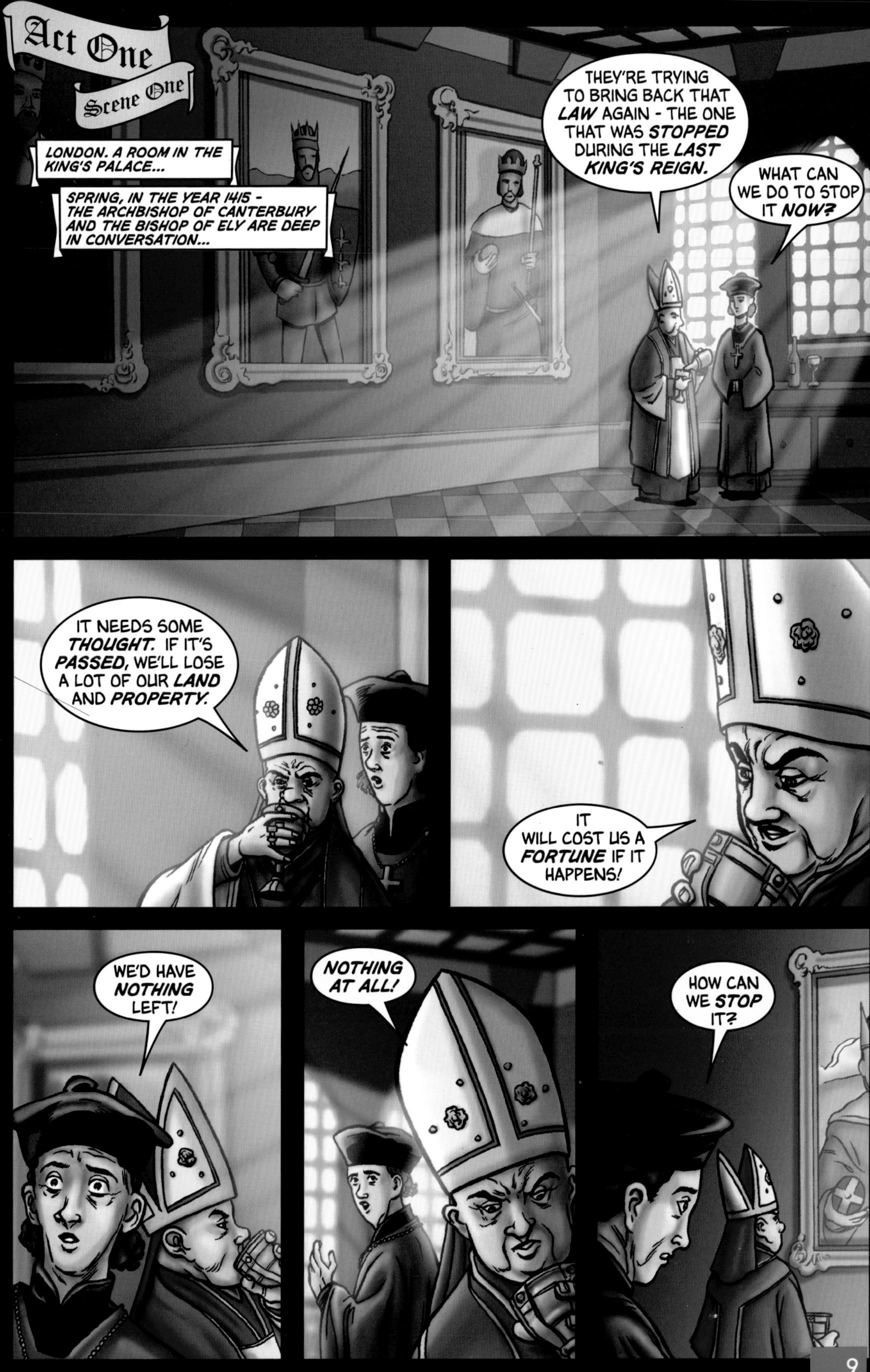
Act One
Scene One
LONDON. A ROOM IN THE KING'S PALACE...
SPRING, IN THE YEAR 1415 - THE ARCHBISHOP OF CANTERBURY AND THE BISHOP OF ELY ARE DEEP IN CONVERSATION...
THEY'RE TRYING TO BRING BACK THAT LAW AGAIN - THE ONE THAT WAS STOPPED DURING THE LAST KING'S REIGN.
WHAT CAN WE DO TO STOP IT NOW?
IT NEEDS SOME THOUGHT. IF IT'S PASSED, WE'LL LOSE A LOT OF OUR LAND AND PROPERTY.
IT WILL COST US A FORTUNE IF IT HAPPENS!
WE'D HAVE NOTHING LEFT!
NOTHING AT ALL!
HOW CAN WE STOP IT?

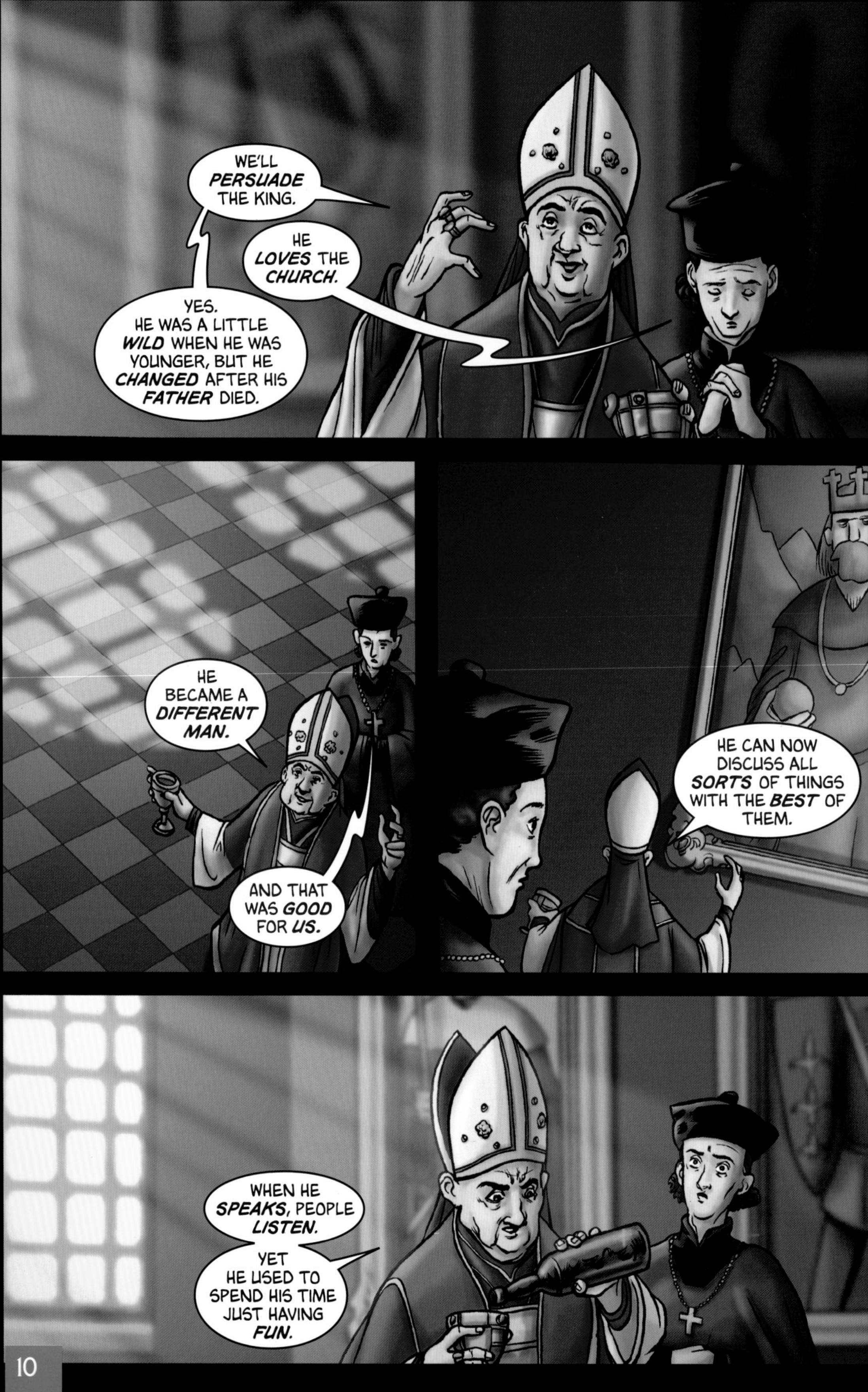
WE'LL PERSUADE THE KING.
YES. HE WAS A LITTLE WILD WHEN HE WAS YOUNGER, BUT HE CHANGED AFTER HIS FATHER DIED.
HE LOVES THE CHURCH.
HE BECAME A DIFFERENT MAN.
AND THAT WAS GOOD FOR US.
HE CAN NOW DISCUSS ALL SORTS OF THINGS WITH THE BEST OF THEM.
WHEN HE SPEAKS, PEOPLE LISTEN.
YET HE USED TO SPEND HIS TIME JUST HAVING FUN.

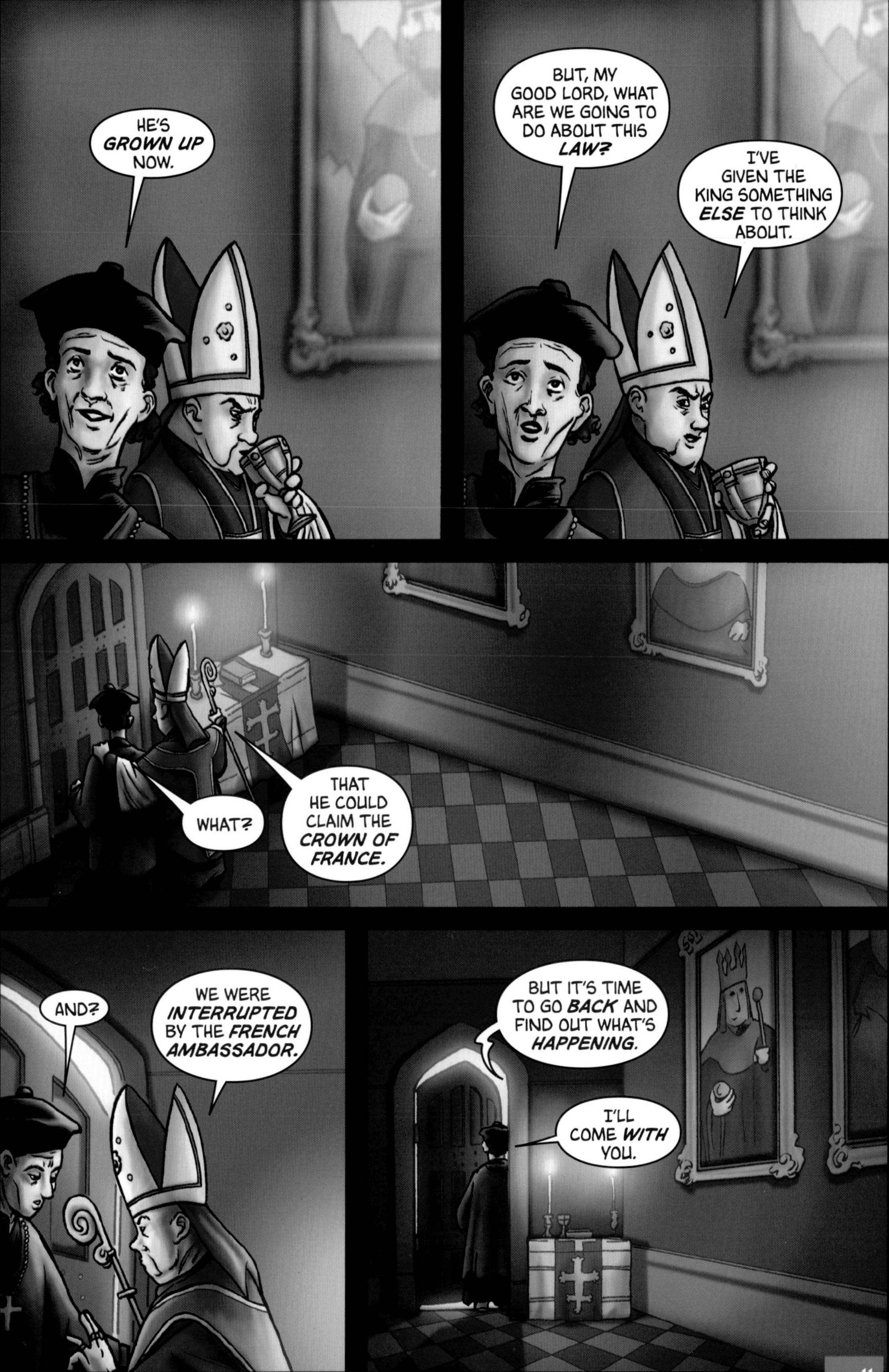
HE'S GROWN UP NOW.
BUT, MY GOOD LORD, WHAT ARE WE GOING TO DO ABOUT THIS LAW?
I'VE GIVEN THE KING SOMETHING ELSE TO THINK ABOUT.
WHAT?
THAT HE COULD CLAIM THE CROWN OF FRANCE.
AND?
WE WERE INTERRUPTED BY THE FRENCH AMBASSADOR.
BUT IT'S TIME TO GO BACK AND FIND OUT WHAT'S HAPPENING.
I'LL COME WITH YOU.

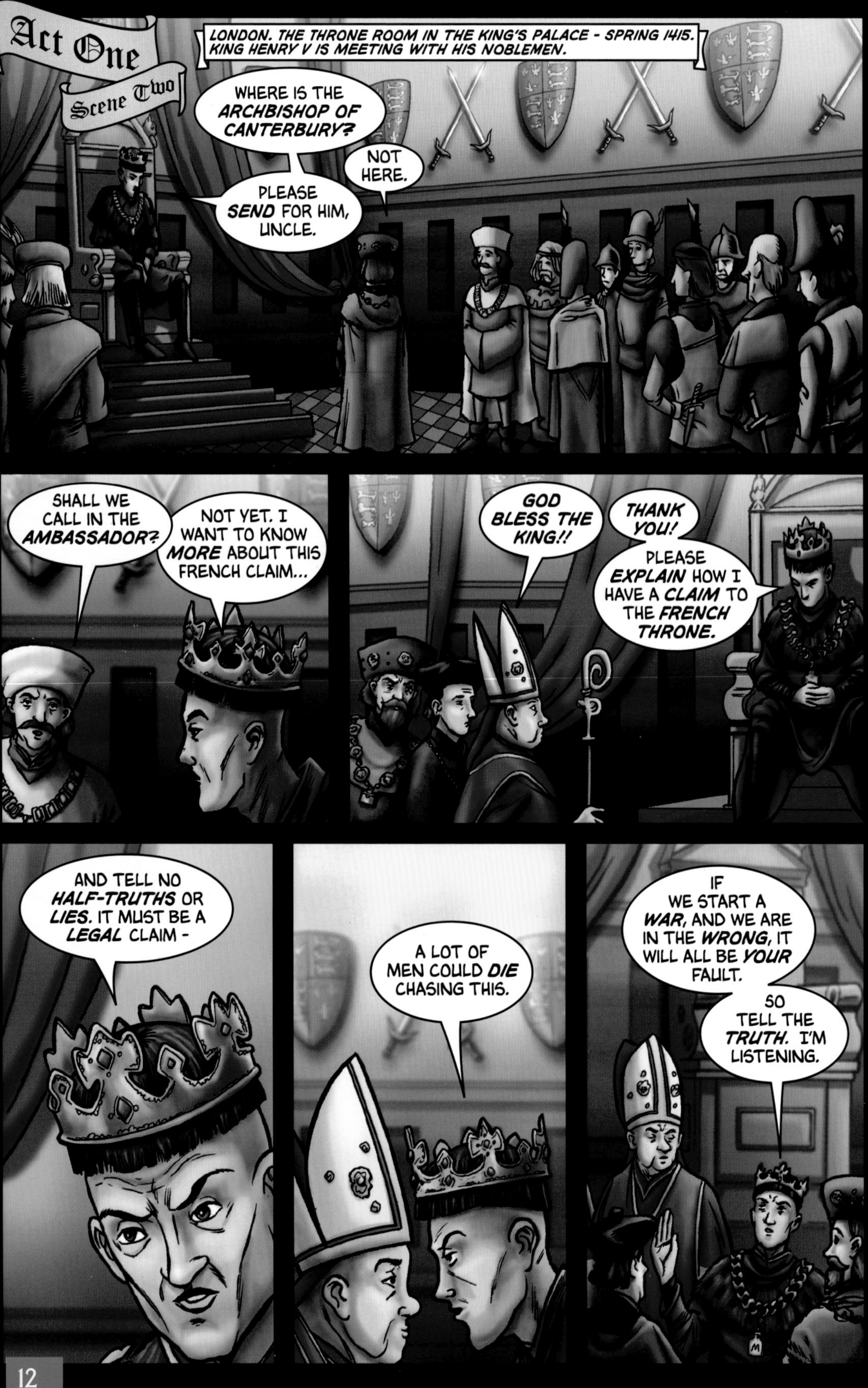
Act One
Scene Two
LONDON. THE THRONE ROOM IN THE KING'S PALACE - SPRING 1415. KING HENRY V IS MEETING WITH HIS NOBLEMEN.
WHERE IS THE ARCHBISHOP OF CANTERBURY?
NOT HERE.
PLEASE SEND FOR HIM, UNCLE.
SHALL WE CALL IN THE AMBASSADOR?
NOT YET. I WANT TO KNOW MORE ABOUT THIS FRENCH CLAIM...
GOD BLESS THE KING!!
THANK YOU!
PLEASE EXPLAIN HOW I HAVE A CLAIM TO THE FRENCH THRONE.
AND TELL NO HALF-TRUTHS OR LIES. IT MUST BE A LEGAL CLAIM -
A LOT OF MEN COULD DIE CHASING THIS.
IF WE START A WAR, AND WE ARE IN THE WRONG, IT WILL ALL BE YOUR FAULT.
SO TELL THE TRUTH. I'M LISTENING.

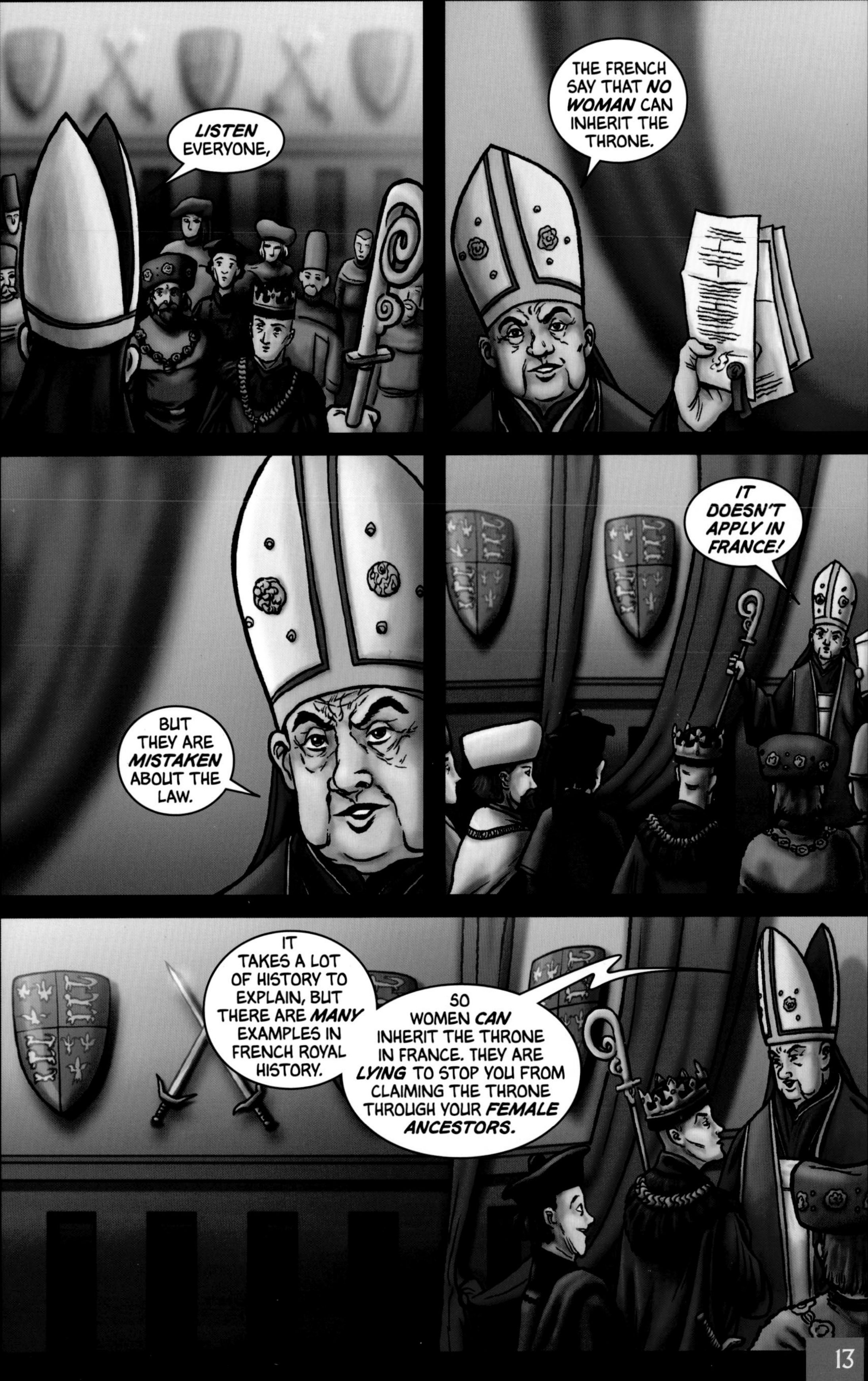

LISTEN EVERYONE,
THE FRENCH SAY THAT NO WOMAN CAN INHERIT THE THRONE.
BUT THEY ARE MISTAKEN ABOUT THE LAW.
IT DOESN'T APPLY IN FRANCE!
IT TAKES A LOT OF HISTORY TO EXPLAIN, BUT THERE ARE MANY EXAMPLES IN FRENCH ROYAL HISTORY.
SO WOMEN CAN INHERIT THE THRONE IN FRANCE. THEY ARE LYING TO STOP YOU FROM CLAIMING THE THRONE THROUGH YOUR FEMALE ANCESTORS.

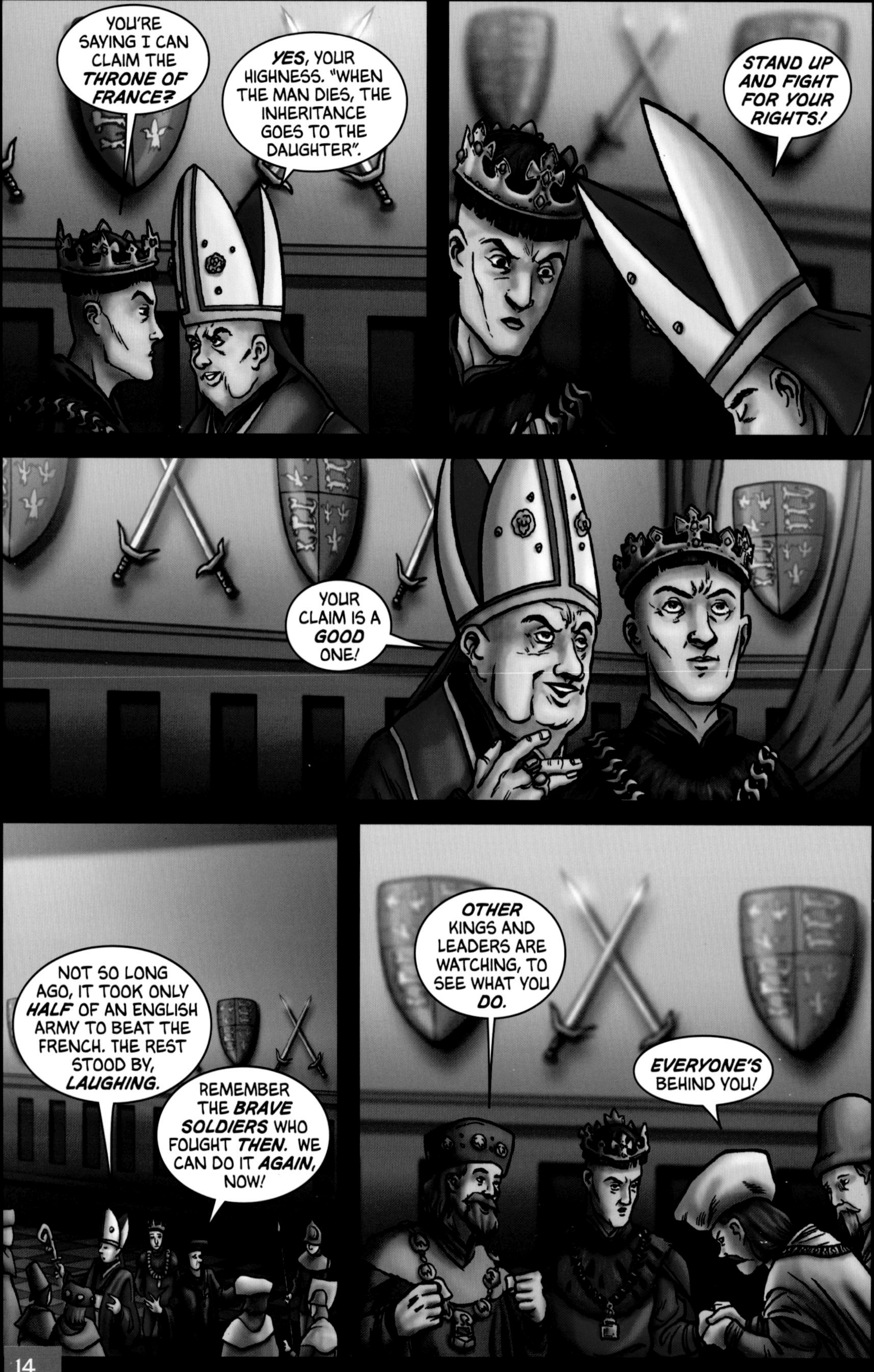
YOU'RE SAYING I CAN CLAIM THE THRONE OF FRANCE?
YES, YOUR HIGHNESS. "WHEN THE MAN DIES, THE INHERITANCE GOES TO THE DAUGHTER".
STAND UP AND FIGHT FOR YOUR RIGHTS!
YOUR CLAIM IS A GOOD ONE!
NOT SO LONG AGO, IT TOOK ONLY HALF OF AN ENGLISH ARMY TO BEAT THE FRENCH. THE REST STOOD BY, LAUGHING.
REMEMBER THE BRAVE SOLDIERS WHO FOUGHT THEN. WE CAN DO IT AGAIN, NOW!
OTHER KINGS AND LEADERS ARE WATCHING, TO SEE WHAT YOU DO.
EVERYONE'S BEHIND YOU!

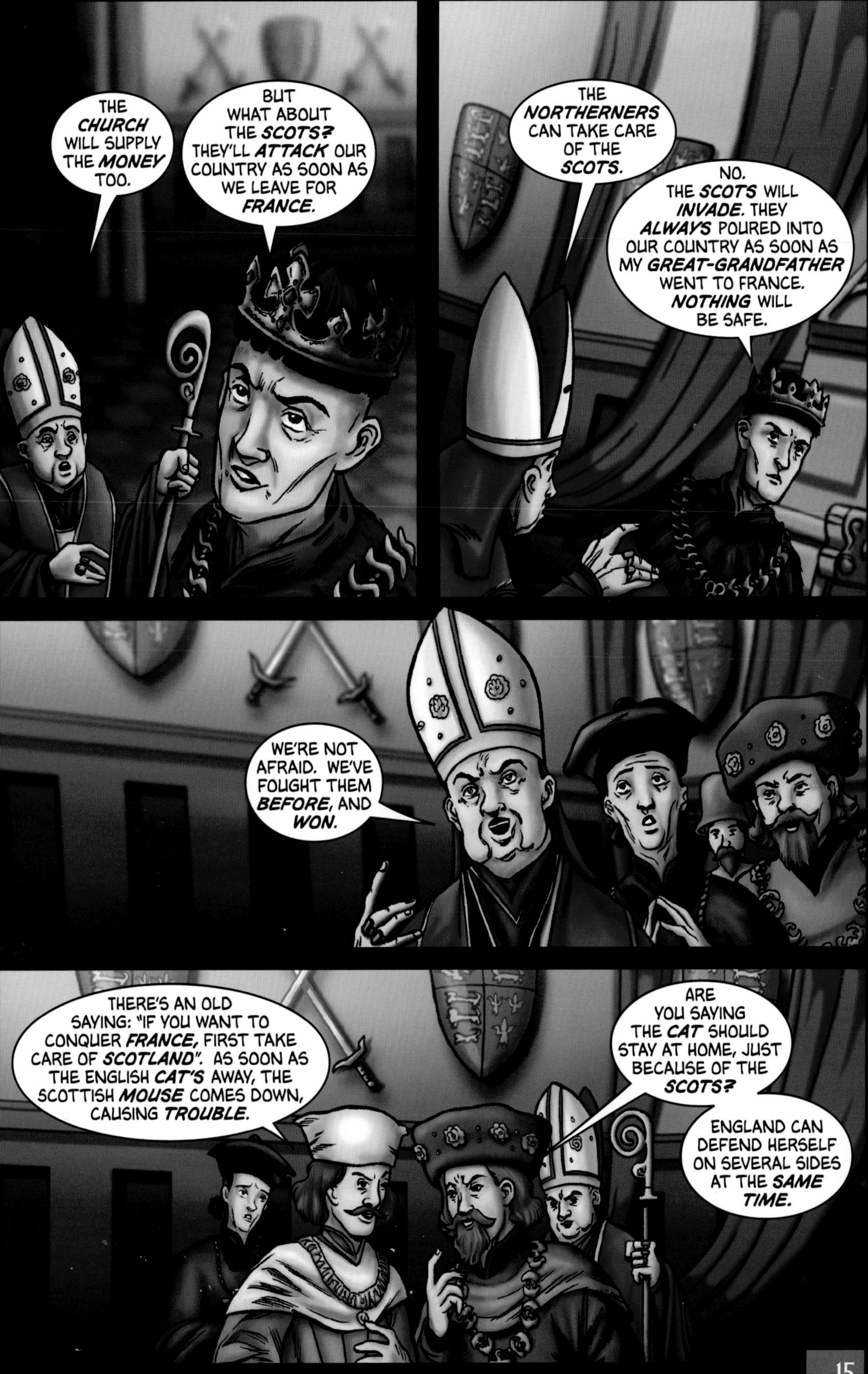
THE CHURCH WILL SUPPLY THE MONEY TOO.
BUT WHAT ABOUT THE SCOTS? THEY'LL ATTACK OUR COUNTRY AS SOON AS WE LEAVE FOR FRANCE.
THE NORTHERNERS CAN TAKE CARE OF THE SCOTS.
NO. THE SCOTS WILL INVADE. THEY ALWAYS POURED INTO OUR COUNTRY AS SOON AS MY GREAT-GRANDFATHER WENT TO FRANCE. NOTHING WILL BE SAFE.
WE'RE NOT AFRAID. WE'VE FOUGHT THEM BEFORE, AND WON.
THERE'S AN OLD SAYING: "IF YOU WANT TO CONQUER FRANCE, FIRST TAKE CARE OF SCOTLAND". AS SOON AS THE ENGLISH CAT'S AWAY, THE SCOTTISH MOUSE COMES DOWN, CAUSING TROUBLE.
ARE YOU SAYING THE CAT SHOULD STAY AT HOME, JUST BECAUSE OF THE SCOTS?
ENGLAND CAN DEFEND HERSELF ON SEVERAL SIDES AT THE SAME TIME.

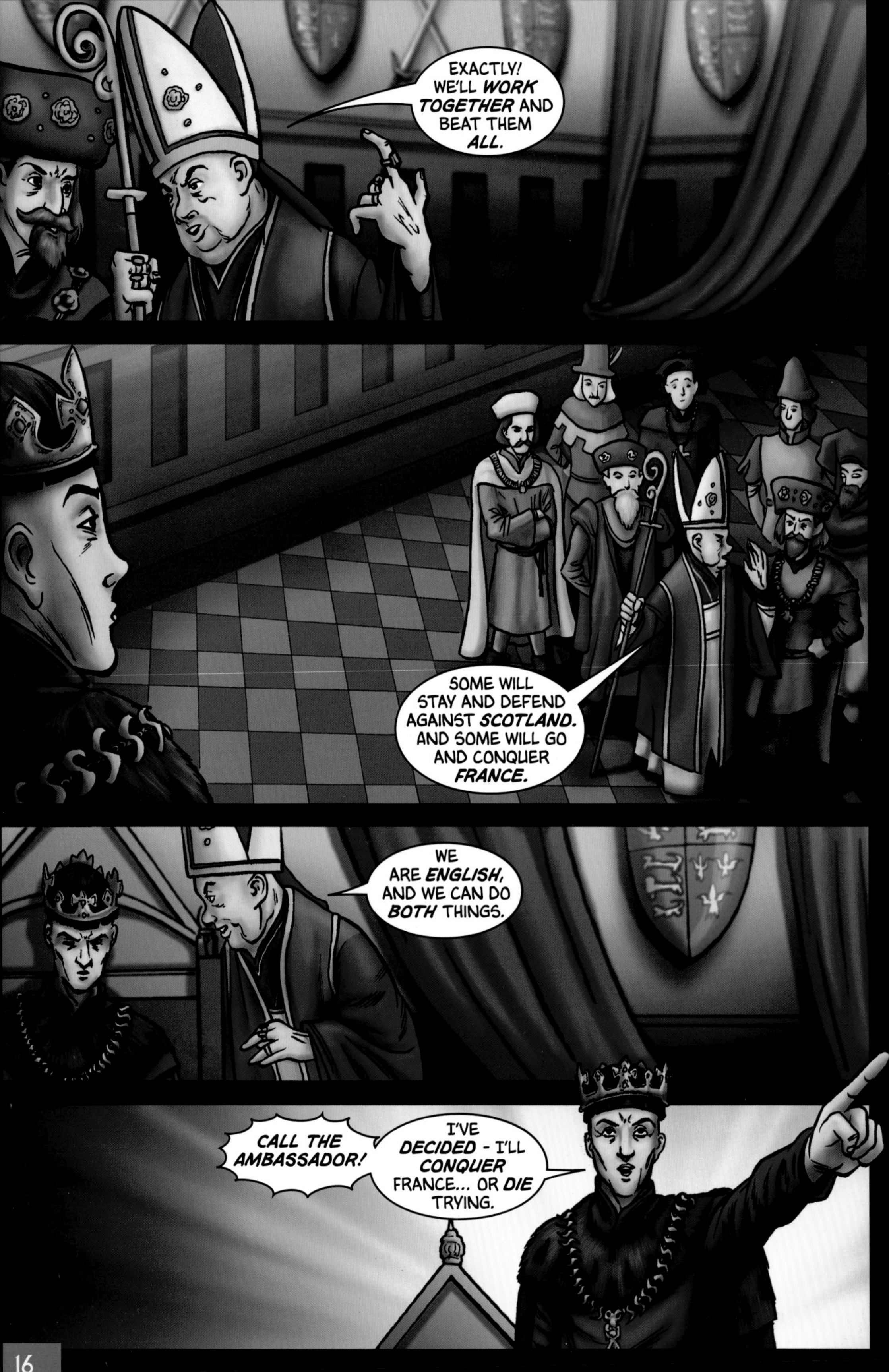
EXACTLY! WE'LL WORK TOGETHER AND BEAT THEM ALL.
SOME WILL STAY AND DEFEND AGAINST SCOTLAND. AND SOME WILL GO AND CONQUER FRANCE.
WE ARE ENGLISH, AND WE CAN DO BOTH THINGS.
CALL THE AMBASSADOR!
I'VE DECIDED - I'LL CONQUER FRANCE... OR DIE TRYING.

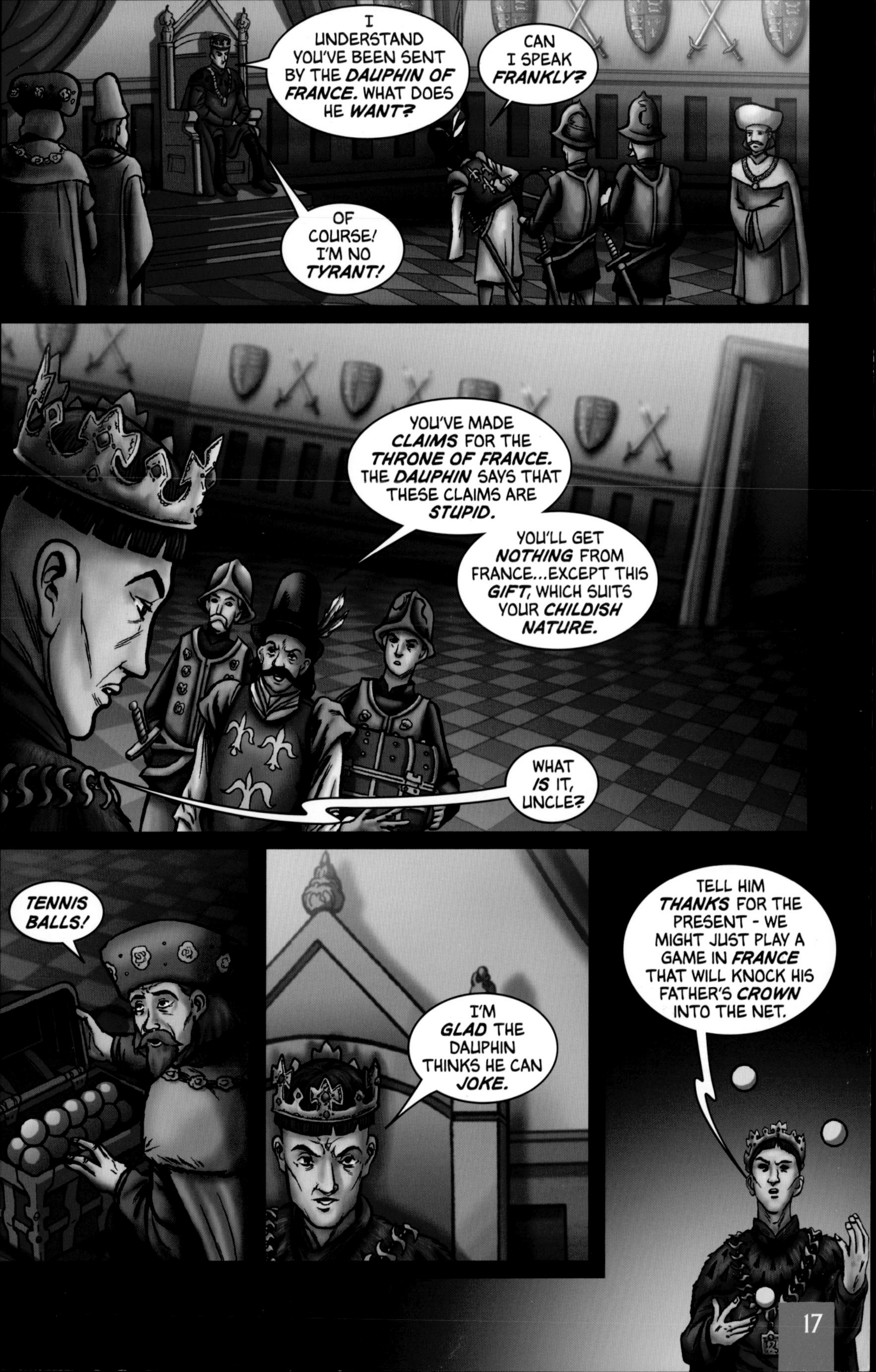
I UNDERSTAND YOU'VE BEEN SENT BY THE DAUPHIN OF FRANCE. WHAT DOES HE WANT?
CAN I SPEAK FRANKLY?
OF COURSE! I'M NO TYRANT!
YOU'VE MADE CLAIMS FOR THE THRONE OF FRANCE. THE DAUPHIN SAYS THAT THESE CLAIMS ARE STUPID.
YOU'LL GET NOTHING FROM FRANCE...EXCEPT THIS GIFT, WHICH SUITS YOUR CHILDISH NATURE.
WHAT IS IT, UNCLE?
TENNIS BALLS!
I'M GLAD THE DAUPHIN THINKS HE CAN JOKE.
TELL HIM THANKS FOR THE PRESENT - WE MIGHT JUST PLAY A GAME IN FRANCE THAT WILL KNOCK HIS FATHER'S CROWN INTO THE NET.

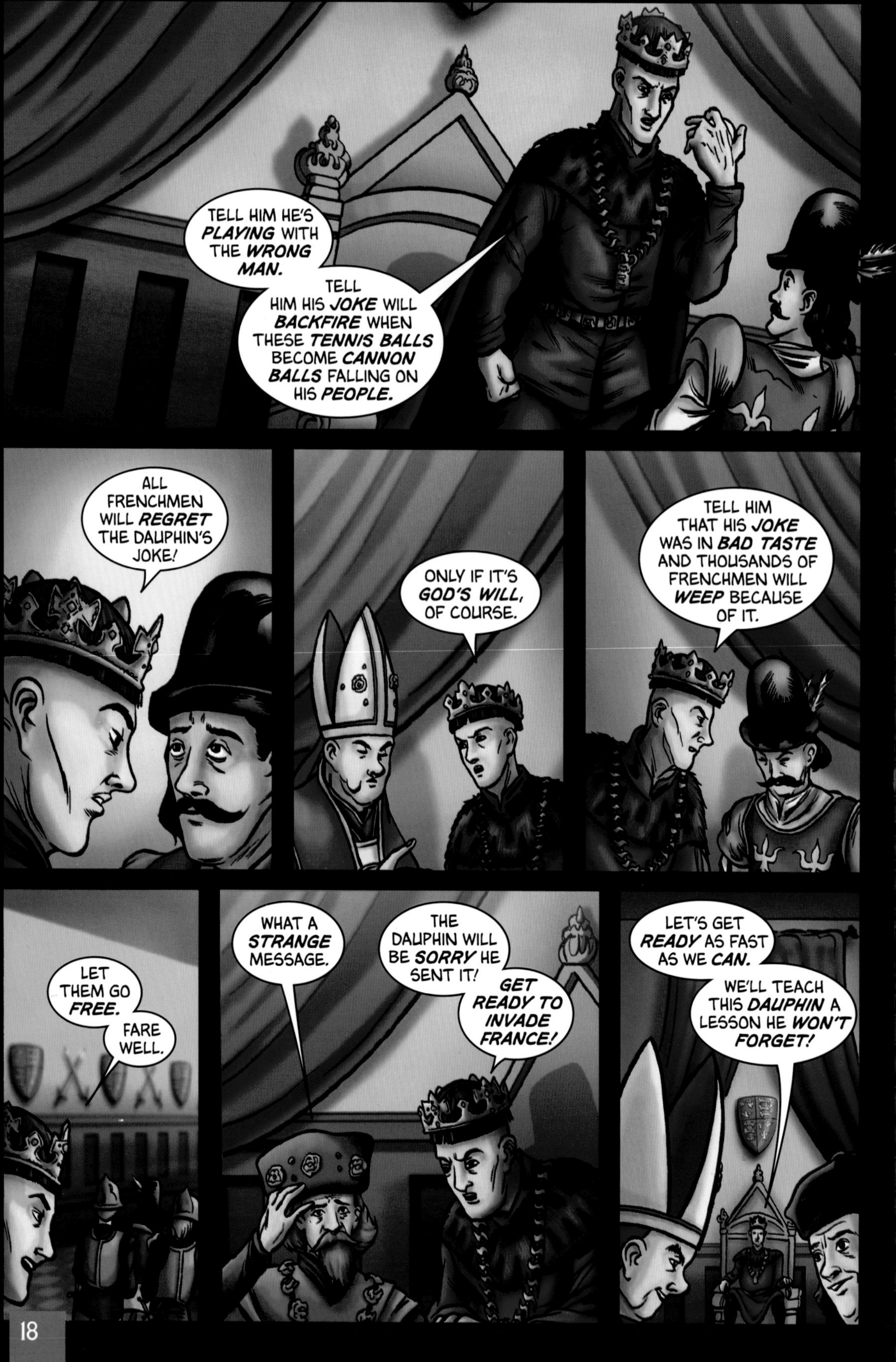

TELL HIM HE'S PLAYING WITH THE WRONG MAN.
TELL HIM HIS JOKE WILL BACKFIRE WHEN THESE TENNIS BALLS BECOME CANNON BALLS FALLING ON HIS PEOPLE.
ALL FRENCHMEN WILL REGRET THE DAUPHIN'S JOKE!
ONLY IF IT'S GOD'S WILL, OF COURSE.
TELL HIM THAT HIS JOKE WAS IN BAD TASTE AND THOUSANDS OF FRENCHMEN WILL WEEP BECAUSE OF IT.
LET THEM GO FREE.
FARE WELL.
WHAT A STRANGE MESSAGE.
THE DAUPHIN WILL BE SORRY HE SENT IT!
GET READY TO INVADE FRANCE!
LET'S GET READY AS FAST AS WE CAN.
WE'LL TEACH THIS DAUPHIN A LESSON HE WON'T FORGET!

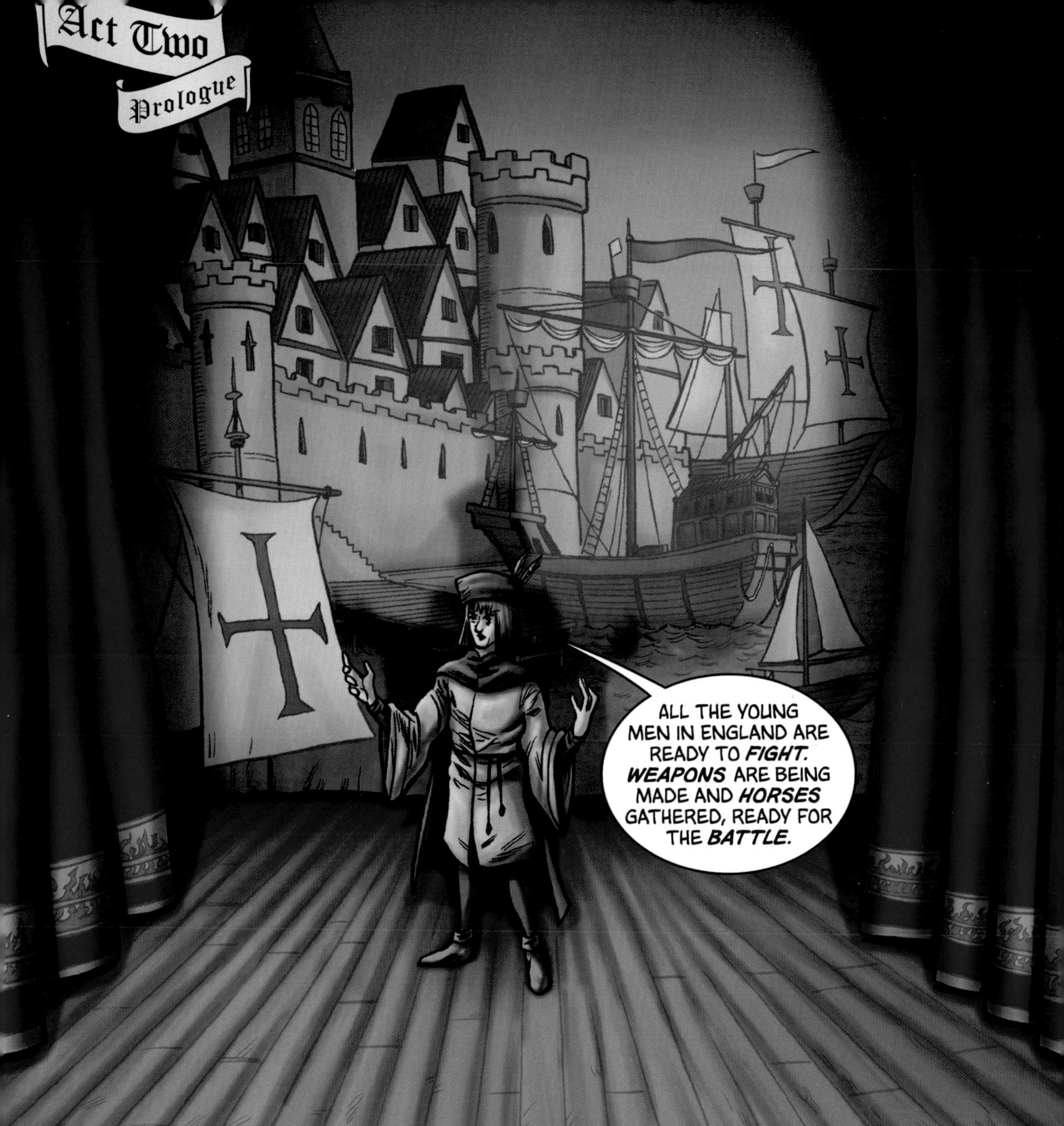
Act Two
Prologue
ALL THE YOUNG MEN IN ENGLAND ARE READY TO *FIGHT*. *WEAPONS* ARE BEING MADE AND *HORSES* GATHERED, READY FOR THE *BATTLE*.

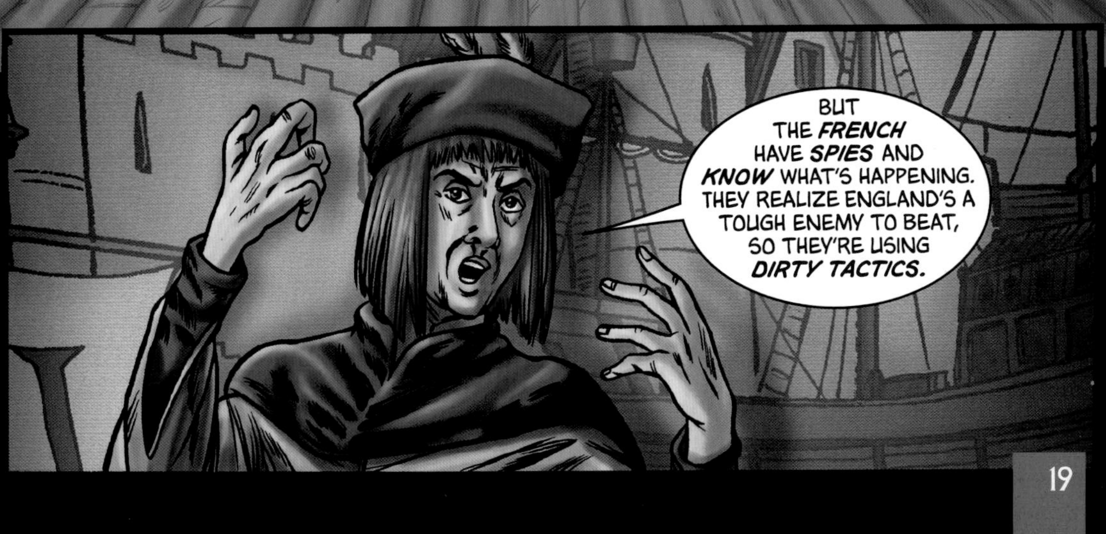
BUT THE *FRENCH* HAVE *SPIES* AND *KNOW* WHAT'S HAPPENING. THEY REALIZE ENGLAND'S A TOUGH ENEMY TO BEAT, SO THEY'RE USING *DIRTY TACTICS*.

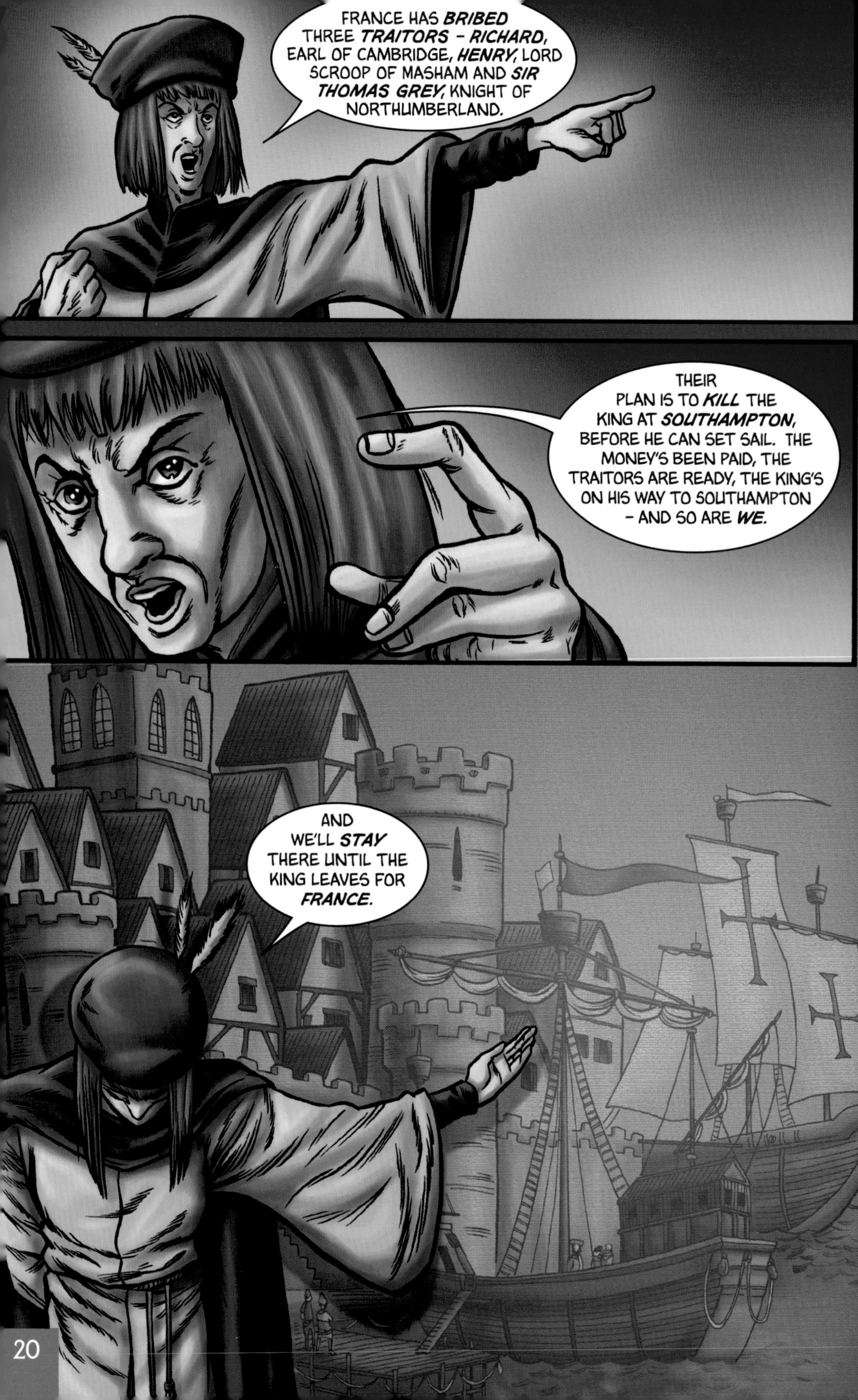
FRANCE HAS BRIBED THREE TRAITORS - RICHARD, EARL OF CAMBRIDGE, HENRY, LORD SCROOP OF MASHAM AND SIR THOMAS GREY, KNIGHT OF NORTHUMBERLAND.
THEIR PLAN IS TO KILL THE KING AT SOUTHAMPTON, BEFORE HE CAN SET SAIL. THE MONEY'S BEEN PAID, THE TRAITORS ARE READY, THE KING'S ON HIS WAY TO SOUTHAMPTON - AND SO ARE WE.
AND WE'LL STAY THERE UNTIL THE KING LEAVES FOR FRANCE.

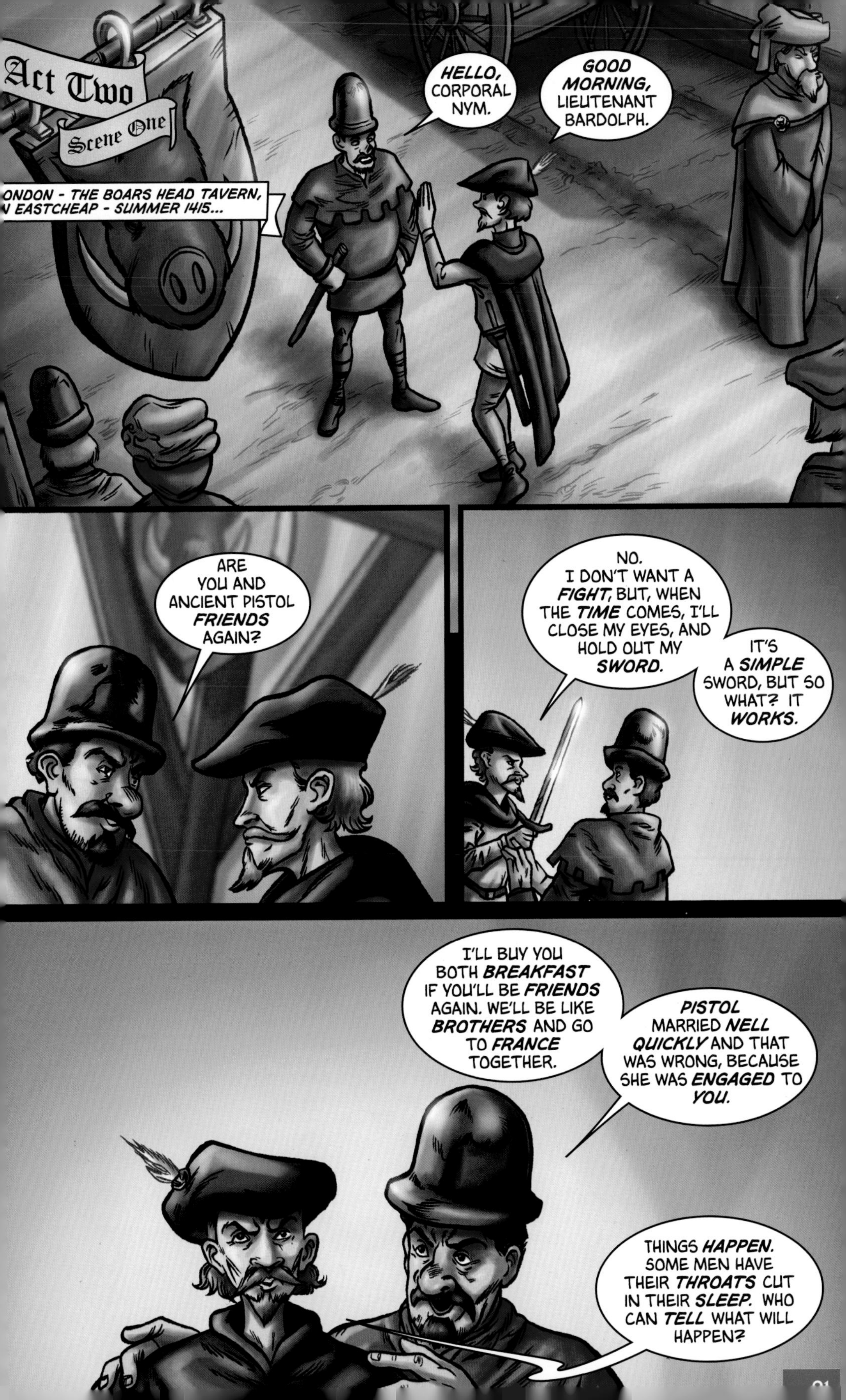
Act Two
Scene One
LONDON - THE BOARS HEAD TAVERN, IN EASTCHEAP - SUMMER 1415...
HELLO, CORPORAL NYM.
GOOD MORNING, LIEUTENANT BARDOLPH.
ARE YOU AND ANCIENT PISTOL FRIENDS AGAIN?
NO. I DON'T WANT A FIGHT, BUT, WHEN THE TIME COMES, I'LL CLOSE MY EYES, AND HOLD OUT MY SWORD.
IT'S A SIMPLE SWORD, BUT SO WHAT? IT WORKS.
I'LL BUY YOU BOTH BREAKFAST IF YOU'LL BE FRIENDS AGAIN. WE'LL BE LIKE BROTHERS AND GO TO FRANCE TOGETHER.
PISTOL MARRIED NELL QUICKLY AND THAT WAS WRONG, BECAUSE SHE WAS ENGAGED TO YOU.
THINGS HAPPEN. SOME MEN HAVE THEIR THROATS CUT IN THEIR SLEEP. WHO CAN TELL WHAT WILL HAPPEN?

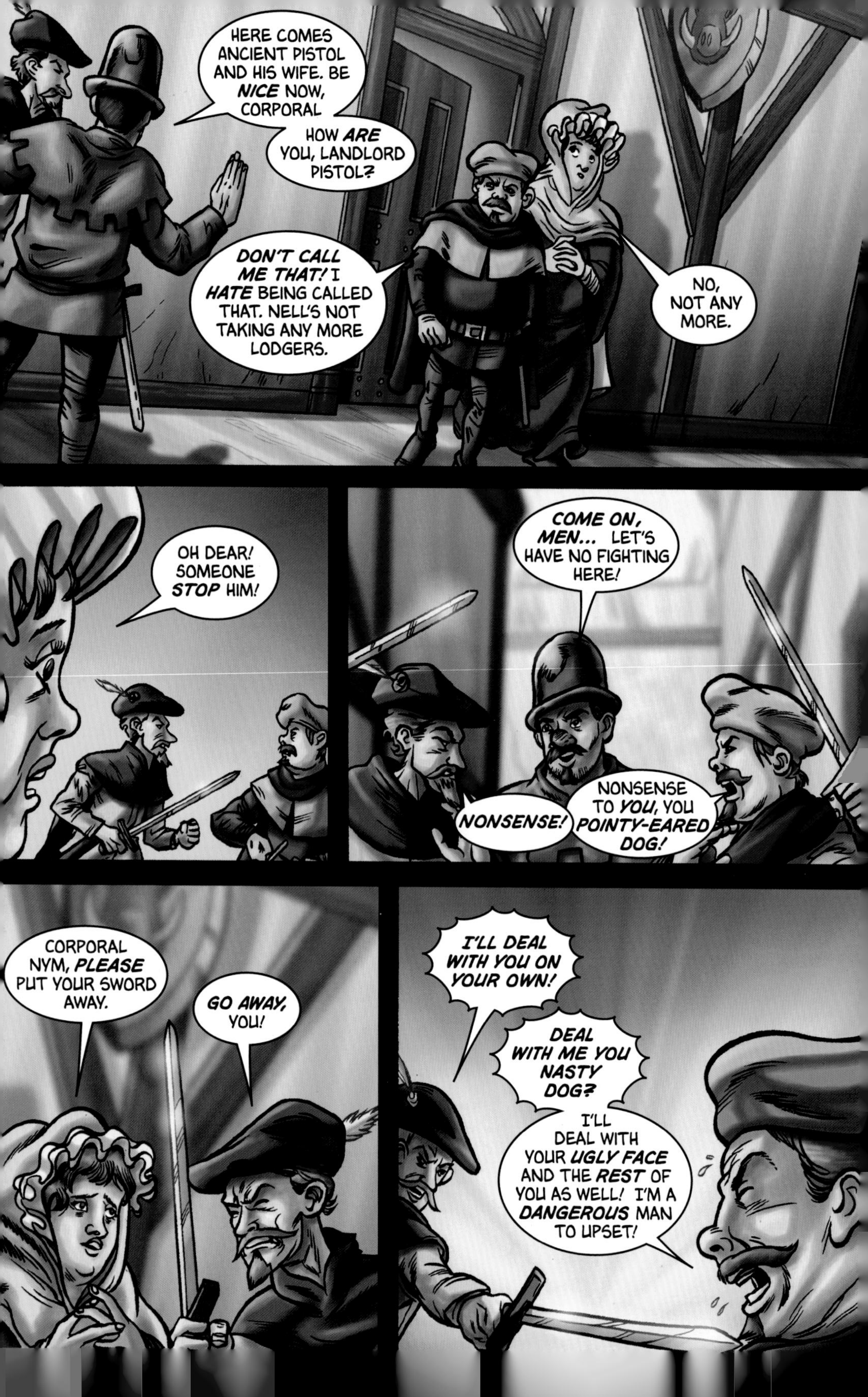
HERE COMES ANCIENT PISTOL AND HIS WIFE. BE NICE NOW, CORPORAL
HOW ARE YOU, LANDLORD PISTOL?
DON'T CALL ME THAT! I HATE BEING CALLED THAT. NELL'S NOT TAKING ANY MORE LODGERS.
NO, NOT ANY MORE.
OH DEAR! SOMEONE STOP HIM!
COME ON, MEN... LET'S HAVE NO FIGHTING HERE!
NONSENSE!
NONSENSE TO YOU, YOU POINTY-EARED DOG!
CORPORAL NYM, PLEASE PUT YOUR SWORD AWAY.
GO AWAY, YOU!
I'LL DEAL WITH YOU ON YOUR OWN!
DEAL WITH ME YOU NASTY DOG?
I'LL DEAL WITH YOUR UGLY FACE AND THE REST OF YOU AS WELL! I'M A DANGEROUS MAN TO UPSET!

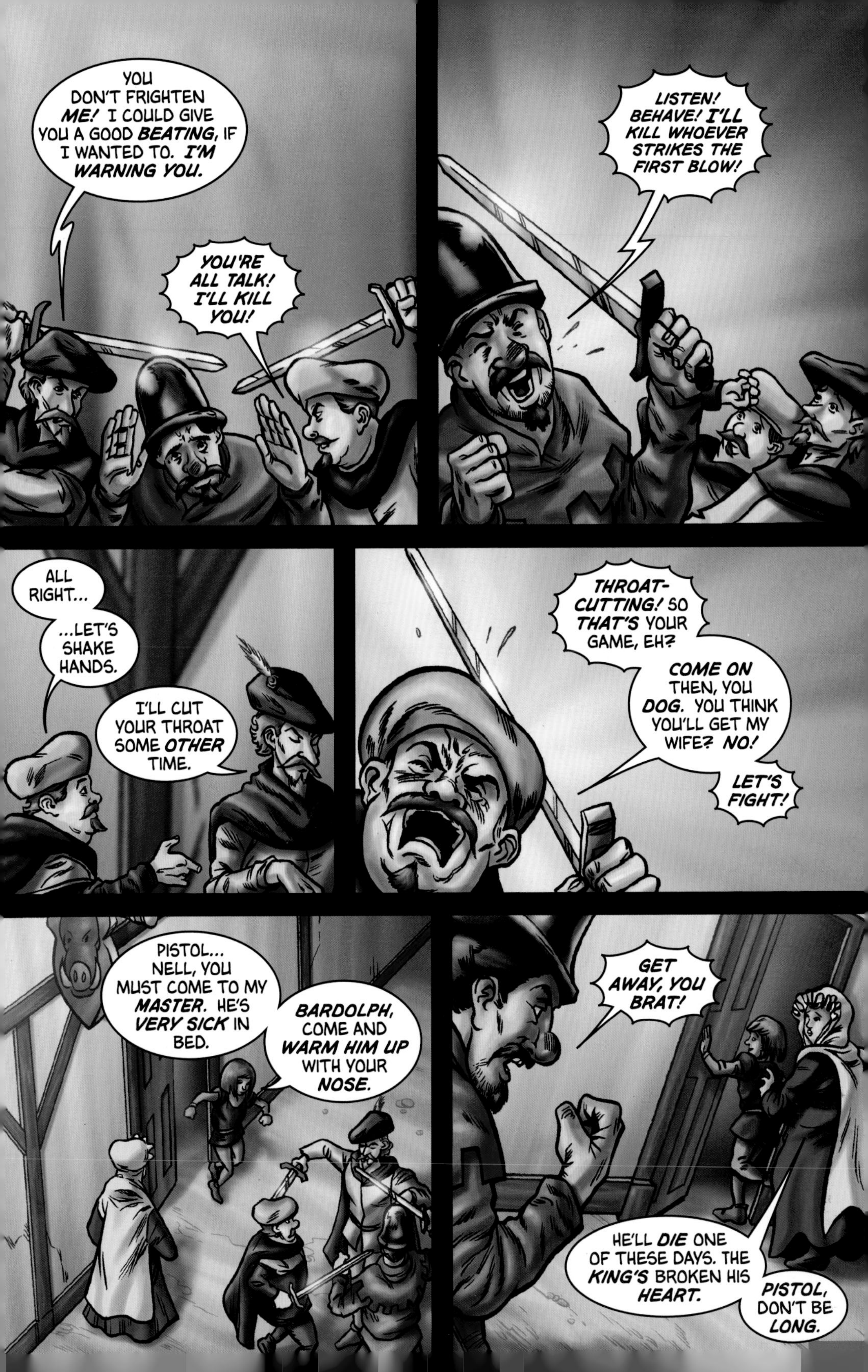
YOU DON'T FRIGHTEN ME! I COULD GIVE YOU A GOOD BEATING, IF I WANTED TO. I'M WARNING YOU.
YOU'RE ALL TALK! I'LL KILL YOU!
LISTEN! BEHAVE! I'LL KILL WHOEVER STRIKES THE FIRST BLOW!
ALL RIGHT...
...LET'S SHAKE HANDS.
I'LL CUT YOUR THROAT SOME OTHER TIME.
THROAT-CUTTING! SO THAT'S YOUR GAME, EH?
COME ON THEN, YOU DOG. YOU THINK YOU'LL GET MY WIFE? NO!
LET'S FIGHT!
PISTOL... NELL, YOU MUST COME TO MY MASTER. HE'S VERY SICK IN BED.
BARDOLPH, COME AND WARM HIM UP WITH YOUR NOSE.
GET AWAY, YOU BRAT!
HE'LL DIE ONE OF THESE DAYS. THE KING'S BROKEN HIS HEART.
PISTOL, DON'T BE LONG.

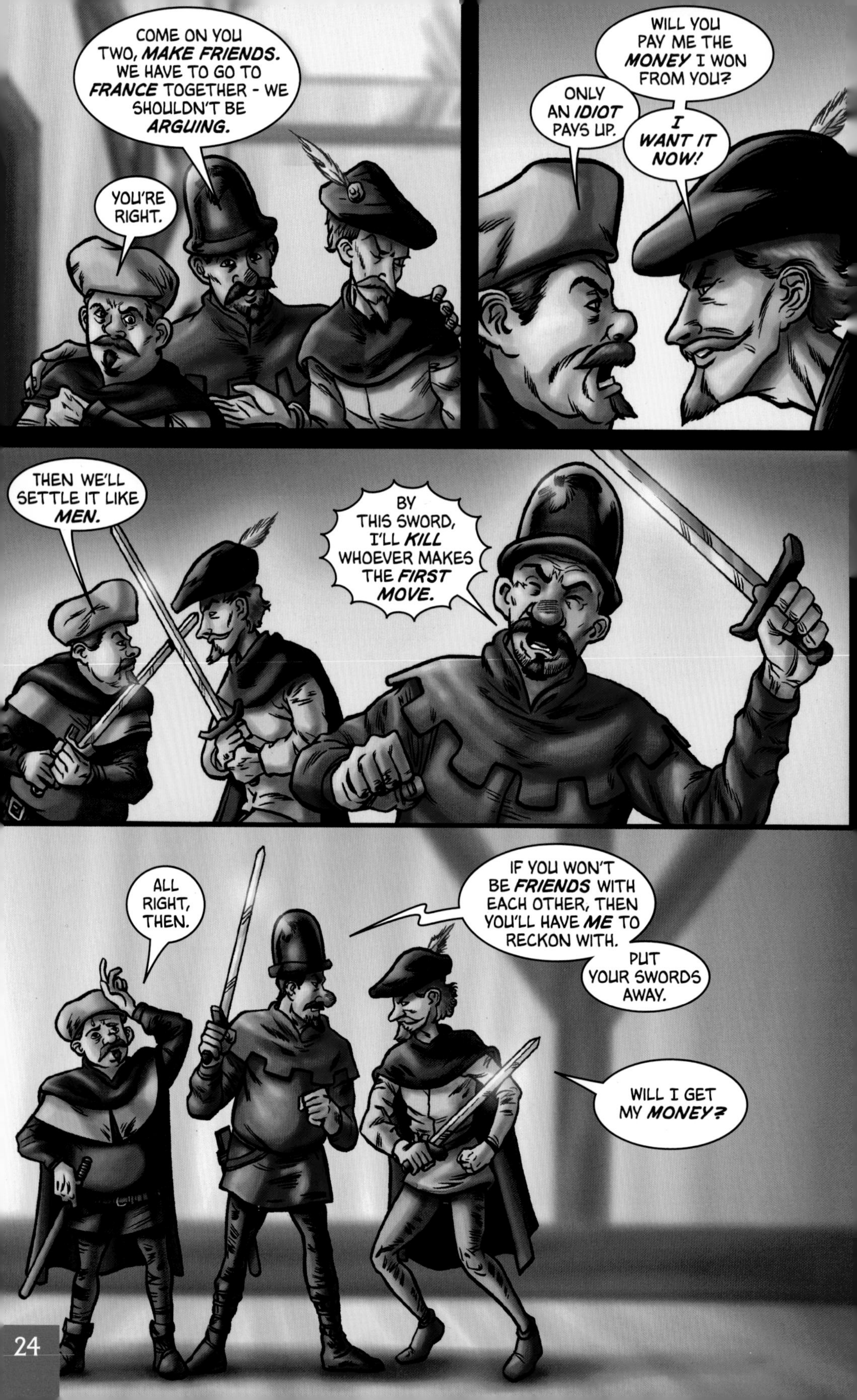
COME ON YOU TWO, MAKE FRIENDS. WE HAVE TO GO TO FRANCE TOGETHER - WE SHOULDN'T BE ARGUING.
YOU'RE RIGHT.
WILL YOU PAY ME THE MONEY I WON FROM YOU?
ONLY AN IDIOT PAYS UP.
I WANT IT NOW!
THEN WE'LL SETTLE IT LIKE MEN.
BY THIS SWORD, I'LL KILL WHOEVER MAKES THE FIRST MOVE.
ALL RIGHT, THEN.
IF YOU WON'T BE FRIENDS WITH EACH OTHER, THEN YOU'LL HAVE ME TO RECKON WITH.
PUT YOUR SWORDS AWAY.
WILL I GET MY MONEY?

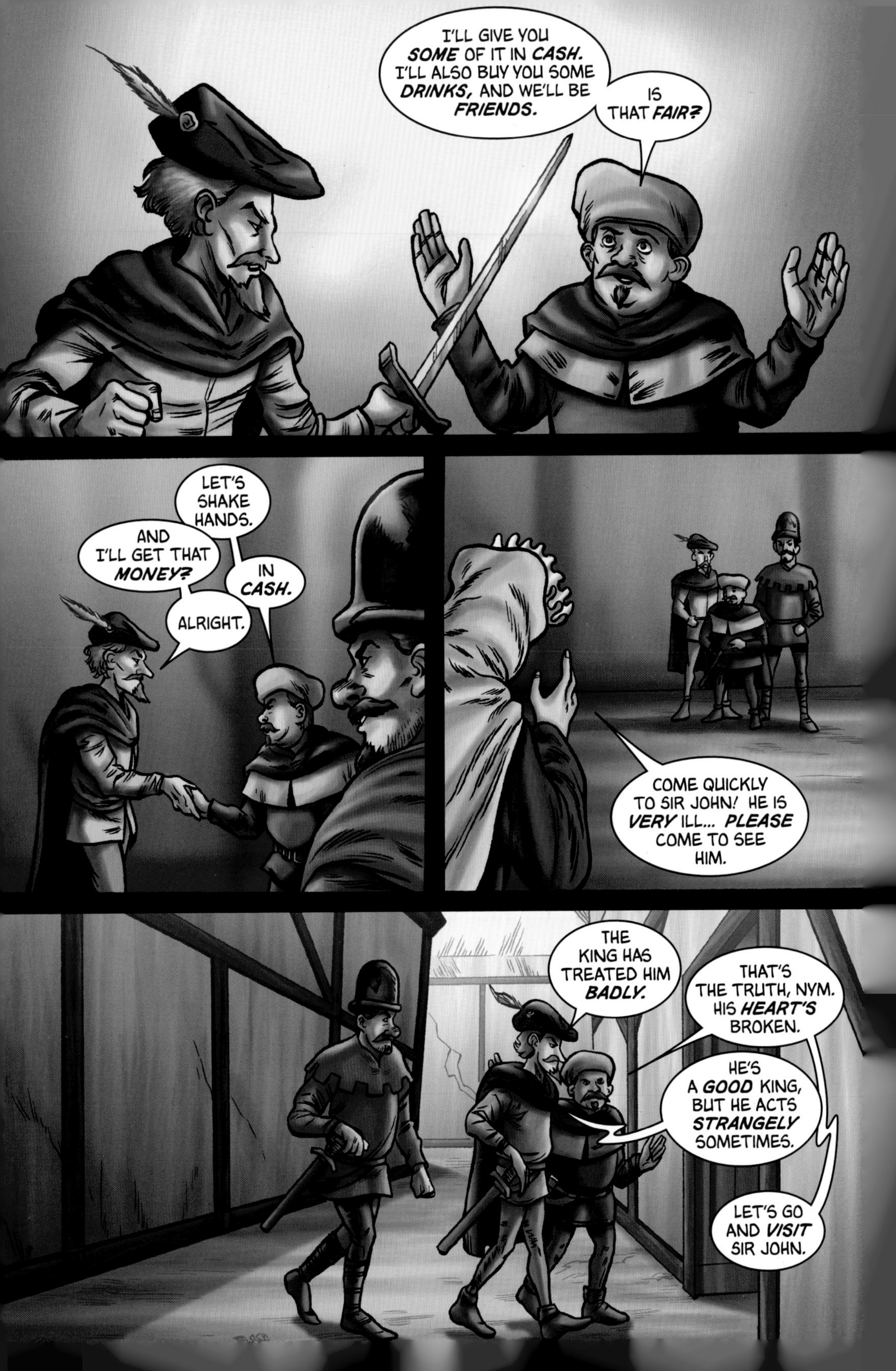
I'LL GIVE YOU SOME OF IT IN CASH. I'LL ALSO BUY YOU SOME DRINKS, AND WE'LL BE FRIENDS.
IS THAT FAIR?
LET'S SHAKE HANDS.
AND I'LL GET THAT MONEY?
IN CASH.
ALRIGHT.
COME QUICKLY TO SIR JOHN! HE IS VERY ILL... PLEASE COME TO SEE HIM.
THE KING HAS TREATED HIM BADLY.
THAT'S THE TRUTH, NYM. HIS HEART'S BROKEN.
HE'S A GOOD KING, BUT HE ACTS STRANGELY SOMETIMES.
LET'S GO AND VISIT SIR JOHN.

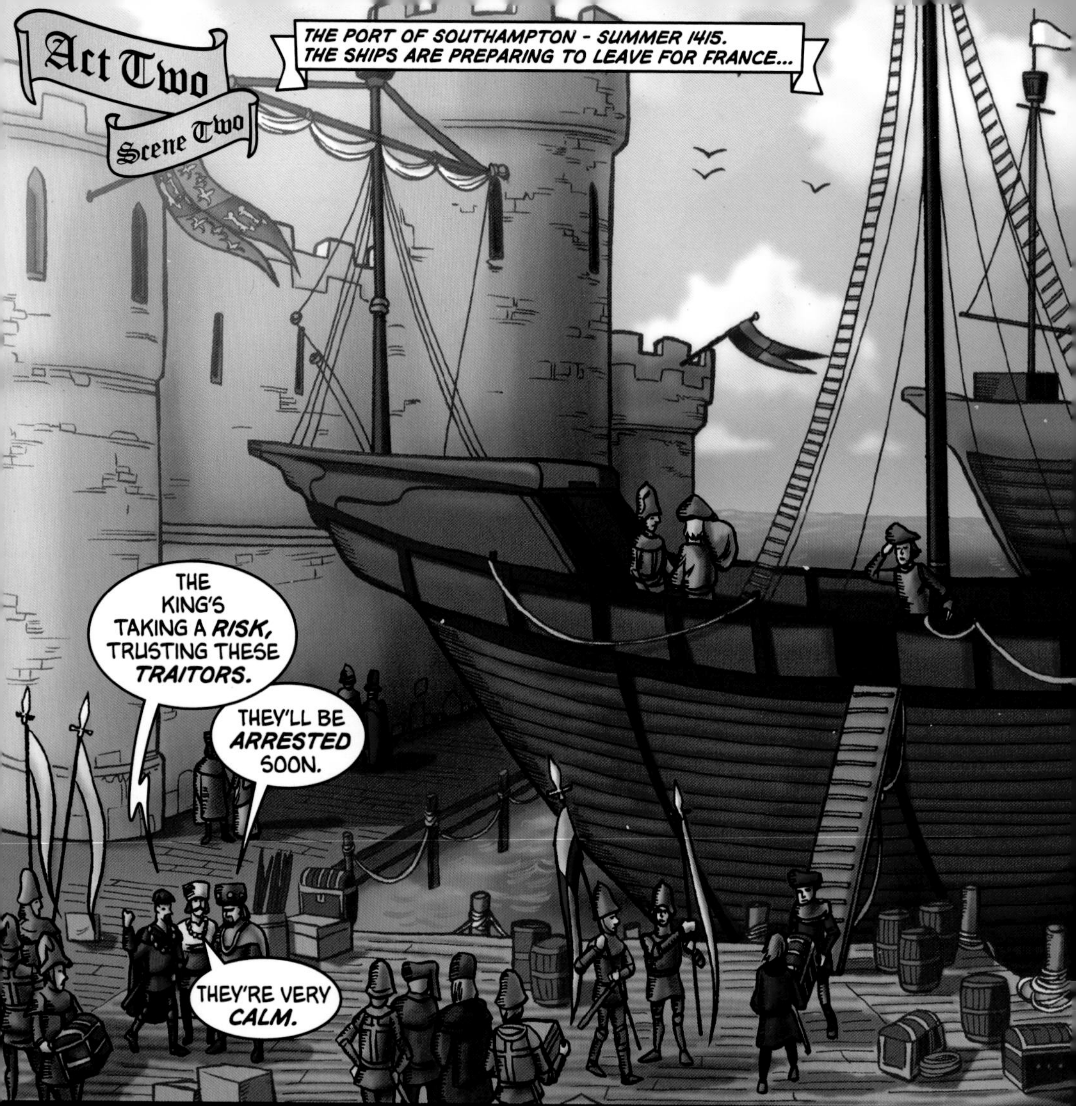
Act Two
Scene Two
THE PORT OF SOUTHAMPTON - SUMMER 1415. THE SHIPS ARE PREPARING TO LEAVE FOR FRANCE...
THE KING'S TAKING A RISK, TRUSTING THESE TRAITORS.
THEY'LL BE ARRESTED SOON.
THEY'RE VERY CALM.

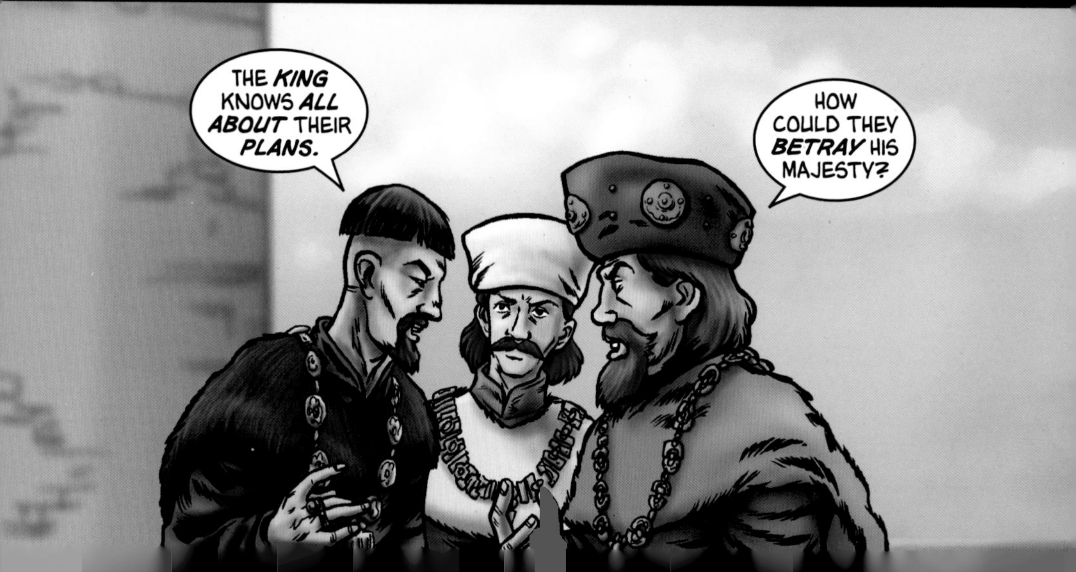
THE KING KNOWS ALL ABOUT THEIR PLANS.
HOW COULD THEY BETRAY HIS MAJESTY?

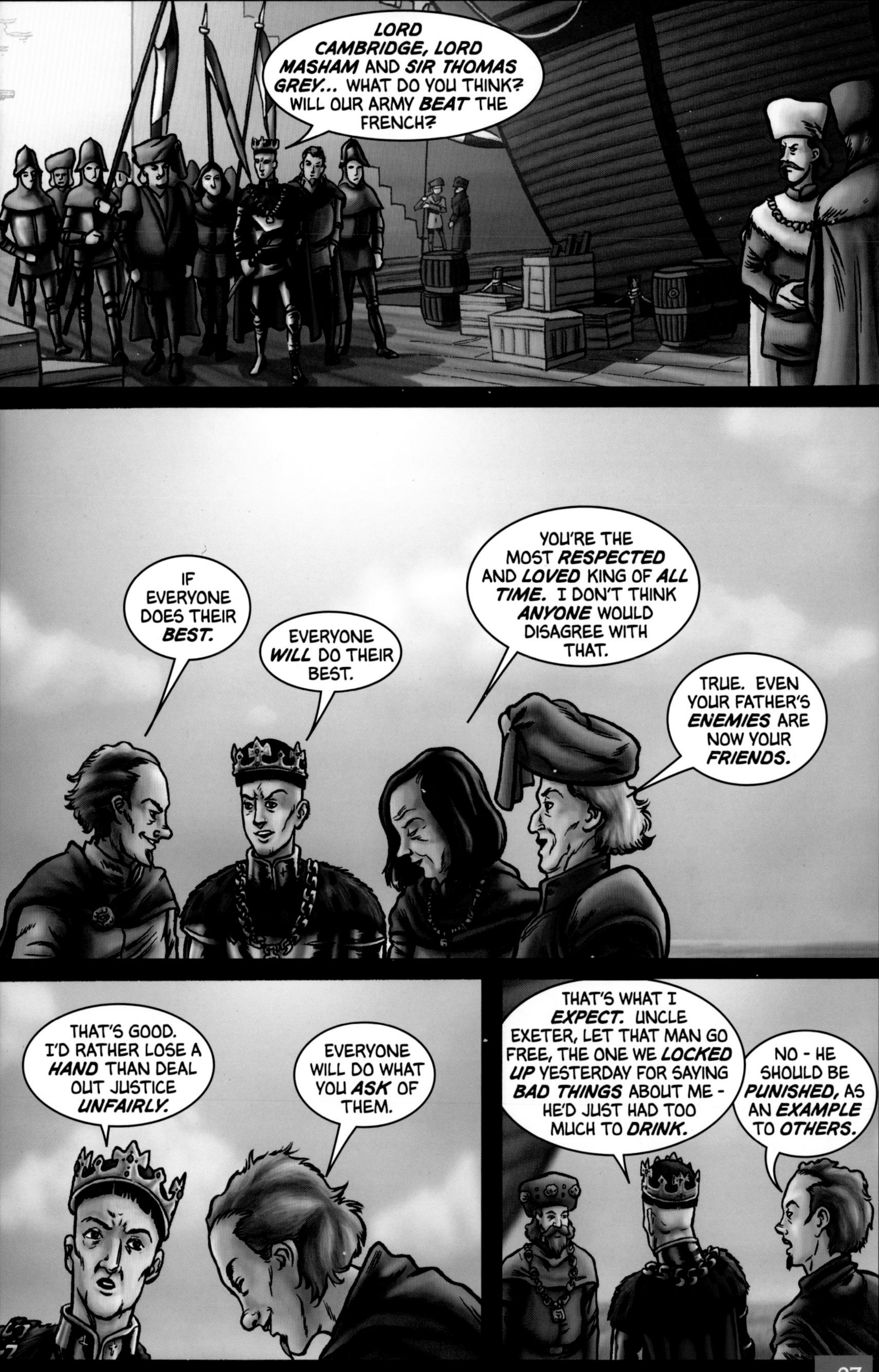
LORD CAMBRIDGE, LORD MASHAM AND SIR THOMAS GREY... WHAT DO YOU THINK? WILL OUR ARMY BEAT THE FRENCH?
IF EVERYONE DOES THEIR BEST.
EVERYONE WILL DO THEIR BEST.
YOU'RE THE MOST RESPECTED AND LOVED KING OF ALL TIME. I DON'T THINK ANYONE WOULD DISAGREE WITH THAT.
TRUE. EVEN YOUR FATHER'S ENEMIES ARE NOW YOUR FRIENDS.
THAT'S GOOD. I'D RATHER LOSE A HAND THAN DEAL OUT JUSTICE UNFAIRLY.
EVERYONE WILL DO WHAT YOU ASK OF THEM.
THAT'S WHAT I EXPECT. UNCLE EXETER, LET THAT MAN GO FREE, THE ONE WE LOCKED UP YESTERDAY FOR SAYING BAD THINGS ABOUT ME - HE'D JUST HAD TOO MUCH TO DRINK.
NO - HE SHOULD BE PUNISHED, AS AN EXAMPLE TO OTHERS.

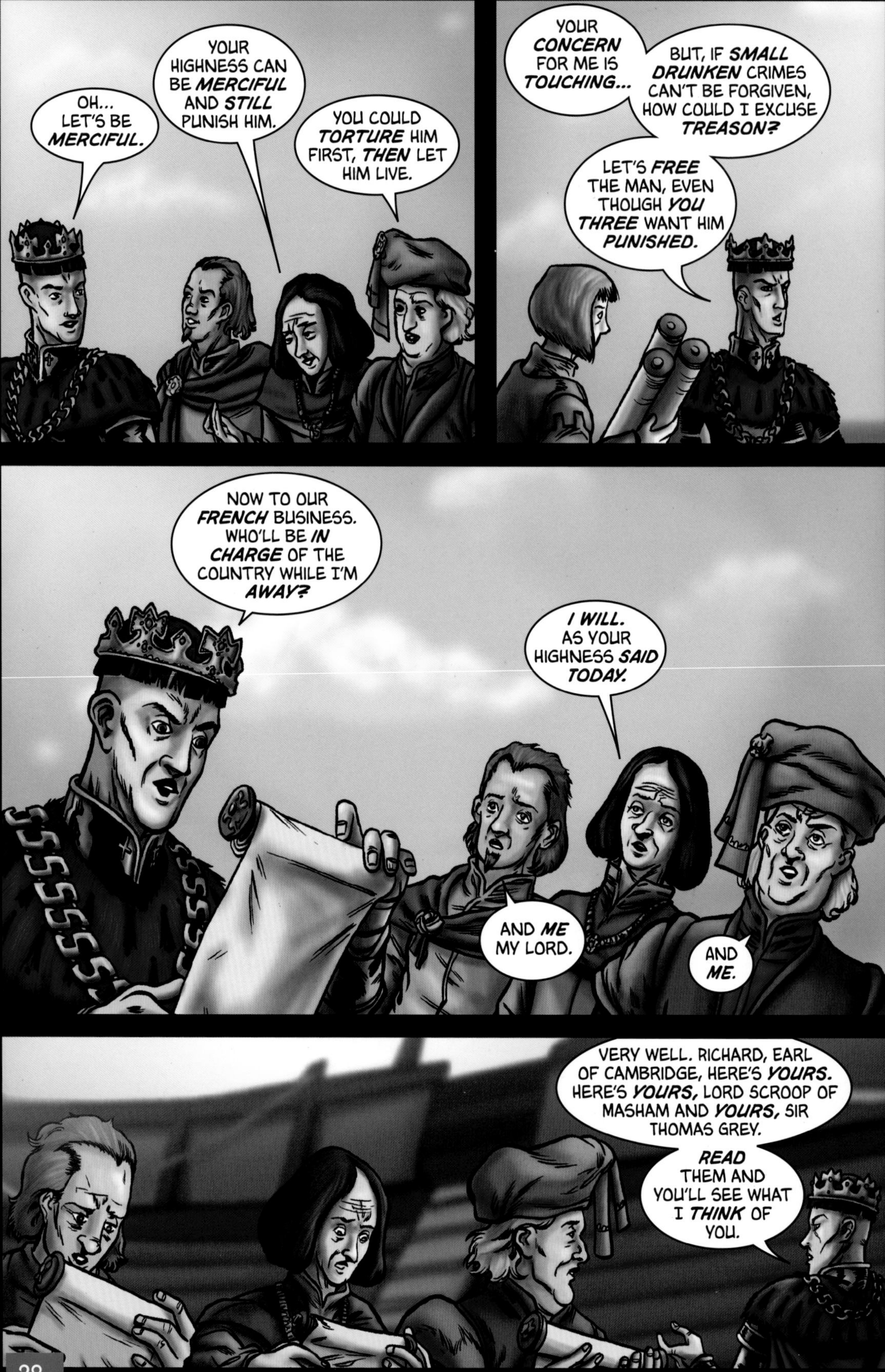
OH... LET'S BE MERCIFUL.
YOUR HIGHNESS CAN BE MERCIFUL AND STILL PUNISH HIM.
YOU COULD TORTURE HIM FIRST, THEN LET HIM LIVE.
YOUR CONCERN FOR ME IS TOUCHING...
BUT, IF SMALL DRUNKEN CRIMES CAN'T BE FORGIVEN, HOW COULD I EXCUSE TREASON?
LET'S FREE THE MAN, EVEN THOUGH YOU THREE WANT HIM PUNISHED.
NOW TO OUR FRENCH BUSINESS. WHO'LL BE IN CHARGE OF THE COUNTRY WHILE I'M AWAY?
I WILL. AS YOUR HIGHNESS SAID TODAY.
AND ME MY LORD.
AND ME.
VERY WELL. RICHARD, EARL OF CAMBRIDGE, HERE'S YOURS. HERE'S YOURS, LORD SCROOP OF MASHAM AND YOURS, SIR THOMAS GREY.
READ THEM AND YOU'LL SEE WHAT I THINK OF YOU.

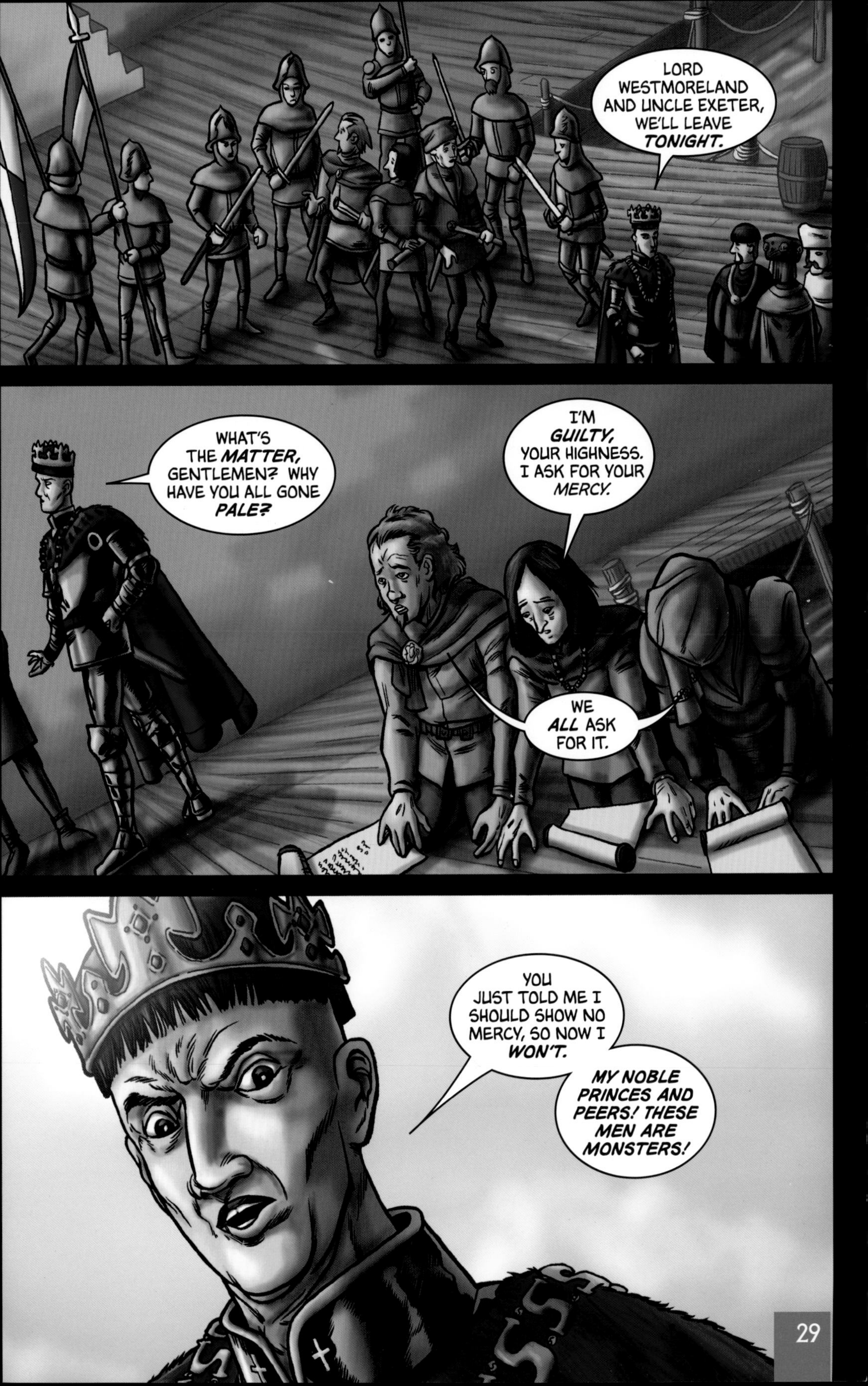
LORD WESTMORELAND AND UNCLE EXETER, WE'LL LEAVE *TONIGHT.*
WHAT'S THE *MATTER,* GENTLEMEN? WHY HAVE YOU ALL GONE *PALE?*
I'M *GUILTY,* YOUR HIGHNESS. I ASK FOR YOUR *MERCY.*
WE *ALL* ASK FOR IT.
YOU JUST TOLD ME I SHOULD SHOW NO MERCY, SO NOW I *WON'T.*
MY NOBLE PRINCES AND PEERS! THESE MEN ARE MONSTERS!

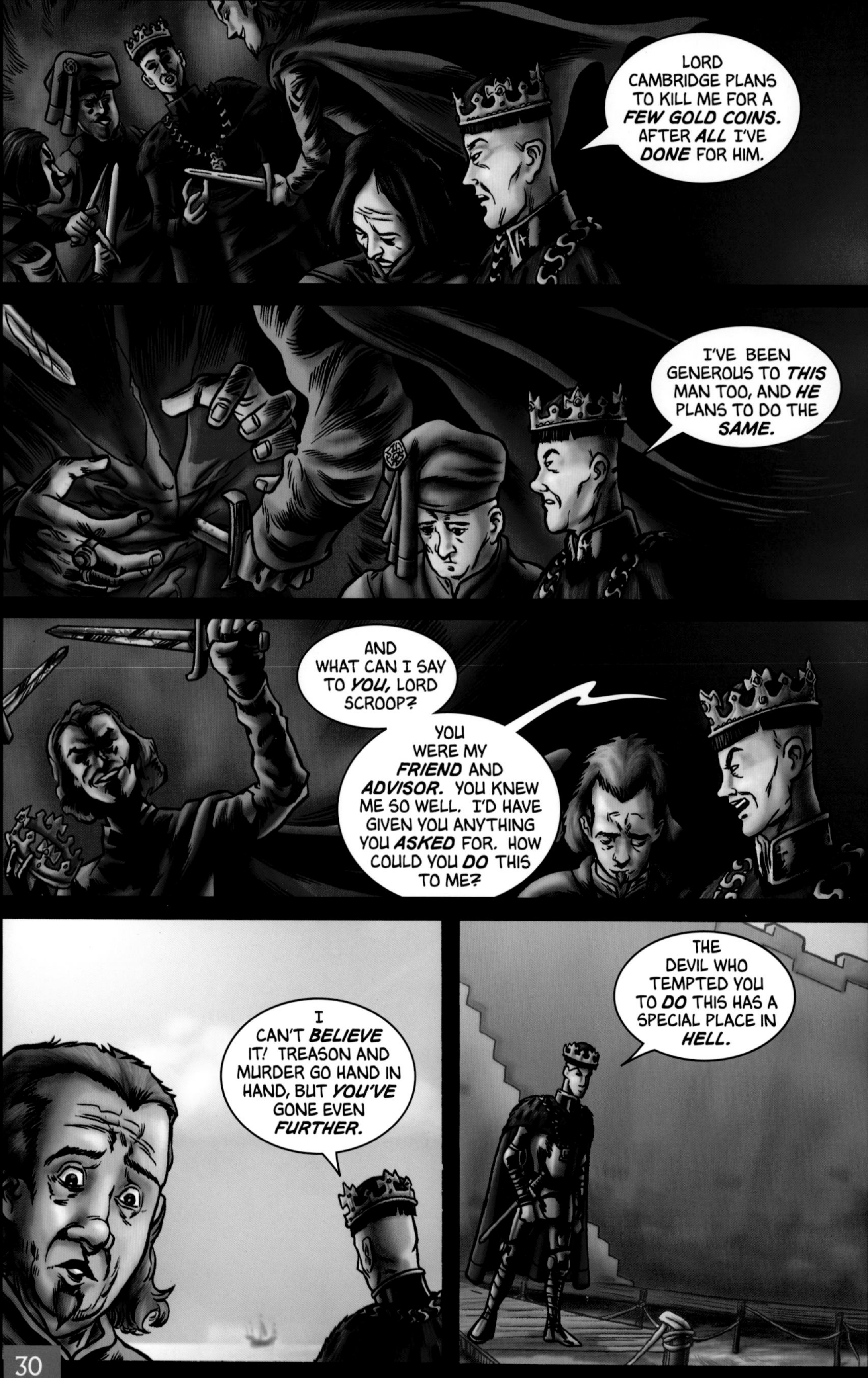
LORD CAMBRIDGE PLANS TO KILL ME FOR A FEW GOLD COINS. AFTER ALL I'VE DONE FOR HIM.
I'VE BEEN GENEROUS TO THIS MAN TOO, AND HE PLANS TO DO THE SAME.
AND WHAT CAN I SAY TO YOU, LORD SCROOP?
YOU WERE MY FRIEND AND ADVISOR. YOU KNEW ME SO WELL. I'D HAVE GIVEN YOU ANYTHING YOU ASKED FOR. HOW COULD YOU DO THIS TO ME?
I CAN'T BELIEVE IT! TREASON AND MURDER GO HAND IN HAND, BUT YOU'VE GONE EVEN FURTHER.
THE DEVIL WHO TEMPTED YOU TO DO THIS HAS A SPECIAL PLACE IN HELL.

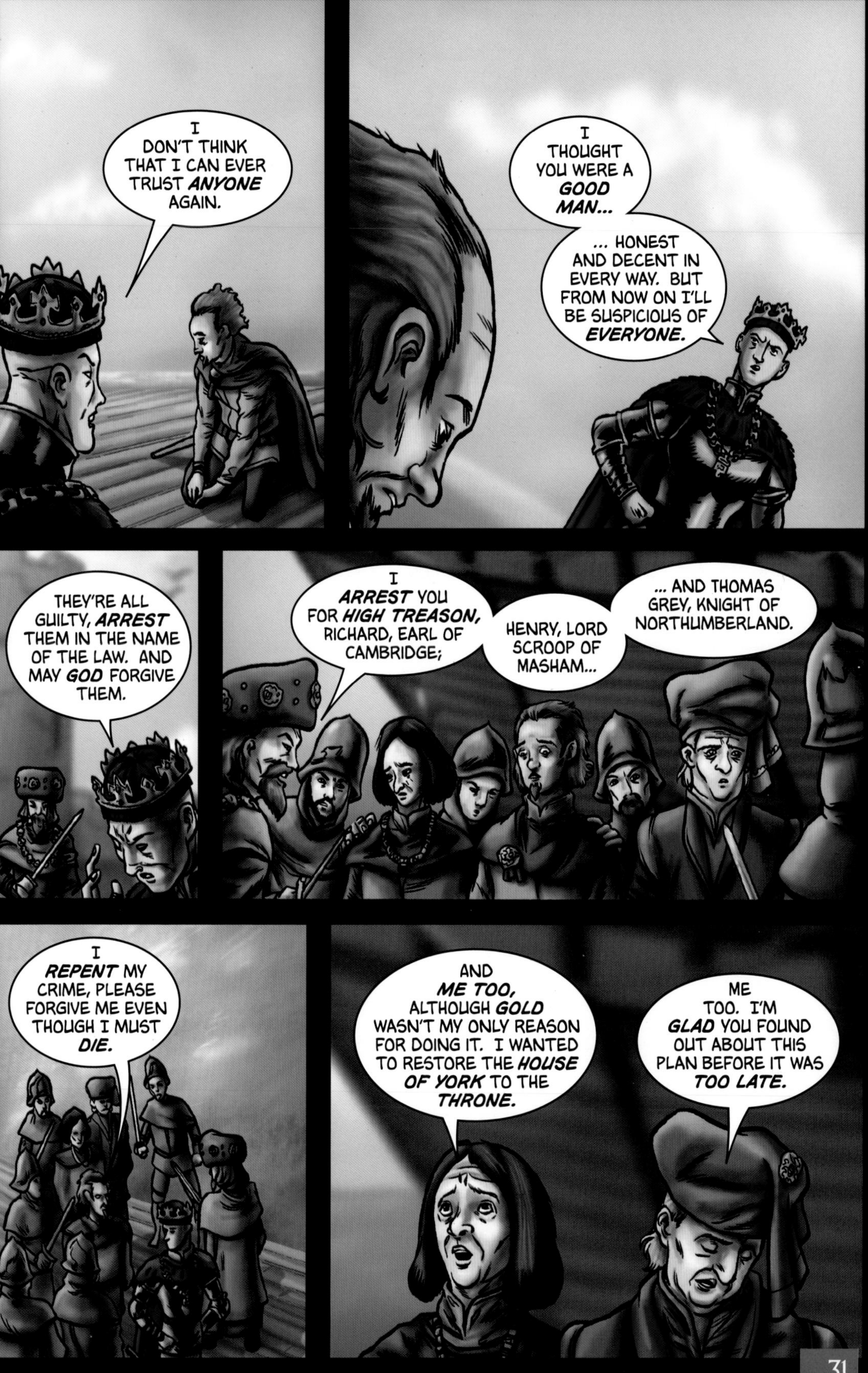
I DON'T THINK THAT I CAN EVER TRUST ANYONE AGAIN.
I THOUGHT YOU WERE A GOOD MAN...
... HONEST AND DECENT IN EVERY WAY. BUT FROM NOW ON I'LL BE SUSPICIOUS OF EVERYONE.
THEY'RE ALL GUILTY, ARREST THEM IN THE NAME OF THE LAW. AND MAY GOD FORGIVE THEM.
I ARREST YOU FOR HIGH TREASON, RICHARD, EARL OF CAMBRIDGE;
HENRY, LORD SCROOP OF MASHAM...
... AND THOMAS GREY, KNIGHT OF NORTHUMBERLAND.
I REPENT MY CRIME, PLEASE FORGIVE ME EVEN THOUGH I MUST DIE.
AND ME TOO, ALTHOUGH GOLD WASN'T MY ONLY REASON FOR DOING IT. I WANTED TO RESTORE THE HOUSE OF YORK TO THE THRONE.
ME TOO. I'M GLAD YOU FOUND OUT ABOUT THIS PLAN BEFORE IT WAS TOO LATE.

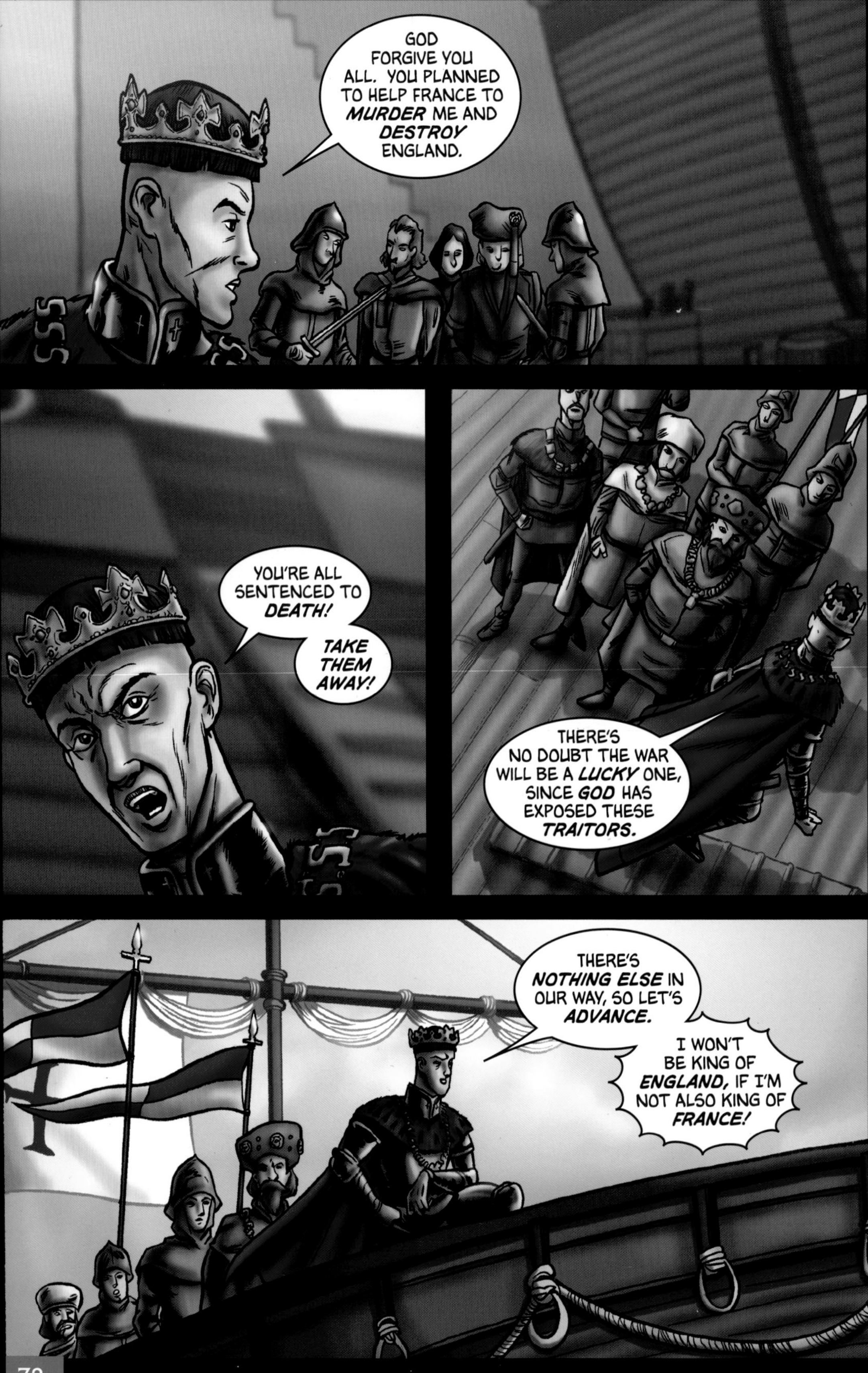
GOD FORGIVE YOU ALL. YOU PLANNED TO HELP FRANCE TO MURDER ME AND DESTROY ENGLAND.
YOU'RE ALL SENTENCED TO DEATH!
TAKE THEM AWAY!
THERE'S NO DOUBT THE WAR WILL BE A LUCKY ONE, SINCE GOD HAS EXPOSED THESE TRAITORS.
THERE'S NOTHING ELSE IN OUR WAY, SO LET'S ADVANCE.
I WON'T BE KING OF ENGLAND, IF I'M NOT ALSO KING OF FRANCE!

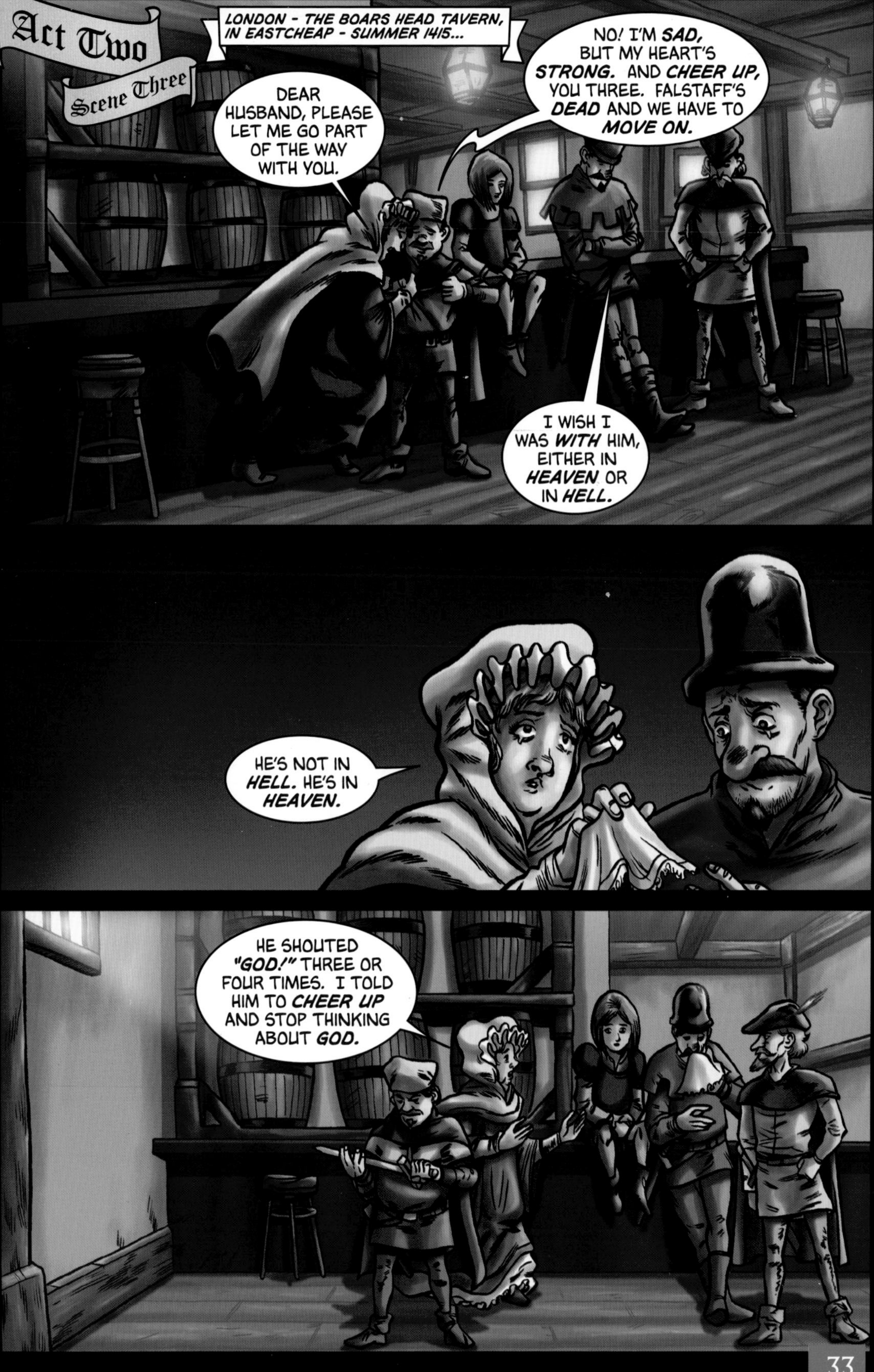
Act Two
Scene Three
LONDON - THE BOARS HEAD TAVERN, IN EASTCHEAP - SUMMER 1415...
DEAR HUSBAND, PLEASE LET ME GO PART OF THE WAY WITH YOU.
NO! I'M SAD, BUT MY HEART'S STRONG. AND CHEER UP, YOU THREE. FALSTAFF'S DEAD AND WE HAVE TO MOVE ON.
I WISH I WAS WITH HIM, EITHER IN HEAVEN OR IN HELL.
HE'S NOT IN HELL. HE'S IN HEAVEN.
HE SHOUTED "GOD!" THREE OR FOUR TIMES. I TOLD HIM TO CHEER UP AND STOP THINKING ABOUT GOD.

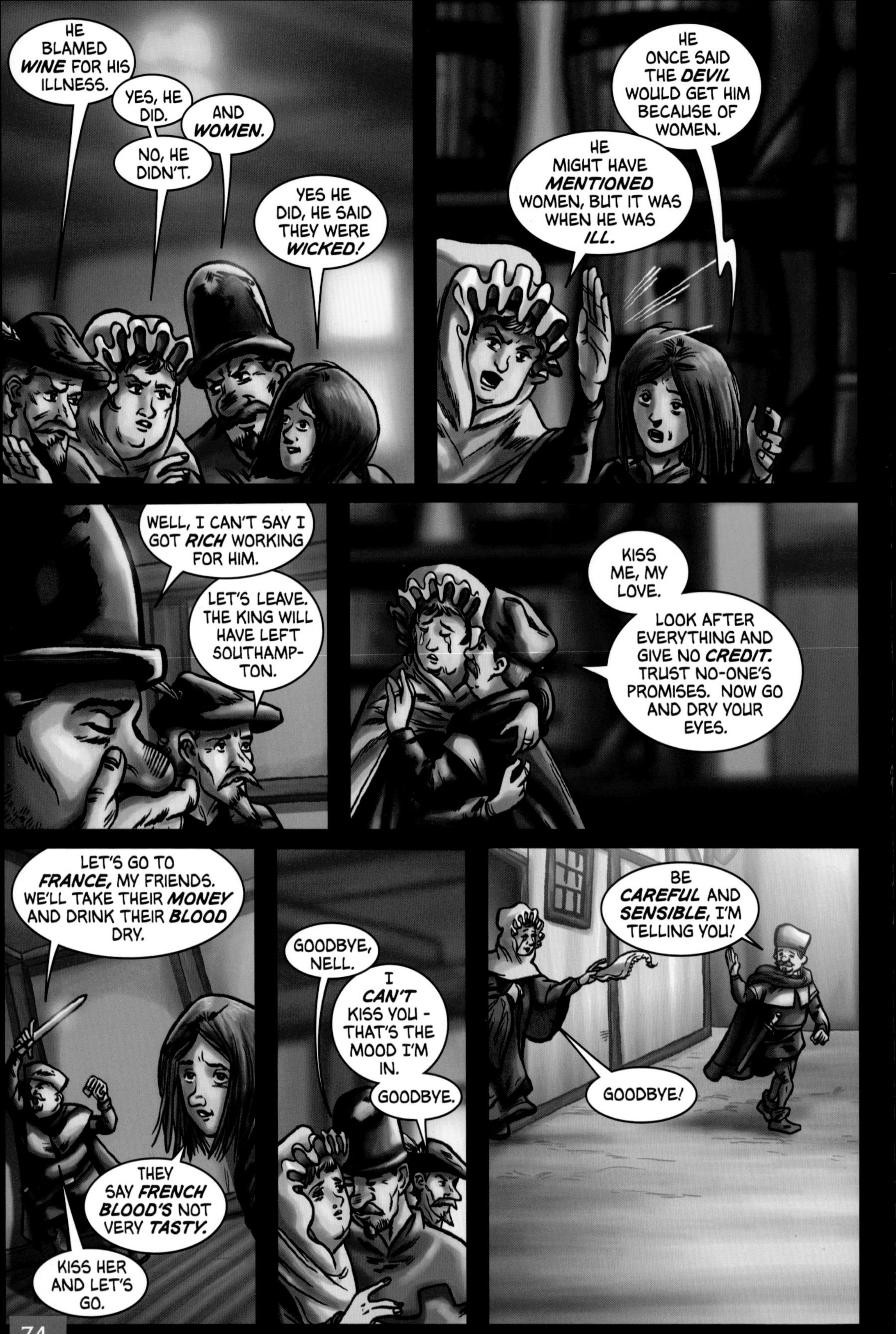
HE BLAMED WINE FOR HIS ILLNESS.
YES, HE DID.
NO, HE DIDN'T.
AND WOMEN.
YES HE DID, HE SAID THEY WERE WICKED!
HE ONCE SAID THE DEVIL WOULD GET HIM BECAUSE OF WOMEN.
HE MIGHT HAVE MENTIONED WOMEN, BUT IT WAS WHEN HE WAS ILL.
WELL, I CAN'T SAY I GOT RICH WORKING FOR HIM.
LET'S LEAVE. THE KING WILL HAVE LEFT SOUTHAMPTON.
KISS ME, MY LOVE.
LOOK AFTER EVERYTHING AND GIVE NO CREDIT. TRUST NO-ONE'S PROMISES. NOW GO AND DRY YOUR EYES.
LET'S GO TO FRANCE, MY FRIENDS. WE'LL TAKE THEIR MONEY AND DRINK THEIR BLOOD DRY.
THEY SAY FRENCH BLOOD'S NOT VERY TASTY.
KISS HER AND LET'S GO.
GOODBYE, NELL.
I CAN'T KISS YOU - THAT'S THE MOOD I'M IN.
GOODBYE.
BE CAREFUL AND SENSIBLE, I'M TELLING YOU!
GOODBYE!

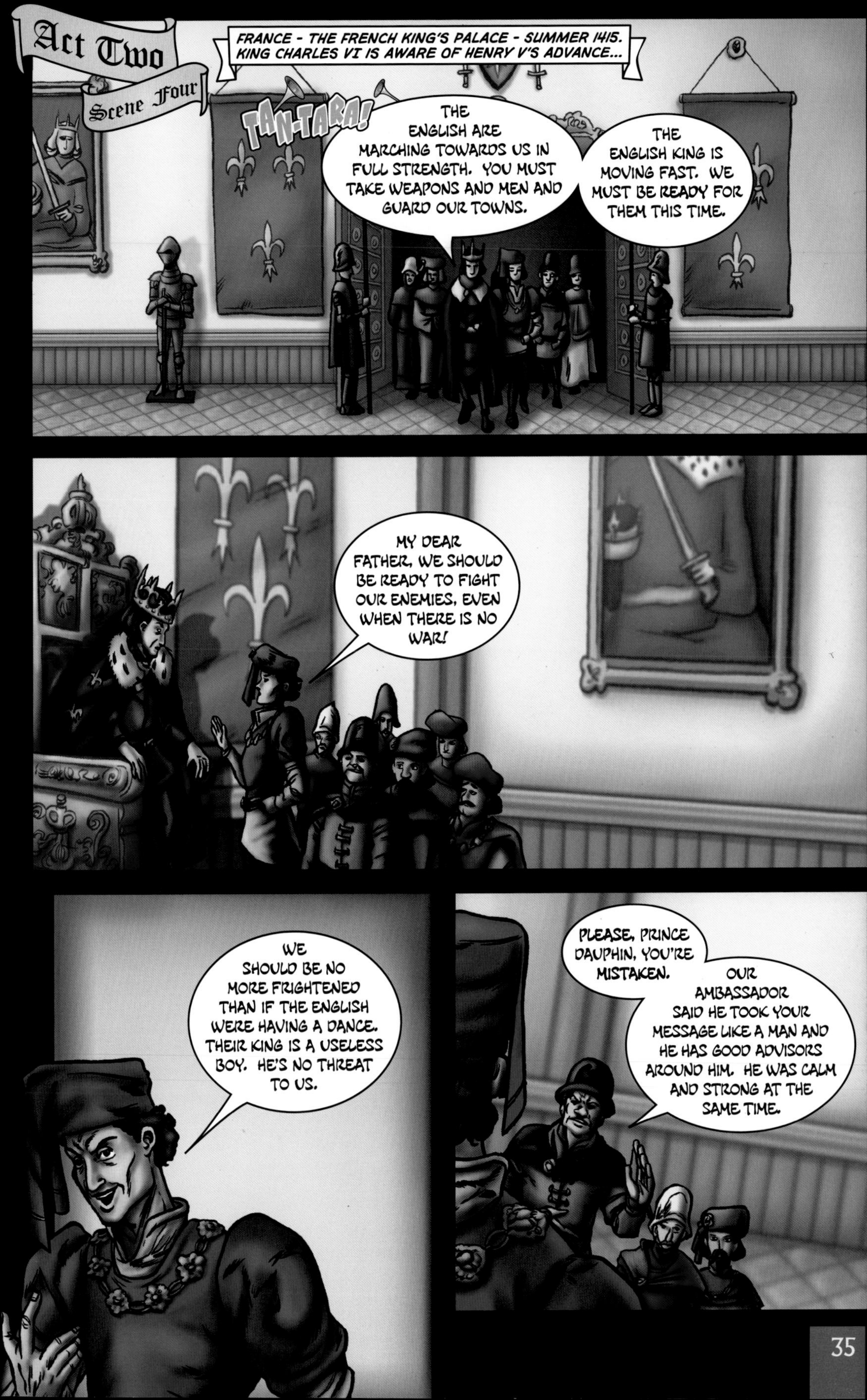
Act Two
Scene Four
FRANCE - THE FRENCH KING'S PALACE - SUMMER 1415. KING CHARLES VI IS AWARE OF HENRY V'S ADVANCE...
TAN-TARA!
THE ENGLISH ARE MARCHING TOWARDS US IN FULL STRENGTH. YOU MUST TAKE WEAPONS AND MEN AND GUARD OUR TOWNS.
THE ENGLISH KING IS MOVING FAST. WE MUST BE READY FOR THEM THIS TIME.
MY DEAR FATHER, WE SHOULD BE READY TO FIGHT OUR ENEMIES, EVEN WHEN THERE IS NO WAR!
WE SHOULD BE NO MORE FRIGHTENED THAN IF THE ENGLISH WERE HAVING A DANCE. THEIR KING IS A USELESS BOY. HE'S NO THREAT TO US.
PLEASE, PRINCE DAUPHIN, YOU'RE MISTAKEN.
OUR AMBASSADOR SAID HE TOOK YOUR MESSAGE LIKE A MAN AND HE HAS GOOD ADVISORS AROUND HIM. HE WAS CALM AND STRONG AT THE SAME TIME.

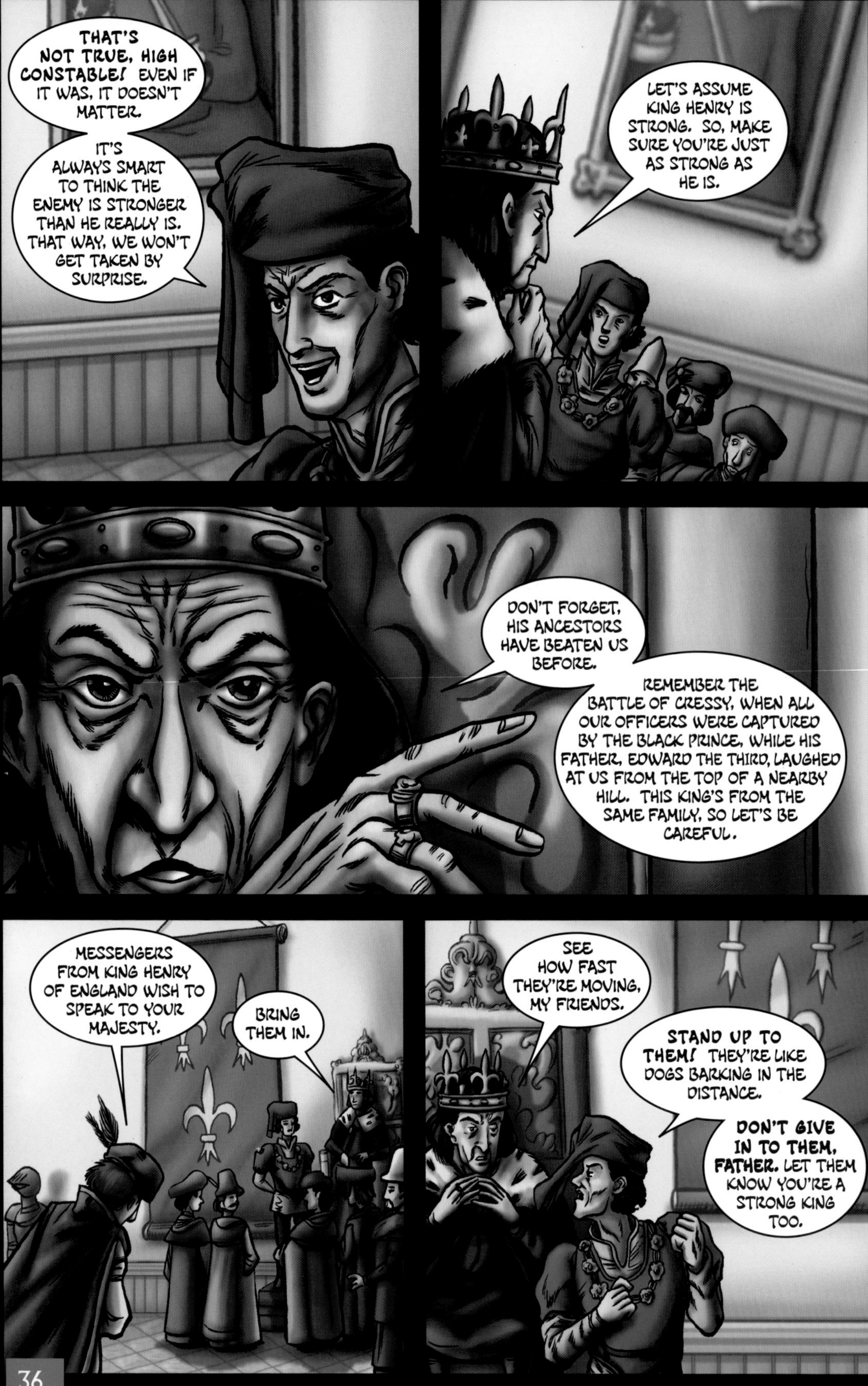
THAT'S NOT TRUE, HIGH CONSTABLE! EVEN IF IT WAS, IT DOESN'T MATTER.
IT'S ALWAYS SMART TO THINK THE ENEMY IS STRONGER THAN HE REALLY IS. THAT WAY, WE WON'T GET TAKEN BY SURPRISE.
LET'S ASSUME KING HENRY IS STRONG. SO, MAKE SURE YOU'RE JUST AS STRONG AS HE IS.
DON'T FORGET, HIS ANCESTORS HAVE BEATEN US BEFORE.
REMEMBER THE BATTLE OF CRESSY, WHEN ALL OUR OFFICERS WERE CAPTURED BY THE BLACK PRINCE, WHILE HIS FATHER, EDWARD THE THIRD, LAUGHED AT US FROM THE TOP OF A NEARBY HILL. THIS KING'S FROM THE SAME FAMILY, SO LET'S BE CAREFUL.
MESSENGERS FROM KING HENRY OF ENGLAND WISH TO SPEAK TO YOUR MAJESTY.
BRING THEM IN.
SEE HOW FAST THEY'RE MOVING, MY FRIENDS.
STAND UP TO THEM! THEY'RE LIKE DOGS BARKING IN THE DISTANCE.
DON'T GIVE IN TO THEM, FATHER. LET THEM KNOW YOU'RE A STRONG KING TOO.

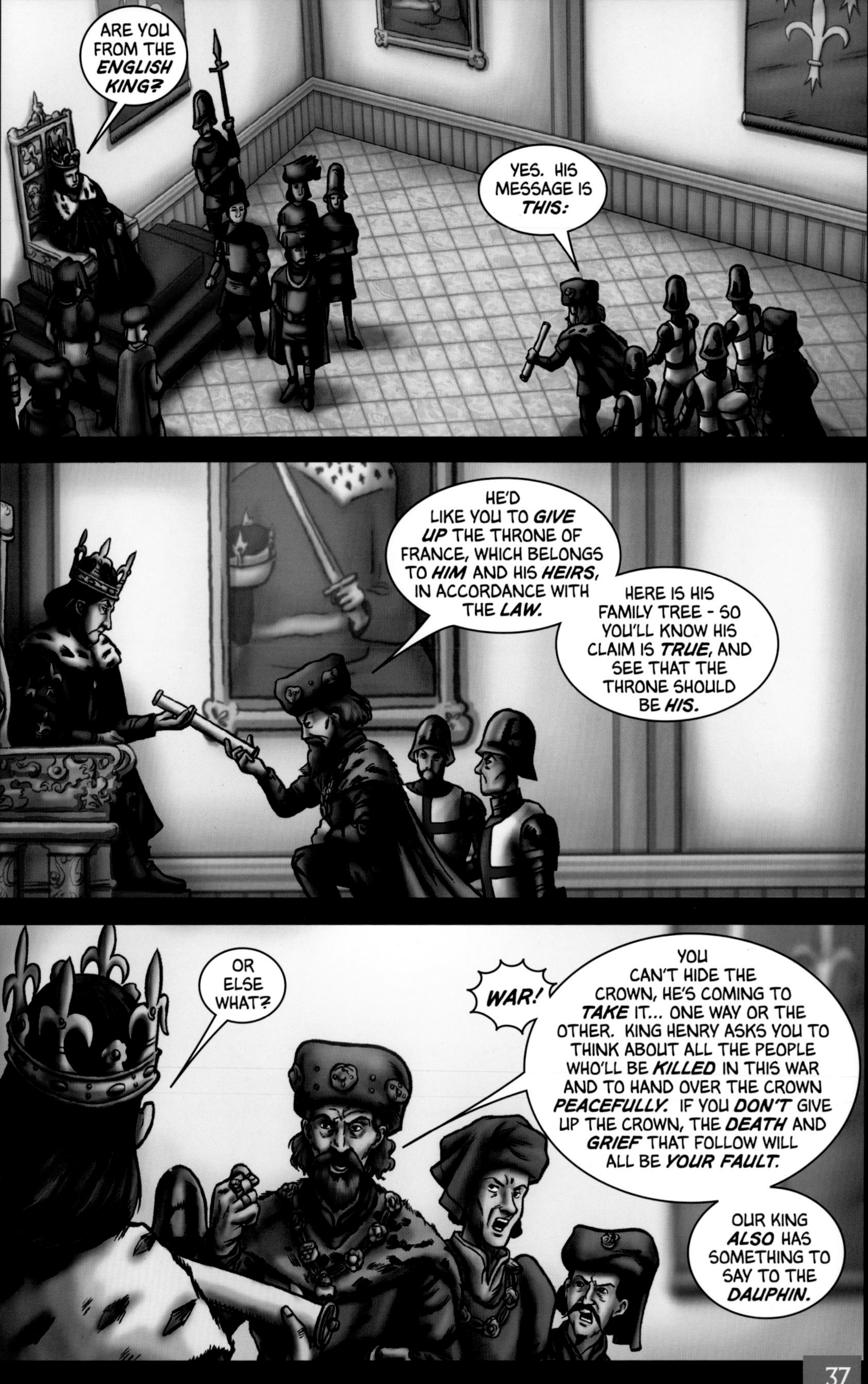
ARE YOU FROM THE ENGLISH KING?
YES. HIS MESSAGE IS THIS:
HE'D LIKE YOU TO GIVE UP THE THRONE OF FRANCE, WHICH BELONGS TO HIM AND HIS HEIRS, IN ACCORDANCE WITH THE LAW.
HERE IS HIS FAMILY TREE - SO YOU'LL KNOW HIS CLAIM IS TRUE, AND SEE THAT THE THRONE SHOULD BE HIS.
OR ELSE WHAT?
WAR!
YOU CAN'T HIDE THE CROWN, HE'S COMING TO TAKE IT... ONE WAY OR THE OTHER. KING HENRY ASKS YOU TO THINK ABOUT ALL THE PEOPLE WHO'LL BE KILLED IN THIS WAR AND TO HAND OVER THE CROWN PEACEFULLY. IF YOU DON'T GIVE UP THE CROWN, THE DEATH AND GRIEF THAT FOLLOW WILL ALL BE YOUR FAULT.
OUR KING ALSO HAS SOMETHING TO SAY TO THE DAUPHIN.

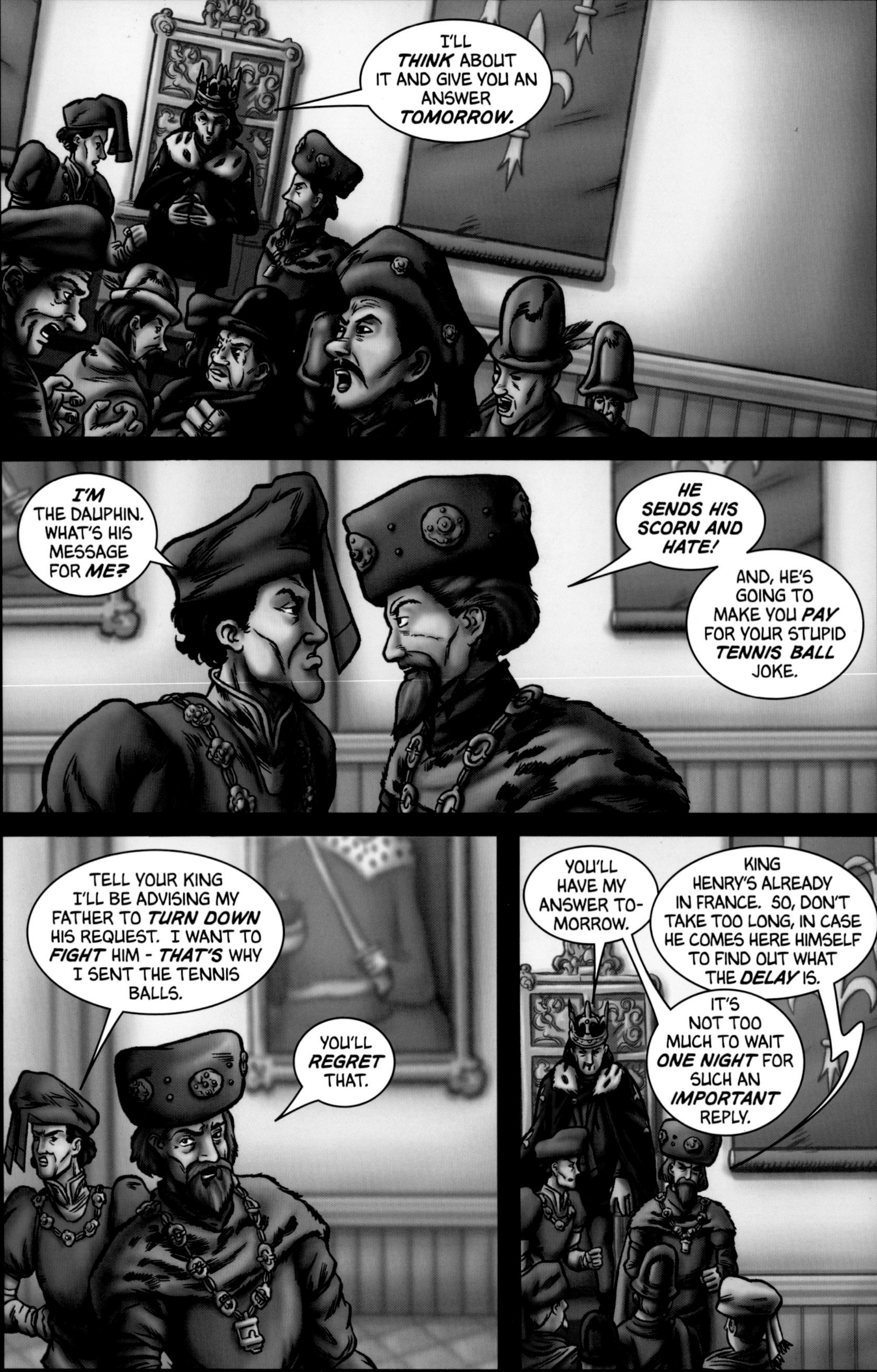
I'LL *THINK* ABOUT IT AND GIVE YOU AN ANSWER *TOMORROW.*
I'M THE DAUPHIN. WHAT'S HIS MESSAGE FOR *ME?*
HE SENDS HIS SCORN AND HATE!
AND, HE'S GOING TO MAKE YOU *PAY* FOR YOUR STUPID *TENNIS BALL* JOKE.
TELL YOUR KING I'LL BE ADVISING MY FATHER TO *TURN DOWN* HIS REQUEST. I WANT TO *FIGHT* HIM - *THAT'S* WHY I SENT THE TENNIS BALLS.
YOU'LL *REGRET* THAT.
YOU'LL HAVE MY ANSWER TO-MORROW.
KING HENRY'S ALREADY IN FRANCE. SO, DON'T TAKE TOO LONG, IN CASE HE COMES HERE HIMSELF TO FIND OUT WHAT THE *DELAY* IS.
IT'S NOT TOO MUCH TO WAIT *ONE NIGHT* FOR SUCH AN *IMPORTANT* REPLY.

Act Three
Prologue

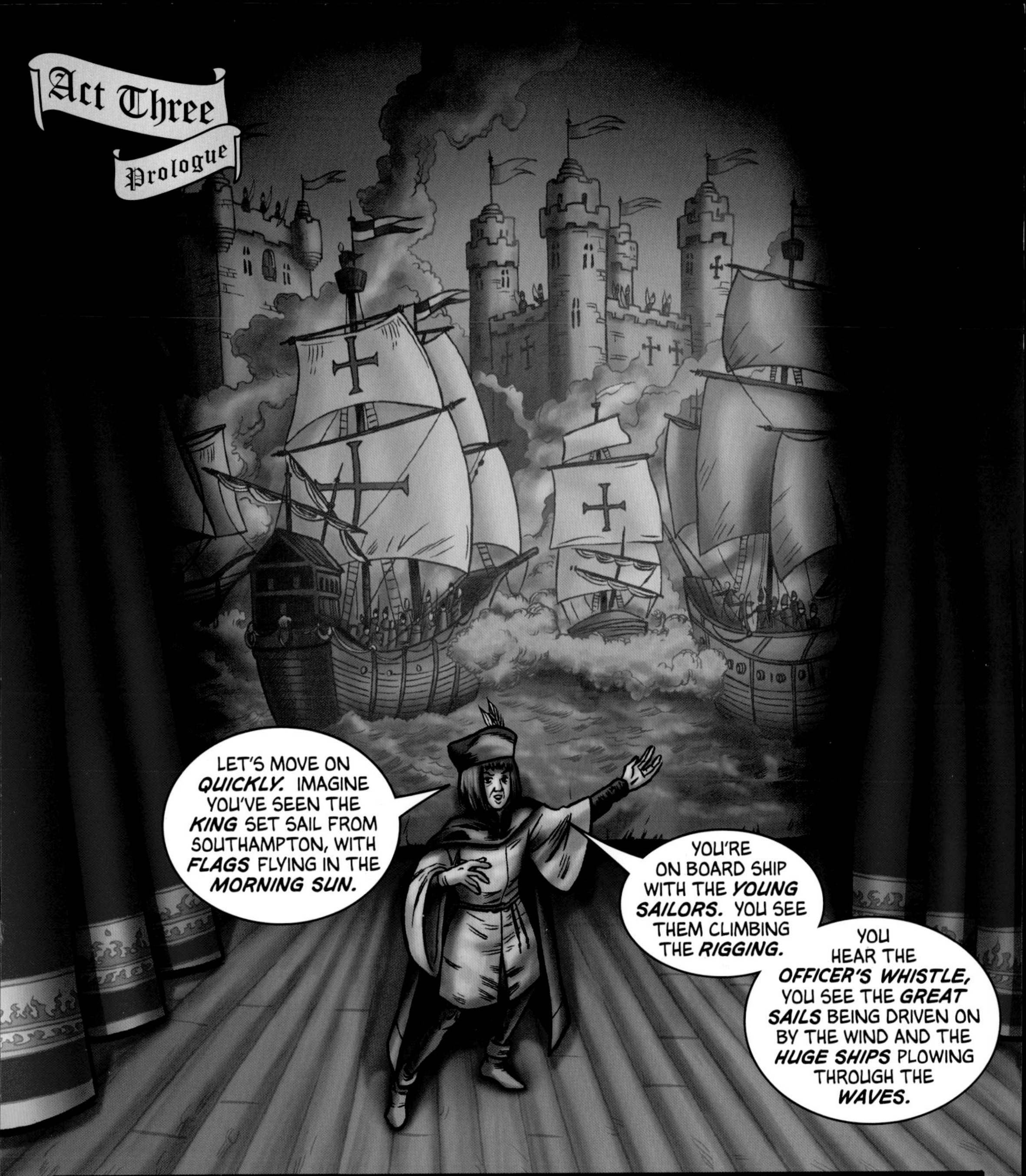
LET'S MOVE ON QUICKLY. IMAGINE YOU'VE SEEN THE KING SET SAIL FROM SOUTHAMPTON, WITH FLAGS FLYING IN THE MORNING SUN.
YOU'RE ON BOARD SHIP WITH THE YOUNG SAILORS. YOU SEE THEM CLIMBING THE RIGGING.
YOU HEAR THE OFFICER'S WHISTLE, YOU SEE THE GREAT SAILS BEING DRIVEN ON BY THE WIND AND THE HUGE SHIPS PLOWING THROUGH THE WAVES.

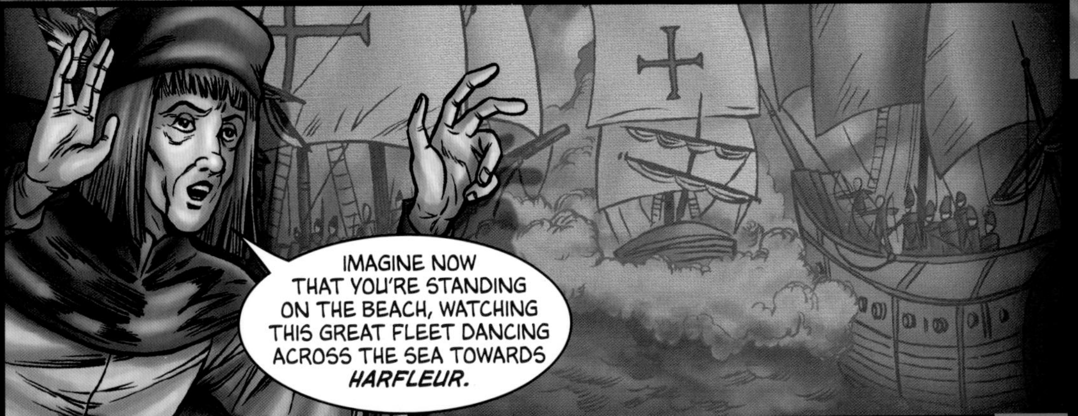
IMAGINE NOW THAT YOU'RE STANDING ON THE BEACH, WATCHING THIS GREAT FLEET DANCING ACROSS THE SEA TOWARDS HARFLEUR.

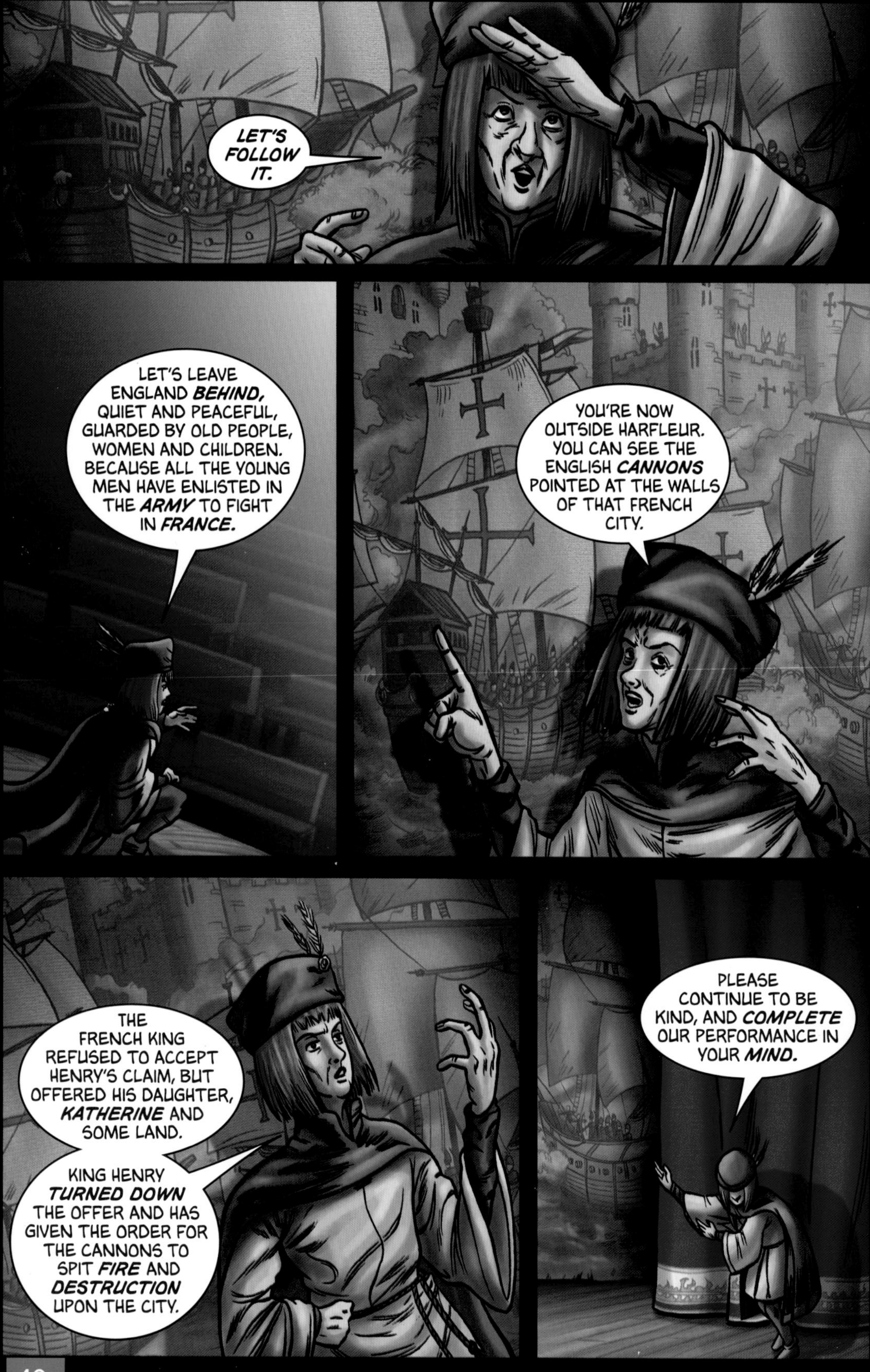
LET'S FOLLOW IT.
LET'S LEAVE ENGLAND BEHIND, QUIET AND PEACEFUL, GUARDED BY OLD PEOPLE, WOMEN AND CHILDREN. BECAUSE ALL THE YOUNG MEN HAVE ENLISTED IN THE ARMY TO FIGHT IN FRANCE.
YOU'RE NOW OUTSIDE HARFLEUR. YOU CAN SEE THE ENGLISH CANNONS POINTED AT THE WALLS OF THAT FRENCH CITY.
THE FRENCH KING REFUSED TO ACCEPT HENRY'S CLAIM, BUT OFFERED HIS DAUGHTER, KATHERINE AND SOME LAND.
KING HENRY TURNED DOWN THE OFFER AND HAS GIVEN THE ORDER FOR THE CANNONS TO SPIT FIRE AND DESTRUCTION UPON THE CITY.
PLEASE CONTINUE TO BE KIND, AND COMPLETE OUR PERFORMANCE IN YOUR MIND.

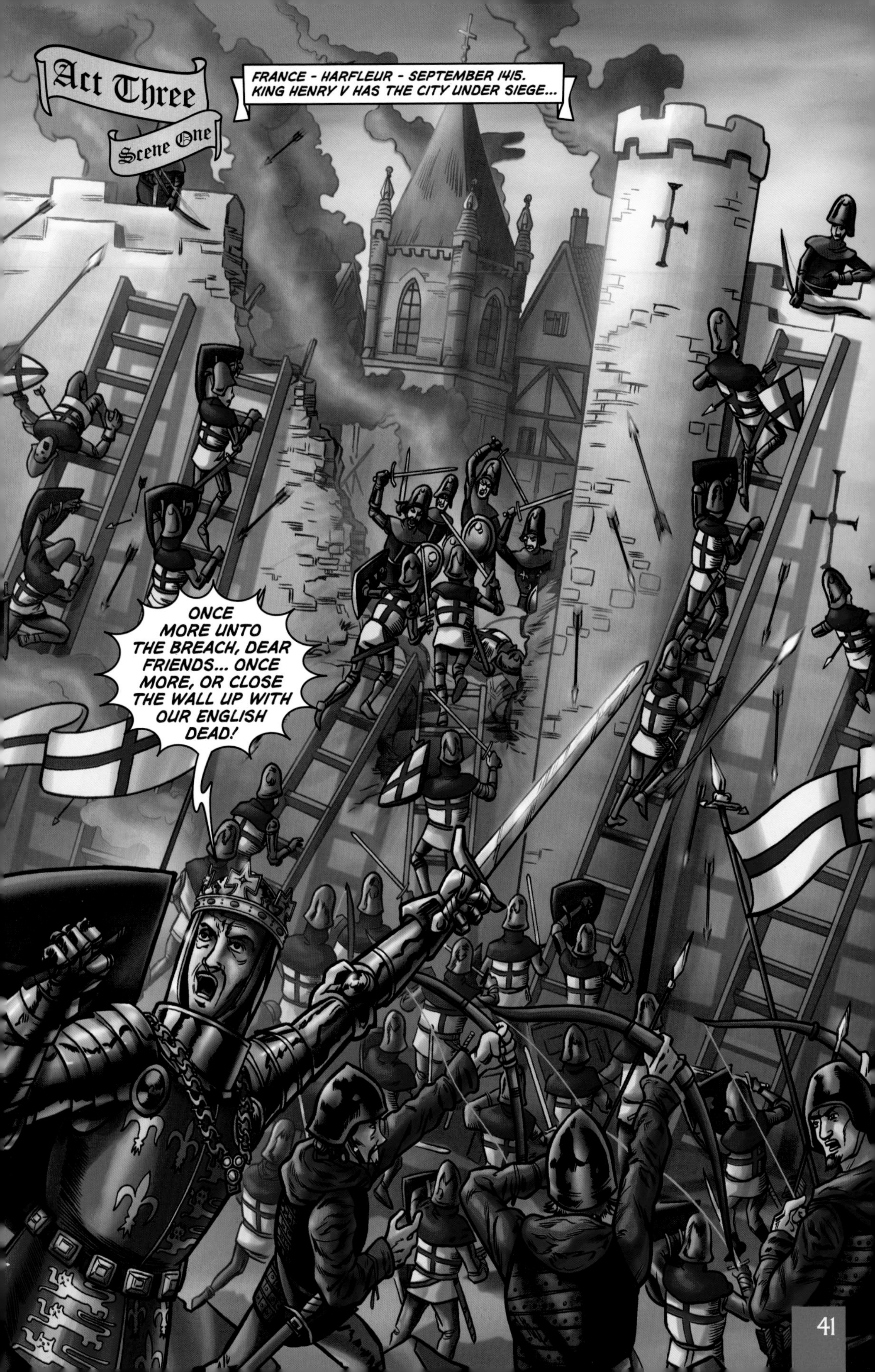
Act Three
Scene One
FRANCE - HARFLEUR - SEPTEMBER 1415. KING HENRY V HAS THE CITY UNDER SIEGE...
ONCE MORE UNTO THE BREACH, DEAR FRIENDS... ONCE MORE, OR CLOSE THE WALL UP WITH OUR ENGLISH DEAD!

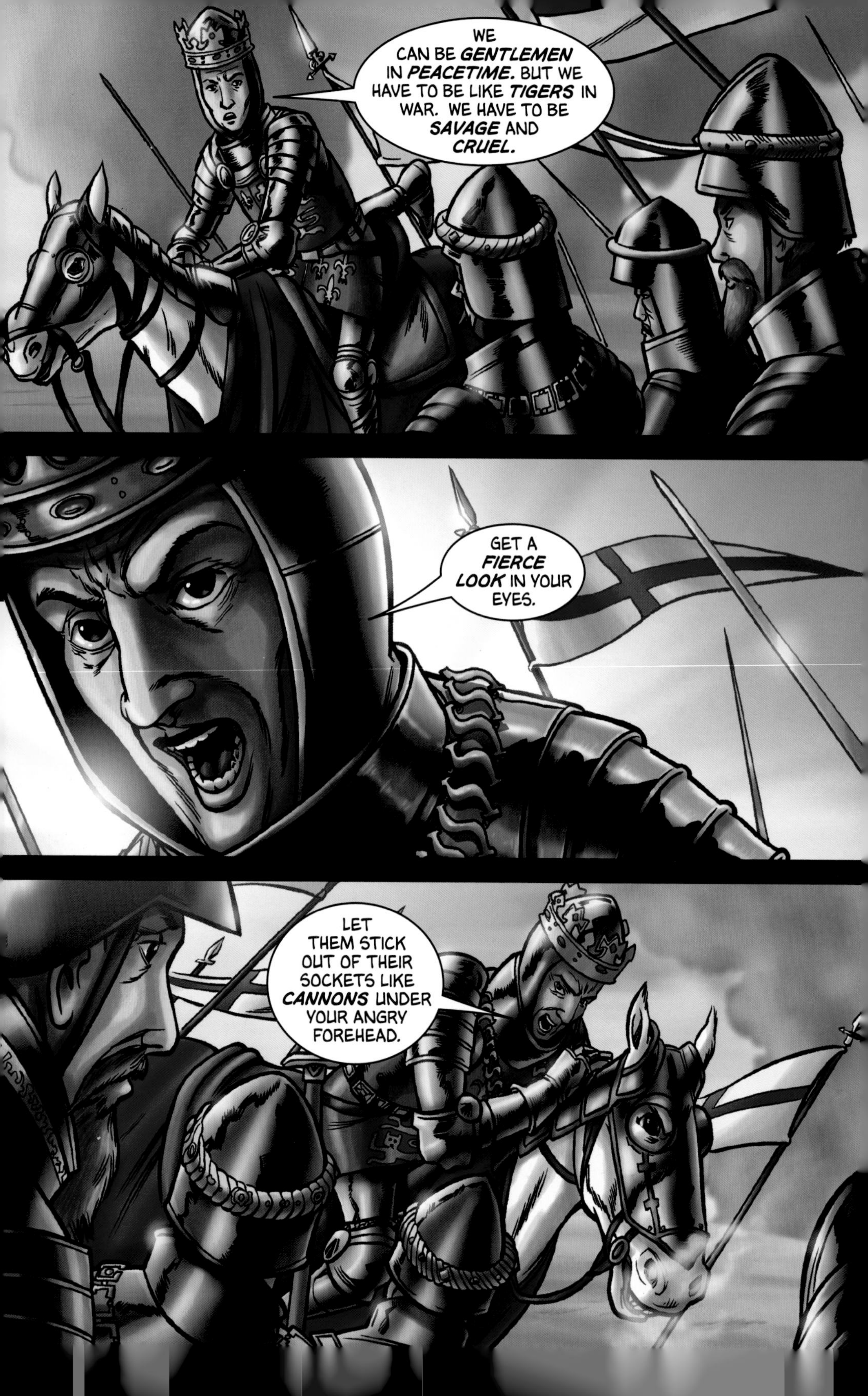
WE CAN BE GENTLEMEN IN PEACETIME. BUT WE HAVE TO BE LIKE TIGERS IN WAR. WE HAVE TO BE SAVAGE AND CRUEL.
GET A FIERCE LOOK IN YOUR EYES.
LET THEM STICK OUT OF THEIR SOCKETS LIKE CANNONS UNDER YOUR ANGRY FOREHEAD.

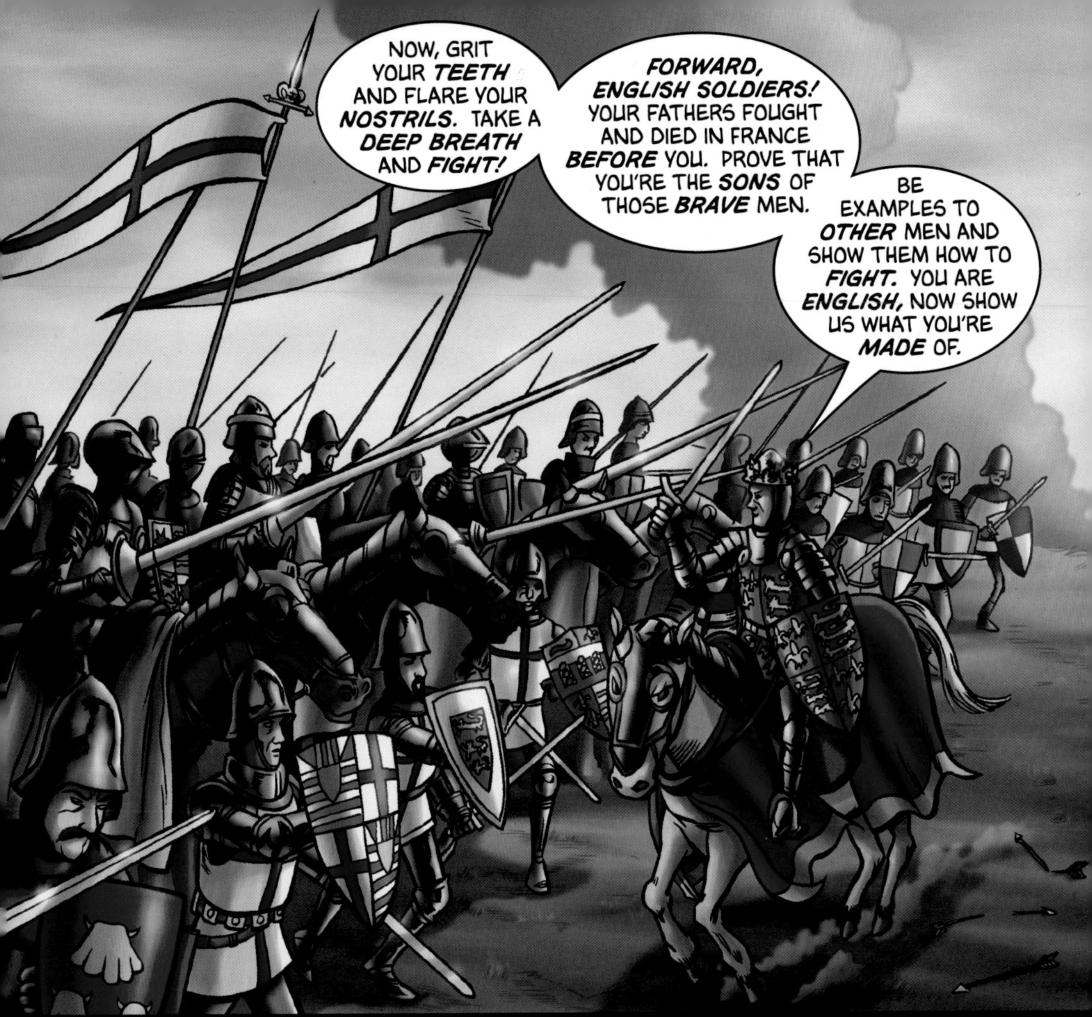
NOW, GRIT YOUR TEETH AND FLARE YOUR NOSTRILS. TAKE A DEEP BREATH AND FIGHT!
FORWARD, ENGLISH SOLDIERS! YOUR FATHERS FOUGHT AND DIED IN FRANCE BEFORE YOU. PROVE THAT YOU'RE THE SONS OF THOSE BRAVE MEN.
BE EXAMPLES TO OTHER MEN AND SHOW THEM HOW TO FIGHT. YOU ARE ENGLISH, NOW SHOW US WHAT YOU'RE MADE OF.

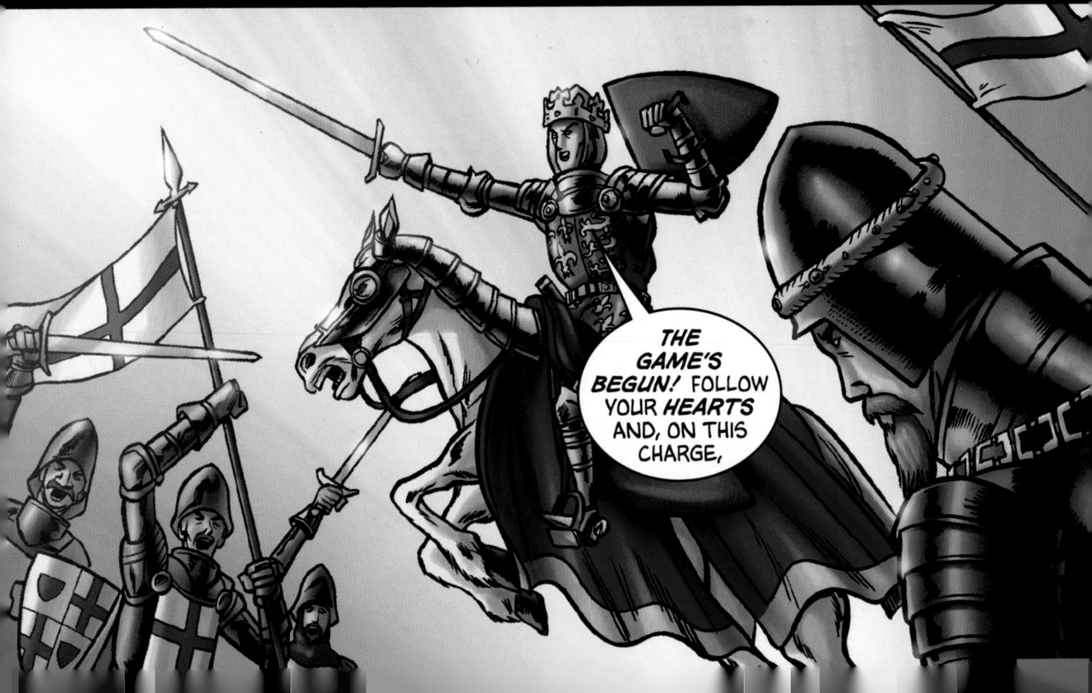
THE GAME'S BEGUN! FOLLOW YOUR HEARTS AND, ON THIS CHARGE,

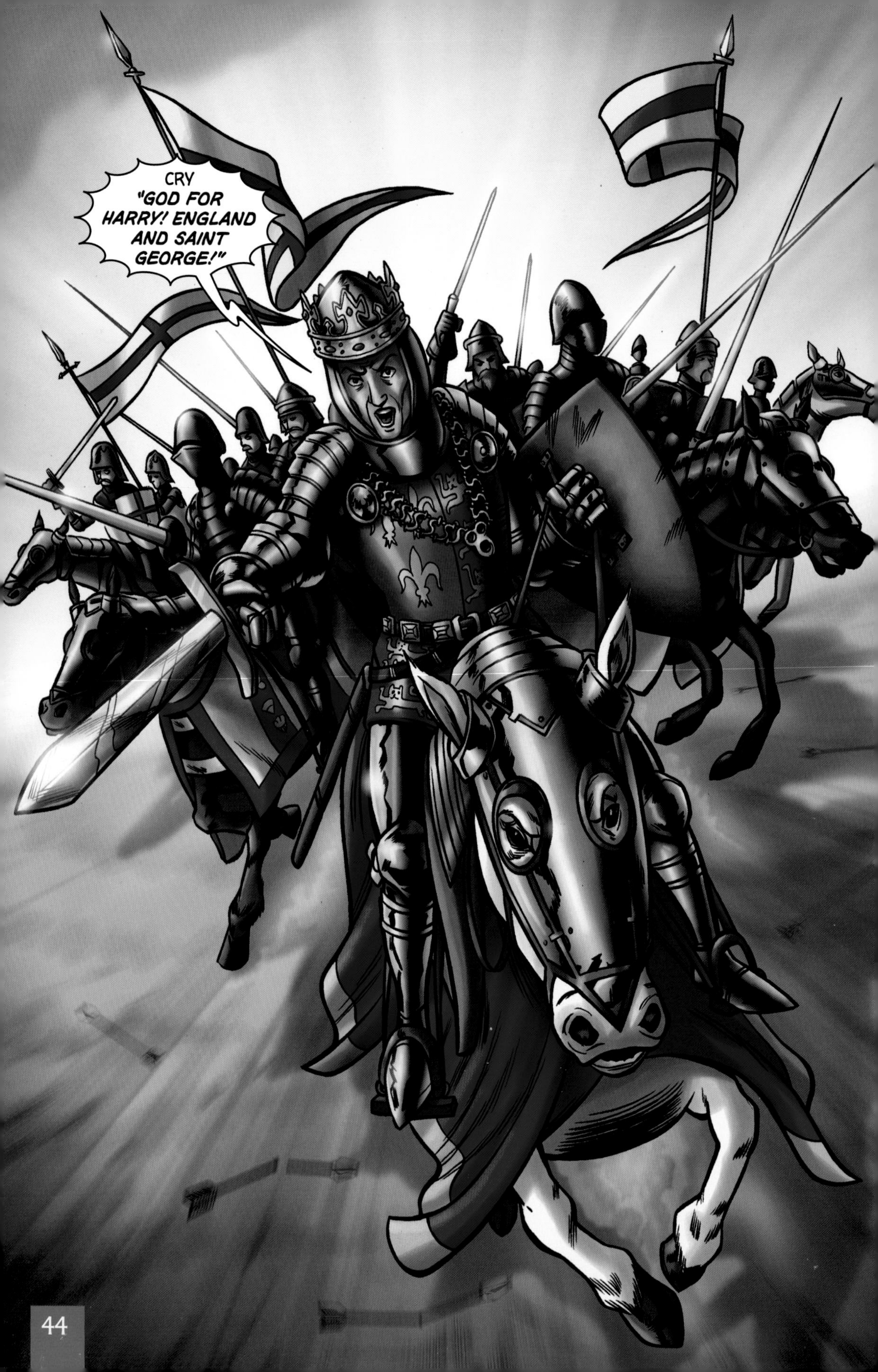
CRY "GOD FOR HARRY! ENGLAND AND SAINT GEORGE!"

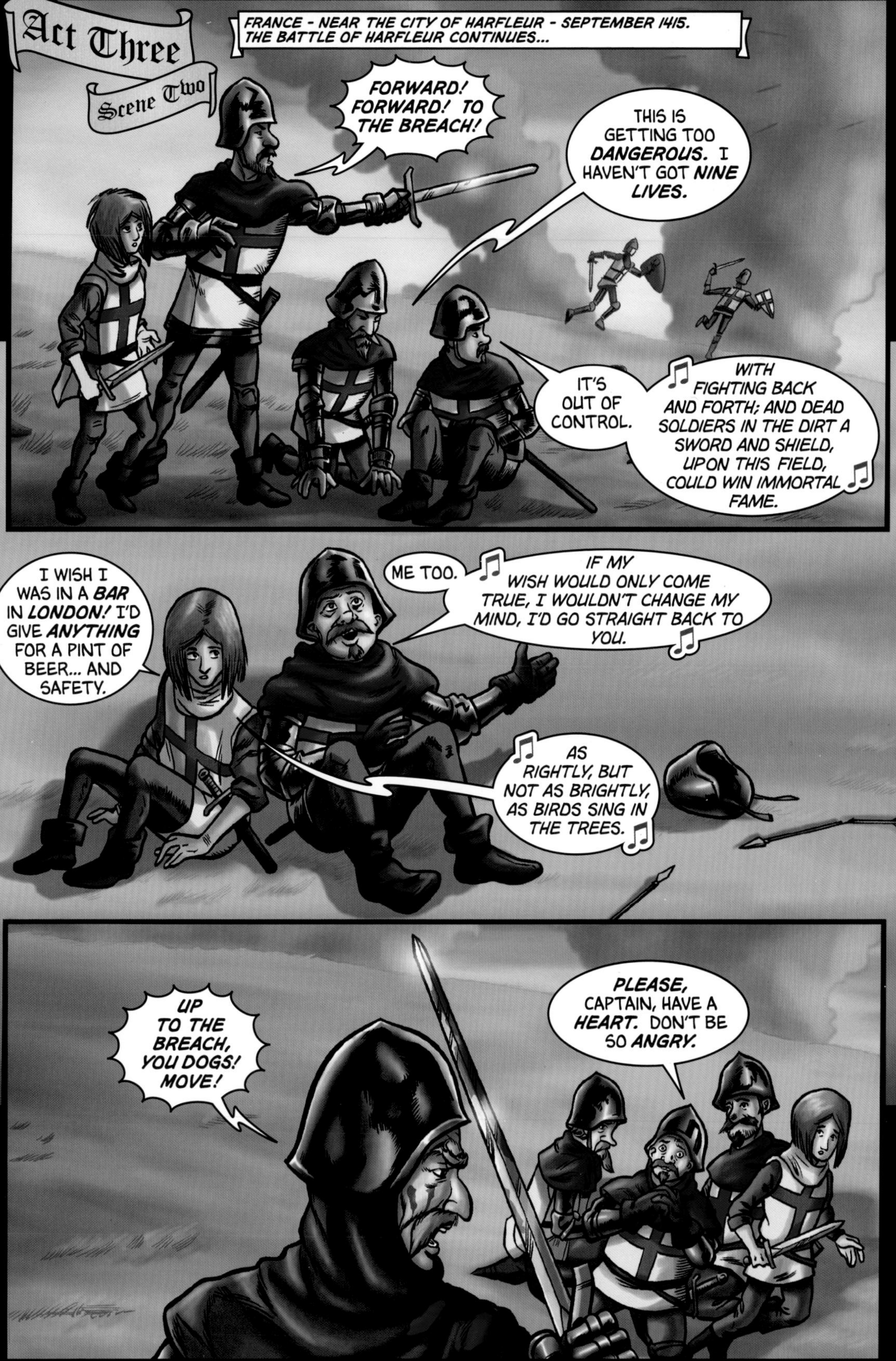
Act Three
Scene Two
FRANCE - NEAR THE CITY OF HARFLEUR - SEPTEMBER 1415. THE BATTLE OF HARFLEUR CONTINUES...
FORWARD! FORWARD! TO THE BREACH!
THIS IS GETTING TOO DANGEROUS. I HAVEN'T GOT NINE LIVES.
IT'S OUT OF CONTROL.
WITH FIGHTING BACK AND FORTH; AND DEAD SOLDIERS IN THE DIRT A SWORD AND SHIELD, UPON THIS FIELD, COULD WIN IMMORTAL FAME.
I WISH I WAS IN A BAR IN LONDON! I'D GIVE ANYTHING FOR A PINT OF BEER... AND SAFETY.
ME TOO.
IF MY WISH WOULD ONLY COME TRUE, I WOULDN'T CHANGE MY MIND, I'D GO STRAIGHT BACK TO YOU.
AS RIGHTLY, BUT NOT AS BRIGHTLY, AS BIRDS SING IN THE TREES.
UP TO THE BREACH, YOU DOGS! MOVE!
PLEASE, CAPTAIN, HAVE A HEART. DON'T BE SO ANGRY.

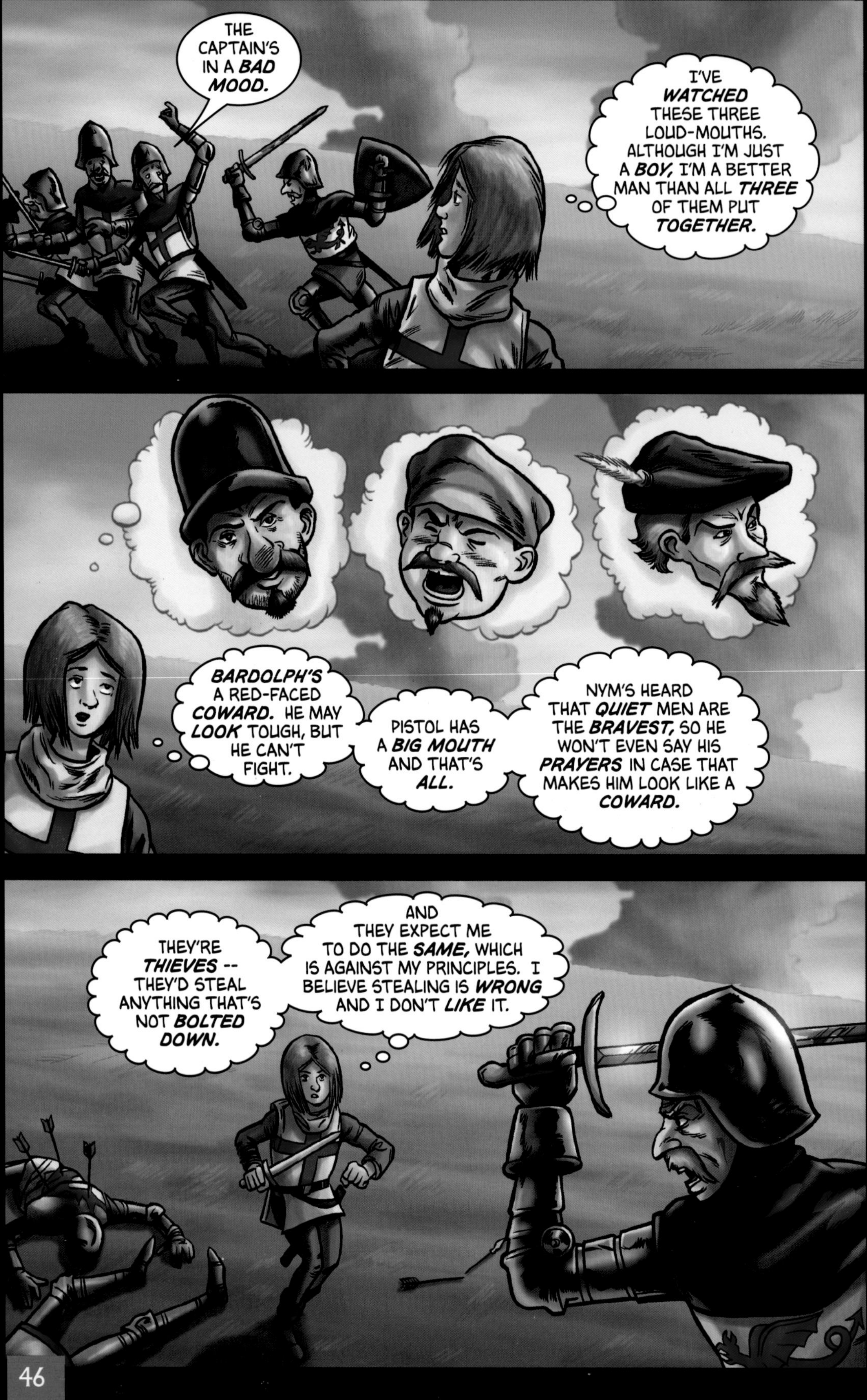
THE CAPTAIN'S IN A BAD MOOD.
I'VE WATCHED THESE THREE LOUD-MOUTHS. ALTHOUGH I'M JUST A BOY, I'M A BETTER MAN THAN ALL THREE OF THEM PUT TOGETHER.
BARDOLPH'S A RED-FACED COWARD. HE MAY LOOK TOUGH, BUT HE CAN'T FIGHT.
PISTOL HAS A BIG MOUTH AND THAT'S ALL.
NYM'S HEARD THAT QUIET MEN ARE THE BRAVEST, SO HE WON'T EVEN SAY HIS PRAYERS IN CASE THAT MAKES HIM LOOK LIKE A COWARD.
THEY'RE THIEVES -- THEY'D STEAL ANYTHING THAT'S NOT BOLTED DOWN.
AND THEY EXPECT ME TO DO THE SAME, WHICH IS AGAINST MY PRINCIPLES. I BELIEVE STEALING IS WRONG AND I DON'T LIKE IT.

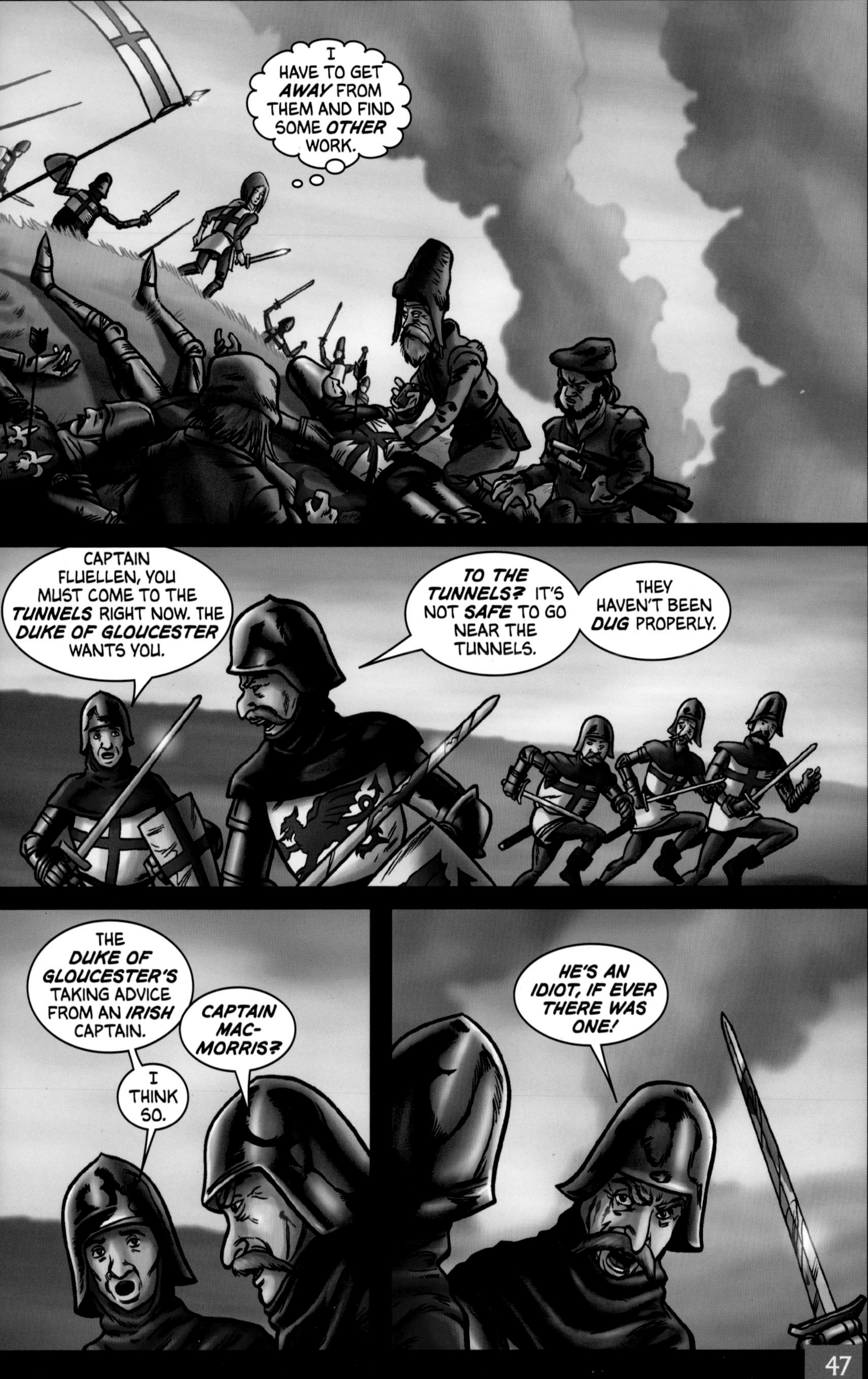
I HAVE TO GET AWAY FROM THEM AND FIND SOME OTHER WORK.
CAPTAIN FLUELLEN, YOU MUST COME TO THE TUNNELS RIGHT NOW. THE DUKE OF GLOUCESTER WANTS YOU.
TO THE TUNNELS? IT'S NOT SAFE TO GO NEAR THE TUNNELS.
THEY HAVEN'T BEEN DUG PROPERLY.
THE DUKE OF GLOUCESTER'S TAKING ADVICE FROM AN IRISH CAPTAIN.
CAPTAIN MAC-MORRIS?
I THINK SO.
HE'S AN IDIOT, IF EVER THERE WAS ONE!

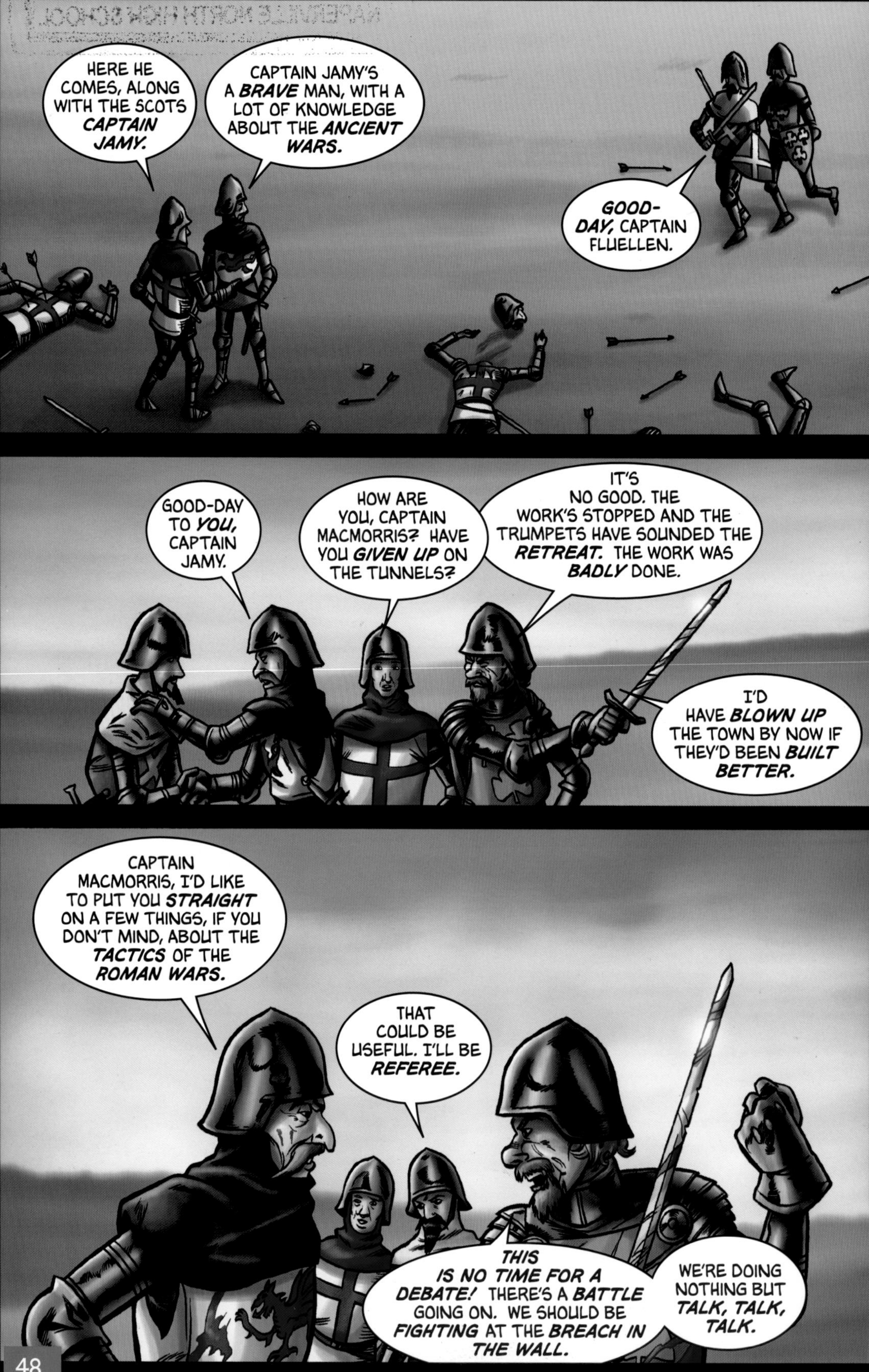
HERE HE COMES, ALONG WITH THE SCOTS CAPTAIN JAMY.
CAPTAIN JAMY'S A BRAVE MAN, WITH A LOT OF KNOWLEDGE ABOUT THE ANCIENT WARS.
GOOD-DAY, CAPTAIN FLUELLEN.
GOOD-DAY TO YOU, CAPTAIN JAMY.
HOW ARE YOU, CAPTAIN MACMORRIS? HAVE YOU GIVEN UP ON THE TUNNELS?
IT'S NO GOOD. THE WORK'S STOPPED AND THE TRUMPETS HAVE SOUNDED THE RETREAT. THE WORK WAS BADLY DONE.
I'D HAVE BLOWN UP THE TOWN BY NOW IF THEY'D BEEN BUILT BETTER.
CAPTAIN MACMORRIS, I'D LIKE TO PUT YOU STRAIGHT ON A FEW THINGS, IF YOU DON'T MIND, ABOUT THE TACTICS OF THE ROMAN WARS.
THAT COULD BE USEFUL. I'LL BE REFEREE.
THIS IS NO TIME FOR A DEBATE! THERE'S A BATTLE GOING ON. WE SHOULD BE FIGHTING AT THE BREACH IN THE WALL.
WE'RE DOING NOTHING BUT TALK, TALK, TALK.

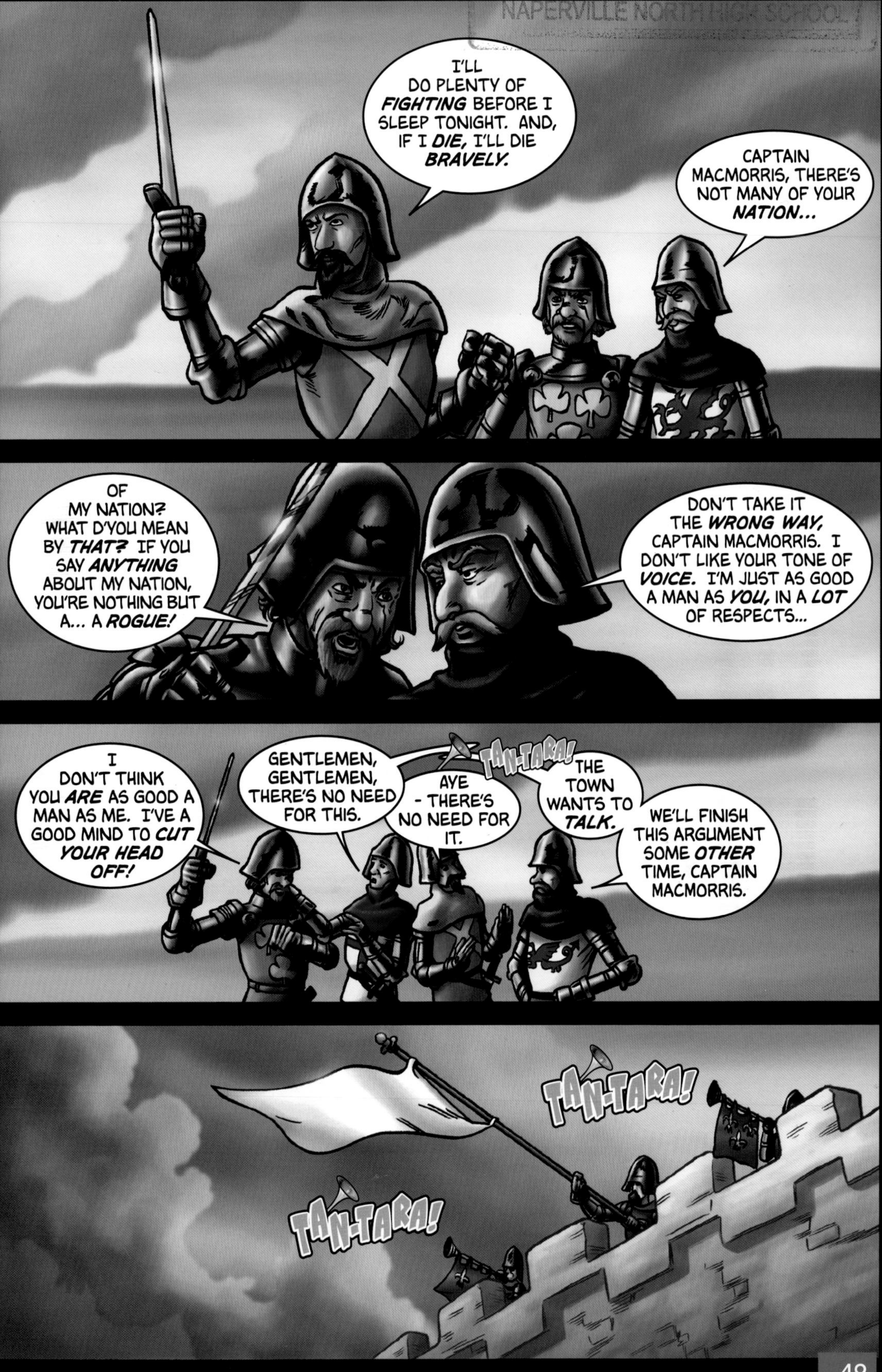
I'LL DO PLENTY OF *FIGHTING* BEFORE I SLEEP TONIGHT. AND, IF I *DIE,* I'LL DIE *BRAVELY.*
CAPTAIN MACMORRIS, THERE'S NOT MANY OF YOUR *NATION...*
OF MY NATION? WHAT D'YOU MEAN BY *THAT?* IF YOU SAY *ANYTHING* ABOUT MY NATION, YOU'RE NOTHING BUT A... A *ROGUE!*
DON'T TAKE IT THE *WRONG WAY,* CAPTAIN MACMORRIS. I DON'T LIKE YOUR TONE OF *VOICE.* I'M JUST AS GOOD A MAN AS *YOU,* IN A *LOT* OF RESPECTS...
I DON'T THINK YOU *ARE* AS GOOD A MAN AS ME. I'VE A GOOD MIND TO *CUT YOUR HEAD OFF!*
GENTLEMEN, GENTLEMEN, THERE'S NO NEED FOR THIS.
AYE - THERE'S NO NEED FOR IT.
TAN-TARA!
THE TOWN WANTS TO *TALK.*
WE'LL FINISH THIS ARGUMENT SOME *OTHER* TIME, CAPTAIN MACMORRIS.
TAN-TARA!
TAN-TARA!

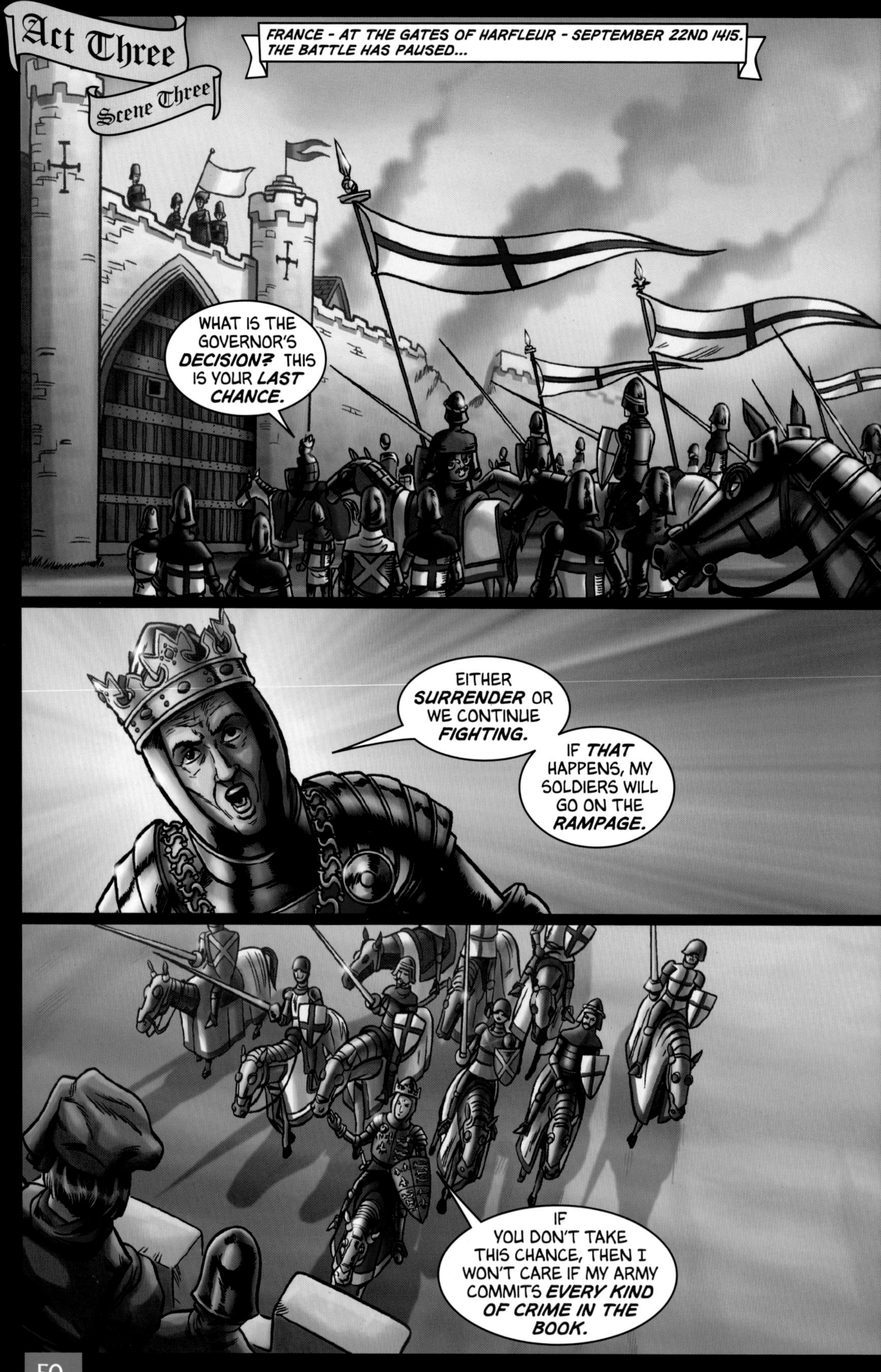
Act Three
Scene Three
FRANCE - AT THE GATES OF HARFLEUR - SEPTEMBER 22ND 1415. THE BATTLE HAS PAUSED...
WHAT IS THE GOVERNOR'S DECISION? THIS IS YOUR LAST CHANCE.
EITHER SURRENDER OR WE CONTINUE FIGHTING.
IF THAT HAPPENS, MY SOLDIERS WILL GO ON THE RAMPAGE.
IF YOU DON'T TAKE THIS CHANCE, THEN I WON'T CARE IF MY ARMY COMMITS EVERY KIND OF CRIME IN THE BOOK.

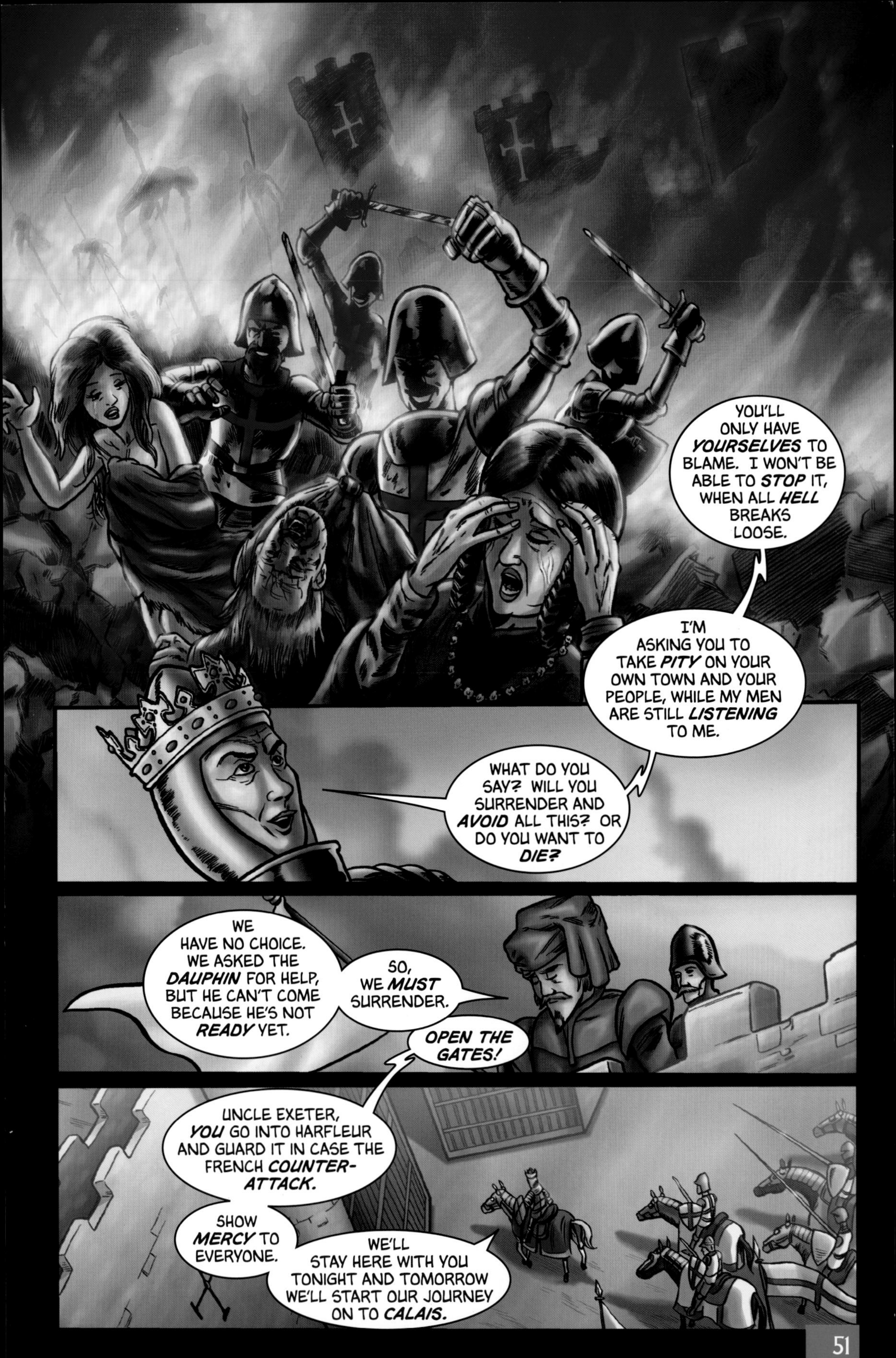
YOU'LL ONLY HAVE YOURSELVES TO BLAME. I WON'T BE ABLE TO STOP IT, WHEN ALL HELL BREAKS LOOSE.
I'M ASKING YOU TO TAKE PITY ON YOUR OWN TOWN AND YOUR PEOPLE, WHILE MY MEN ARE STILL LISTENING TO ME.
WHAT DO YOU SAY? WILL YOU SURRENDER AND AVOID ALL THIS? OR DO YOU WANT TO DIE?
WE HAVE NO CHOICE. WE ASKED THE DAUPHIN FOR HELP, BUT HE CAN'T COME BECAUSE HE'S NOT READY YET.
SO, WE MUST SURRENDER.
OPEN THE GATES!
UNCLE EXETER, YOU GO INTO HARFLEUR AND GUARD IT IN CASE THE FRENCH COUNTER-ATTACK.
SHOW MERCY TO EVERYONE.
WE'LL STAY HERE WITH YOU TONIGHT AND TOMORROW WE'LL START OUR JOURNEY ON TO CALAIS.

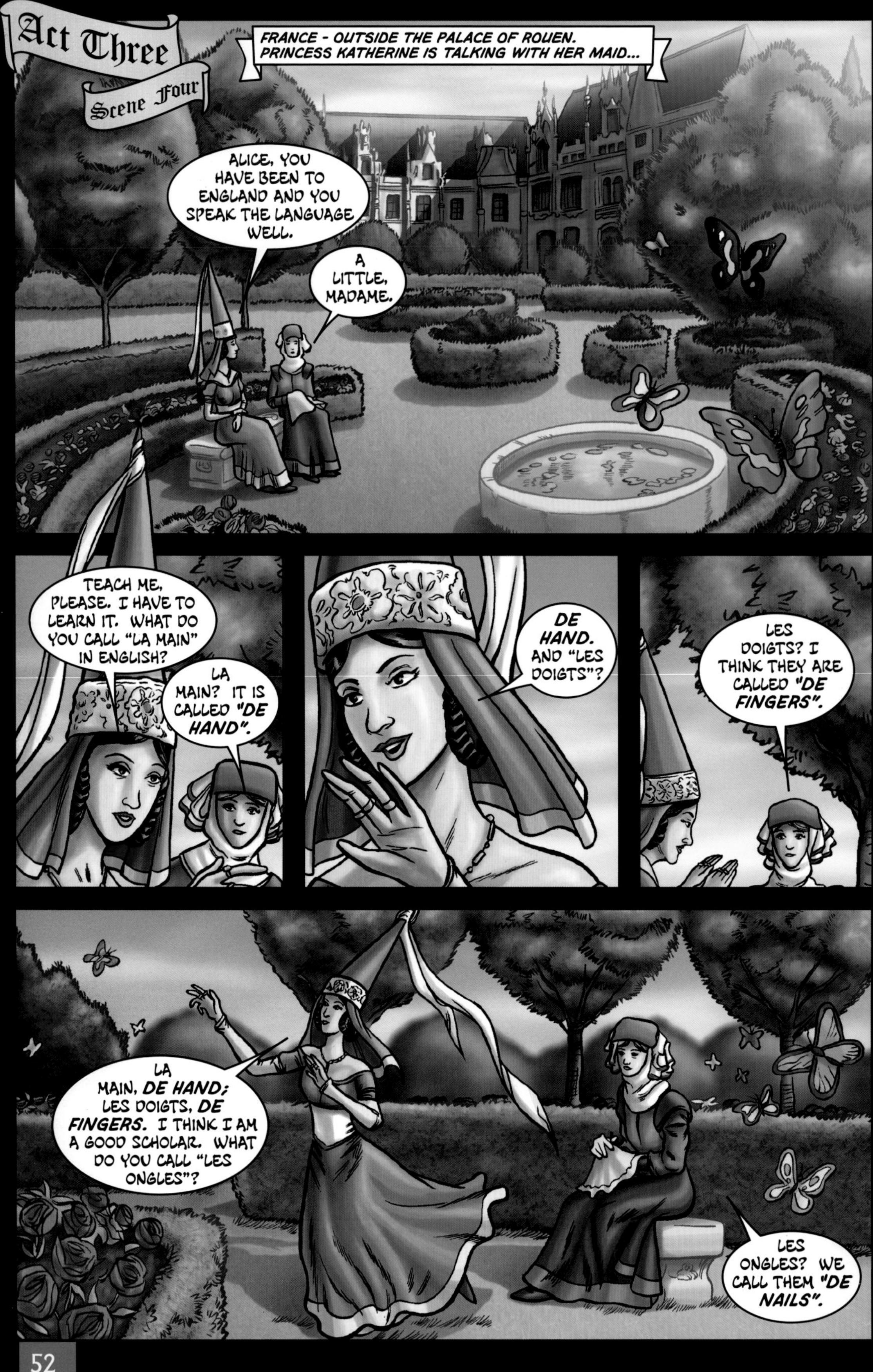
Act Three
Scene Four
FRANCE - OUTSIDE THE PALACE OF ROUEN. PRINCESS KATHERINE IS TALKING WITH HER MAID...
ALICE, YOU HAVE BEEN TO ENGLAND AND YOU SPEAK THE LANGUAGE WELL.
A LITTLE, MADAME.
TEACH ME, PLEASE. I HAVE TO LEARN IT. WHAT DO YOU CALL "LA MAIN" IN ENGLISH?
LA MAIN? IT IS CALLED "DE HAND".
DE HAND. AND "LES DOIGTS"?
LES DOIGTS? I THINK THEY ARE CALLED "DE FINGERS".
LA MAIN, DE HAND; LES DOIGTS, DE FINGERS. I THINK I AM A GOOD SCHOLAR. WHAT DO YOU CALL "LES ONGLES"?
LES ONGLES? WE CALL THEM "DE NAILS".

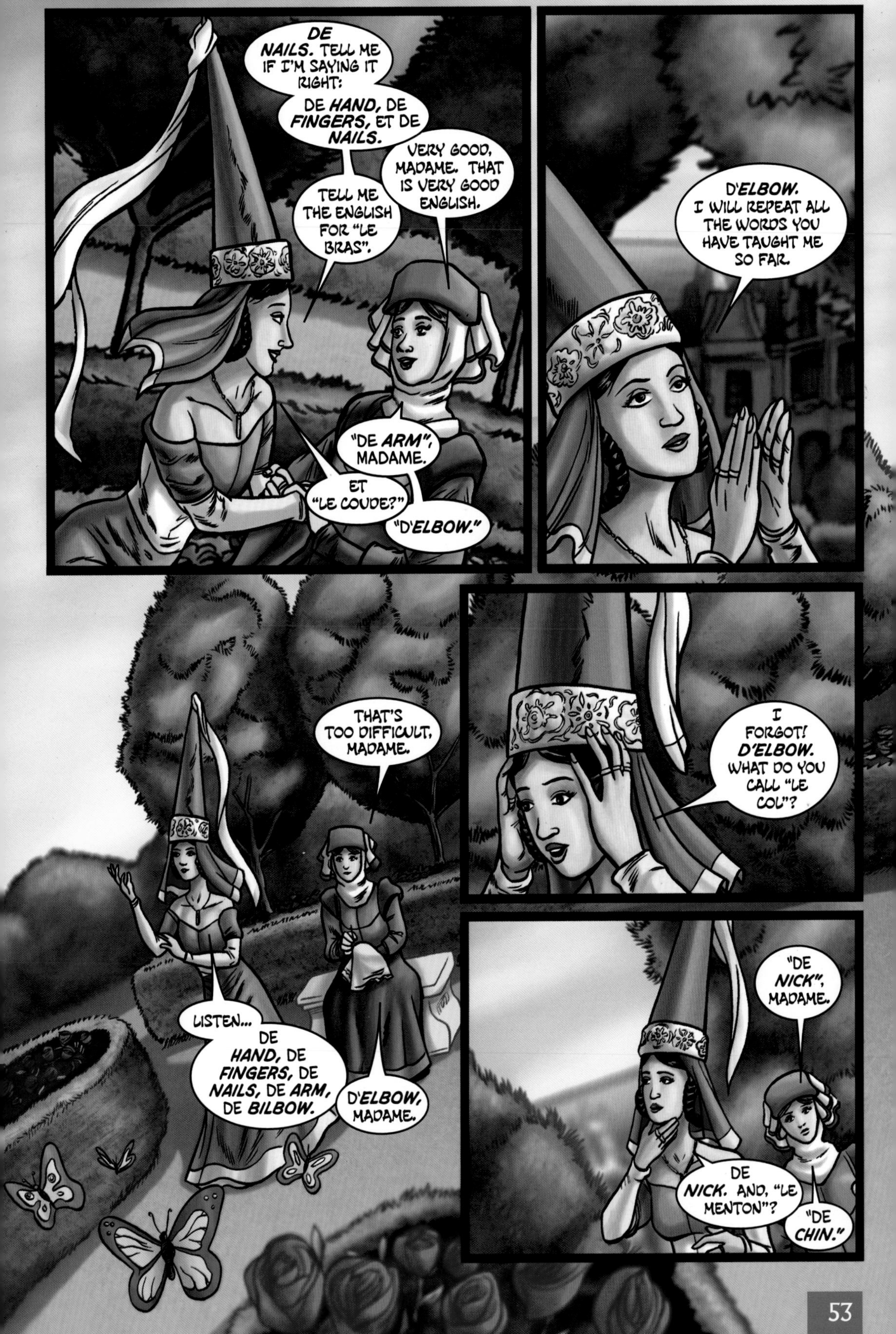
DE NAILS. TELL ME IF I'M SAYING IT RIGHT:
DE HAND, DE FINGERS, ET DE NAILS.
VERY GOOD, MADAME. THAT IS VERY GOOD ENGLISH.
TELL ME THE ENGLISH FOR "LE BRAS".
"DE ARM", MADAME.
ET "LE COUDE?"
"D'ELBOW."
D'ELBOW. I WILL REPEAT ALL THE WORDS YOU HAVE TAUGHT ME SO FAR.
LISTEN... DE HAND, DE FINGERS, DE NAILS, DE ARM, DE BILBOW.
D'ELBOW, MADAME.
THAT'S TOO DIFFICULT, MADAME.
I FORGOT! D'ELBOW. WHAT DO YOU CALL "LE COL"?
"DE NICK", MADAME.
DE NICK. AND, "LE MENTON"?
"DE CHIN."

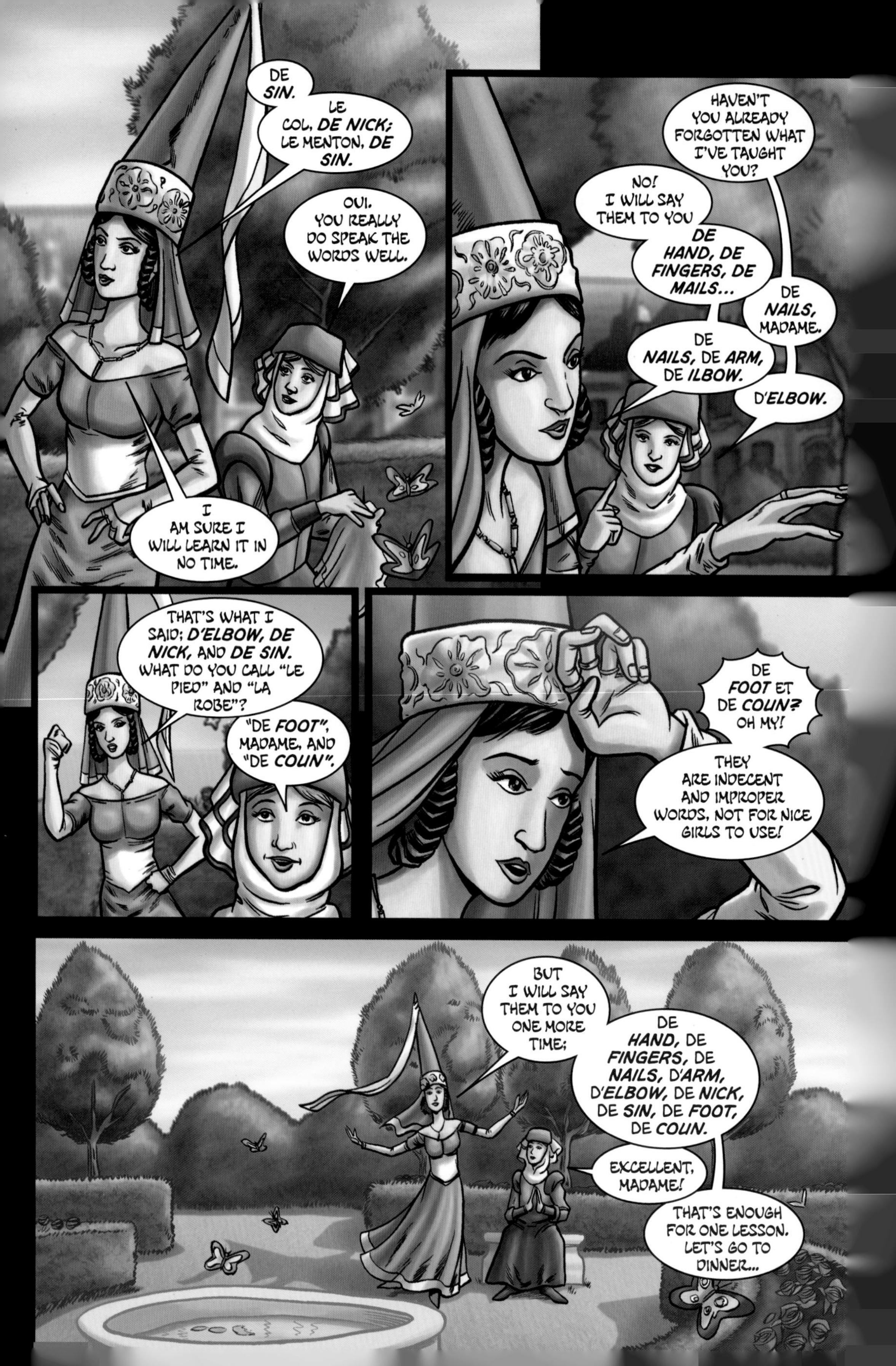

DE SIN.
LE COL, DE NICK; LE MENTON, DE SIN.
OUI. YOU REALLY DO SPEAK THE WORDS WELL.
I AM SURE I WILL LEARN IT IN NO TIME.
HAVEN'T YOU ALREADY FORGOTTEN WHAT I'VE TAUGHT YOU?
NO! I WILL SAY THEM TO YOU
DE HAND, DE FINGERS, DE MAILS...
DE NAILS, MADAME.
DE NAILS, DE ARM, DE ILBOW.
D'ELBOW.
THAT'S WHAT I SAID; D'ELBOW, DE NICK, AND DE SIN. WHAT DO YOU CALL "LE PIED" AND "LA ROBE"?
"DE FOOT", MADAME, AND "DE COUN".
DE FOOT ET DE COUN? OH MY!
THEY ARE INDECENT AND IMPROPER WORDS, NOT FOR NICE GIRLS TO USE!
BUT I WILL SAY THEM TO YOU ONE MORE TIME;
DE HAND, DE FINGERS, DE NAILS, D'ARM, D'ELBOW, DE NICK, DE SIN, DE FOOT, DE COUN.
EXCELLENT, MADAME!
THAT'S ENOUGH FOR ONE LESSON. LET'S GO TO DINNER...

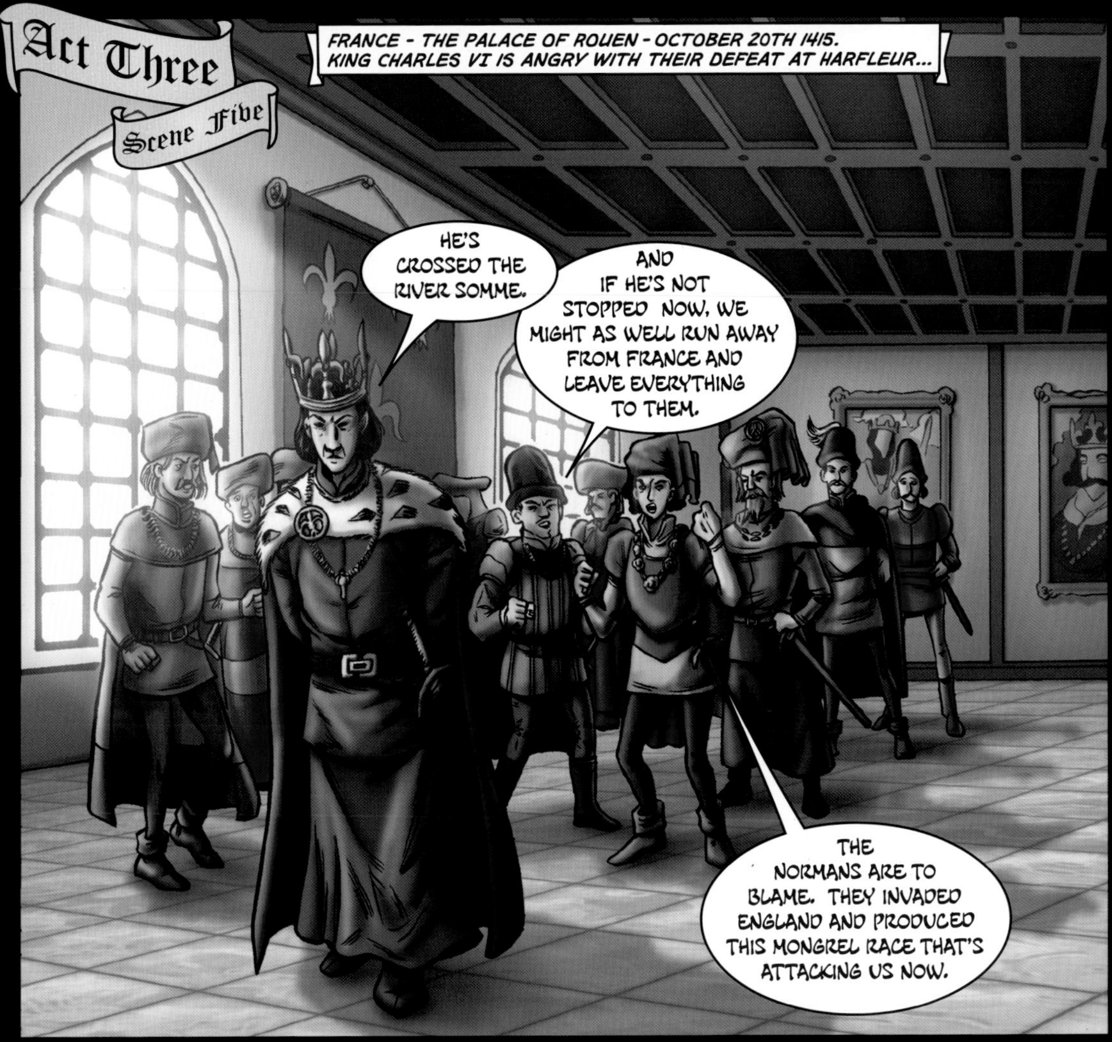
Act Three
Scene Five
FRANCE - THE PALACE OF ROUEN - OCTOBER 20TH 1415. KING CHARLES VI IS ANGRY WITH THEIR DEFEAT AT HARFLEUR...
HE'S CROSSED THE RIVER SOMME.
AND IF HE'S NOT STOPPED NOW, WE MIGHT AS WELL RUN AWAY FROM FRANCE AND LEAVE EVERYTHING TO THEM.
THE NORMANS ARE TO BLAME. THEY INVADED ENGLAND AND PRODUCED THIS MONGREL RACE THAT'S ATTACKING US NOW.

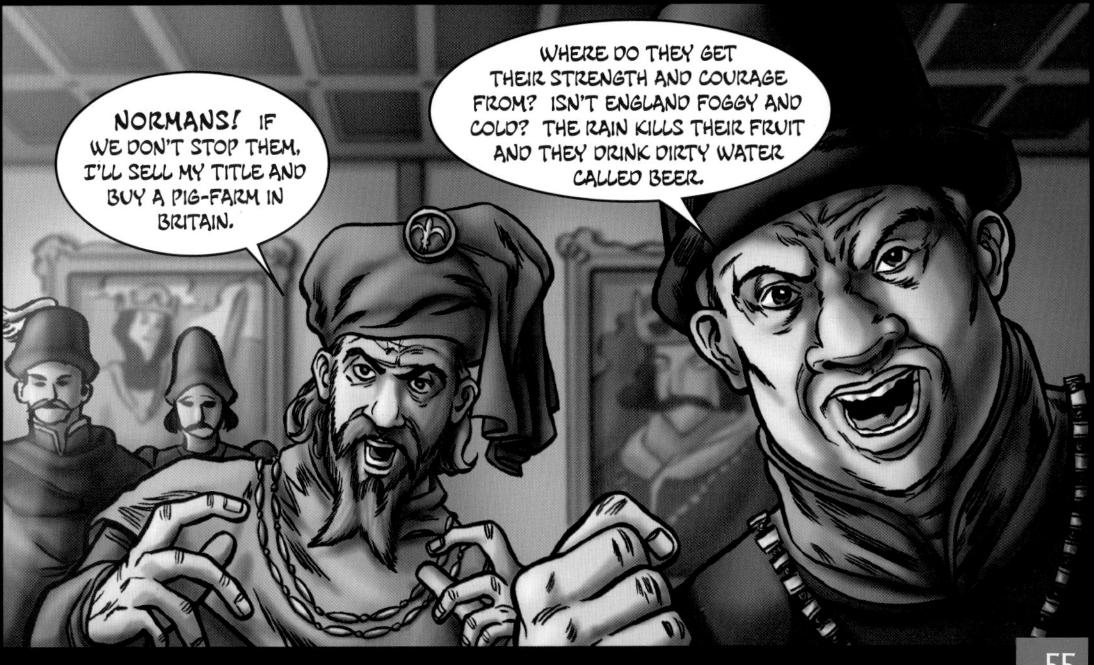
NORMANS! IF WE DON'T STOP THEM, I'LL SELL MY TITLE AND BUY A PIG-FARM IN BRITAIN.
WHERE DO THEY GET THEIR STRENGTH AND COURAGE FROM? ISN'T ENGLAND FOGGY AND COLD? THE RAIN KILLS THEIR FRUIT AND THEY DRINK DIRTY WATER CALLED BEER.

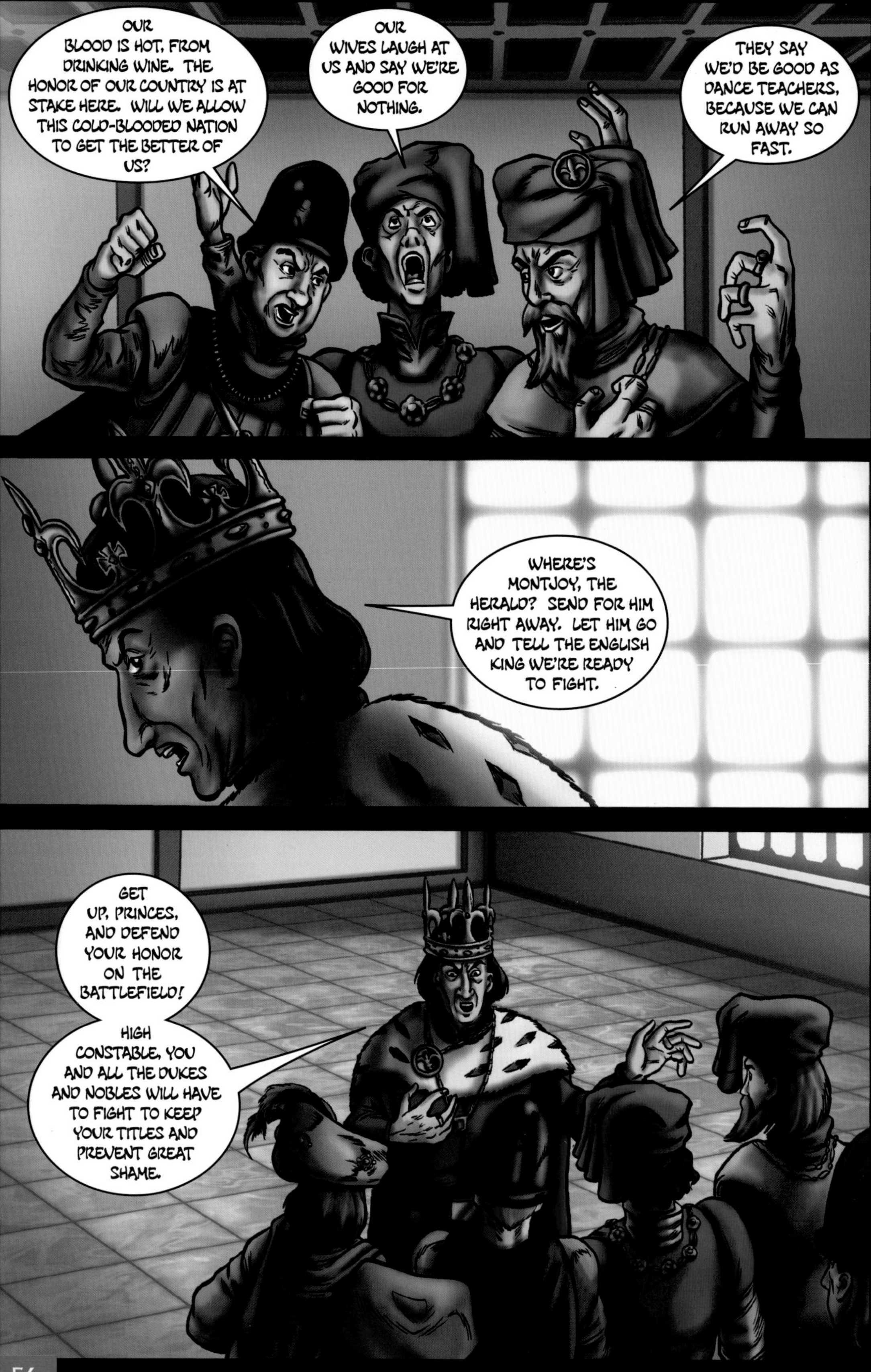
OUR BLOOD IS HOT, FROM DRINKING WINE. THE HONOR OF OUR COUNTRY IS AT STAKE HERE. WILL WE ALLOW THIS COLD-BLOODED NATION TO GET THE BETTER OF US?
OUR WIVES LAUGH AT US AND SAY WE'RE GOOD FOR NOTHING.
THEY SAY WE'D BE GOOD AS DANCE TEACHERS, BECAUSE WE CAN RUN AWAY SO FAST.
WHERE'S MONTJOY, THE HERALD? SEND FOR HIM RIGHT AWAY. LET HIM GO AND TELL THE ENGLISH KING WE'RE READY TO FIGHT.
GET UP, PRINCES, AND DEFEND YOUR HONOR ON THE BATTLEFIELD!
HIGH CONSTABLE, YOU AND ALL THE DUKES AND NOBLES WILL HAVE TO FIGHT TO KEEP YOUR TITLES AND PREVENT GREAT SHAME.

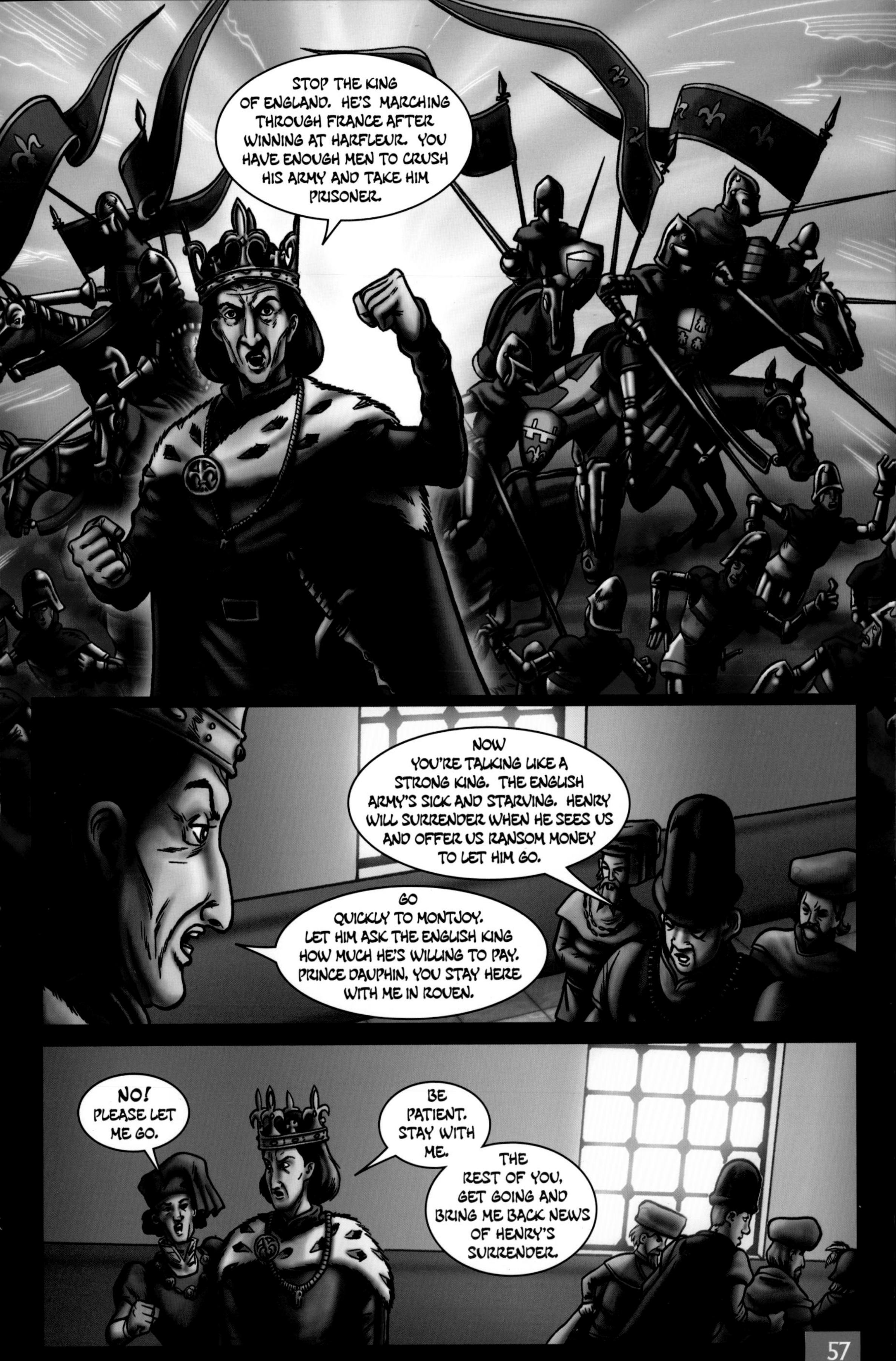
STOP THE KING OF ENGLAND. HE'S MARCHING THROUGH FRANCE AFTER WINNING AT HARFLEUR. YOU HAVE ENOUGH MEN TO CRUSH HIS ARMY AND TAKE HIM PRISONER.
NOW YOU'RE TALKING LIKE A STRONG KING. THE ENGLISH ARMY'S SICK AND STARVING. HENRY WILL SURRENDER WHEN HE SEES US AND OFFER US RANSOM MONEY TO LET HIM GO.
GO QUICKLY TO MONTJOY. LET HIM ASK THE ENGLISH KING HOW MUCH HE'S WILLING TO PAY. PRINCE DAUPHIN, YOU STAY HERE WITH ME IN ROUEN.
NO! PLEASE LET ME GO.
BE PATIENT. STAY WITH ME.
THE REST OF YOU, GET GOING AND BRING ME BACK NEWS OF HENRY'S SURRENDER.

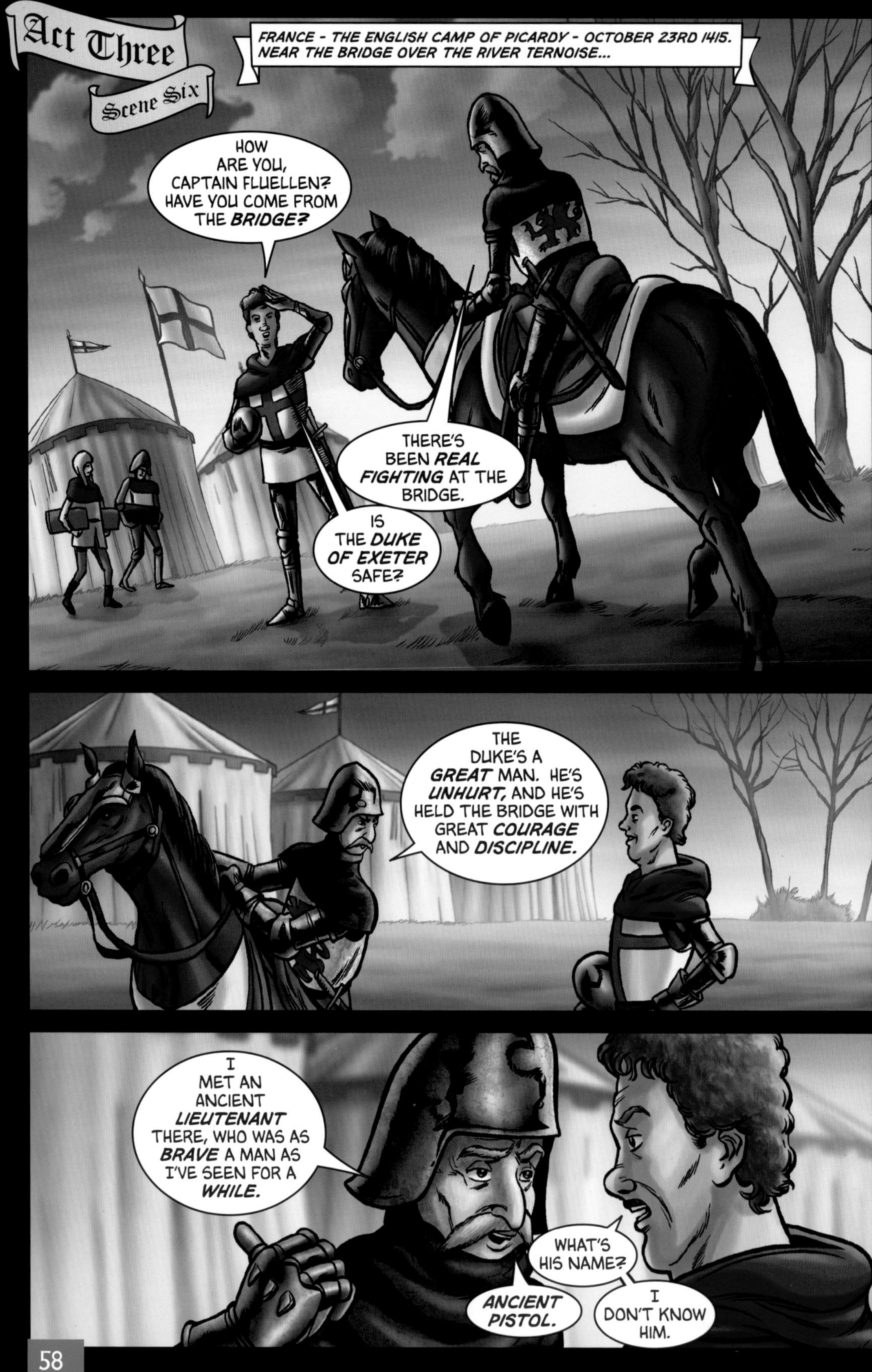
Act Three
Scene Six
FRANCE - THE ENGLISH CAMP OF PICARDY - OCTOBER 23RD 1415. NEAR THE BRIDGE OVER THE RIVER TERNOISE...
HOW ARE YOU, CAPTAIN FLUELLEN? HAVE YOU COME FROM THE BRIDGE?
THERE'S BEEN REAL FIGHTING AT THE BRIDGE.
IS THE DUKE OF EXETER SAFE?
THE DUKE'S A GREAT MAN. HE'S UNHURT, AND HE'S HELD THE BRIDGE WITH GREAT COURAGE AND DISCIPLINE.
I MET AN ANCIENT LIEUTENANT THERE, WHO WAS AS BRAVE A MAN AS I'VE SEEN FOR A WHILE.
WHAT'S HIS NAME?
ANCIENT PISTOL.
I DON'T KNOW HIM.

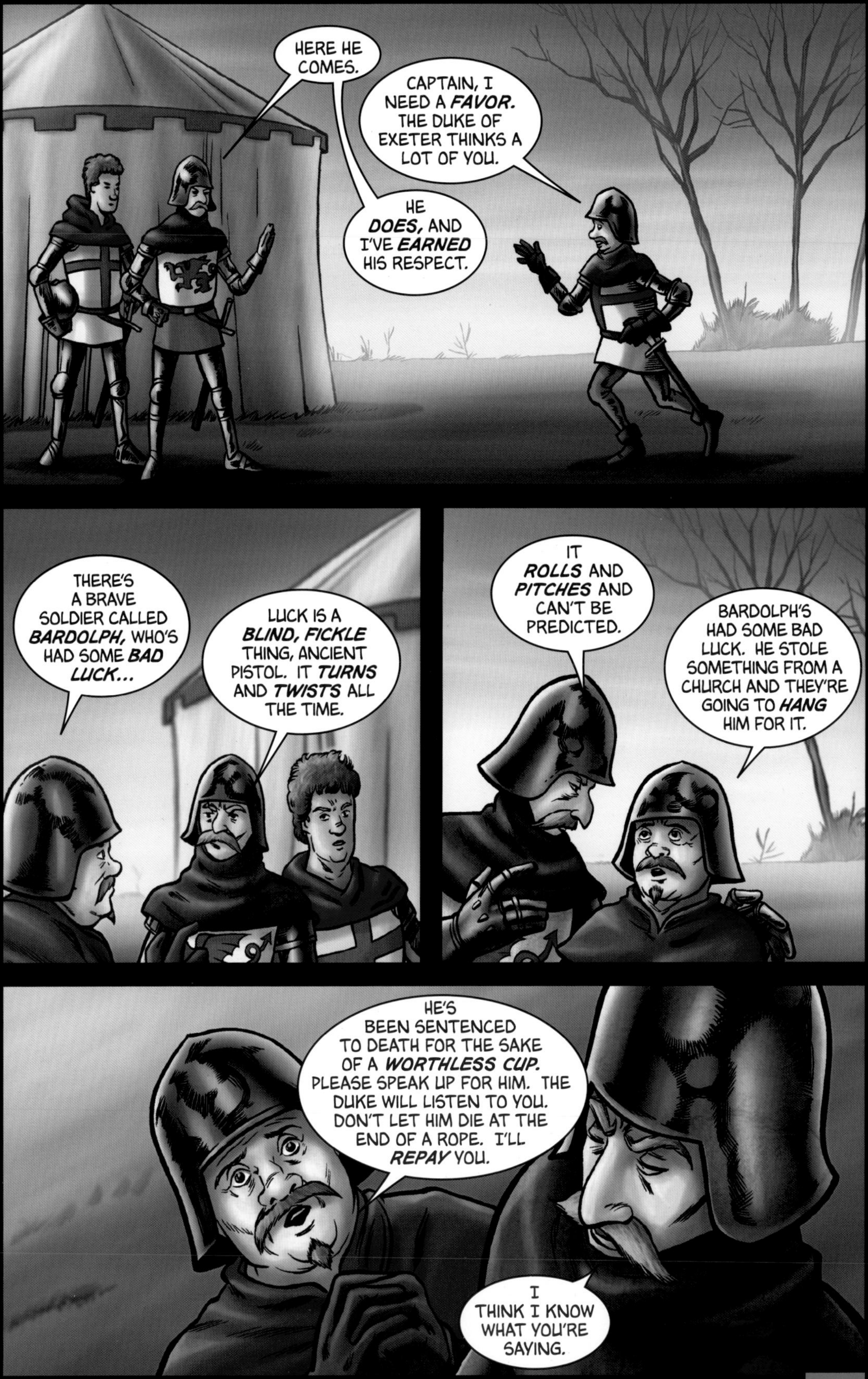
HERE HE COMES.
CAPTAIN, I NEED A *FAVOR.* THE DUKE OF EXETER THINKS A LOT OF YOU.
HE *DOES,* AND I'VE *EARNED* HIS RESPECT.
THERE'S A BRAVE SOLDIER CALLED *BARDOLPH,* WHO'S HAD SOME *BAD LUCK...*
LUCK IS A *BLIND, FICKLE* THING, ANCIENT PISTOL. IT *TURNS* AND *TWISTS* ALL THE TIME.
IT *ROLLS* AND *PITCHES* AND CAN'T BE PREDICTED.
BARDOLPH'S HAD SOME BAD LUCK. HE STOLE SOMETHING FROM A CHURCH AND THEY'RE GOING TO *HANG* HIM FOR IT.
HE'S BEEN SENTENCED TO DEATH FOR THE SAKE OF A *WORTHLESS CUP.* PLEASE SPEAK UP FOR HIM. THE DUKE WILL LISTEN TO YOU. DON'T LET HIM DIE AT THE END OF A ROPE. I'LL *REPAY* YOU.
I THINK I KNOW WHAT YOU'RE SAYING.

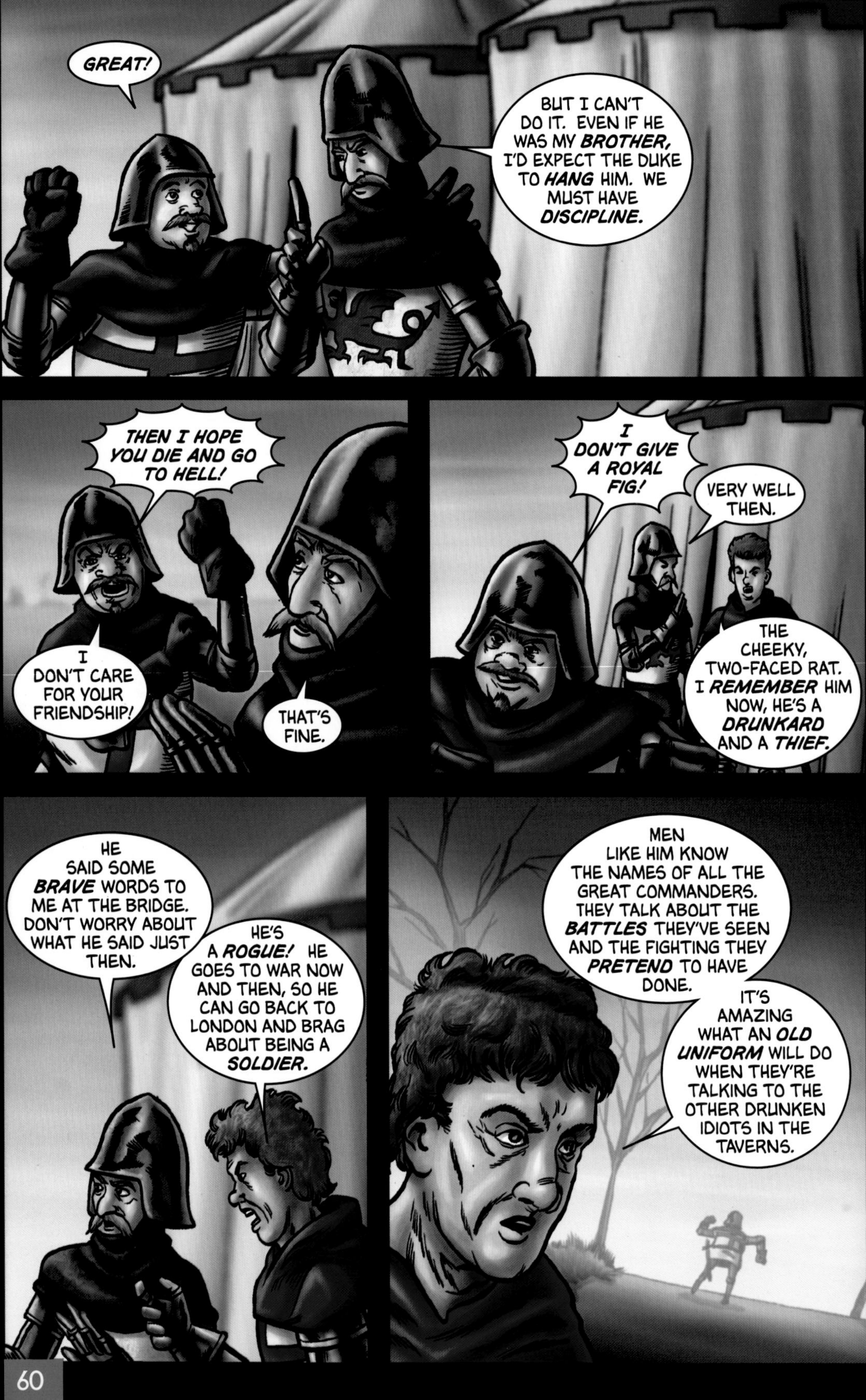
GREAT!
BUT I CAN'T DO IT. EVEN IF HE WAS MY BROTHER, I'D EXPECT THE DUKE TO HANG HIM. WE MUST HAVE DISCIPLINE.
THEN I HOPE YOU DIE AND GO TO HELL!
I DON'T CARE FOR YOUR FRIENDSHIP!
THAT'S FINE.
I DON'T GIVE A ROYAL FIG!
VERY WELL THEN.
THE CHEEKY, TWO-FACED RAT. I REMEMBER HIM NOW, HE'S A DRUNKARD AND A THIEF.
HE SAID SOME BRAVE WORDS TO ME AT THE BRIDGE. DON'T WORRY ABOUT WHAT HE SAID JUST THEN.
HE'S A ROGUE! HE GOES TO WAR NOW AND THEN, SO HE CAN GO BACK TO LONDON AND BRAG ABOUT BEING A SOLDIER.
MEN LIKE HIM KNOW THE NAMES OF ALL THE GREAT COMMANDERS. THEY TALK ABOUT THE BATTLES THEY'VE SEEN AND THE FIGHTING THEY PRETEND TO HAVE DONE.
IT'S AMAZING WHAT AN OLD UNIFORM WILL DO WHEN THEY'RE TALKING TO THE OTHER DRUNKEN IDIOTS IN THE TAVERNS.

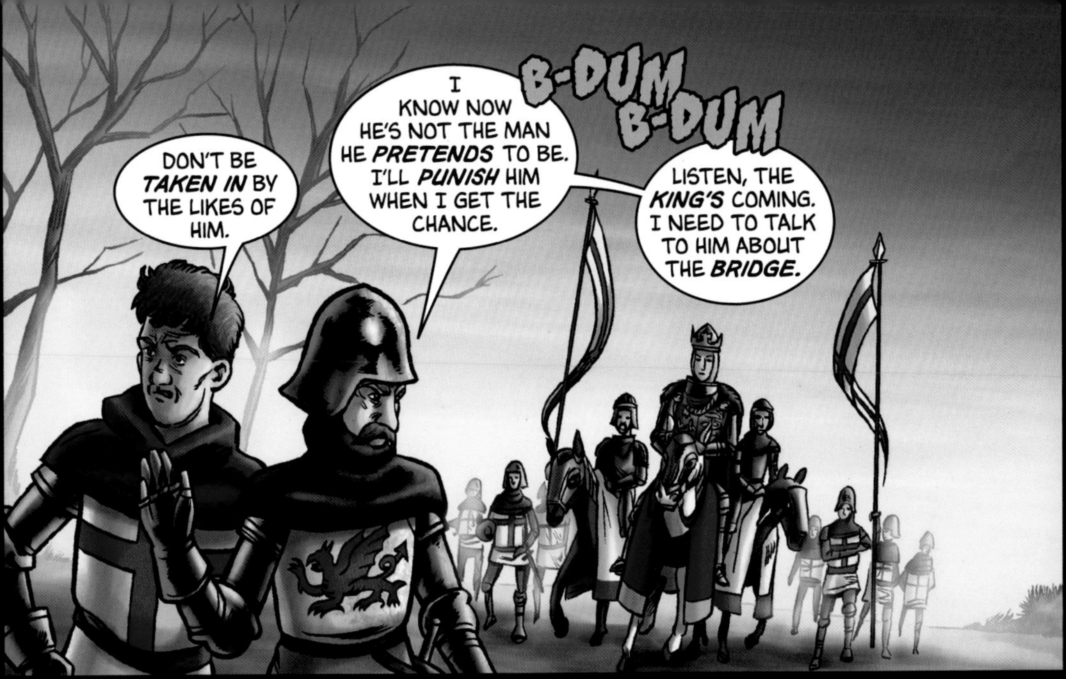
B-DUM B-DUM
DON'T BE TAKEN IN BY THE LIKES OF HIM.
I KNOW NOW HE'S NOT THE MAN HE PRETENDS TO BE. I'LL PUNISH HIM WHEN I GET THE CHANCE.
LISTEN, THE KING'S COMING. I NEED TO TALK TO HIM ABOUT THE BRIDGE.

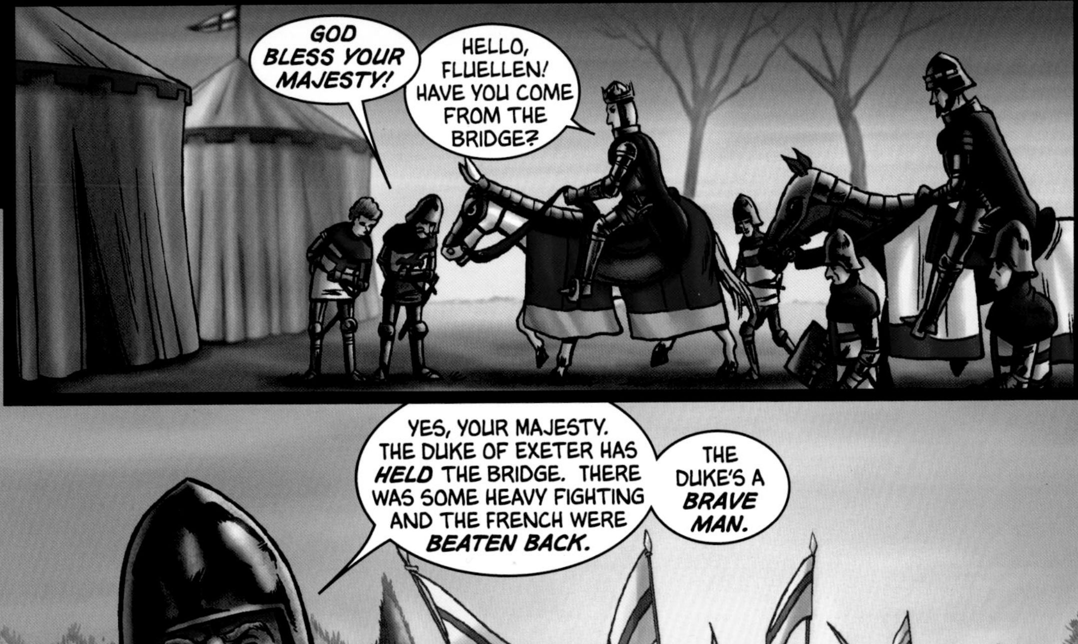
GOD BLESS YOUR MAJESTY!
HELLO, FLUELLEN! HAVE YOU COME FROM THE BRIDGE?

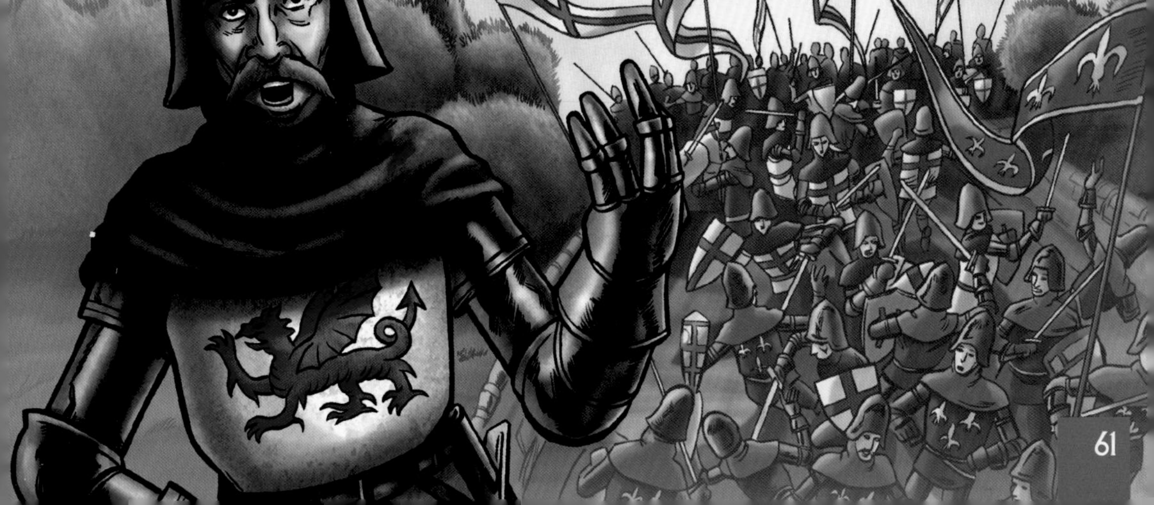
YES, YOUR MAJESTY. THE DUKE OF EXETER HAS HELD THE BRIDGE. THERE WAS SOME HEAVY FIGHTING AND THE FRENCH WERE BEATEN BACK.
THE DUKE'S A BRAVE MAN.

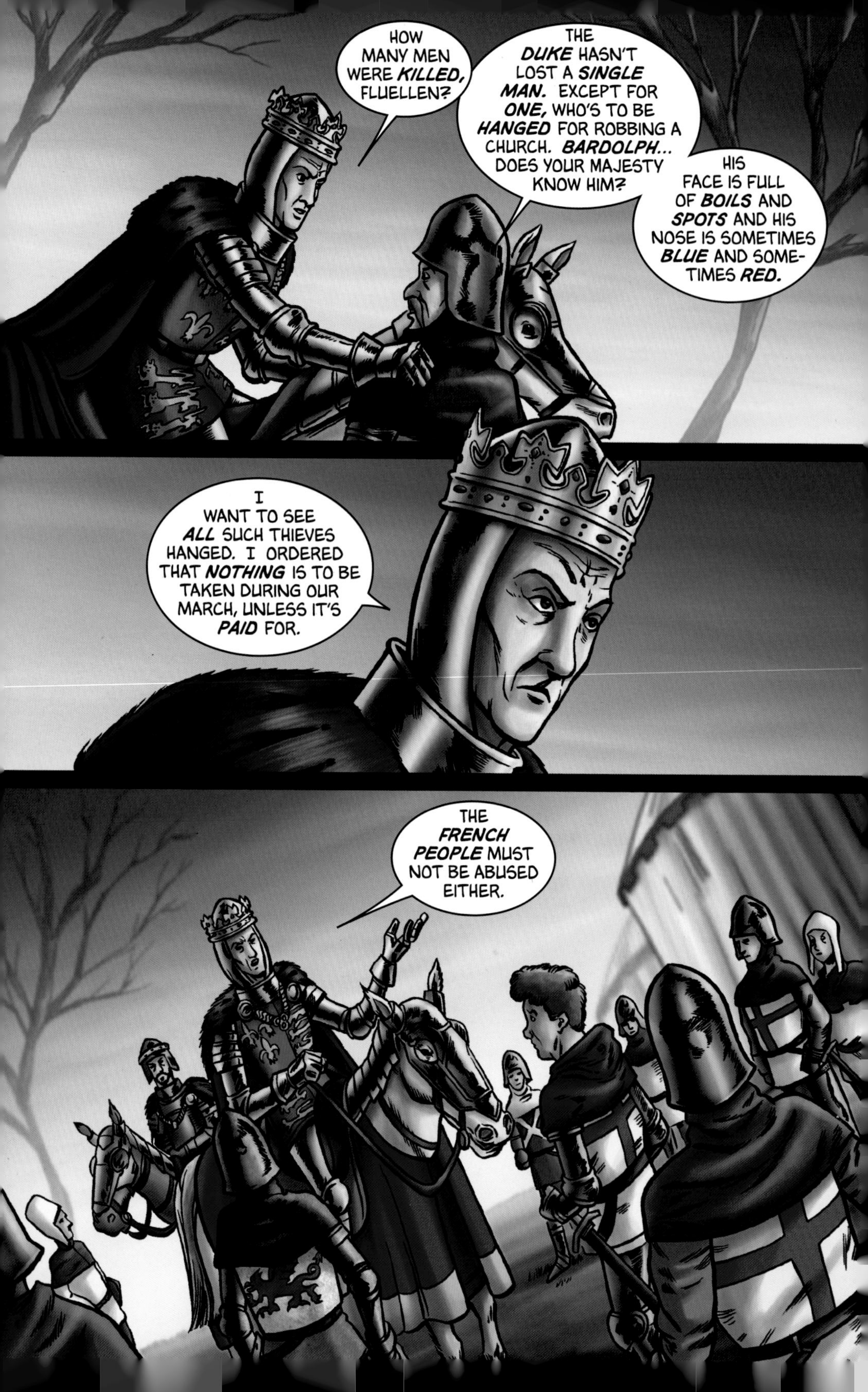
HOW MANY MEN WERE KILLED, FLUELLEN?
THE DUKE HASN'T LOST A SINGLE MAN. EXCEPT FOR ONE, WHO'S TO BE HANGED FOR ROBBING A CHURCH. BARDOLPH... DOES YOUR MAJESTY KNOW HIM?
HIS FACE IS FULL OF BOILS AND SPOTS AND HIS NOSE IS SOMETIMES BLUE AND SOMETIMES RED.
I WANT TO SEE ALL SUCH THIEVES HANGED. I ORDERED THAT NOTHING IS TO BE TAKEN DURING OUR MARCH, UNLESS IT'S PAID FOR.
THE FRENCH PEOPLE MUST NOT BE ABUSED EITHER.

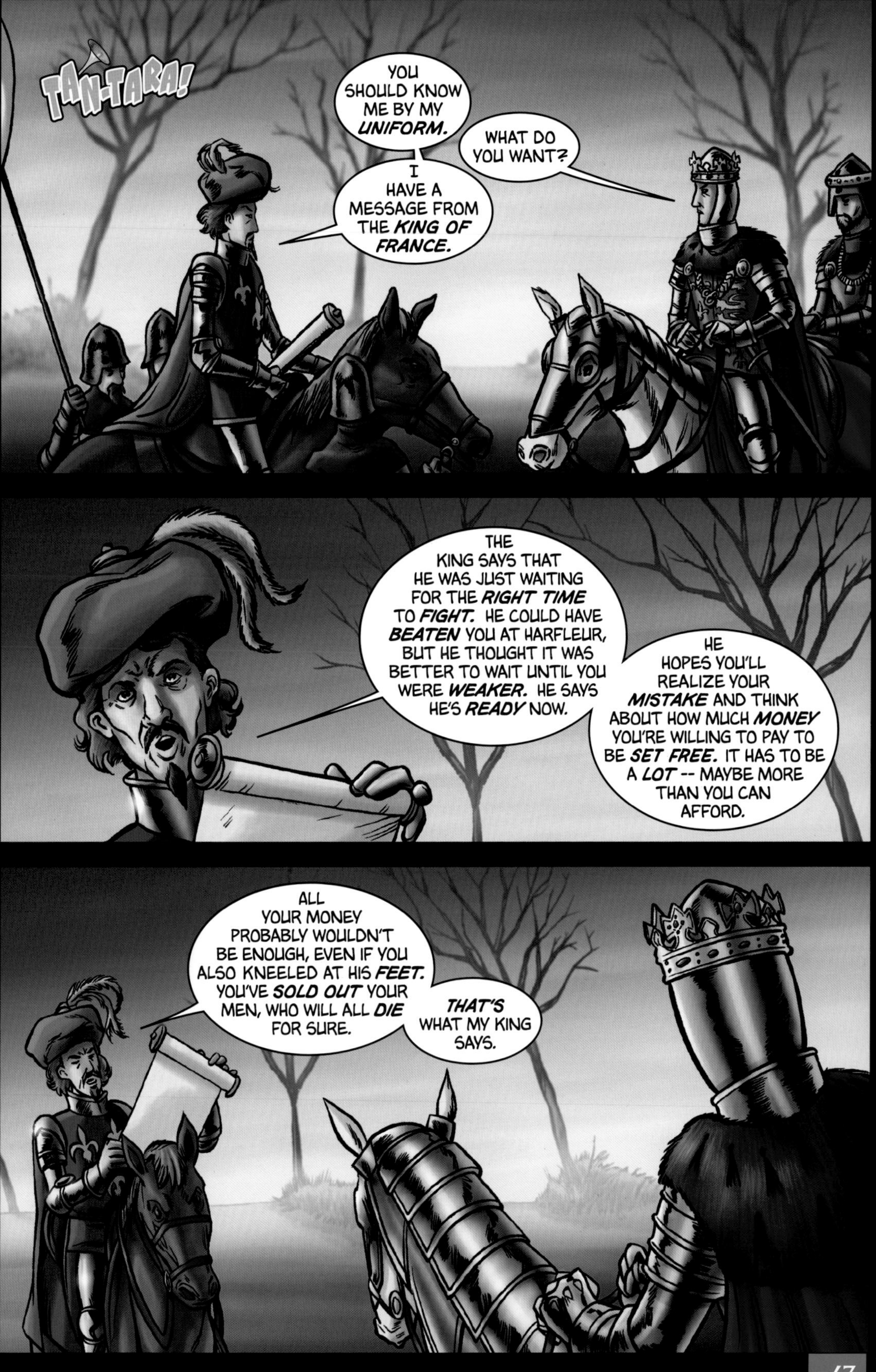
TAN-TARA!
YOU SHOULD KNOW ME BY MY UNIFORM.
WHAT DO YOU WANT?
I HAVE A MESSAGE FROM THE KING OF FRANCE.
THE KING SAYS THAT HE WAS JUST WAITING FOR THE RIGHT TIME TO FIGHT. HE COULD HAVE BEATEN YOU AT HARFLEUR, BUT HE THOUGHT IT WAS BETTER TO WAIT UNTIL YOU WERE WEAKER. HE SAYS HE'S READY NOW.
HE HOPES YOU'LL REALIZE YOUR MISTAKE AND THINK ABOUT HOW MUCH MONEY YOU'RE WILLING TO PAY TO BE SET FREE. IT HAS TO BE A LOT -- MAYBE MORE THAN YOU CAN AFFORD.
ALL YOUR MONEY PROBABLY WOULDN'T BE ENOUGH, EVEN IF YOU ALSO KNEELED AT HIS FEET. YOU'VE SOLD OUT YOUR MEN, WHO WILL ALL DIE FOR SURE.
THAT'S WHAT MY KING SAYS.

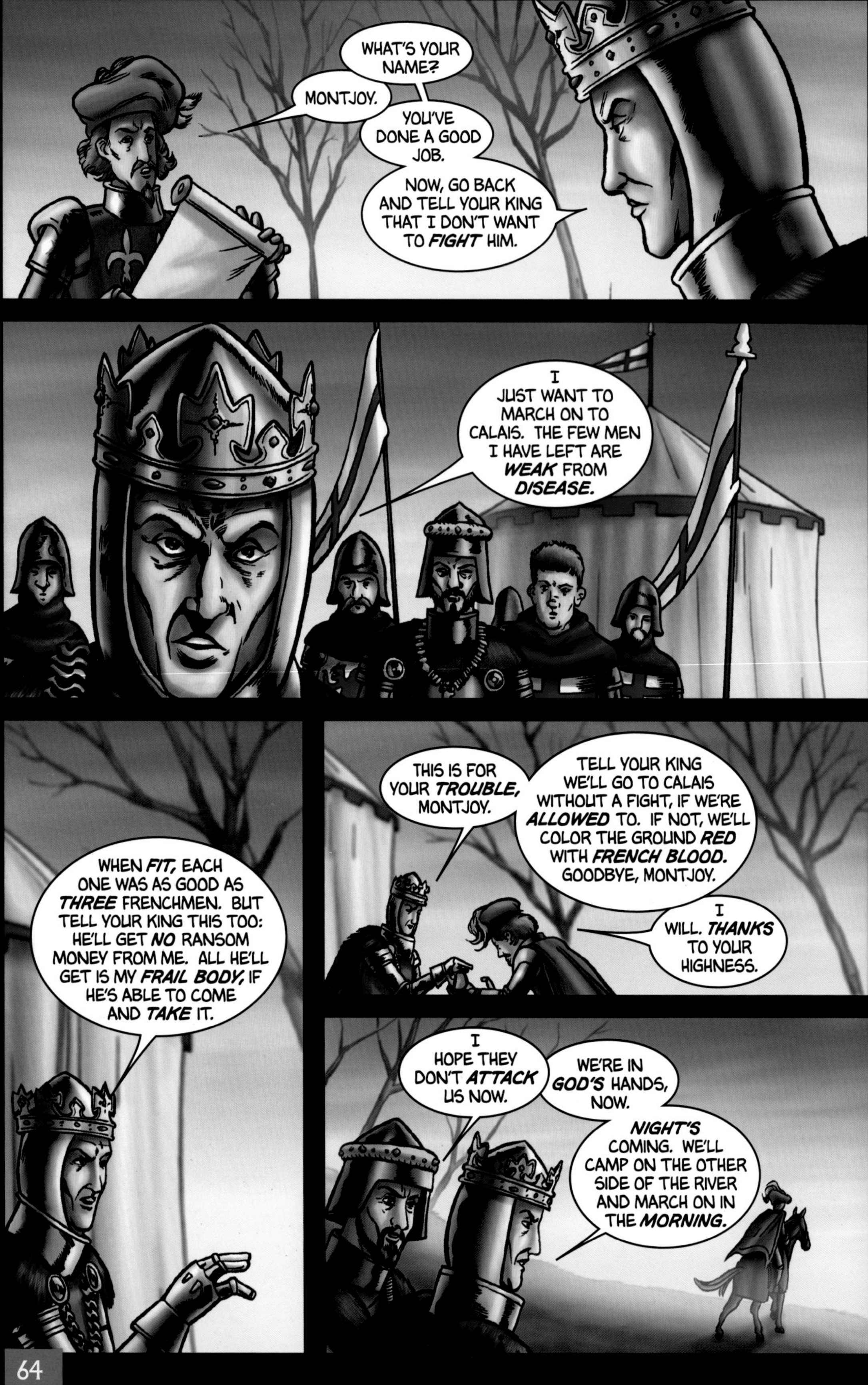
WHAT'S YOUR NAME?
MONTJOY.
YOU'VE DONE A GOOD JOB.
NOW, GO BACK AND TELL YOUR KING THAT I DON'T WANT TO FIGHT HIM.
I JUST WANT TO MARCH ON TO CALAIS. THE FEW MEN I HAVE LEFT ARE WEAK FROM DISEASE.
WHEN FIT, EACH ONE WAS AS GOOD AS THREE FRENCHMEN. BUT TELL YOUR KING THIS TOO: HE'LL GET NO RANSOM MONEY FROM ME. ALL HE'LL GET IS MY FRAIL BODY, IF HE'S ABLE TO COME AND TAKE IT.
THIS IS FOR YOUR TROUBLE, MONTJOY.
TELL YOUR KING WE'LL GO TO CALAIS WITHOUT A FIGHT, IF WE'RE ALLOWED TO. IF NOT, WE'LL COLOR THE GROUND RED WITH FRENCH BLOOD. GOODBYE, MONTJOY.
I WILL. THANKS TO YOUR HIGHNESS.
I HOPE THEY DON'T ATTACK US NOW.
WE'RE IN GOD'S HANDS, NOW.
NIGHT'S COMING. WE'LL CAMP ON THE OTHER SIDE OF THE RIVER AND MARCH ON IN THE MORNING.

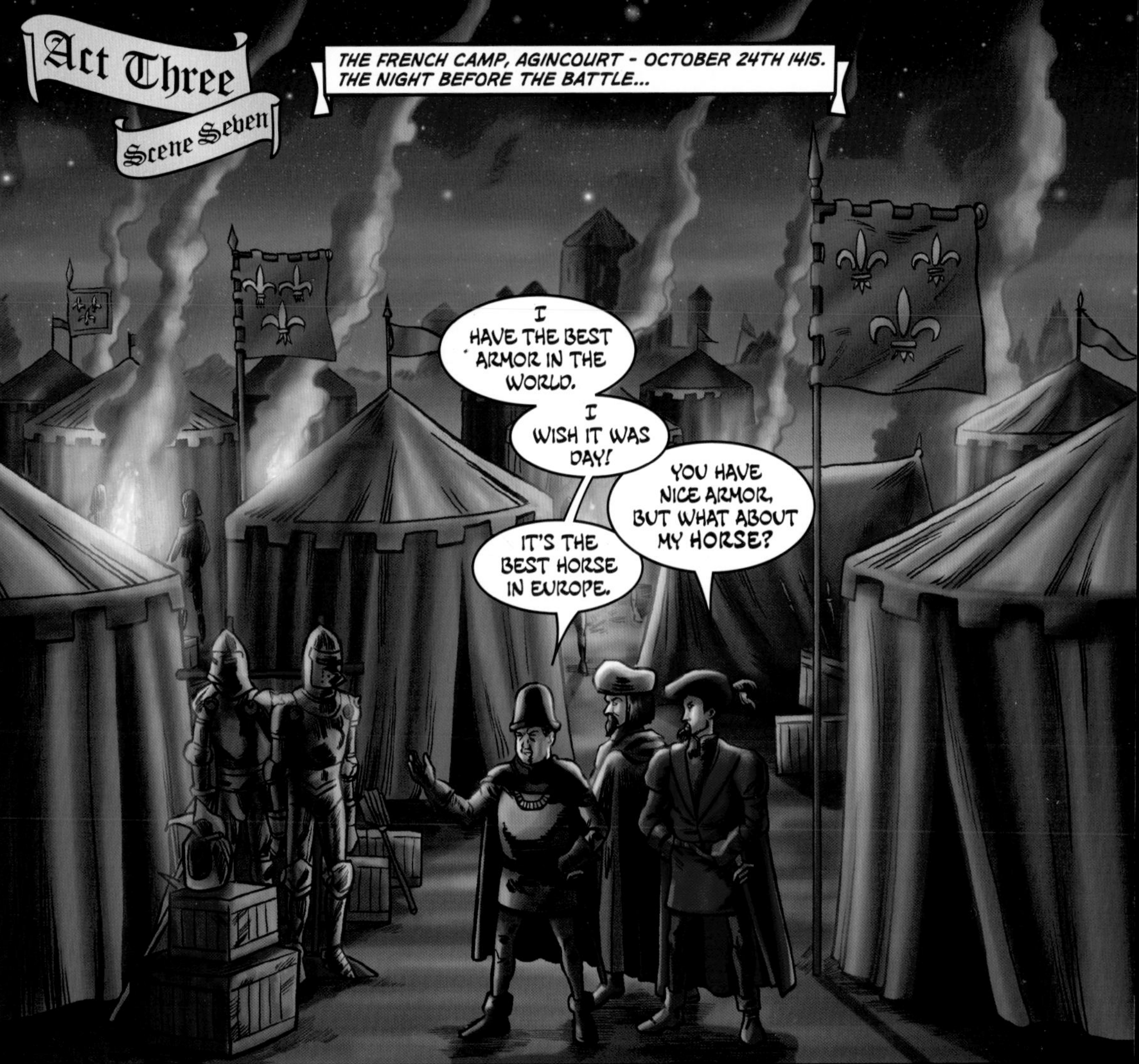
Act Three
Scene Seven
THE FRENCH CAMP, AGINCOURT - OCTOBER 24TH 1415. THE NIGHT BEFORE THE BATTLE...
I HAVE THE BEST ARMOR IN THE WORLD.
I WISH IT WAS DAY!
IT'S THE BEST HORSE IN EUROPE.
YOU HAVE NICE ARMOR, BUT WHAT ABOUT MY HORSE?

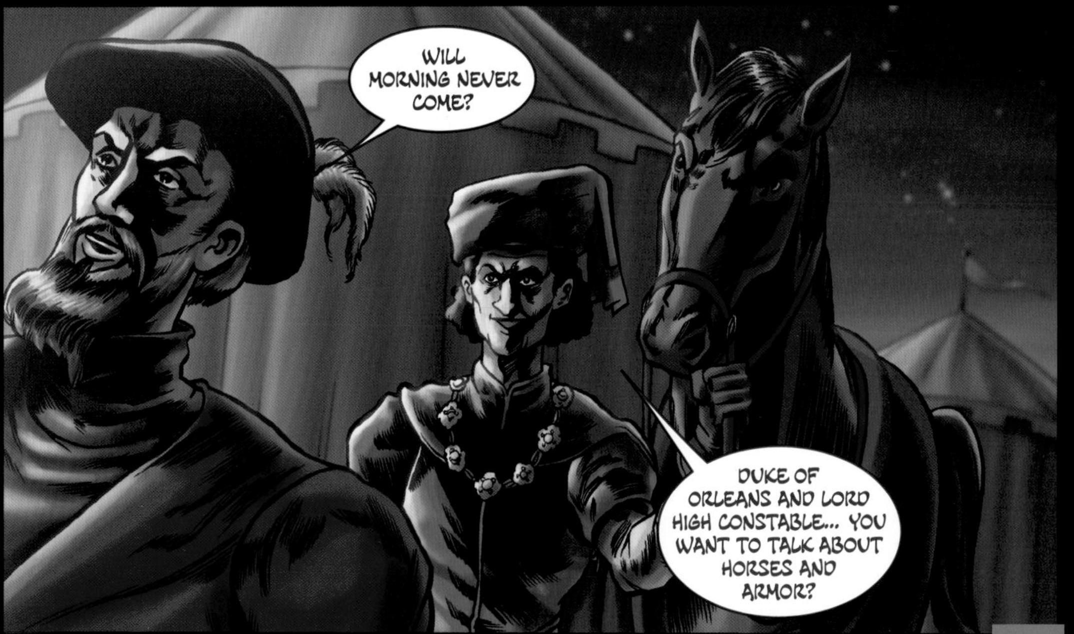
WILL MORNING NEVER COME?
DUKE OF ORLEANS AND LORD HIGH CONSTABLE... YOU WANT TO TALK ABOUT HORSES AND ARMOR?

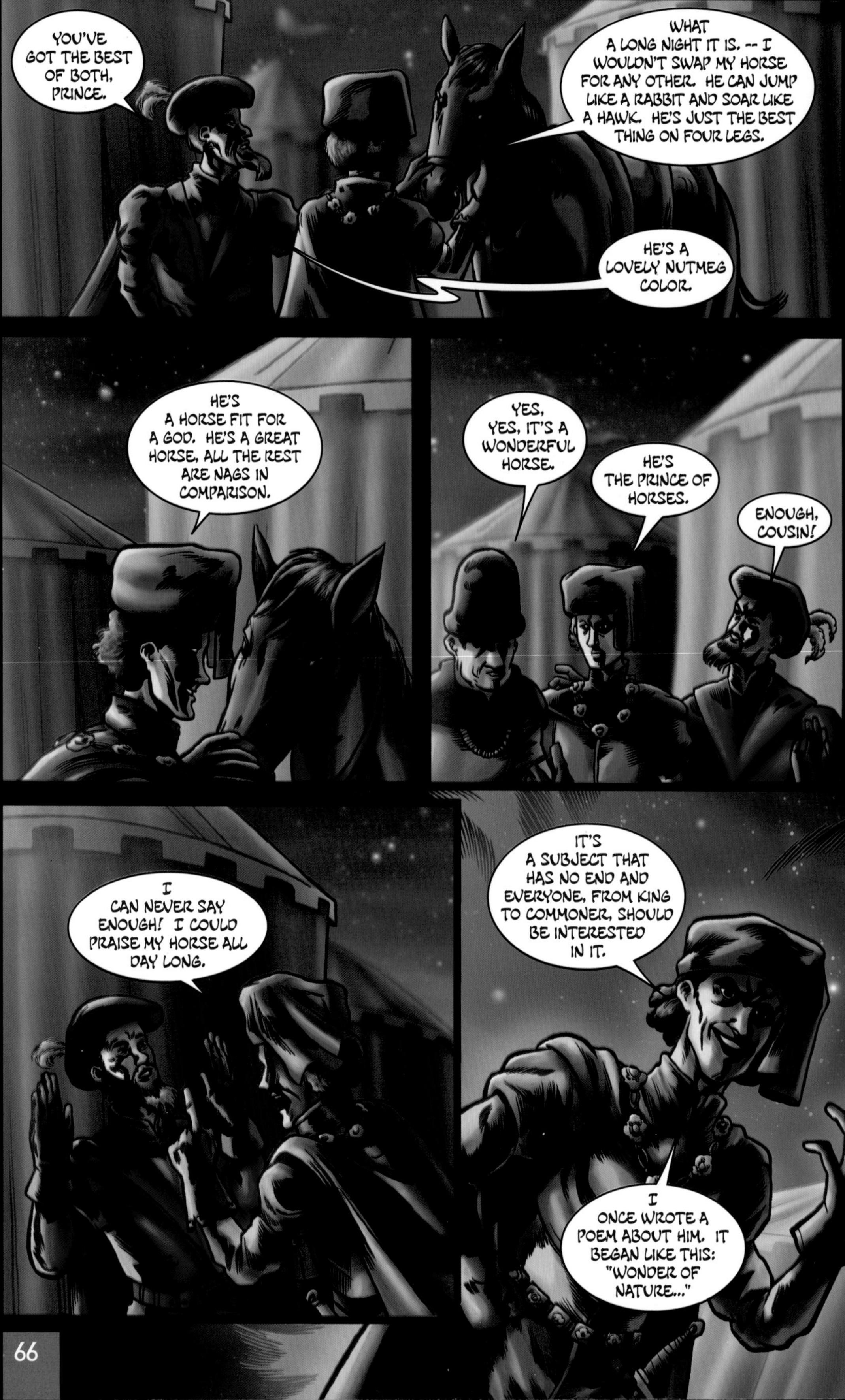
YOU'VE GOT THE BEST OF BOTH, PRINCE.
WHAT A LONG NIGHT IT IS. -- I WOULDN'T SWAP MY HORSE FOR ANY OTHER. HE CAN JUMP LIKE A RABBIT AND SOAR LIKE A HAWK. HE'S JUST THE BEST THING ON FOUR LEGS.
HE'S A LOVELY NUTMEG COLOR.
HE'S A HORSE FIT FOR A GOD. HE'S A GREAT HORSE, ALL THE REST ARE NAGS IN COMPARISON.
YES, YES, IT'S A WONDERFUL HORSE.
HE'S THE PRINCE OF HORSES.
ENOUGH, COUSIN!
I CAN NEVER SAY ENOUGH! I COULD PRAISE MY HORSE ALL DAY LONG.
IT'S A SUBJECT THAT HAS NO END AND EVERYONE, FROM KING TO COMMONER, SHOULD BE INTERESTED IN IT.
I ONCE WROTE A POEM ABOUT HIM. IT BEGAN LIKE THIS: "WONDER OF NATURE..."

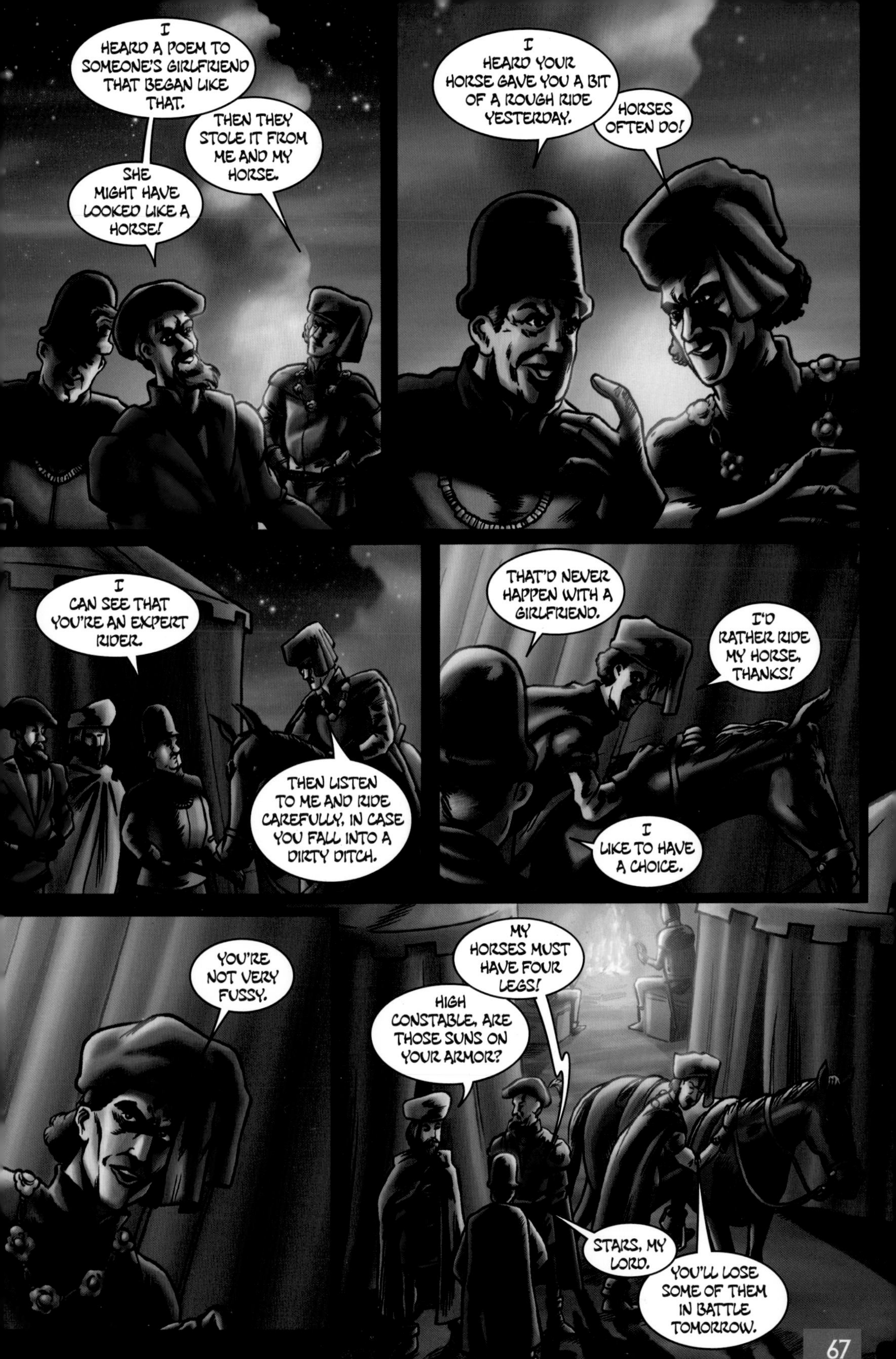
I HEARD A POEM TO SOMEONE'S GIRLFRIEND THAT BEGAN LIKE THAT.
SHE MIGHT HAVE LOOKED LIKE A HORSE!
THEN THEY STOLE IT FROM ME AND MY HORSE.
I HEARD YOUR HORSE GAVE YOU A BIT OF A ROUGH RIDE YESTERDAY.
HORSES OFTEN DO!
I CAN SEE THAT YOU'RE AN EXPERT RIDER.
THEN LISTEN TO ME AND RIDE CAREFULLY, IN CASE YOU FALL INTO A DIRTY DITCH.
THAT'D NEVER HAPPEN WITH A GIRLFRIEND.
I'D RATHER RIDE MY HORSE, THANKS!
I LIKE TO HAVE A CHOICE.
YOU'RE NOT VERY FUSSY.
MY HORSES MUST HAVE FOUR LEGS!
HIGH CONSTABLE, ARE THOSE SUNS ON YOUR ARMOR?
STARS, MY LORD.
YOU'LL LOSE SOME OF THEM IN BATTLE TOMORROW.

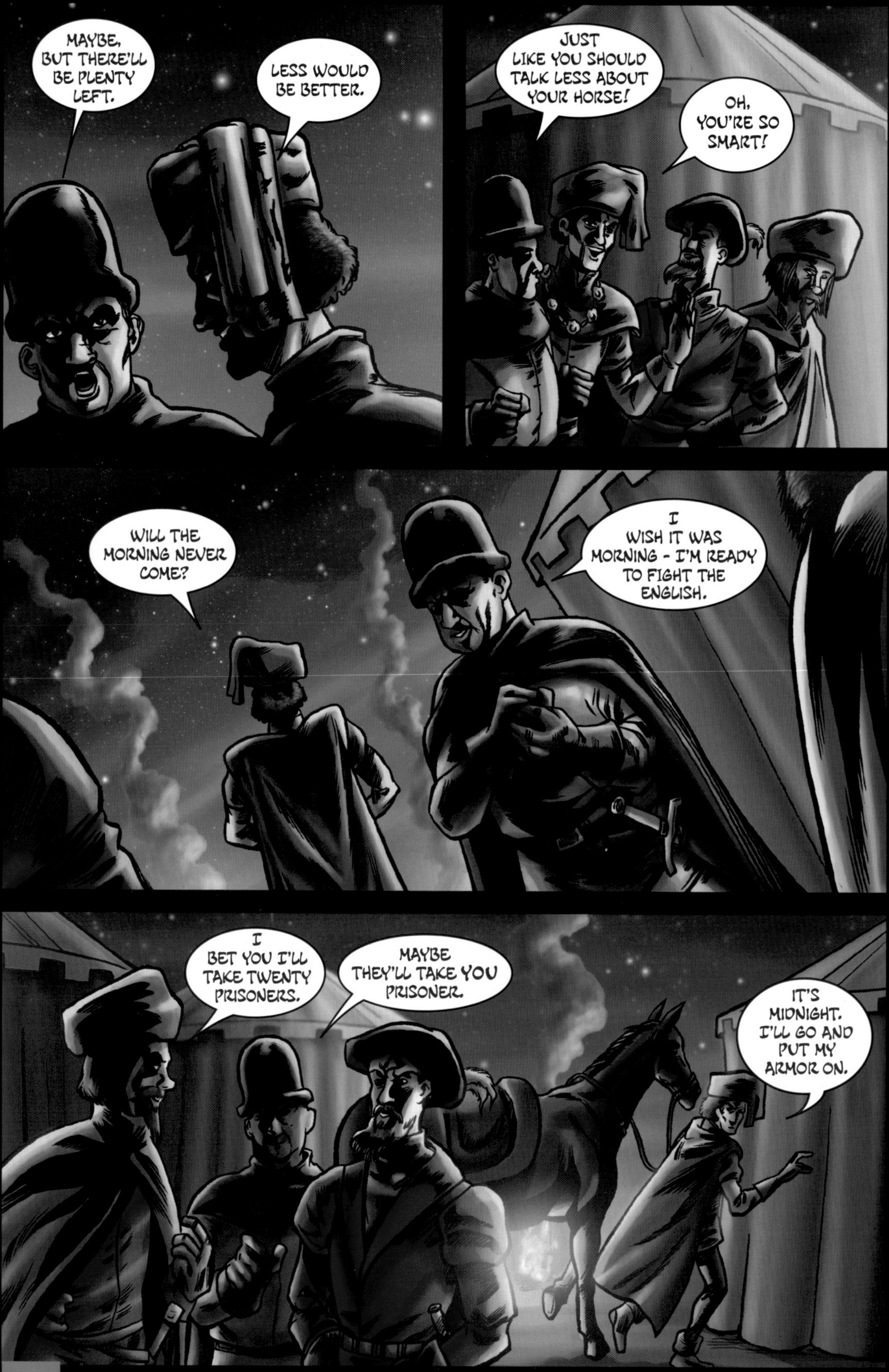
MAYBE, BUT THERE'LL BE PLENTY LEFT.
LESS WOULD BE BETTER.
JUST LIKE YOU SHOULD TALK LESS ABOUT YOUR HORSE!
OH, YOU'RE SO SMART!
WILL THE MORNING NEVER COME?
I WISH IT WAS MORNING - I'M READY TO FIGHT THE ENGLISH.
I BET YOU I'LL TAKE TWENTY PRISONERS.
MAYBE THEY'LL TAKE YOU PRISONER.
IT'S MIDNIGHT. I'LL GO AND PUT MY ARMOR ON.

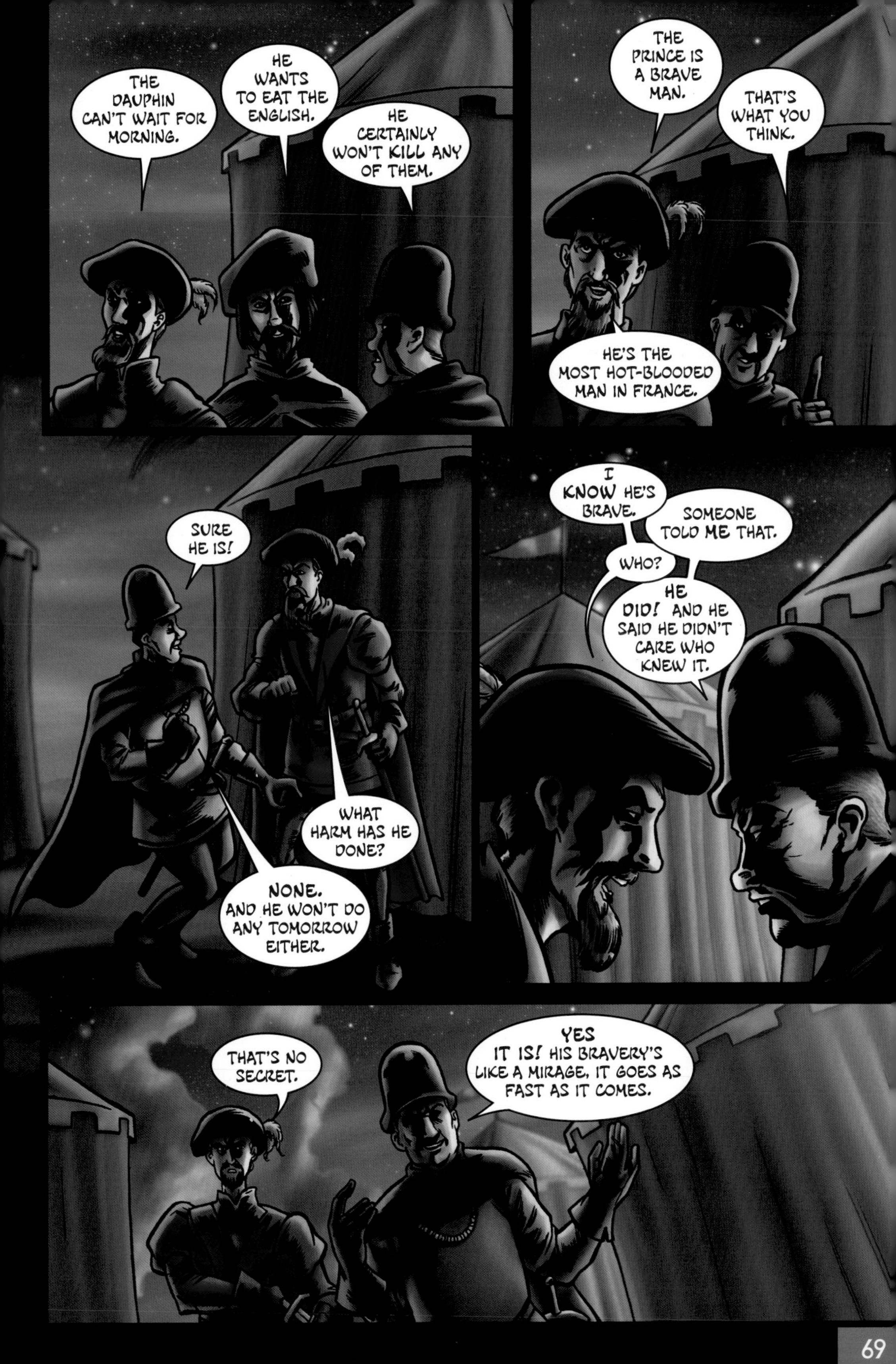
THE DAUPHIN CAN'T WAIT FOR MORNING.
HE WANTS TO EAT THE ENGLISH.
HE CERTAINLY WON'T KILL ANY OF THEM.
THE PRINCE IS A BRAVE MAN.
THAT'S WHAT YOU THINK.
HE'S THE MOST HOT-BLOODED MAN IN FRANCE.
SURE HE IS!
WHAT HARM HAS HE DONE?
NONE. AND HE WON'T DO ANY TOMORROW EITHER.
I KNOW HE'S BRAVE.
SOMEONE TOLD ME THAT.
WHO?
HE DID! AND HE SAID HE DIDN'T CARE WHO KNEW IT.
THAT'S NO SECRET.
YES IT IS! HIS BRAVERY'S LIKE A MIRAGE, IT GOES AS FAST AS IT COMES.

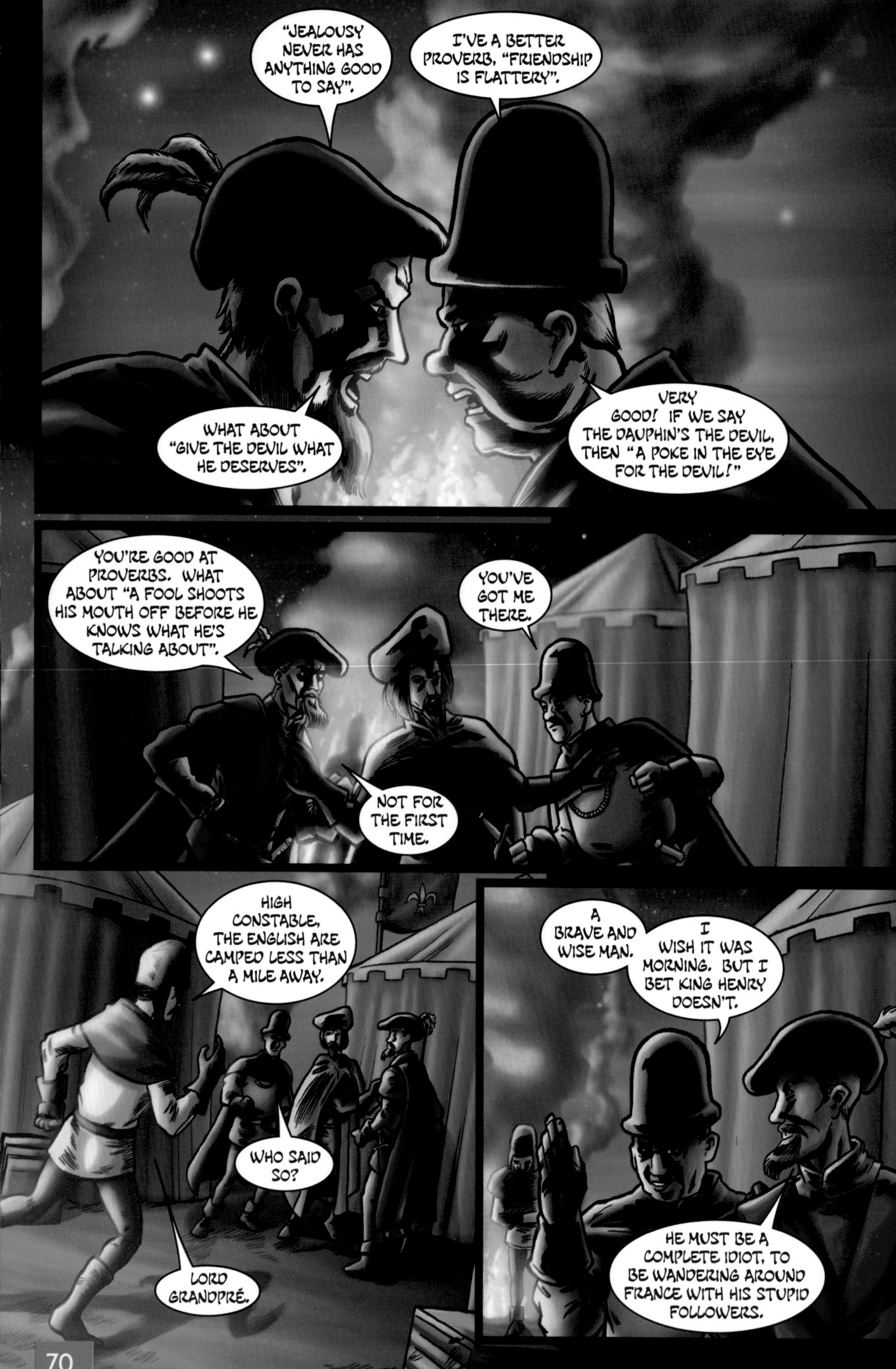
"JEALOUSY NEVER HAS ANYTHING GOOD TO SAY".
I'VE A BETTER PROVERB, "FRIENDSHIP IS FLATTERY".
WHAT ABOUT "GIVE THE DEVIL WHAT HE DESERVES".
VERY GOOD! IF WE SAY THE DAUPHIN'S THE DEVIL, THEN "A POKE IN THE EYE FOR THE DEVIL!"
YOU'RE GOOD AT PROVERBS. WHAT ABOUT "A FOOL SHOOTS HIS MOUTH OFF BEFORE HE KNOWS WHAT HE'S TALKING ABOUT".
YOU'VE GOT ME THERE.
NOT FOR THE FIRST TIME.
HIGH CONSTABLE, THE ENGLISH ARE CAMPED LESS THAN A MILE AWAY.
WHO SAID SO?
LORD GRANDPRÉ.
A BRAVE AND WISE MAN.
I WISH IT WAS MORNING. BUT I BET KING HENRY DOESN'T.
HE MUST BE A COMPLETE IDIOT, TO BE WANDERING AROUND FRANCE WITH HIS STUPID FOLLOWERS.

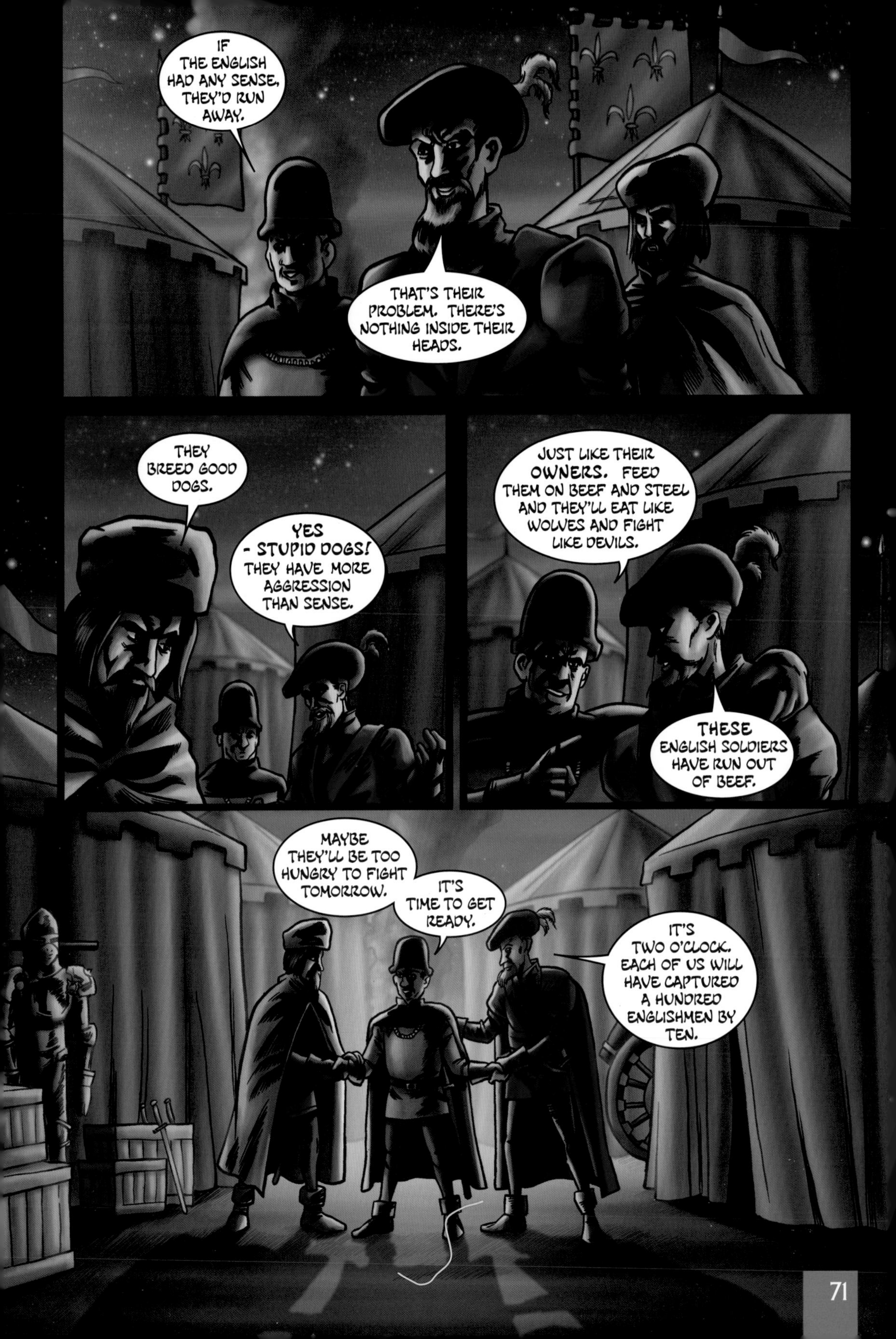
IF THE ENGLISH HAD ANY SENSE, THEY'D RUN AWAY.
THAT'S THEIR PROBLEM. THERE'S NOTHING INSIDE THEIR HEADS.
THEY BREED GOOD DOGS.
YES - STUPID DOGS! THEY HAVE MORE AGGRESSION THAN SENSE.
JUST LIKE THEIR OWNERS. FEED THEM ON BEEF AND STEEL AND THEY'LL EAT LIKE WOLVES AND FIGHT LIKE DEVILS.
THESE ENGLISH SOLDIERS HAVE RUN OUT OF BEEF.
MAYBE THEY'LL BE TOO HUNGRY TO FIGHT TOMORROW.
IT'S TIME TO GET READY.
IT'S TWO O'CLOCK. EACH OF US WILL HAVE CAPTURED A HUNDRED ENGLISHMEN BY TEN.

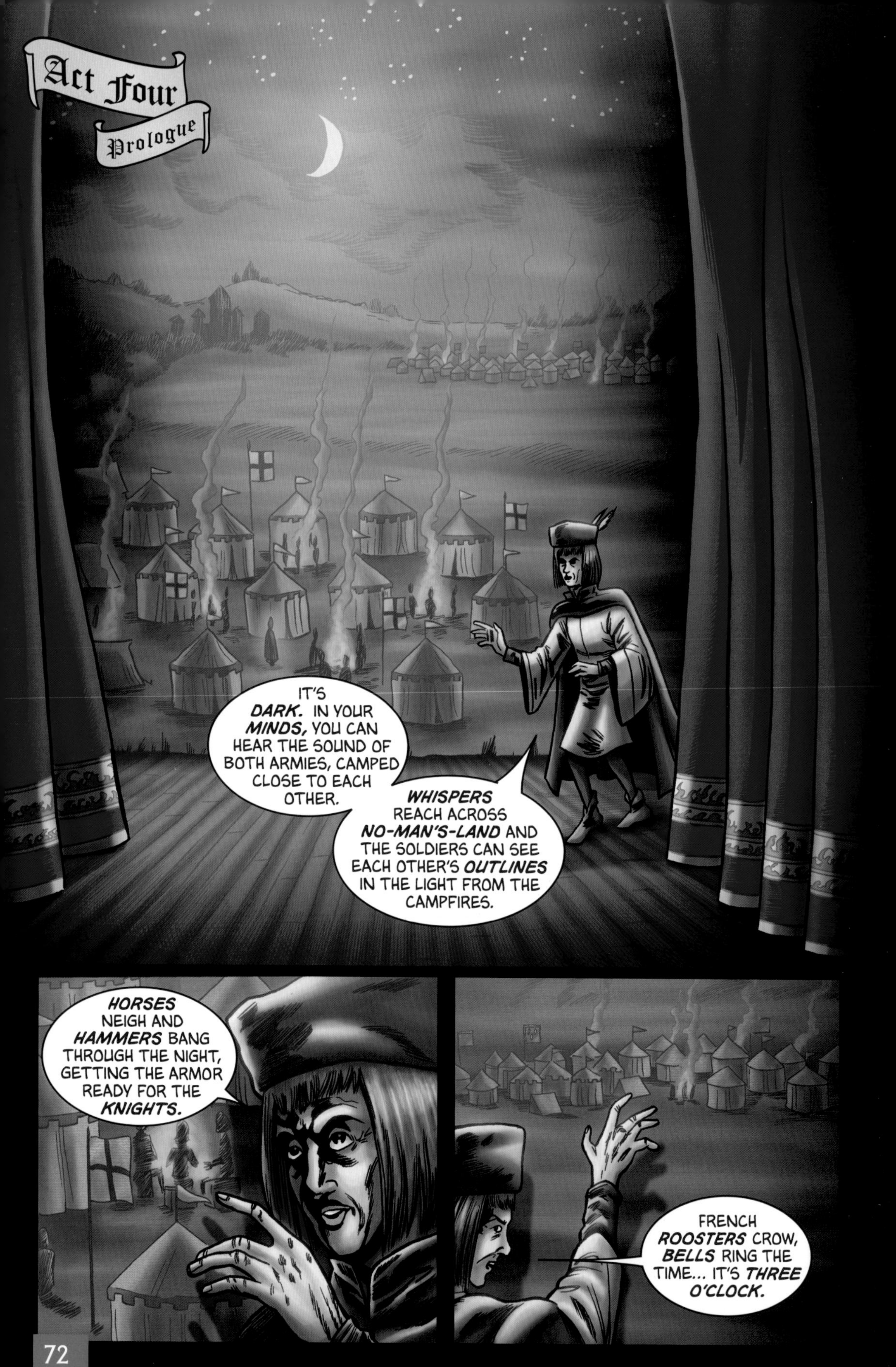
Act Four
Prologue
IT'S DARK. IN YOUR MINDS, YOU CAN HEAR THE SOUND OF BOTH ARMIES, CAMPED CLOSE TO EACH OTHER.
WHISPERS REACH ACROSS NO-MAN'S-LAND AND THE SOLDIERS CAN SEE EACH OTHER'S OUTLINES IN THE LIGHT FROM THE CAMPFIRES.
HORSES NEIGH AND HAMMERS BANG THROUGH THE NIGHT, GETTING THE ARMOR READY FOR THE KNIGHTS.
FRENCH ROOSTERS CROW, BELLS RING THE TIME... IT'S THREE O'CLOCK.

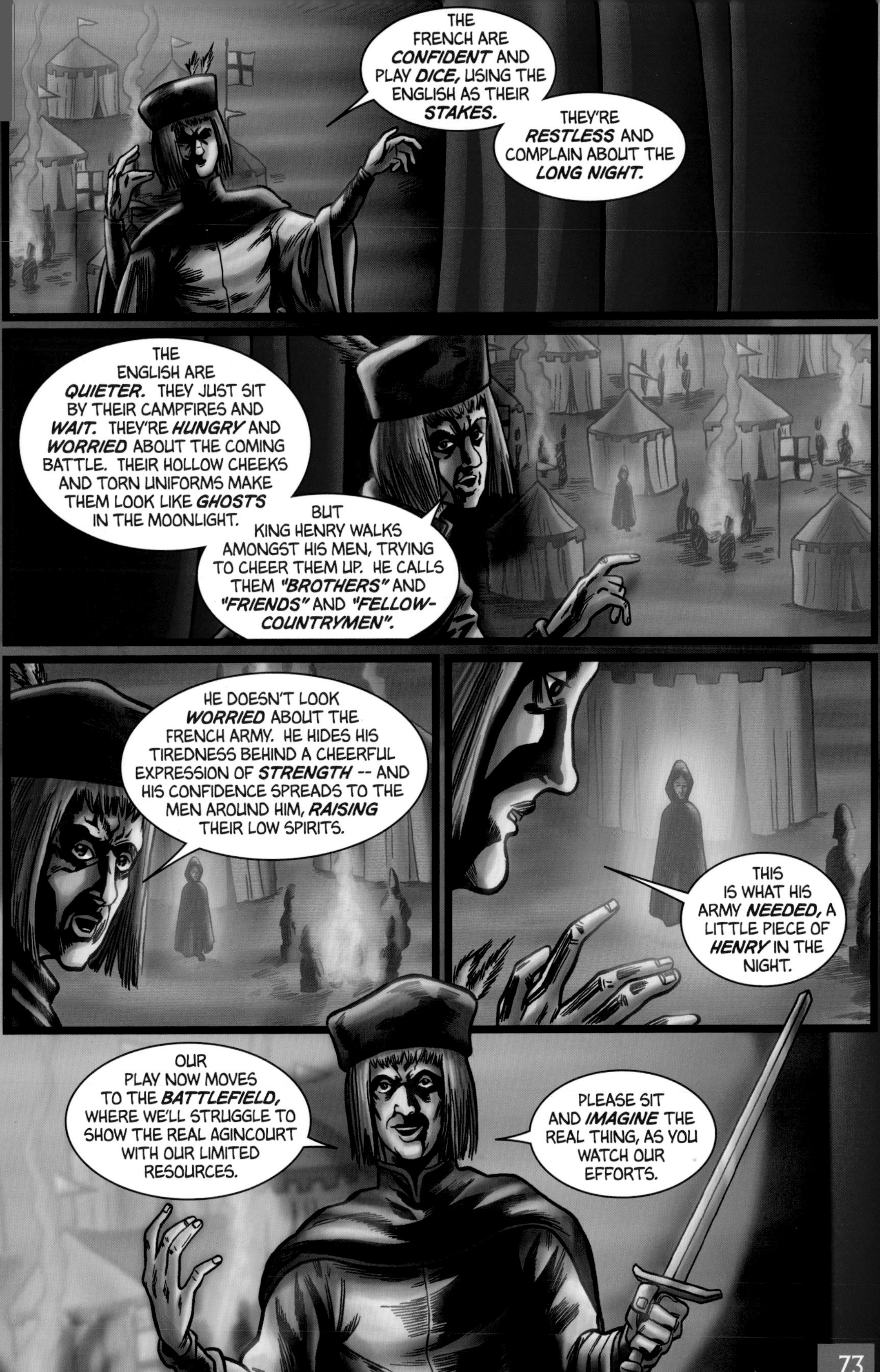
THE FRENCH ARE CONFIDENT AND PLAY DICE, USING THE ENGLISH AS THEIR STAKES.
THEY'RE RESTLESS AND COMPLAIN ABOUT THE LONG NIGHT.
THE ENGLISH ARE QUIETER. THEY JUST SIT BY THEIR CAMPFIRES AND WAIT. THEY'RE HUNGRY AND WORRIED ABOUT THE COMING BATTLE. THEIR HOLLOW CHEEKS AND TORN UNIFORMS MAKE THEM LOOK LIKE GHOSTS IN THE MOONLIGHT.
BUT KING HENRY WALKS AMONGST HIS MEN, TRYING TO CHEER THEM UP. HE CALLS THEM "BROTHERS" AND "FRIENDS" AND "FELLOW-COUNTRYMEN".
HE DOESN'T LOOK WORRIED ABOUT THE FRENCH ARMY. HE HIDES HIS TIREDNESS BEHIND A CHEERFUL EXPRESSION OF STRENGTH -- AND HIS CONFIDENCE SPREADS TO THE MEN AROUND HIM, RAISING THEIR LOW SPIRITS.
THIS IS WHAT HIS ARMY NEEDED, A LITTLE PIECE OF HENRY IN THE NIGHT.
OUR PLAY NOW MOVES TO THE BATTLEFIELD, WHERE WE'LL STRUGGLE TO SHOW THE REAL AGINCOURT WITH OUR LIMITED RESOURCES.
PLEASE SIT AND IMAGINE THE REAL THING, AS YOU WATCH OUR EFFORTS.

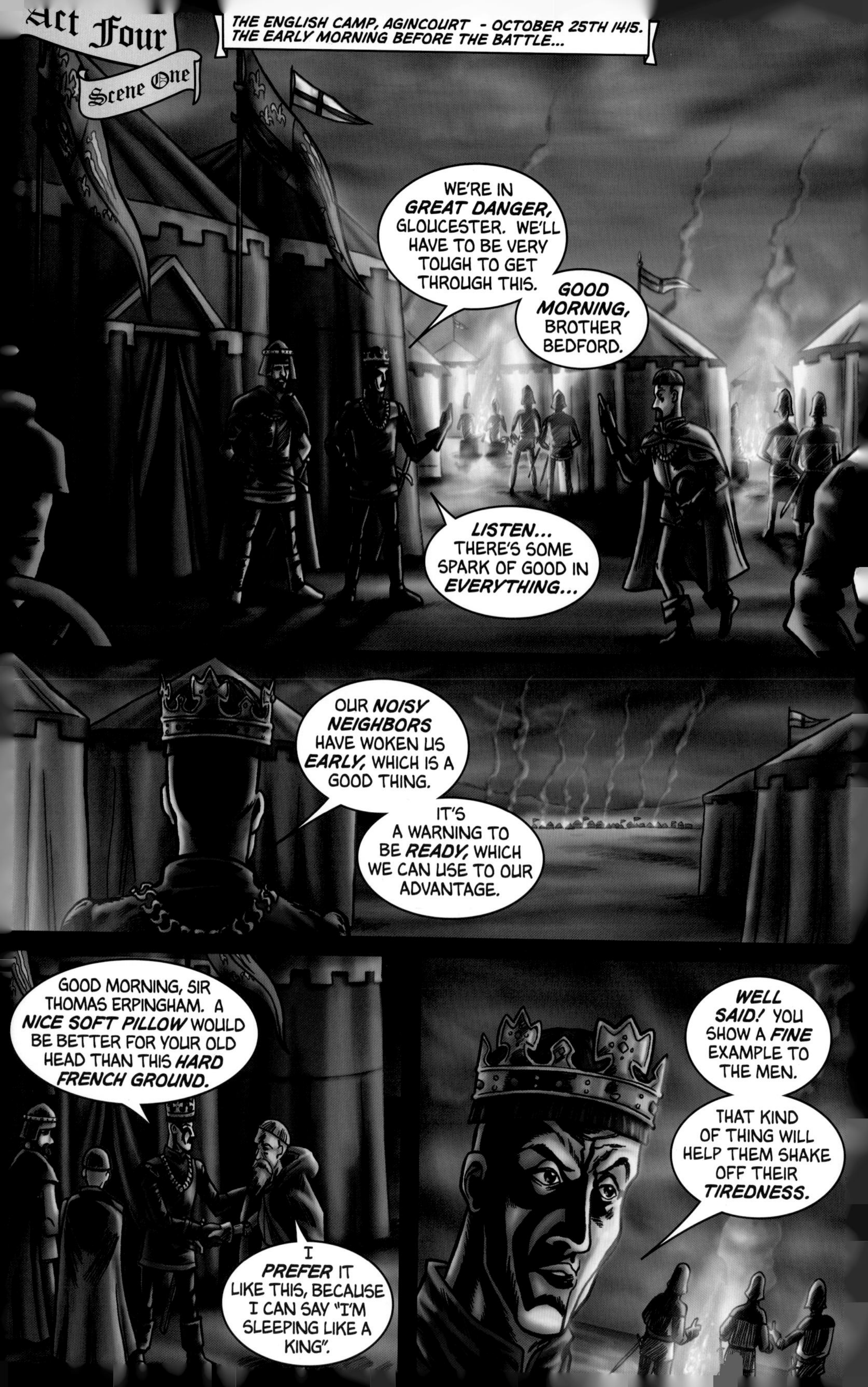
Act Four
Scene One
THE ENGLISH CAMP, AGINCOURT - OCTOBER 25TH 1415. THE EARLY MORNING BEFORE THE BATTLE...
WE'RE IN GREAT DANGER, GLOUCESTER. WE'LL HAVE TO BE VERY TOUGH TO GET THROUGH THIS.
GOOD MORNING, BROTHER BEDFORD.
LISTEN... THERE'S SOME SPARK OF GOOD IN EVERYTHING...
OUR NOISY NEIGHBORS HAVE WOKEN US EARLY, WHICH IS A GOOD THING.
IT'S A WARNING TO BE READY, WHICH WE CAN USE TO OUR ADVANTAGE.
GOOD MORNING, SIR THOMAS ERPINGHAM. A NICE SOFT PILLOW WOULD BE BETTER FOR YOUR OLD HEAD THAN THIS HARD FRENCH GROUND.
I PREFER IT LIKE THIS, BECAUSE I CAN SAY "I'M SLEEPING LIKE A KING".
WELL SAID! YOU SHOW A FINE EXAMPLE TO THE MEN.
THAT KIND OF THING WILL HELP THEM SHAKE OFF THEIR TIREDNESS.

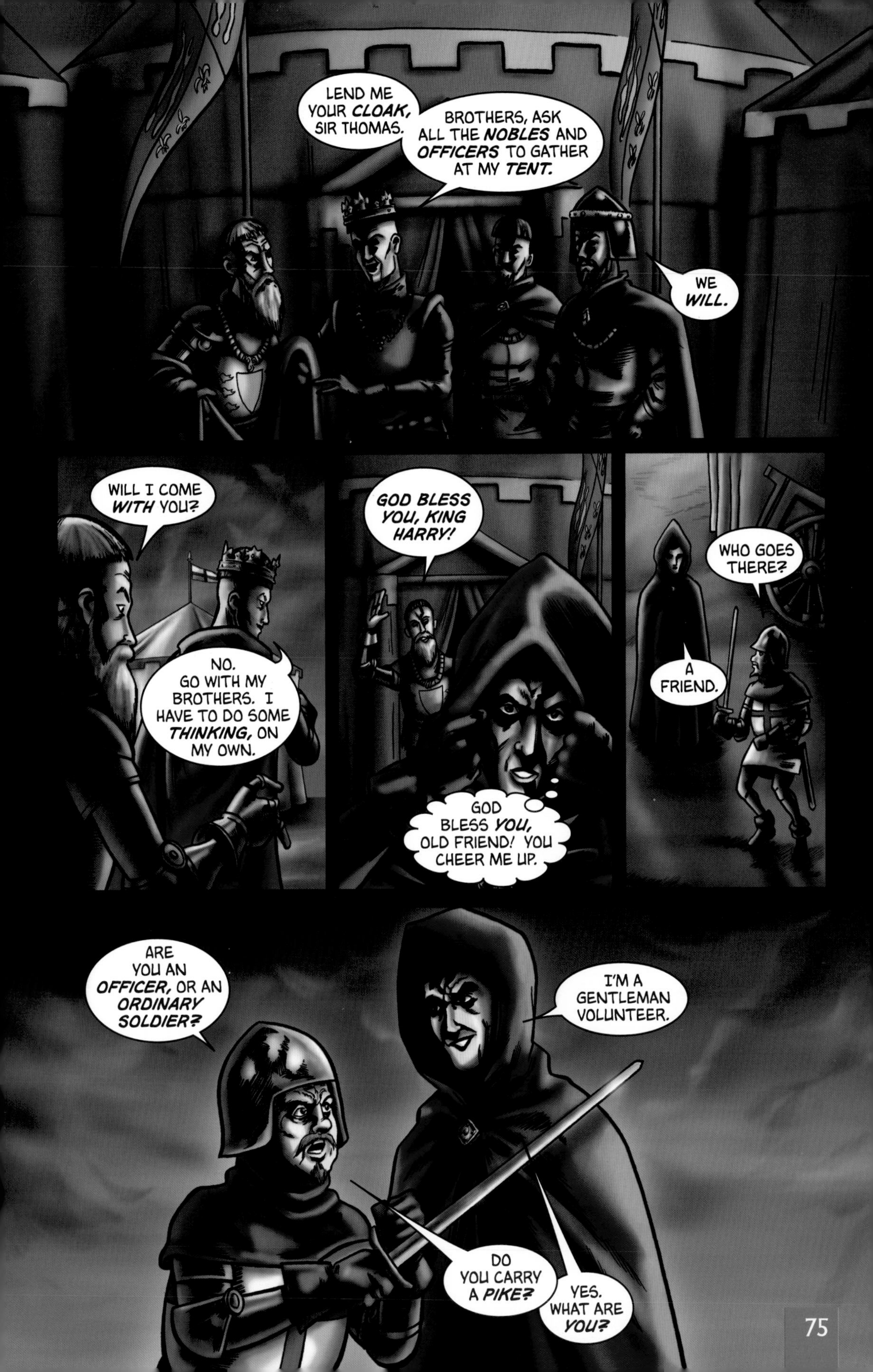
LEND ME YOUR CLOAK, SIR THOMAS.
BROTHERS, ASK ALL THE NOBLES AND OFFICERS TO GATHER AT MY TENT.
WE WILL.
WILL I COME WITH YOU?
NO. GO WITH MY BROTHERS. I HAVE TO DO SOME THINKING, ON MY OWN.
GOD BLESS YOU, KING HARRY!
GOD BLESS YOU, OLD FRIEND! YOU CHEER ME UP.
WHO GOES THERE?
A FRIEND.
ARE YOU AN OFFICER, OR AN ORDINARY SOLDIER?
I'M A GENTLEMAN VOLUNTEER.
DO YOU CARRY A PIKE?
YES. WHAT ARE YOU?

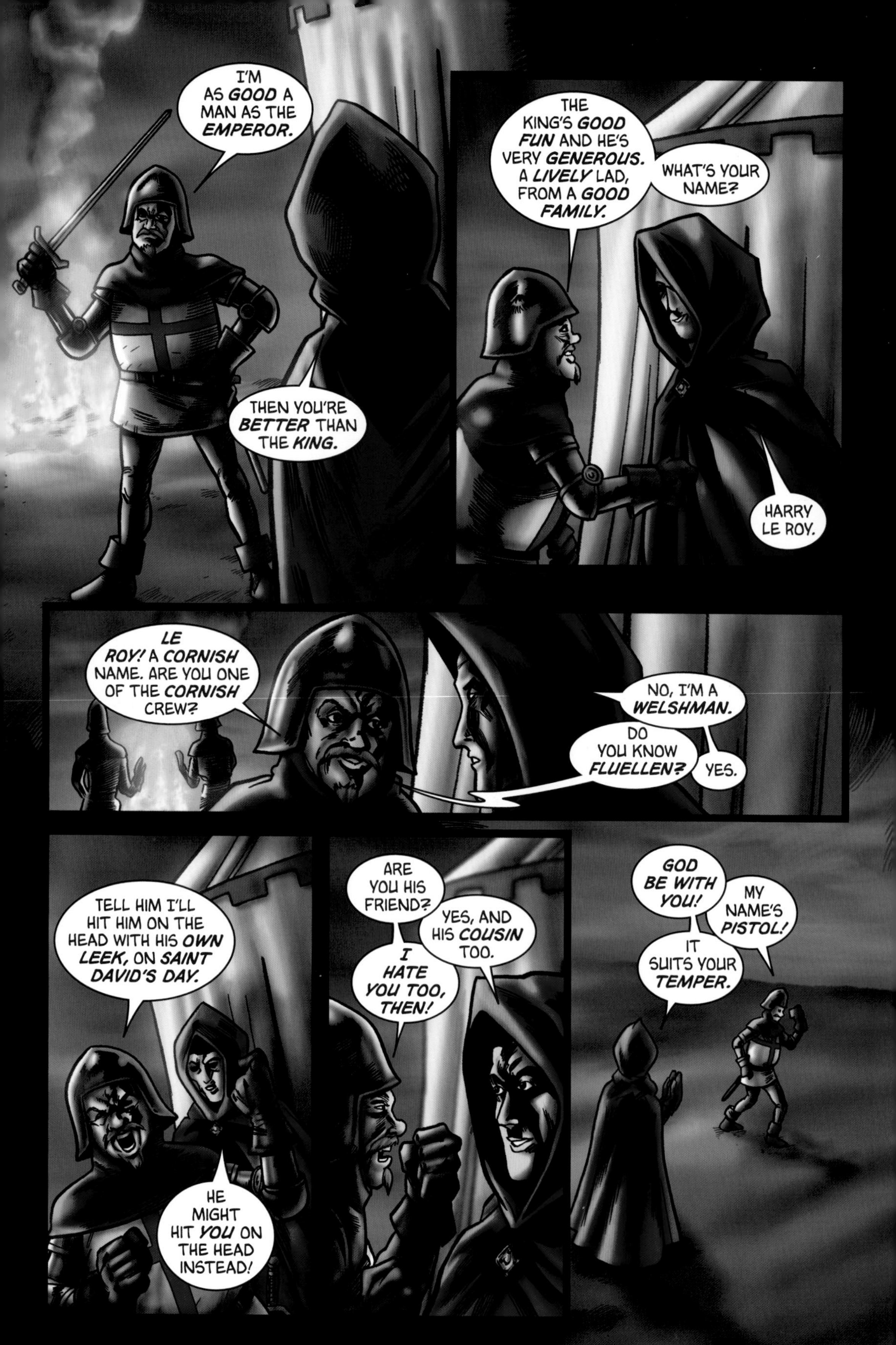
I'M AS GOOD A MAN AS THE EMPEROR.
THEN YOU'RE BETTER THAN THE KING.
THE KING'S GOOD FUN AND HE'S VERY GENEROUS. A LIVELY LAD, FROM A GOOD FAMILY.
WHAT'S YOUR NAME?
HARRY LE ROY.
LE ROY! A CORNISH NAME. ARE YOU ONE OF THE CORNISH CREW?
NO, I'M A WELSHMAN.
DO YOU KNOW FLUELLEN?
YES.
TELL HIM I'LL HIT HIM ON THE HEAD WITH HIS OWN LEEK, ON SAINT DAVID'S DAY.
HE MIGHT HIT YOU ON THE HEAD INSTEAD!
ARE YOU HIS FRIEND?
YES, AND HIS COUSIN TOO.
I HATE YOU TOO, THEN!
GOD BE WITH YOU!
MY NAME'S PISTOL!
IT SUITS YOUR TEMPER.

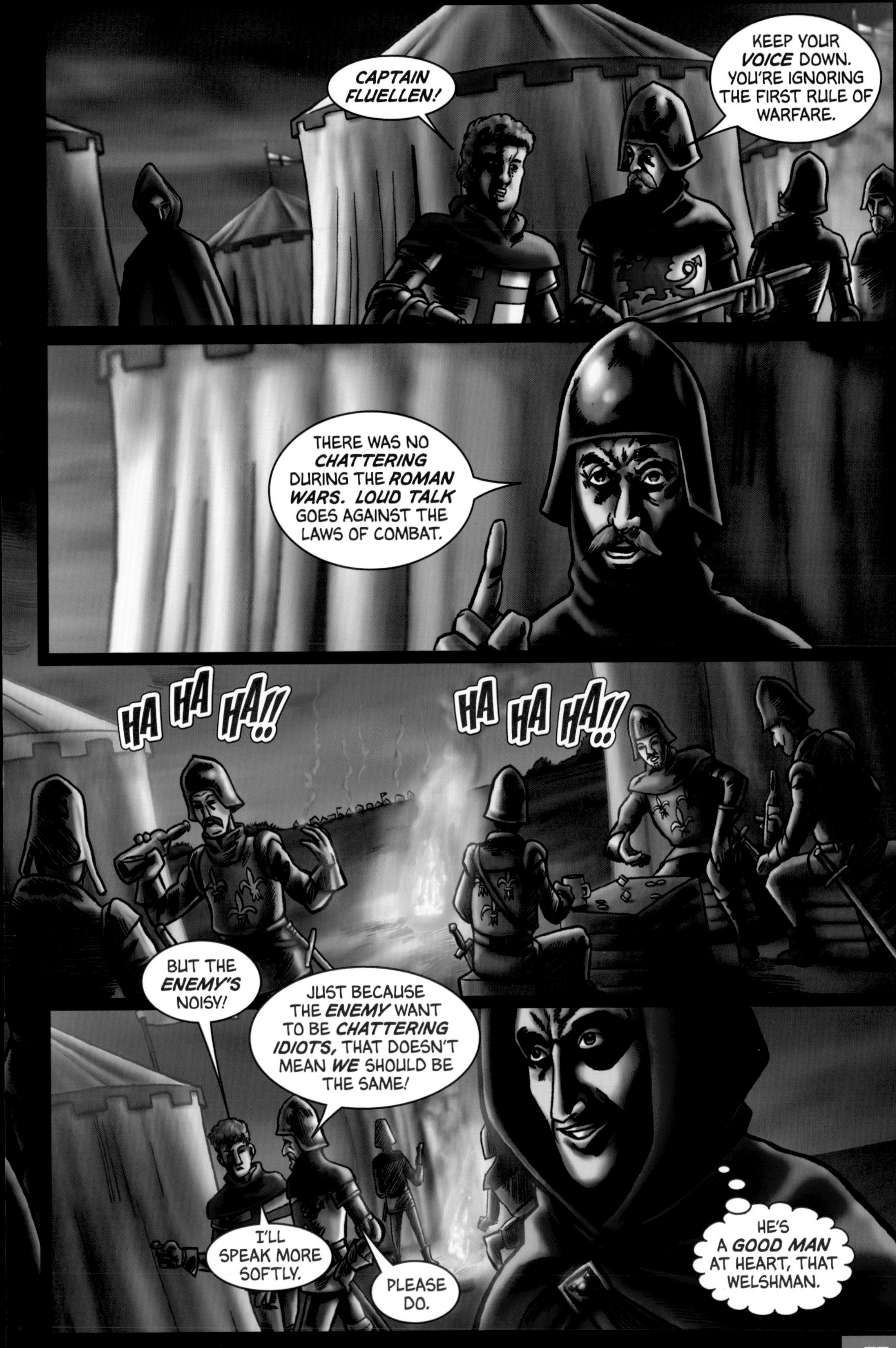
CAPTAIN FLUELLEN!
KEEP YOUR VOICE DOWN. YOU'RE IGNORING THE FIRST RULE OF WARFARE.
THERE WAS NO CHATTERING DURING THE ROMAN WARS. LOUD TALK GOES AGAINST THE LAWS OF COMBAT.
HA HA HA!!
HA HA HA!!
BUT THE ENEMY'S NOISY!
JUST BECAUSE THE ENEMY WANT TO BE CHATTERING IDIOTS, THAT DOESN'T MEAN WE SHOULD BE THE SAME!
I'LL SPEAK MORE SOFTLY.
PLEASE DO.
HE'S A GOOD MAN AT HEART, THAT WELSHMAN.

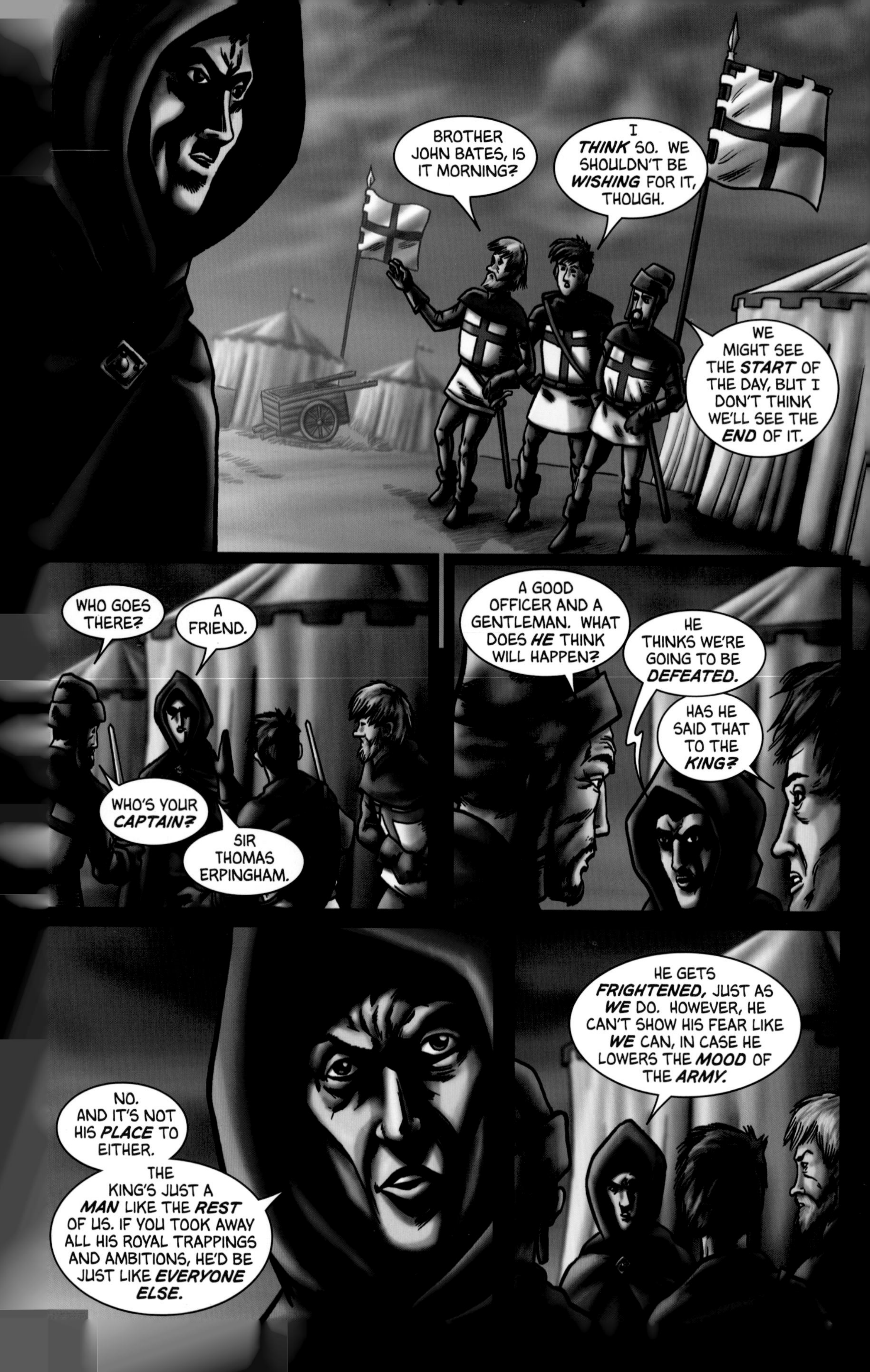
BROTHER JOHN BATES, IS IT MORNING?
I THINK SO. WE SHOULDN'T BE WISHING FOR IT, THOUGH.
WE MIGHT SEE THE START OF THE DAY, BUT I DON'T THINK WE'LL SEE THE END OF IT.
WHO GOES THERE?
A FRIEND.
WHO'S YOUR CAPTAIN?
SIR THOMAS ERPINGHAM.
A GOOD OFFICER AND A GENTLEMAN. WHAT DOES HE THINK WILL HAPPEN?
HE THINKS WE'RE GOING TO BE DEFEATED.
HAS HE SAID THAT TO THE KING?
NO. AND IT'S NOT HIS PLACE TO EITHER.
THE KING'S JUST A MAN LIKE THE REST OF US. IF YOU TOOK AWAY ALL HIS ROYAL TRAPPINGS AND AMBITIONS, HE'D BE JUST LIKE EVERYONE ELSE.
HE GETS FRIGHTENED, JUST AS WE DO. HOWEVER, HE CAN'T SHOW HIS FEAR LIKE WE CAN, IN CASE HE LOWERS THE MOOD OF THE ARMY.

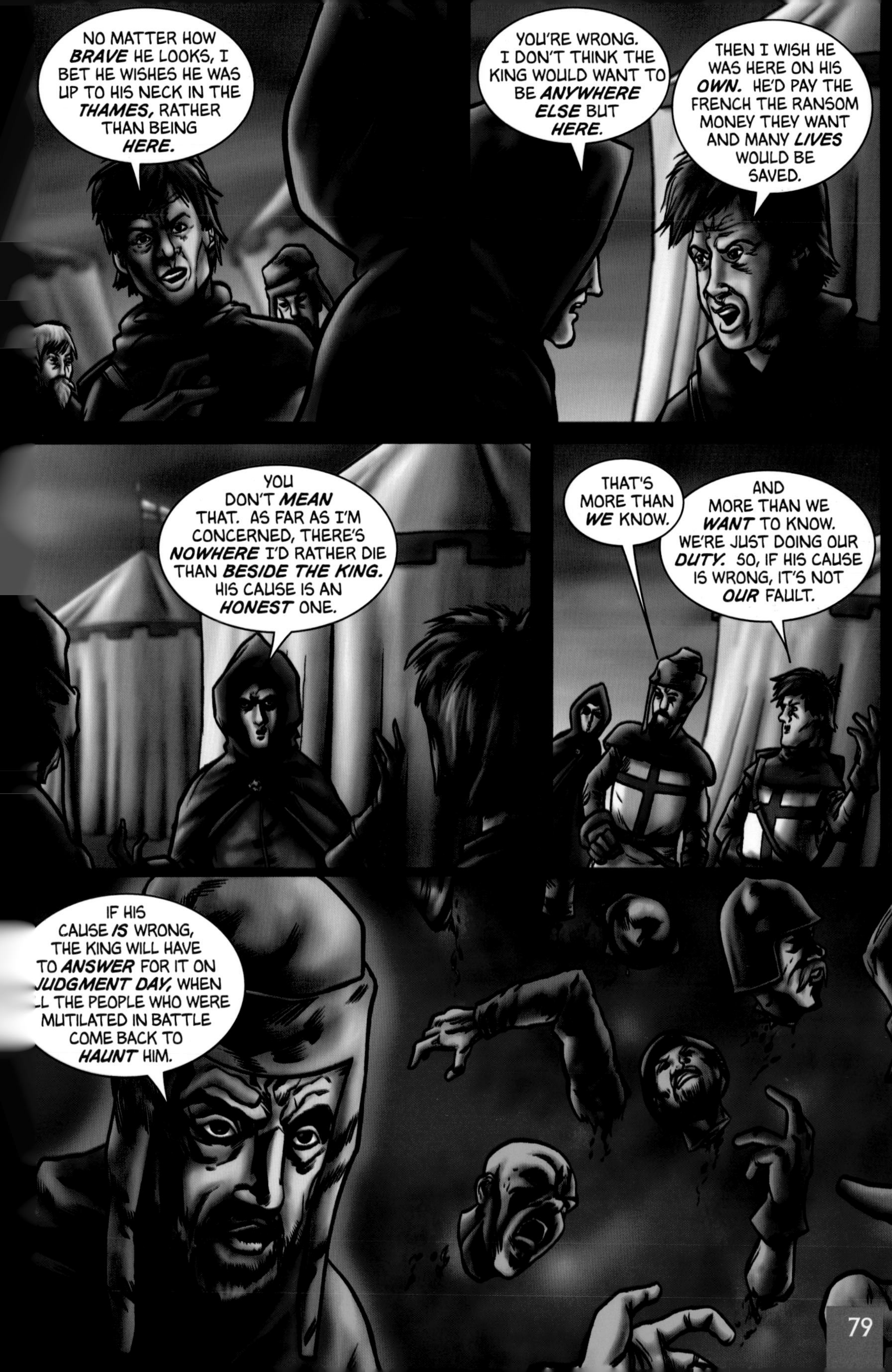
NO MATTER HOW BRAVE HE LOOKS, I BET HE WISHES HE WAS UP TO HIS NECK IN THE THAMES, RATHER THAN BEING HERE.
YOU'RE WRONG. I DON'T THINK THE KING WOULD WANT TO BE ANYWHERE ELSE BUT HERE.
THEN I WISH HE WAS HERE ON HIS OWN. HE'D PAY THE FRENCH THE RANSOM MONEY THEY WANT AND MANY LIVES WOULD BE SAVED.
YOU DON'T MEAN THAT. AS FAR AS I'M CONCERNED, THERE'S NOWHERE I'D RATHER DIE THAN BESIDE THE KING. HIS CAUSE IS AN HONEST ONE.
THAT'S MORE THAN WE KNOW.
AND MORE THAN WE WANT TO KNOW. WE'RE JUST DOING OUR DUTY. SO, IF HIS CAUSE IS WRONG, IT'S NOT OUR FAULT.
IF HIS CAUSE IS WRONG, THE KING WILL HAVE TO ANSWER FOR IT ON JUDGMENT DAY, WHEN ALL THE PEOPLE WHO WERE MUTILATED IN BATTLE COME BACK TO HAUNT HIM.

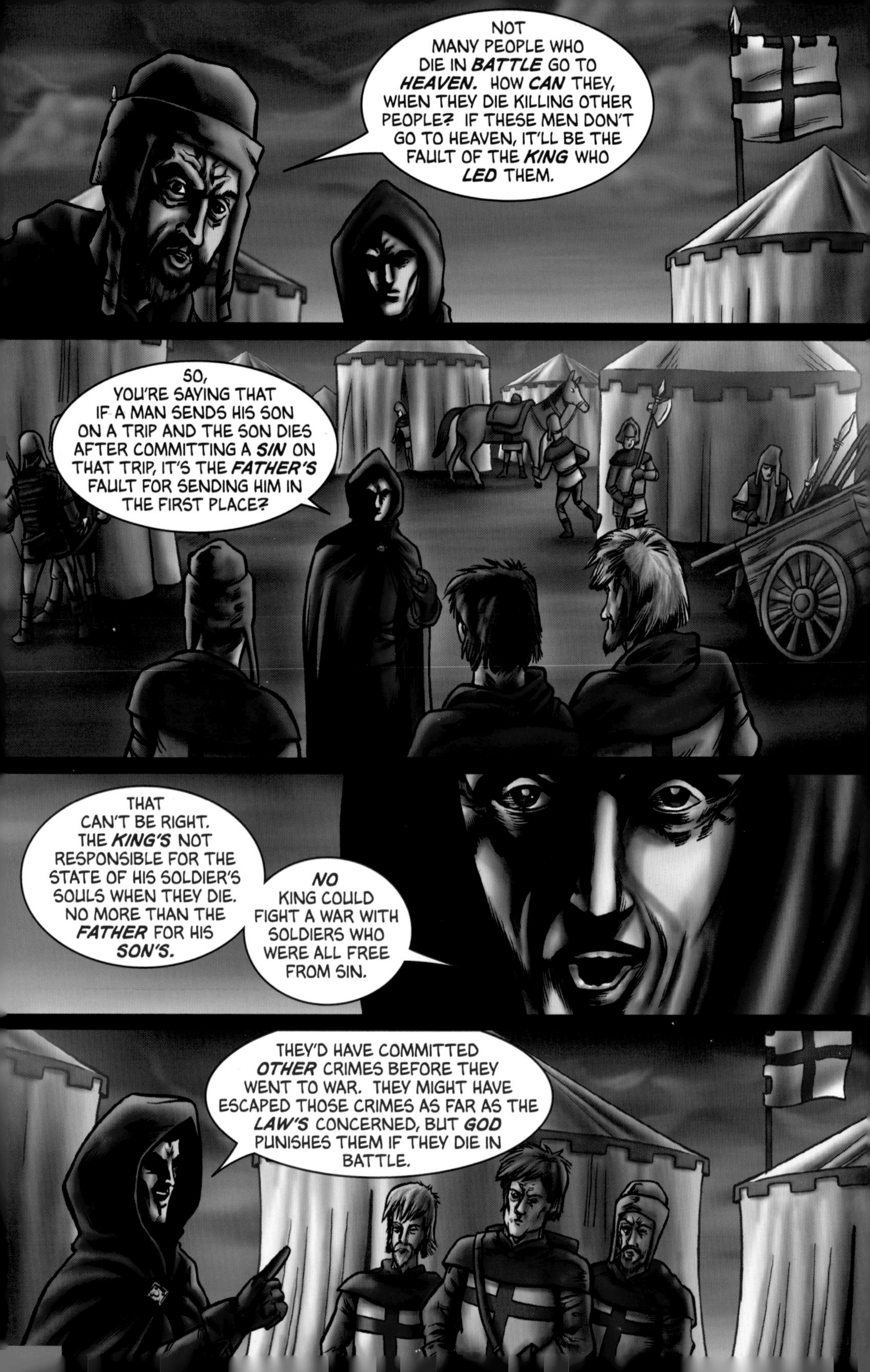
NOT MANY PEOPLE WHO DIE IN BATTLE GO TO HEAVEN. HOW CAN THEY, WHEN THEY DIE KILLING OTHER PEOPLE? IF THESE MEN DON'T GO TO HEAVEN, IT'LL BE THE FAULT OF THE KING WHO LED THEM.
SO, YOU'RE SAYING THAT IF A MAN SENDS HIS SON ON A TRIP AND THE SON DIES AFTER COMMITTING A SIN ON THAT TRIP, IT'S THE FATHER'S FAULT FOR SENDING HIM IN THE FIRST PLACE?
THAT CAN'T BE RIGHT. THE KING'S NOT RESPONSIBLE FOR THE STATE OF HIS SOLDIER'S SOULS WHEN THEY DIE. NO MORE THAN THE FATHER FOR HIS SON'S.
NO KING COULD FIGHT A WAR WITH SOLDIERS WHO WERE ALL FREE FROM SIN.
THEY'D HAVE COMMITTED OTHER CRIMES BEFORE THEY WENT TO WAR. THEY MIGHT HAVE ESCAPED THOSE CRIMES AS FAR AS THE LAW'S CONCERNED, BUT GOD PUNISHES THEM IF THEY DIE IN BATTLE.

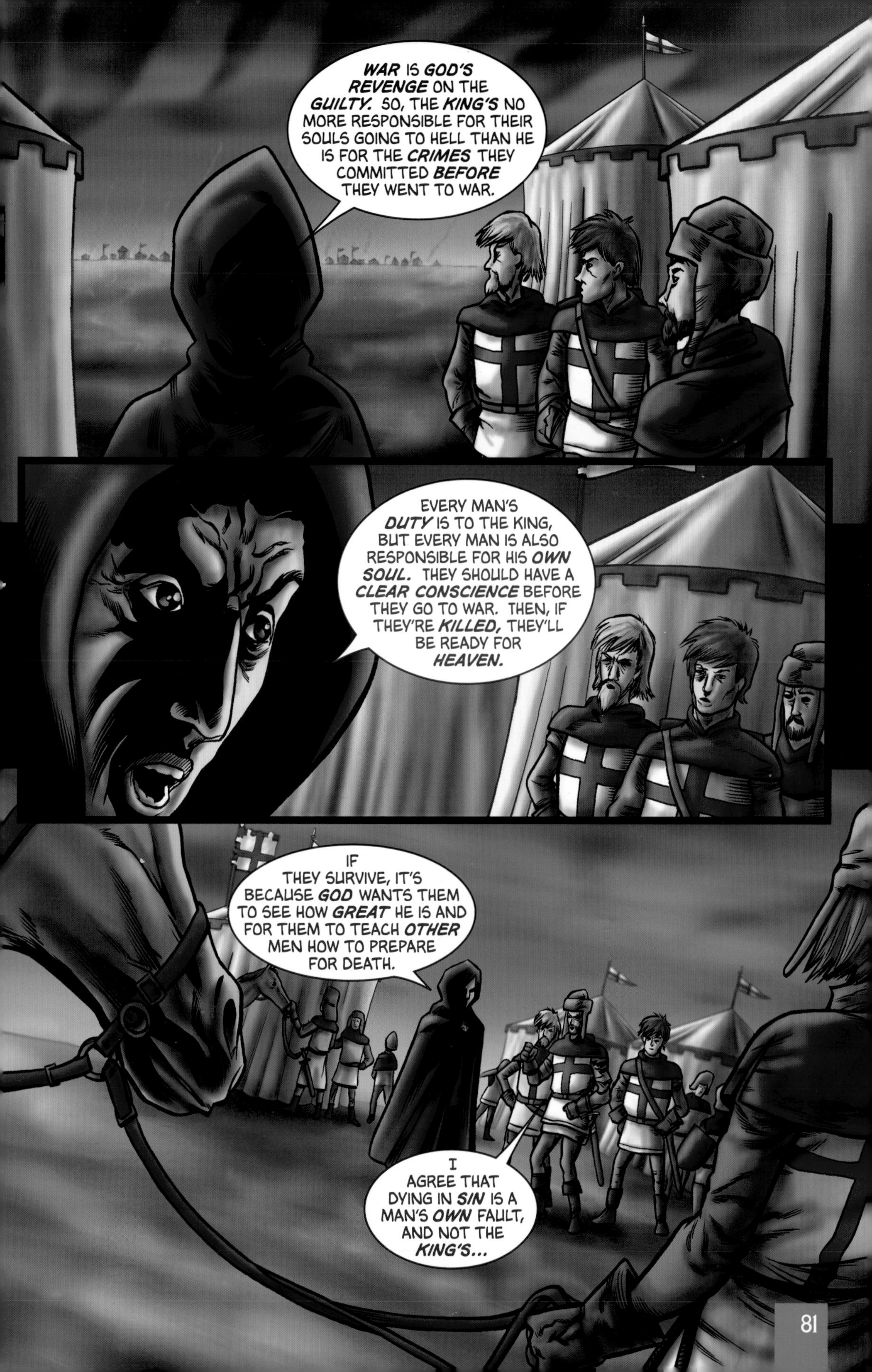
WAR IS GOD'S REVENGE ON THE GUILTY. SO, THE KING'S NO MORE RESPONSIBLE FOR THEIR SOULS GOING TO HELL THAN HE IS FOR THE CRIMES THEY COMMITTED BEFORE THEY WENT TO WAR.
EVERY MAN'S DUTY IS TO THE KING, BUT EVERY MAN IS ALSO RESPONSIBLE FOR HIS OWN SOUL. THEY SHOULD HAVE A CLEAR CONSCIENCE BEFORE THEY GO TO WAR. THEN, IF THEY'RE KILLED, THEY'LL BE READY FOR HEAVEN.
IF THEY SURVIVE, IT'S BECAUSE GOD WANTS THEM TO SEE HOW GREAT HE IS AND FOR THEM TO TEACH OTHER MEN HOW TO PREPARE FOR DEATH.
I AGREE THAT DYING IN SIN IS A MAN'S OWN FAULT, AND NOT THE KING'S...

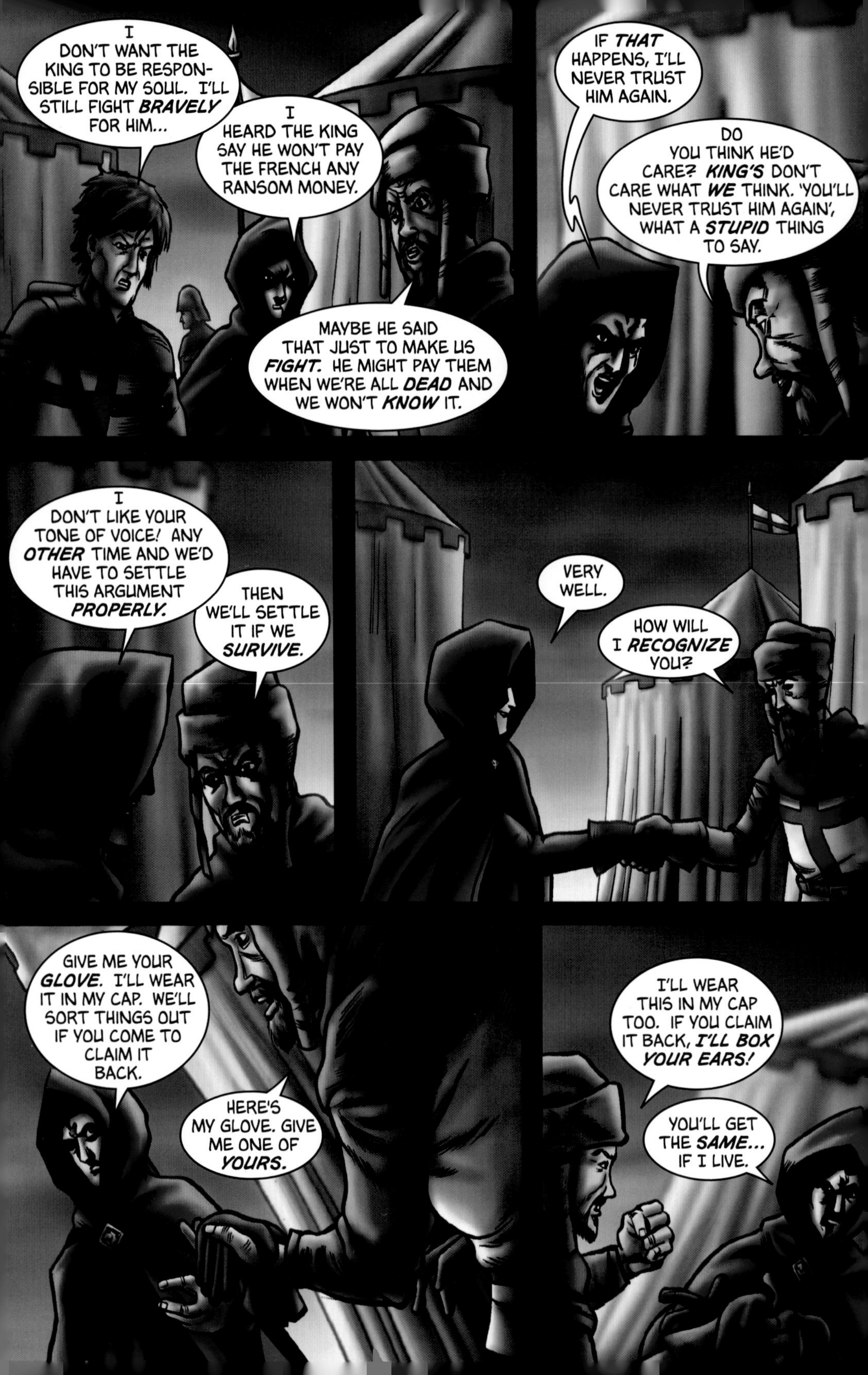
I DON'T WANT THE KING TO BE RESPON-SIBLE FOR MY SOUL. I'LL STILL FIGHT BRAVELY FOR HIM...
I HEARD THE KING SAY HE WON'T PAY THE FRENCH ANY RANSOM MONEY.
MAYBE HE SAID THAT JUST TO MAKE US FIGHT. HE MIGHT PAY THEM WHEN WE'RE ALL DEAD AND WE WON'T KNOW IT.
IF THAT HAPPENS, I'LL NEVER TRUST HIM AGAIN.
DO YOU THINK HE'D CARE? KING'S DON'T CARE WHAT WE THINK. 'YOU'LL NEVER TRUST HIM AGAIN', WHAT A STUPID THING TO SAY.
I DON'T LIKE YOUR TONE OF VOICE! ANY OTHER TIME AND WE'D HAVE TO SETTLE THIS ARGUMENT PROPERLY.
THEN WE'LL SETTLE IT IF WE SURVIVE.
VERY WELL.
HOW WILL I RECOGNIZE YOU?
GIVE ME YOUR GLOVE. I'LL WEAR IT IN MY CAP. WE'LL SORT THINGS OUT IF YOU COME TO CLAIM IT BACK.
HERE'S MY GLOVE. GIVE ME ONE OF YOURS.
I'LL WEAR THIS IN MY CAP TOO. IF YOU CLAIM IT BACK, I'LL BOX YOUR EARS!
YOU'LL GET THE SAME... IF I LIVE.

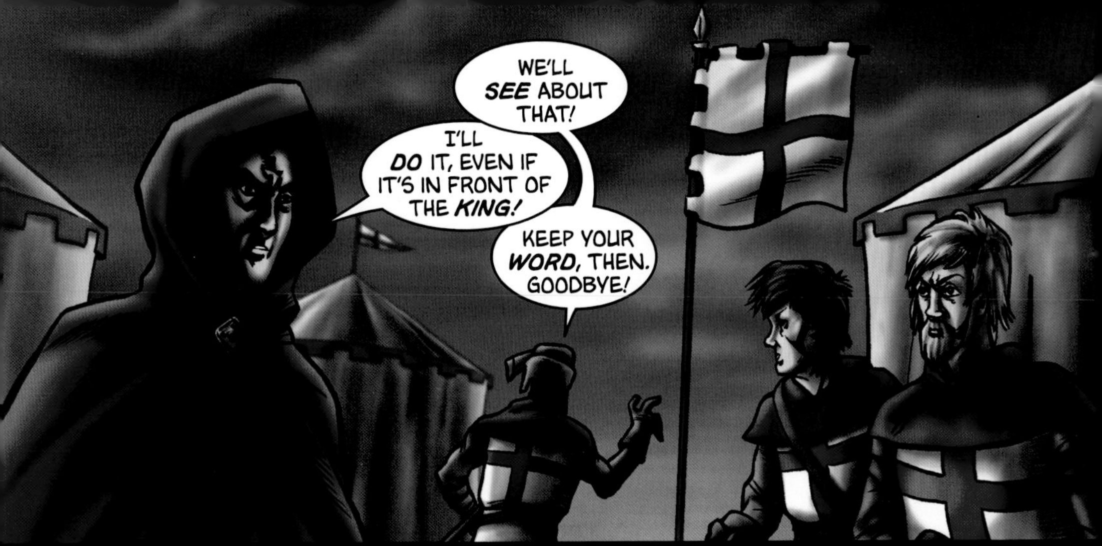
WE'LL SEE ABOUT THAT!
I'LL DO IT, EVEN IF IT'S IN FRONT OF THE KING!
KEEP YOUR WORD, THEN. GOODBYE!

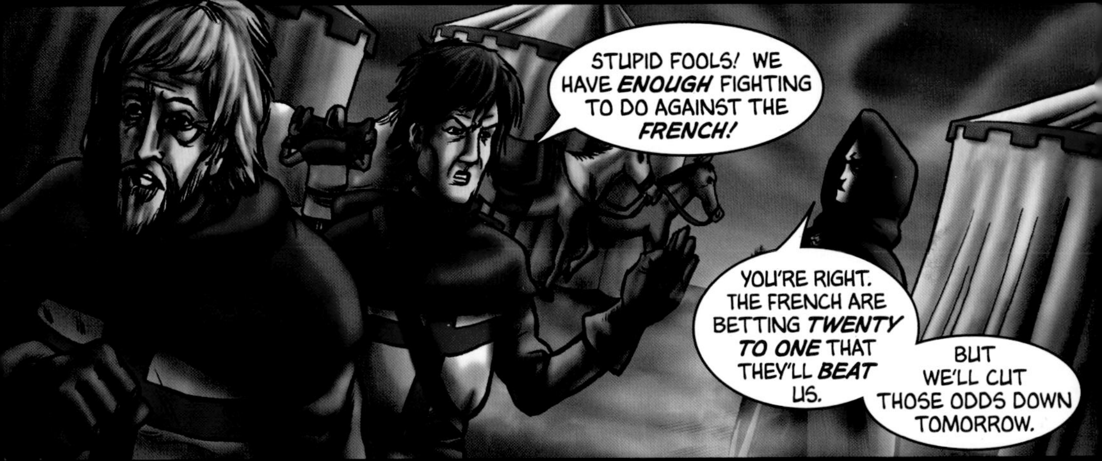
STUPID FOOLS! WE HAVE ENOUGH FIGHTING TO DO AGAINST THE FRENCH!
YOU'RE RIGHT. THE FRENCH ARE BETTING TWENTY TO ONE THAT THEY'LL BEAT US.
BUT WE'LL CUT THOSE ODDS DOWN TOMORROW.

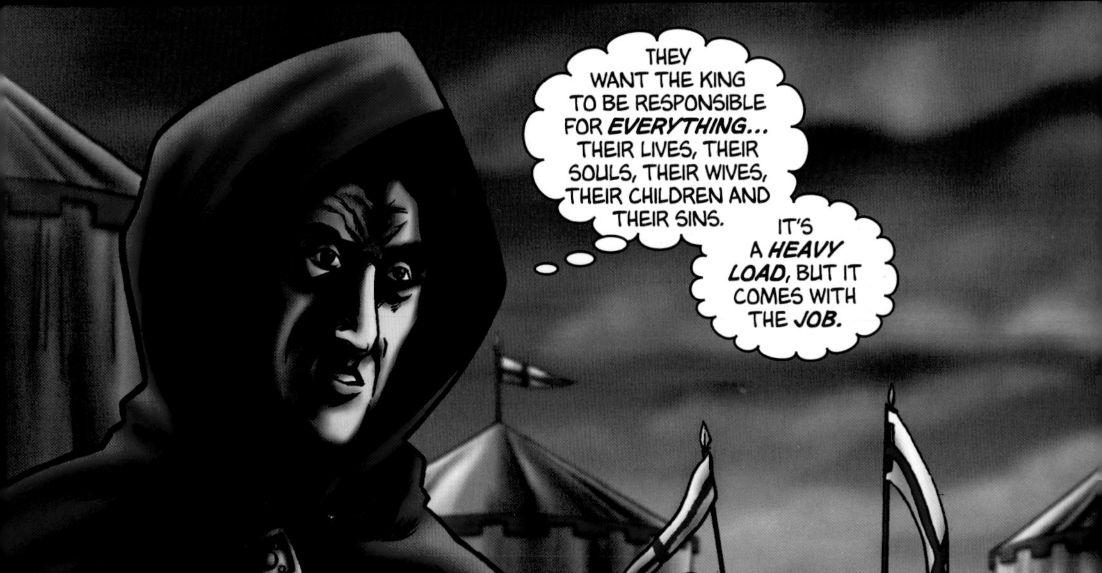
THEY WANT THE KING TO BE RESPONSIBLE FOR EVERYTHING... THEIR LIVES, THEIR SOULS, THEIR WIVES, THEIR CHILDREN AND THEIR SINS.
IT'S A HEAVY LOAD, BUT IT COMES WITH THE JOB.

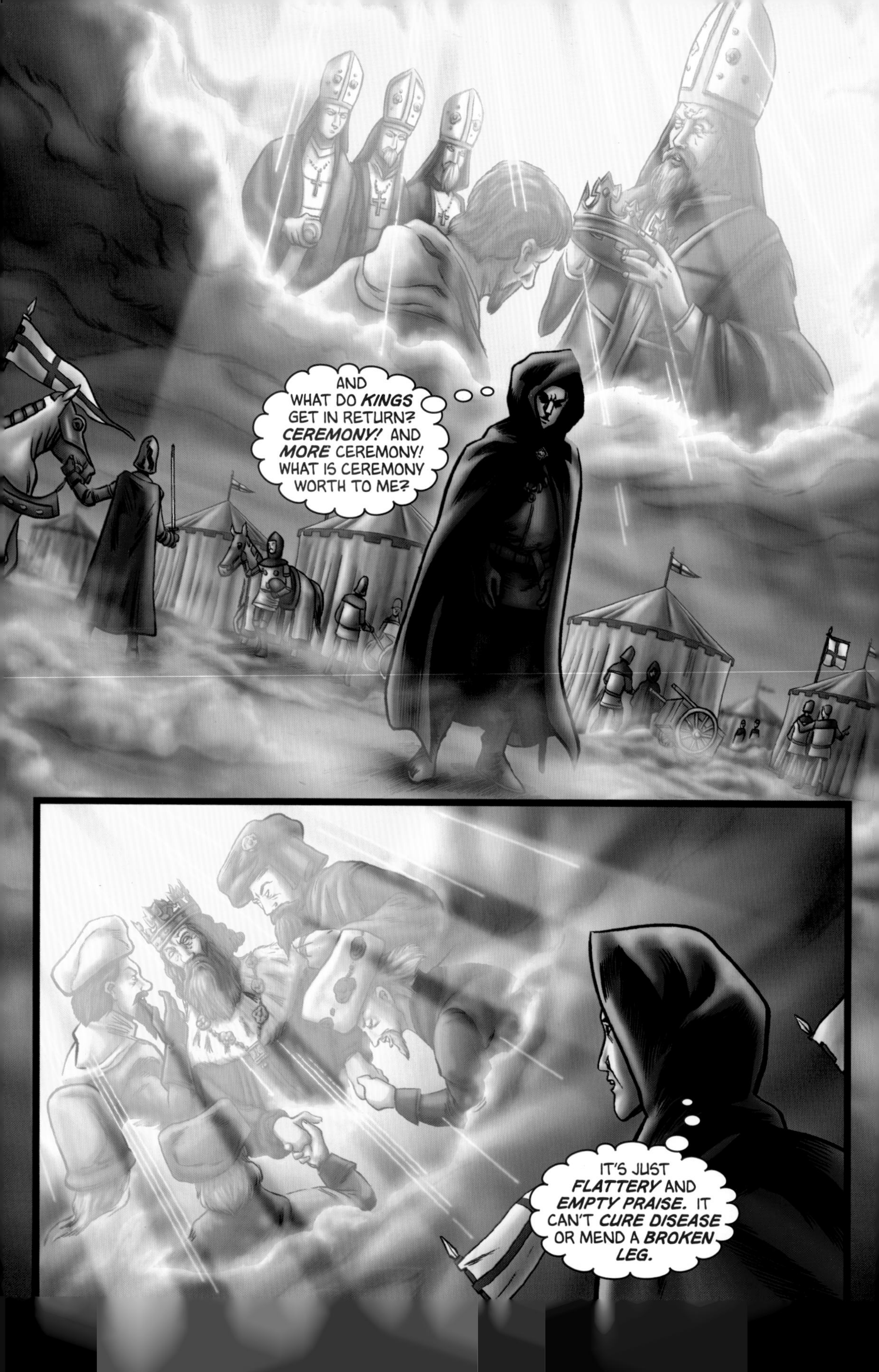
AND WHAT DO KINGS GET IN RETURN? CEREMONY! AND MORE CEREMONY! WHAT IS CEREMONY WORTH TO ME?
IT'S JUST FLATTERY AND EMPTY PRAISE. IT CAN'T CURE DISEASE OR MEND A BROKEN LEG.

NO! IT'S A *VAIN ILLUSION* THAT KINGS HAVE. *I'M* A KING AND *I* SHOULD *KNOW.* IT'S NOT ABOUT THE GOLDEN CROWN, OR THE FINE ROBES, OR EVEN THE THRONE.

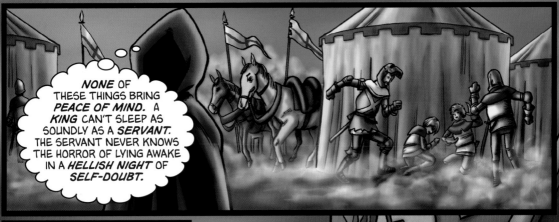

NONE OF THESE THINGS BRING *PEACE OF MIND.* A *KING* CAN'T SLEEP AS SOUNDLY AS A *SERVANT.* THE SERVANT NEVER KNOWS THE HORROR OF LYING AWAKE IN A *HELLISH NIGHT* OF *SELF-DOUBT.*

A KING GETS NO PEACE -- HE HAS TO WORRY ALL THE TIME ABOUT THE *ENTIRE COUNTRY* AND HOW TO MAKE THINGS RIGHT FOR *EVERYBODY.*

MY LORD, THE NOBLES ARE *WORRIED* AND ARE *SEARCHING THE CAMP* FOR YOU.

GET THEM ALL TO GO TO MY *TENT.* I'LL GO THERE NOW.

I'LL *DO* THAT, MY LORD.

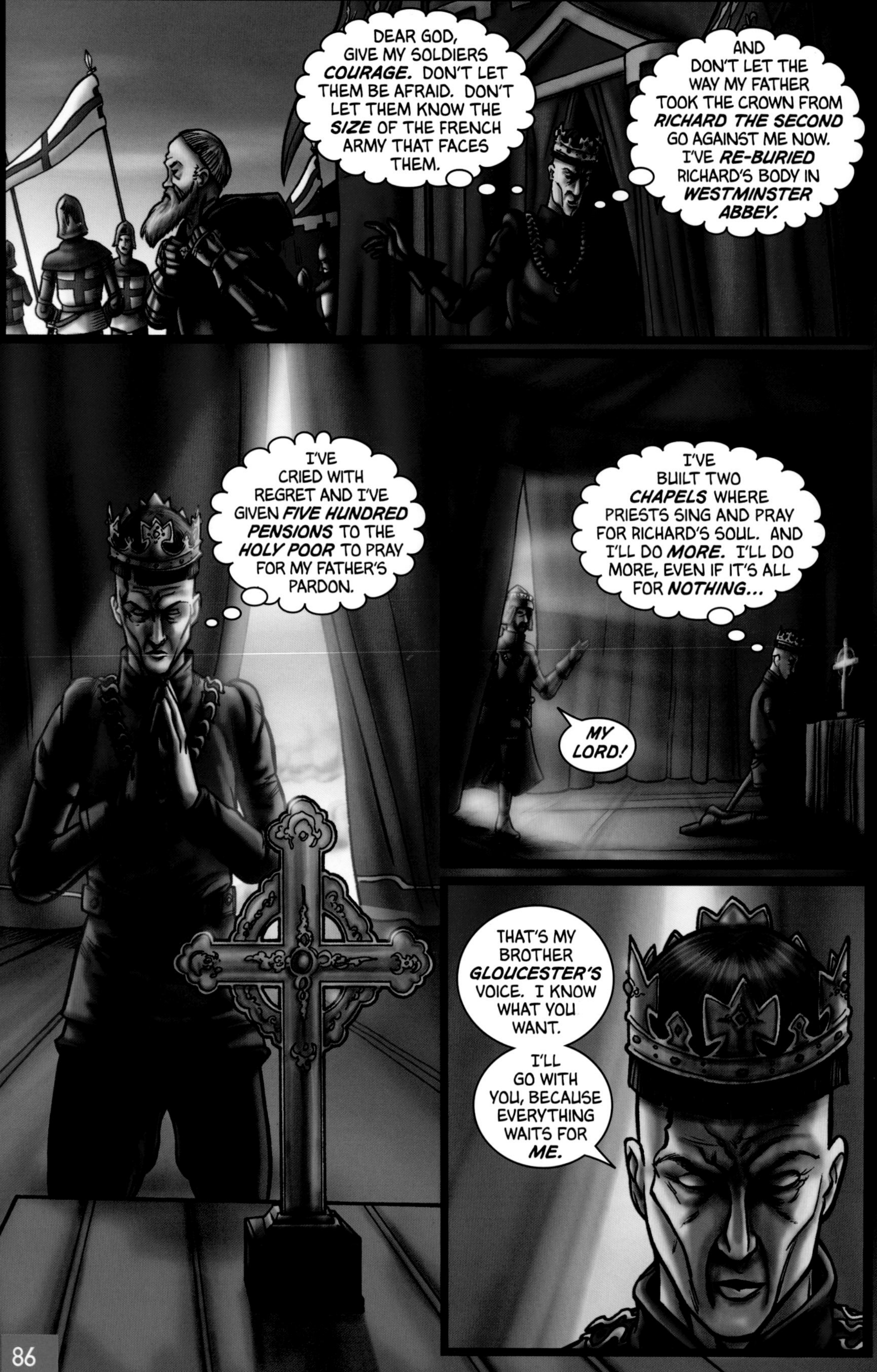
DEAR GOD, GIVE MY SOLDIERS COURAGE. DON'T LET THEM BE AFRAID. DON'T LET THEM KNOW THE SIZE OF THE FRENCH ARMY THAT FACES THEM.
AND DON'T LET THE WAY MY FATHER TOOK THE CROWN FROM RICHARD THE SECOND GO AGAINST ME NOW. I'VE RE-BURIED RICHARD'S BODY IN WESTMINSTER ABBEY.
I'VE CRIED WITH REGRET AND I'VE GIVEN FIVE HUNDRED PENSIONS TO THE HOLY POOR TO PRAY FOR MY FATHER'S PARDON.
I'VE BUILT TWO CHAPELS WHERE PRIESTS SING AND PRAY FOR RICHARD'S SOUL. AND I'LL DO MORE. I'LL DO MORE, EVEN IF IT'S ALL FOR NOTHING...
MY LORD!
THAT'S MY BROTHER GLOUCESTER'S VOICE. I KNOW WHAT YOU WANT.
I'LL GO WITH YOU, BECAUSE EVERYTHING WAITS FOR ME.

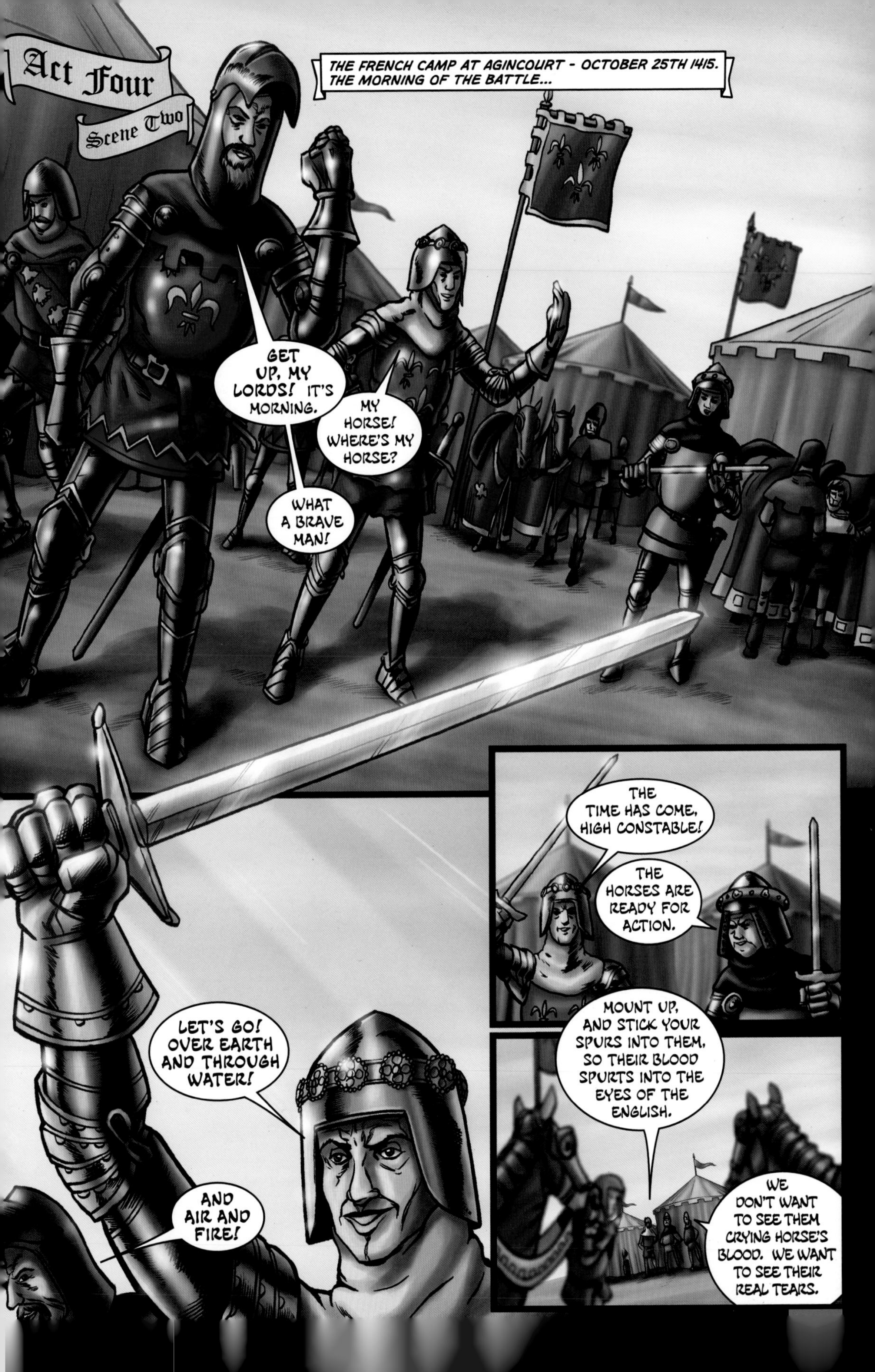
Act Four
Scene Two
THE FRENCH CAMP AT AGINCOURT - OCTOBER 25TH 1415. THE MORNING OF THE BATTLE...
GET UP, MY LORDS! IT'S MORNING.
MY HORSE! WHERE'S MY HORSE?
WHAT A BRAVE MAN!
LET'S GO! OVER EARTH AND THROUGH WATER!
AND AIR AND FIRE!
THE TIME HAS COME, HIGH CONSTABLE!
THE HORSES ARE READY FOR ACTION.
MOUNT UP, AND STICK YOUR SPURS INTO THEM, SO THEIR BLOOD SPURTS INTO THE EYES OF THE ENGLISH.
WE DON'T WANT TO SEE THEM CRYING HORSE'S BLOOD. WE WANT TO SEE THEIR REAL TEARS.

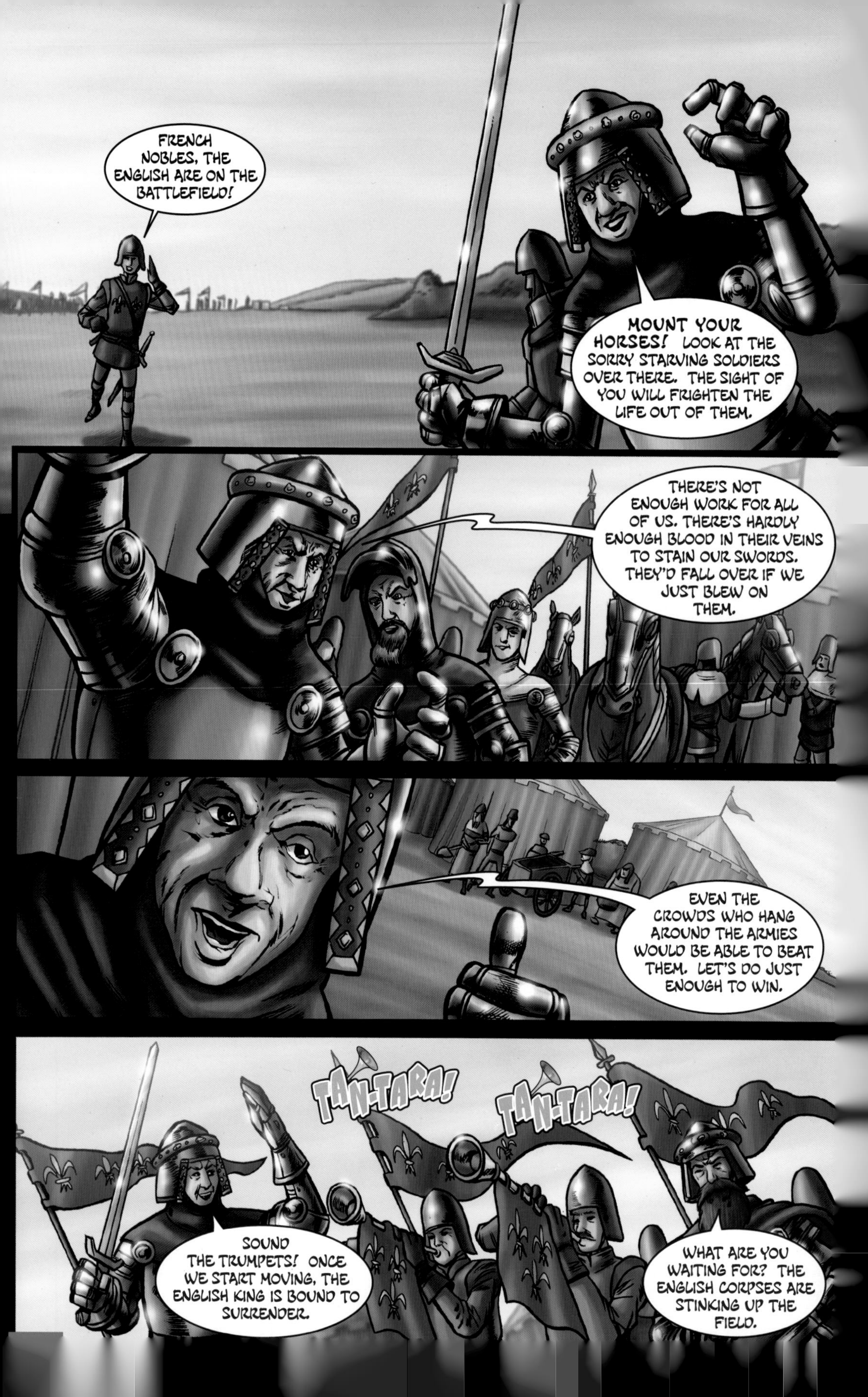
FRENCH NOBLES, THE ENGLISH ARE ON THE BATTLEFIELD!
MOUNT YOUR HORSES! LOOK AT THE SORRY STARVING SOLDIERS OVER THERE. THE SIGHT OF YOU WILL FRIGHTEN THE LIFE OUT OF THEM.
THERE'S NOT ENOUGH WORK FOR ALL OF US. THERE'S HARDLY ENOUGH BLOOD IN THEIR VEINS TO STAIN OUR SWORDS. THEY'D FALL OVER IF WE JUST BLEW ON THEM.
EVEN THE CROWDS WHO HANG AROUND THE ARMIES WOULD BE ABLE TO BEAT THEM. LET'S DO JUST ENOUGH TO WIN.
TAN-TARA!
TAN-TARA!
SOUND THE TRUMPETS! ONCE WE START MOVING, THE ENGLISH KING IS BOUND TO SURRENDER.
WHAT ARE YOU WAITING FOR? THE ENGLISH CORPSES ARE STINKING UP THE FIELD.

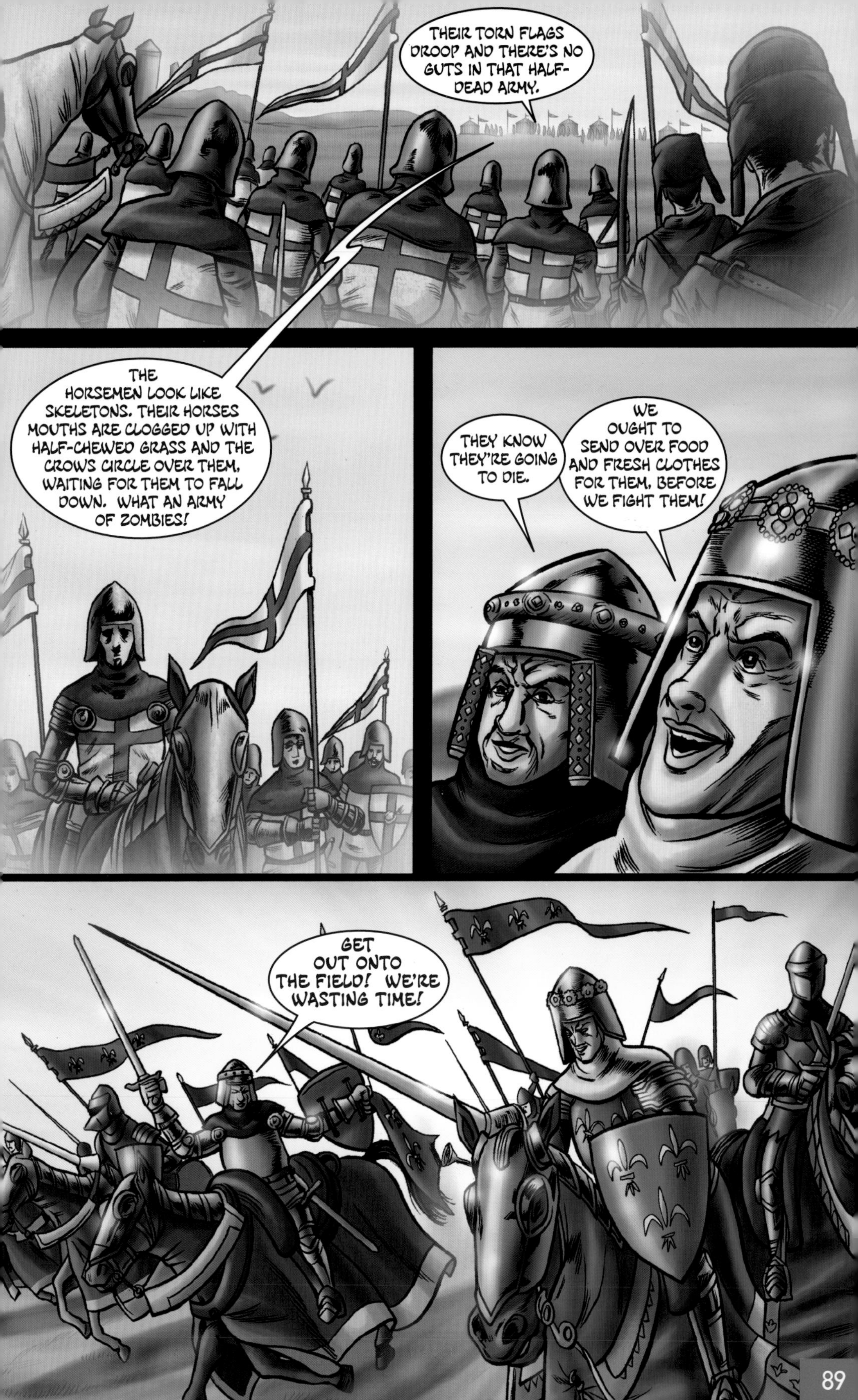
THEIR TORN FLAGS DROOP AND THERE'S NO GUTS IN THAT HALF-DEAD ARMY.
THE HORSEMEN LOOK LIKE SKELETONS. THEIR HORSES MOUTHS ARE CLOGGED UP WITH HALF-CHEWED GRASS AND THE CROWS CIRCLE OVER THEM, WAITING FOR THEM TO FALL DOWN. WHAT AN ARMY OF ZOMBIES!
THEY KNOW THEY'RE GOING TO DIE.
WE OUGHT TO SEND OVER FOOD AND FRESH CLOTHES FOR THEM, BEFORE WE FIGHT THEM!
GET OUT ONTO THE FIELD! WE'RE WASTING TIME!

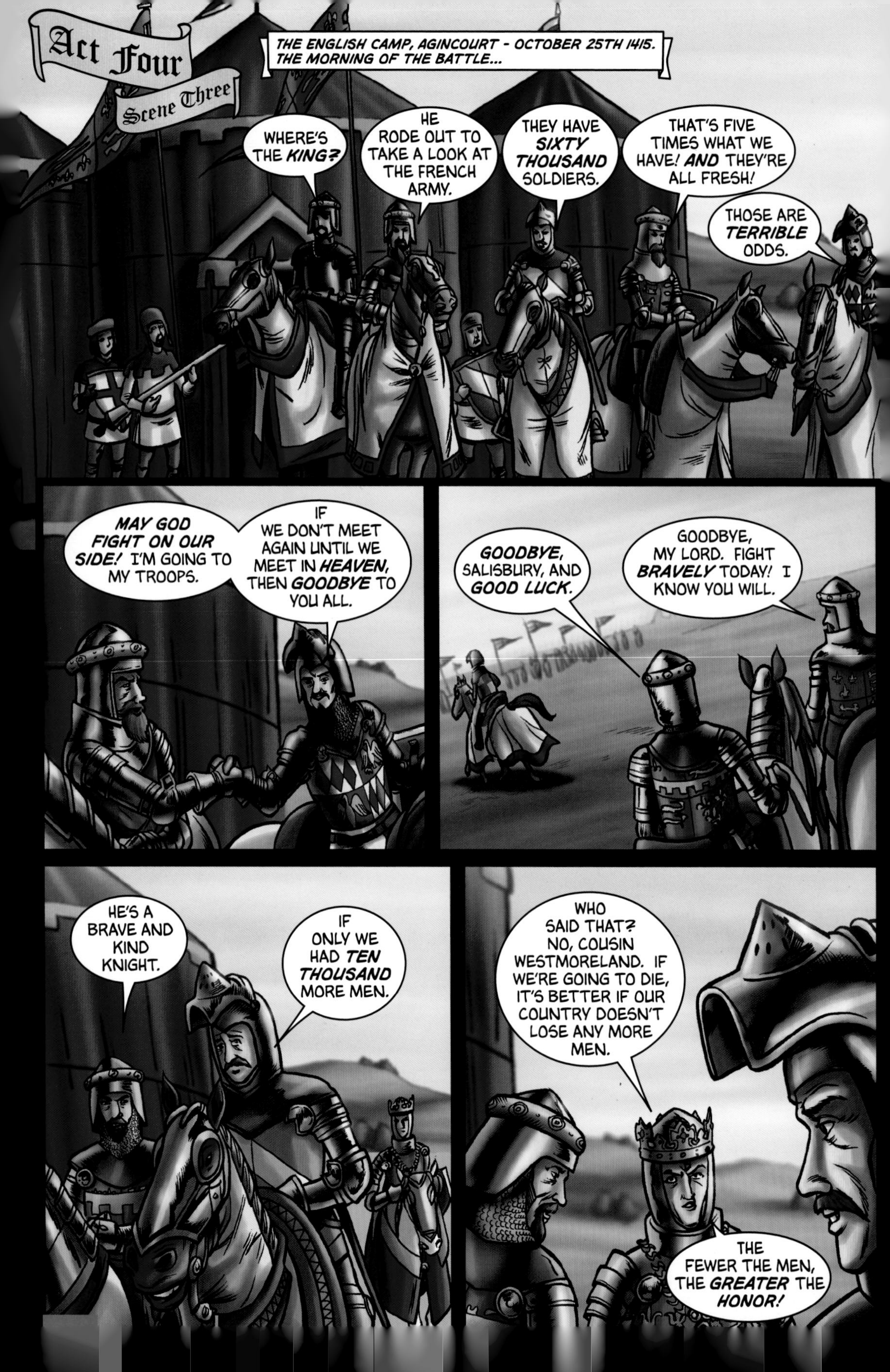
Act Four
Scene Three
THE ENGLISH CAMP, AGINCOURT - OCTOBER 25TH 1415. THE MORNING OF THE BATTLE...
WHERE'S THE KING?
HE RODE OUT TO TAKE A LOOK AT THE FRENCH ARMY.
THEY HAVE SIXTY THOUSAND SOLDIERS.
THAT'S FIVE TIMES WHAT WE HAVE! AND THEY'RE ALL FRESH!
THOSE ARE TERRIBLE ODDS.
MAY GOD FIGHT ON OUR SIDE! I'M GOING TO MY TROOPS.
IF WE DON'T MEET AGAIN UNTIL WE MEET IN HEAVEN, THEN GOODBYE TO YOU ALL.
GOODBYE, SALISBURY, AND GOOD LUCK.
GOODBYE, MY LORD. FIGHT BRAVELY TODAY! I KNOW YOU WILL.
HE'S A BRAVE AND KIND KNIGHT.
IF ONLY WE HAD TEN THOUSAND MORE MEN.
WHO SAID THAT? NO, COUSIN WESTMORELAND. IF WE'RE GOING TO DIE, IT'S BETTER IF OUR COUNTRY DOESN'T LOSE ANY MORE MEN.
THE FEWER THE MEN, THE GREATER THE HONOR!

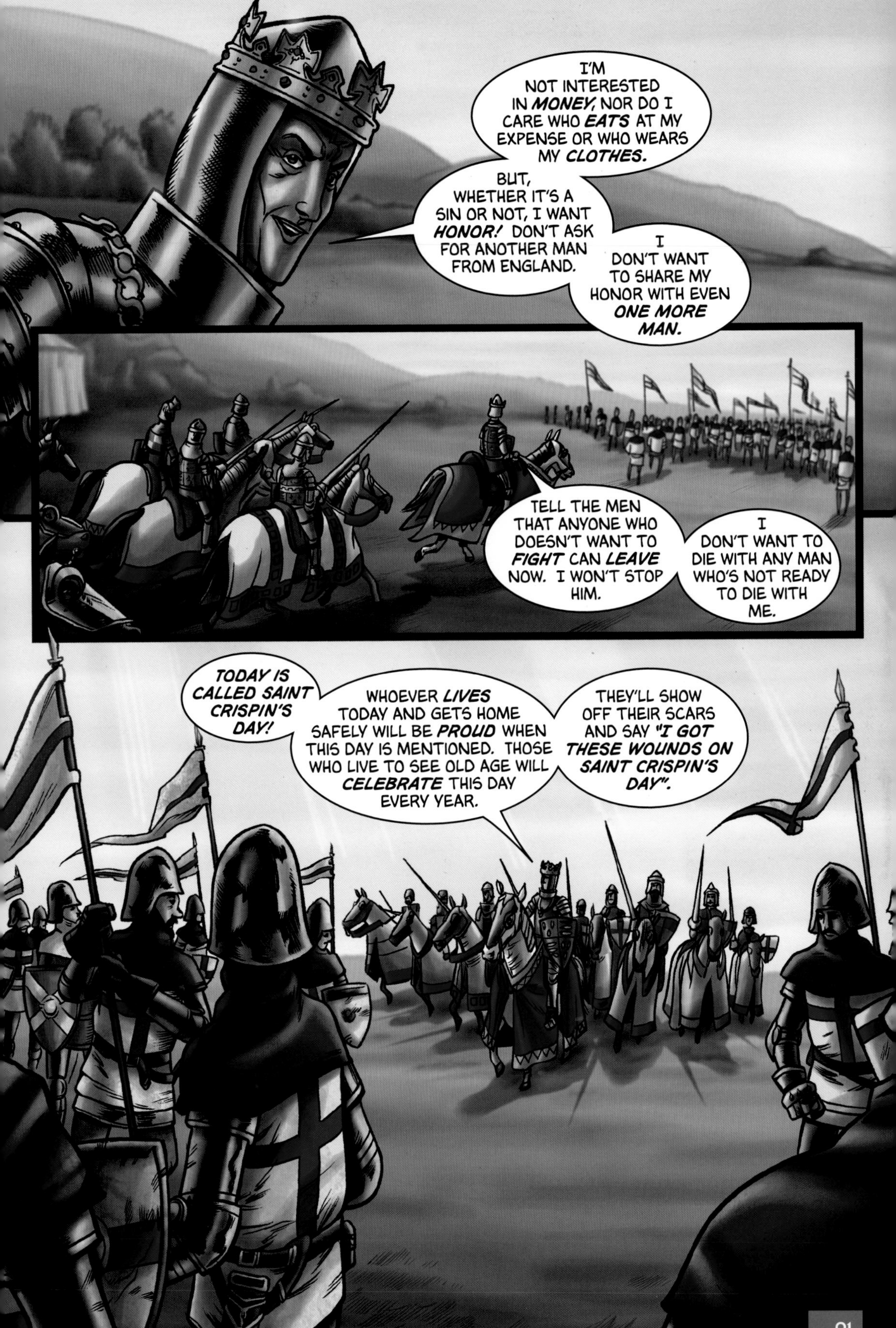
I'M NOT INTERESTED IN *MONEY*, NOR DO I CARE WHO *EATS* AT MY EXPENSE OR WHO WEARS MY *CLOTHES*.
BUT, WHETHER IT'S A SIN OR NOT, I WANT *HONOR!* DON'T ASK FOR ANOTHER MAN FROM ENGLAND.
I DON'T WANT TO SHARE MY HONOR WITH EVEN *ONE MORE MAN*.
TELL THE MEN THAT ANYONE WHO DOESN'T WANT TO *FIGHT* CAN *LEAVE* NOW. I WON'T STOP HIM.
I DON'T WANT TO DIE WITH ANY MAN WHO'S NOT READY TO DIE WITH ME.
TODAY IS CALLED SAINT CRISPIN'S DAY!
WHOEVER *LIVES* TODAY AND GETS HOME SAFELY WILL BE *PROUD* WHEN THIS DAY IS MENTIONED. THOSE WHO LIVE TO SEE OLD AGE WILL *CELEBRATE* THIS DAY EVERY YEAR.
THEY'LL SHOW OFF THEIR SCARS AND SAY *"I GOT THESE WOUNDS ON SAINT CRISPIN'S DAY"*.

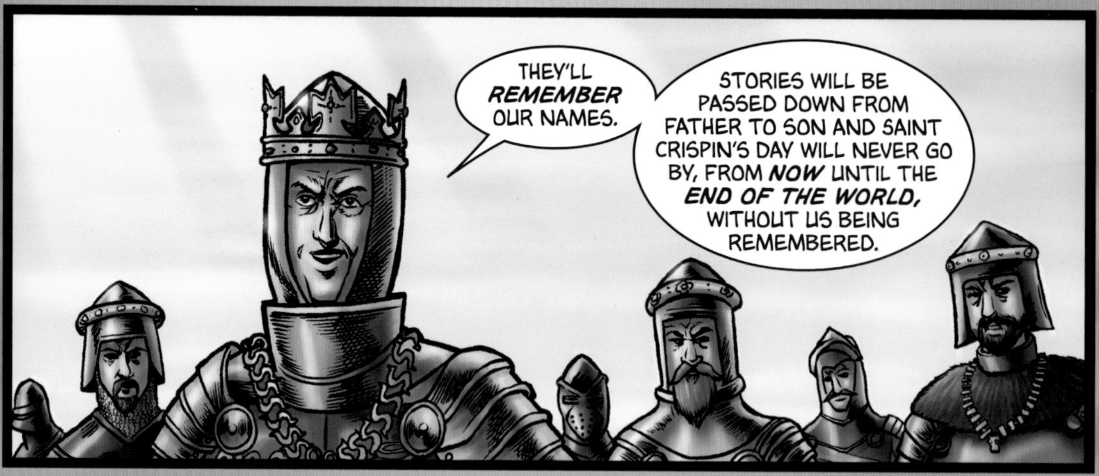
THEY'LL REMEMBER OUR NAMES.
STORIES WILL BE PASSED DOWN FROM FATHER TO SON AND SAINT CRISPIN'S DAY WILL NEVER GO BY, FROM NOW UNTIL THE END OF THE WORLD, WITHOUT US BEING REMEMBERED.

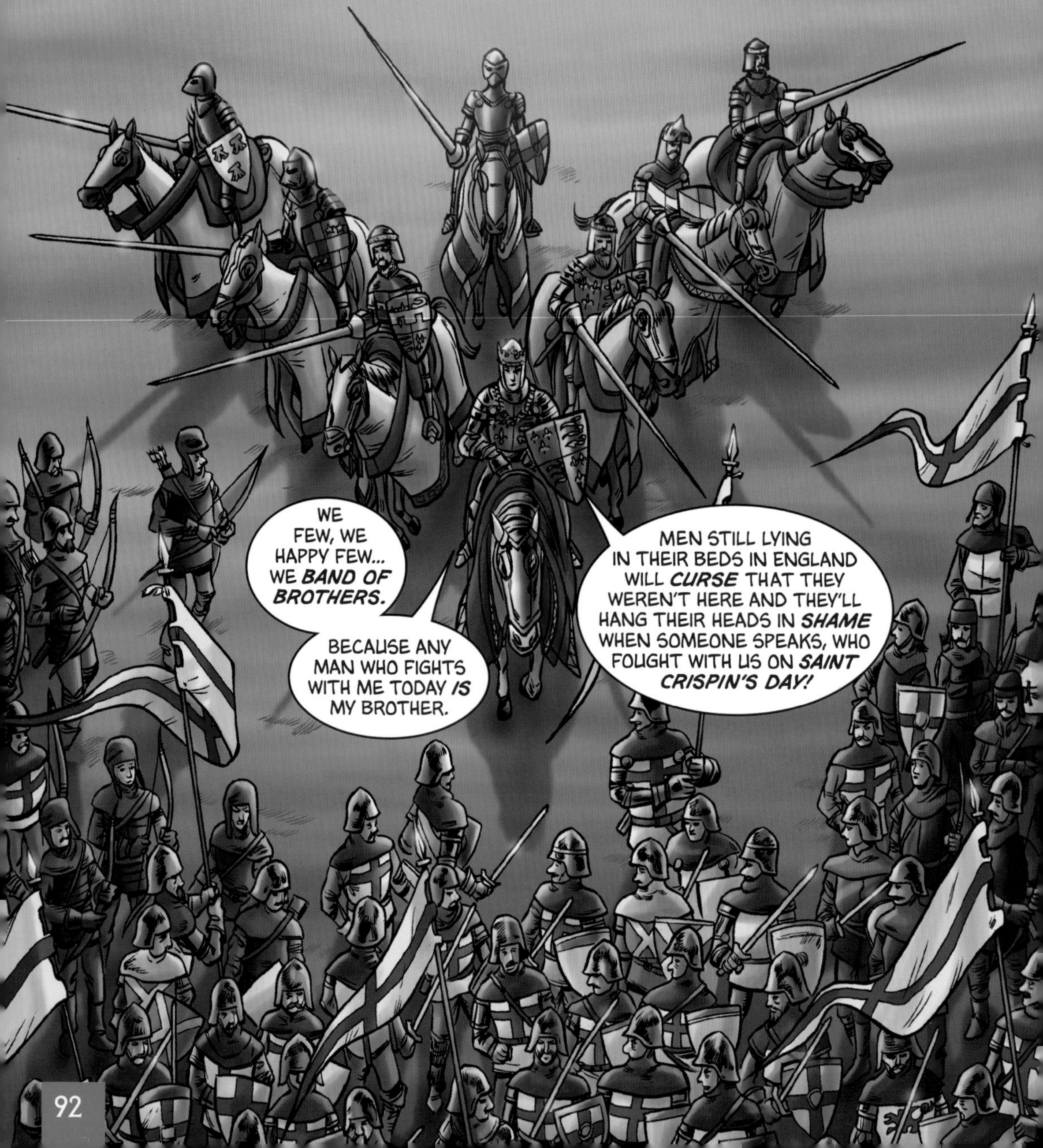
WE FEW, WE HAPPY FEW... WE BAND OF BROTHERS.
BECAUSE ANY MAN WHO FIGHTS WITH ME TODAY IS MY BROTHER.
MEN STILL LYING IN THEIR BEDS IN ENGLAND WILL CURSE THAT THEY WEREN'T HERE AND THEY'LL HANG THEIR HEADS IN SHAME WHEN SOMEONE SPEAKS, WHO FOUGHT WITH US ON SAINT CRISPIN'S DAY!

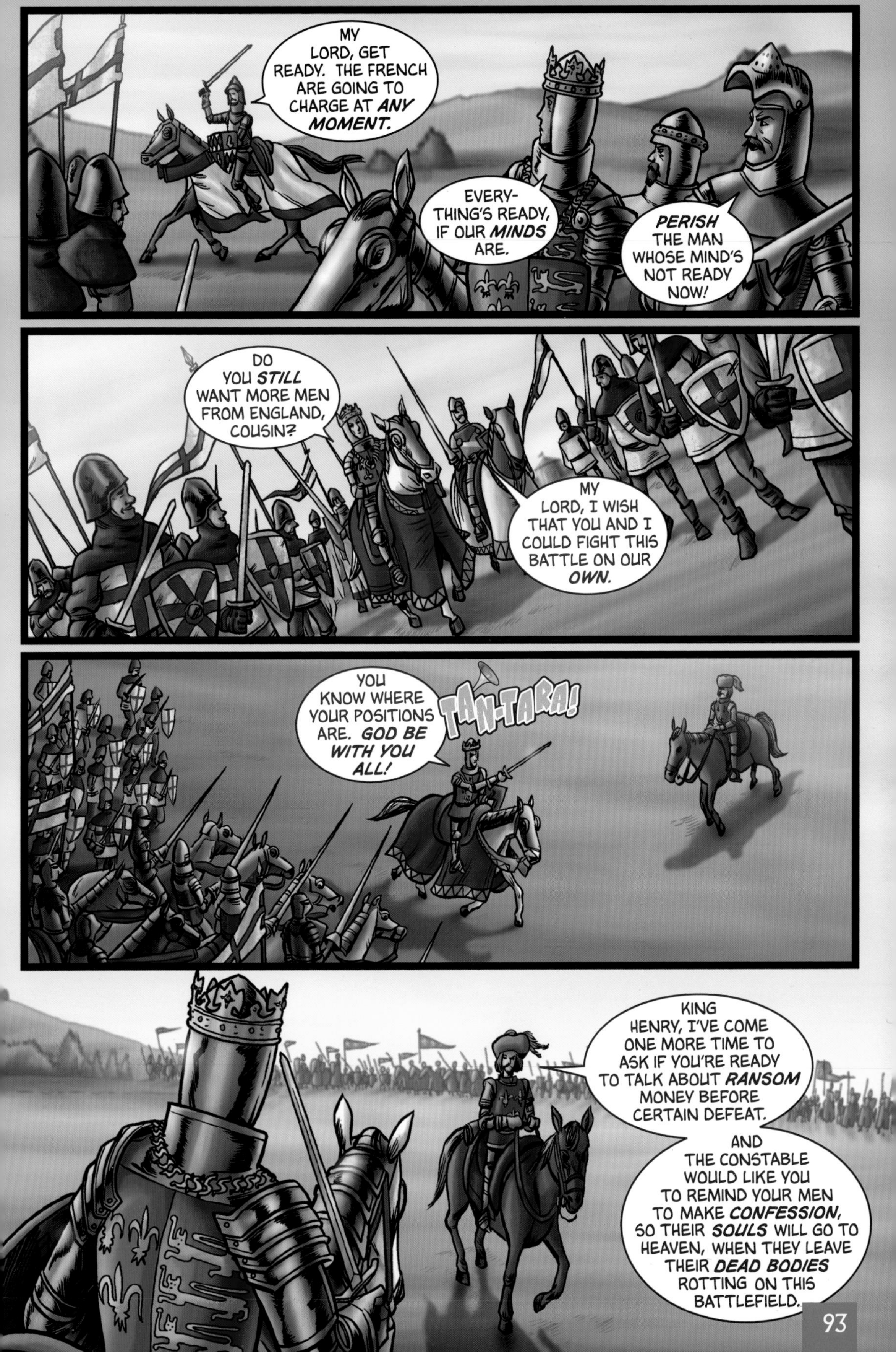
MY LORD, GET READY. THE FRENCH ARE GOING TO CHARGE AT ANY MOMENT.
EVERY-THING'S READY, IF OUR MINDS ARE.
PERISH THE MAN WHOSE MIND'S NOT READY NOW!
DO YOU STILL WANT MORE MEN FROM ENGLAND, COUSIN?
MY LORD, I WISH THAT YOU AND I COULD FIGHT THIS BATTLE ON OUR OWN.
YOU KNOW WHERE YOUR POSITIONS ARE. GOD BE WITH YOU ALL!
TAN-TARA!
KING HENRY, I'VE COME ONE MORE TIME TO ASK IF YOU'RE READY TO TALK ABOUT RANSOM MONEY BEFORE CERTAIN DEFEAT.
AND THE CONSTABLE WOULD LIKE YOU TO REMIND YOUR MEN TO MAKE CONFESSION, SO THEIR SOULS WILL GO TO HEAVEN, WHEN THEY LEAVE THEIR DEAD BODIES ROTTING ON THIS BATTLEFIELD.

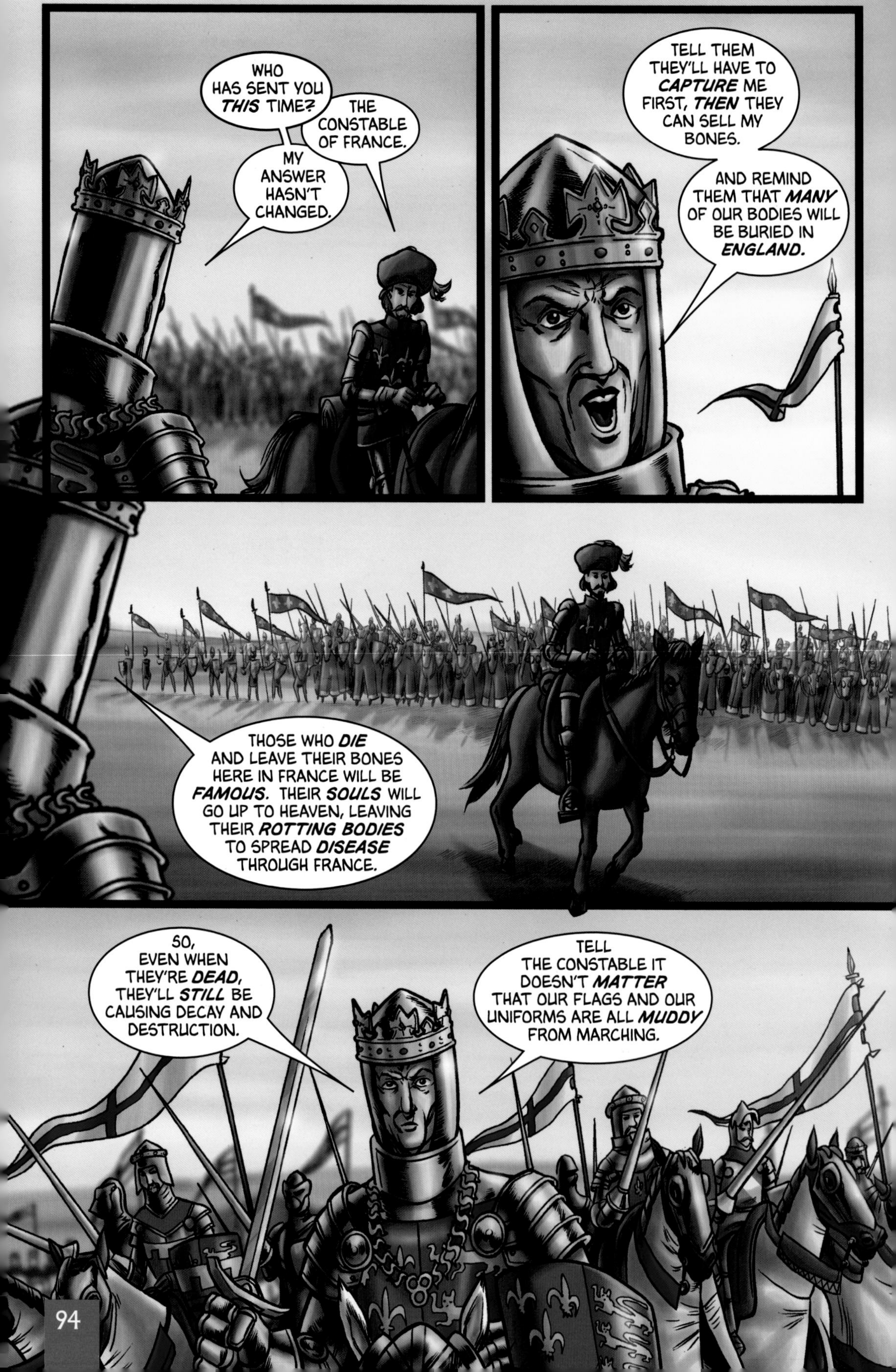
WHO HAS SENT YOU THIS TIME?
THE CONSTABLE OF FRANCE.
MY ANSWER HASN'T CHANGED.
TELL THEM THEY'LL HAVE TO CAPTURE ME FIRST, THEN THEY CAN SELL MY BONES.
AND REMIND THEM THAT MANY OF OUR BODIES WILL BE BURIED IN ENGLAND.
THOSE WHO DIE AND LEAVE THEIR BONES HERE IN FRANCE WILL BE FAMOUS. THEIR SOULS WILL GO UP TO HEAVEN, LEAVING THEIR ROTTING BODIES TO SPREAD DISEASE THROUGH FRANCE.
SO, EVEN WHEN THEY'RE DEAD, THEY'LL STILL BE CAUSING DECAY AND DESTRUCTION.
TELL THE CONSTABLE IT DOESN'T MATTER THAT OUR FLAGS AND OUR UNIFORMS ARE ALL MUDDY FROM MARCHING.

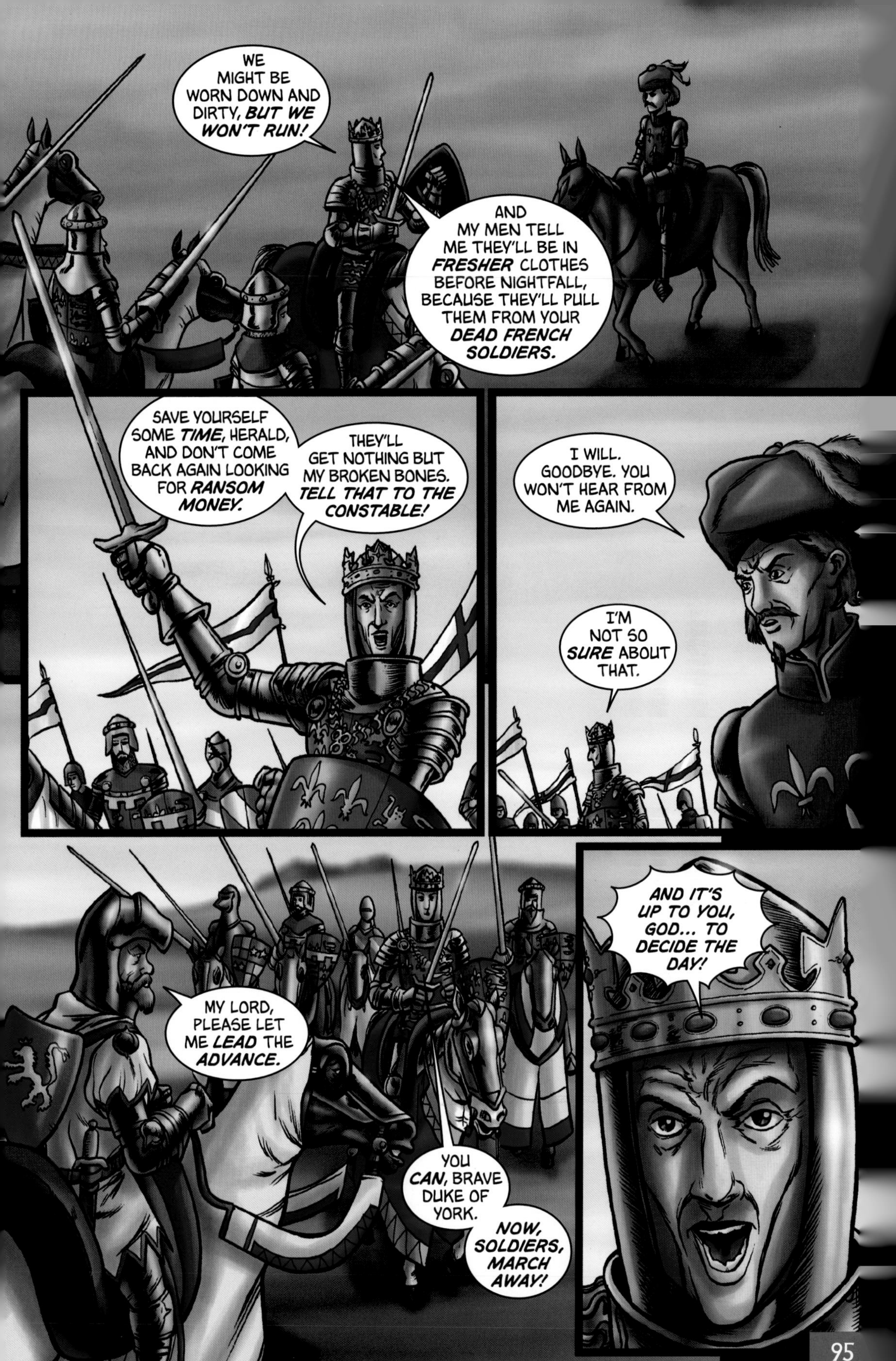
WE MIGHT BE WORN DOWN AND DIRTY, BUT WE WON'T RUN!
AND MY MEN TELL ME THEY'LL BE IN FRESHER CLOTHES BEFORE NIGHTFALL, BECAUSE THEY'LL PULL THEM FROM YOUR DEAD FRENCH SOLDIERS.
SAVE YOURSELF SOME TIME, HERALD, AND DON'T COME BACK AGAIN LOOKING FOR RANSOM MONEY.
THEY'LL GET NOTHING BUT MY BROKEN BONES. TELL THAT TO THE CONSTABLE!
I WILL. GOODBYE. YOU WON'T HEAR FROM ME AGAIN.
I'M NOT SO SURE ABOUT THAT.
MY LORD, PLEASE LET ME LEAD THE ADVANCE.
YOU CAN, BRAVE DUKE OF YORK.
NOW, SOLDIERS, MARCH AWAY!
AND IT'S UP TO YOU, GOD... TO DECIDE THE DAY!

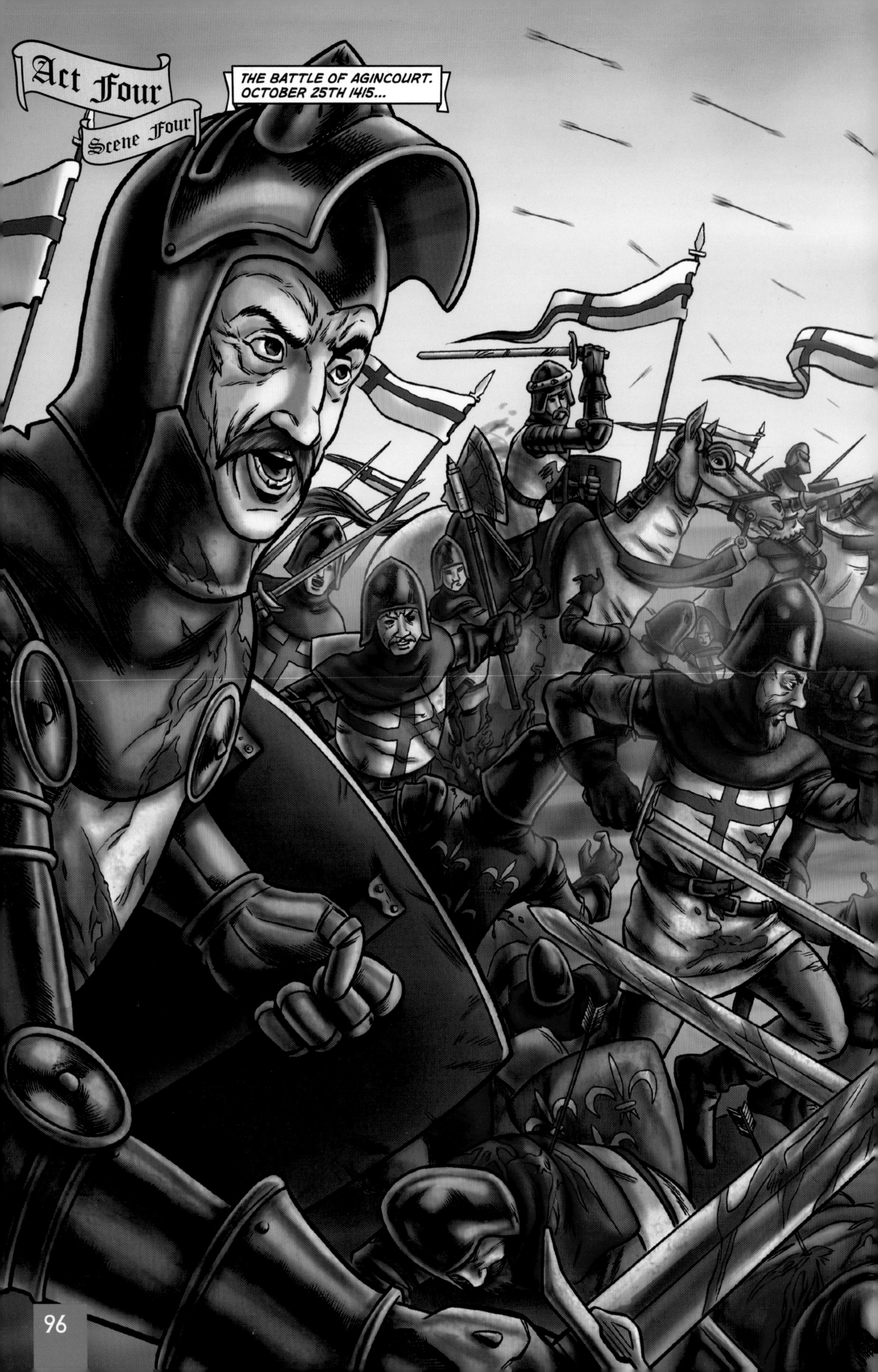
Act Four
Scene Four
THE BATTLE OF AGINCOURT. OCTOBER 25TH 1415...

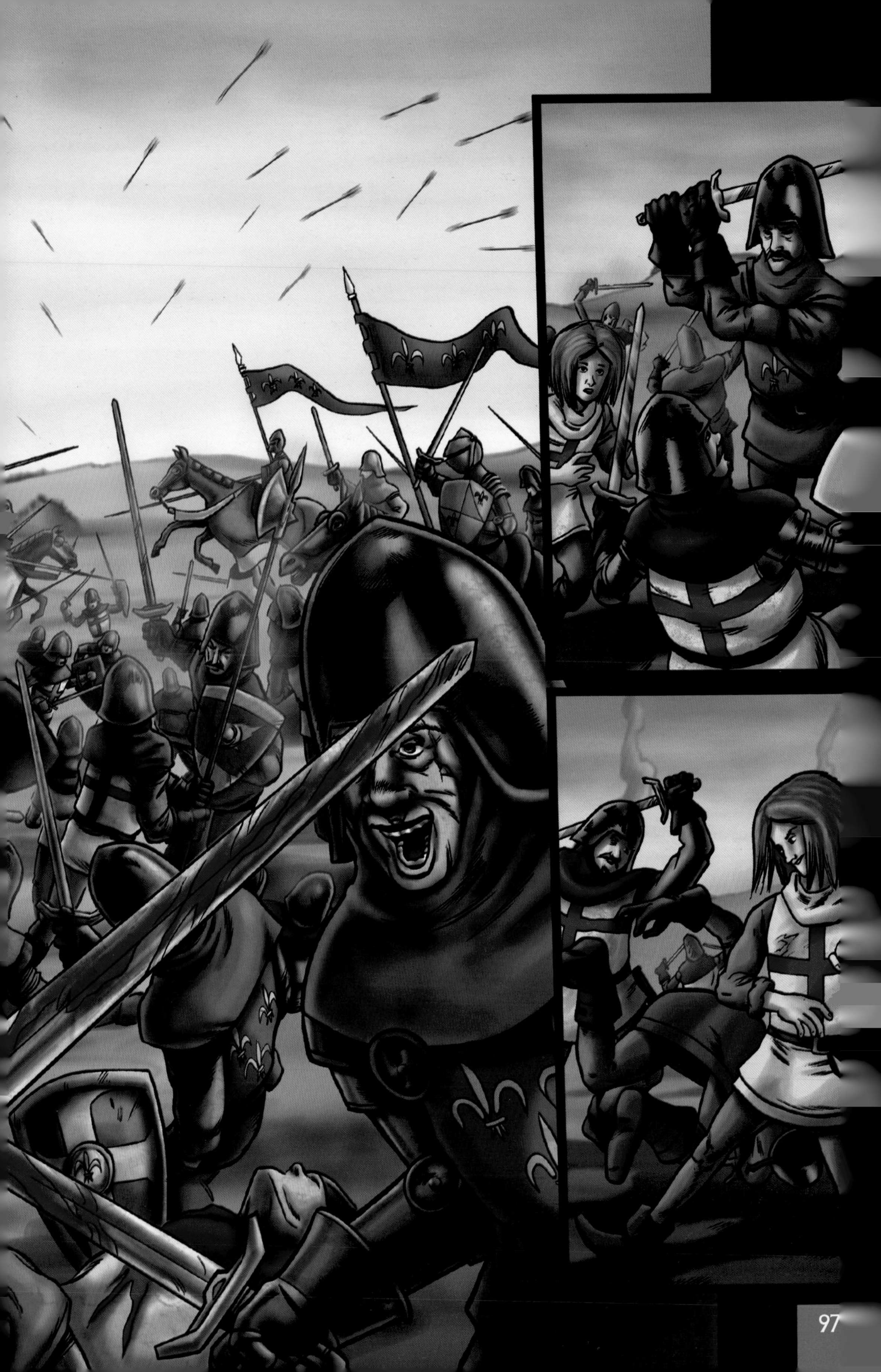

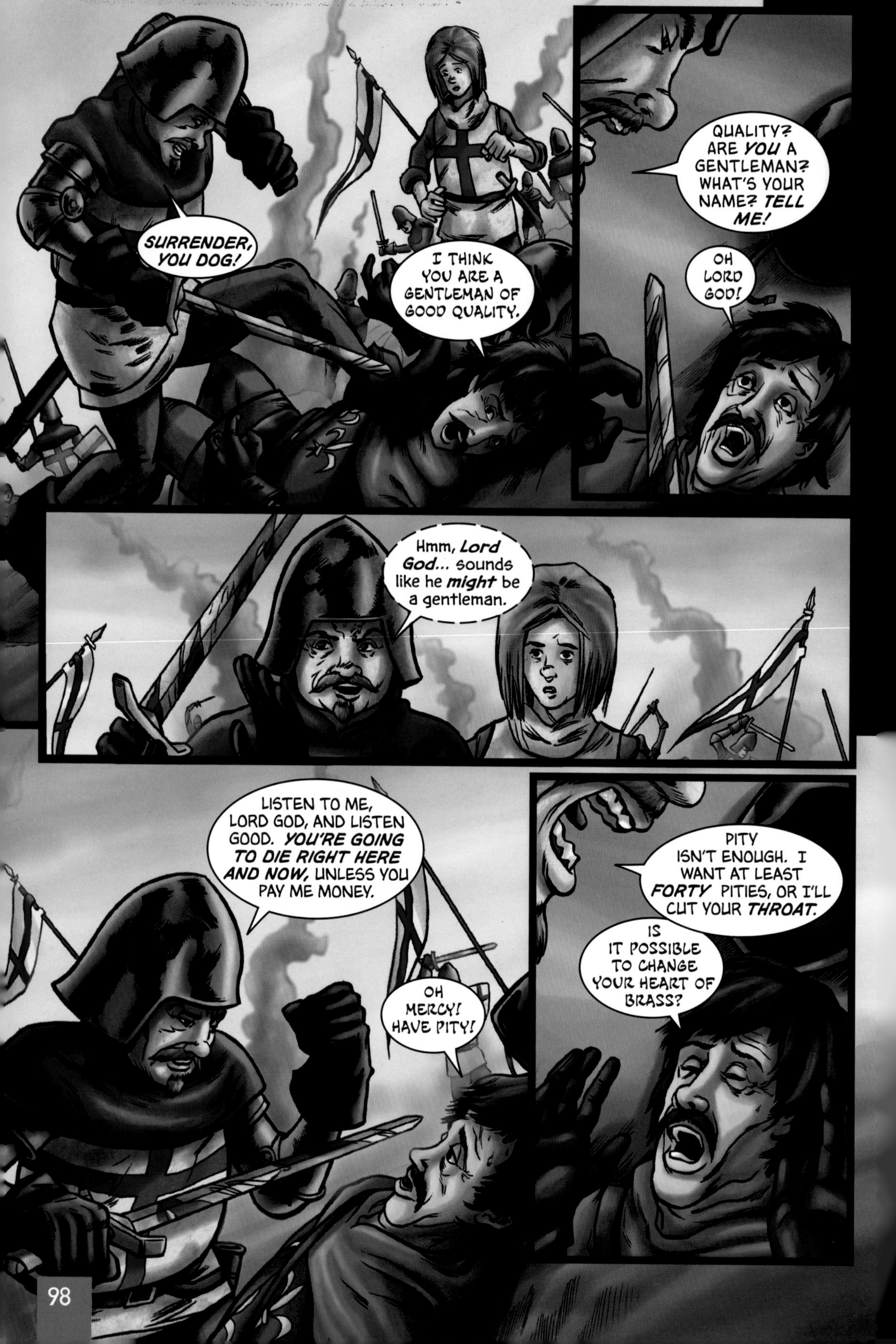
SURRENDER, YOU DOG!
I THINK YOU ARE A GENTLEMAN OF GOOD QUALITY.
QUALITY? ARE YOU A GENTLEMAN? WHAT'S YOUR NAME? TELL ME!
OH LORD GOD!
Hmm, Lord God... sounds like he might be a gentleman.
LISTEN TO ME, LORD GOD, AND LISTEN GOOD. YOU'RE GOING TO DIE RIGHT HERE AND NOW, UNLESS YOU PAY ME MONEY.
OH MERCY! HAVE PITY!
PITY ISN'T ENOUGH. I WANT AT LEAST FORTY PITIES, OR I'LL CUT YOUR THROAT.
IS IT POSSIBLE TO CHANGE YOUR HEART OF BRASS?

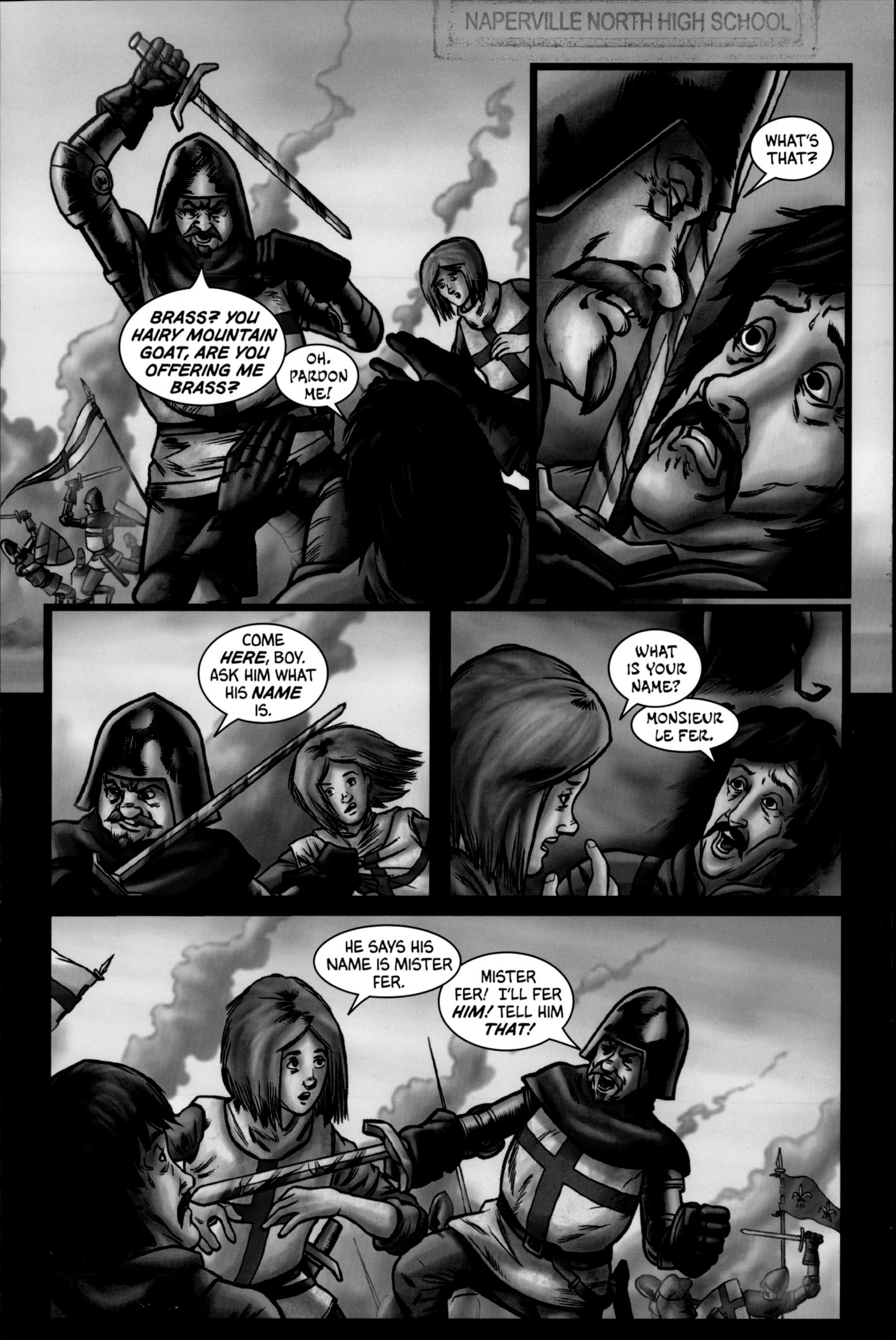
BRASS? YOU HAIRY MOUNTAIN GOAT, ARE YOU OFFERING ME BRASS?
OH. PARDON ME!
WHAT'S THAT?
COME *HERE*, BOY. ASK HIM WHAT HIS *NAME* IS.
WHAT IS YOUR NAME?
MONSIEUR LE FER.
HE SAYS HIS NAME IS MISTER FER.
MISTER FER! I'LL FER *HIM!* TELL HIM *THAT!*

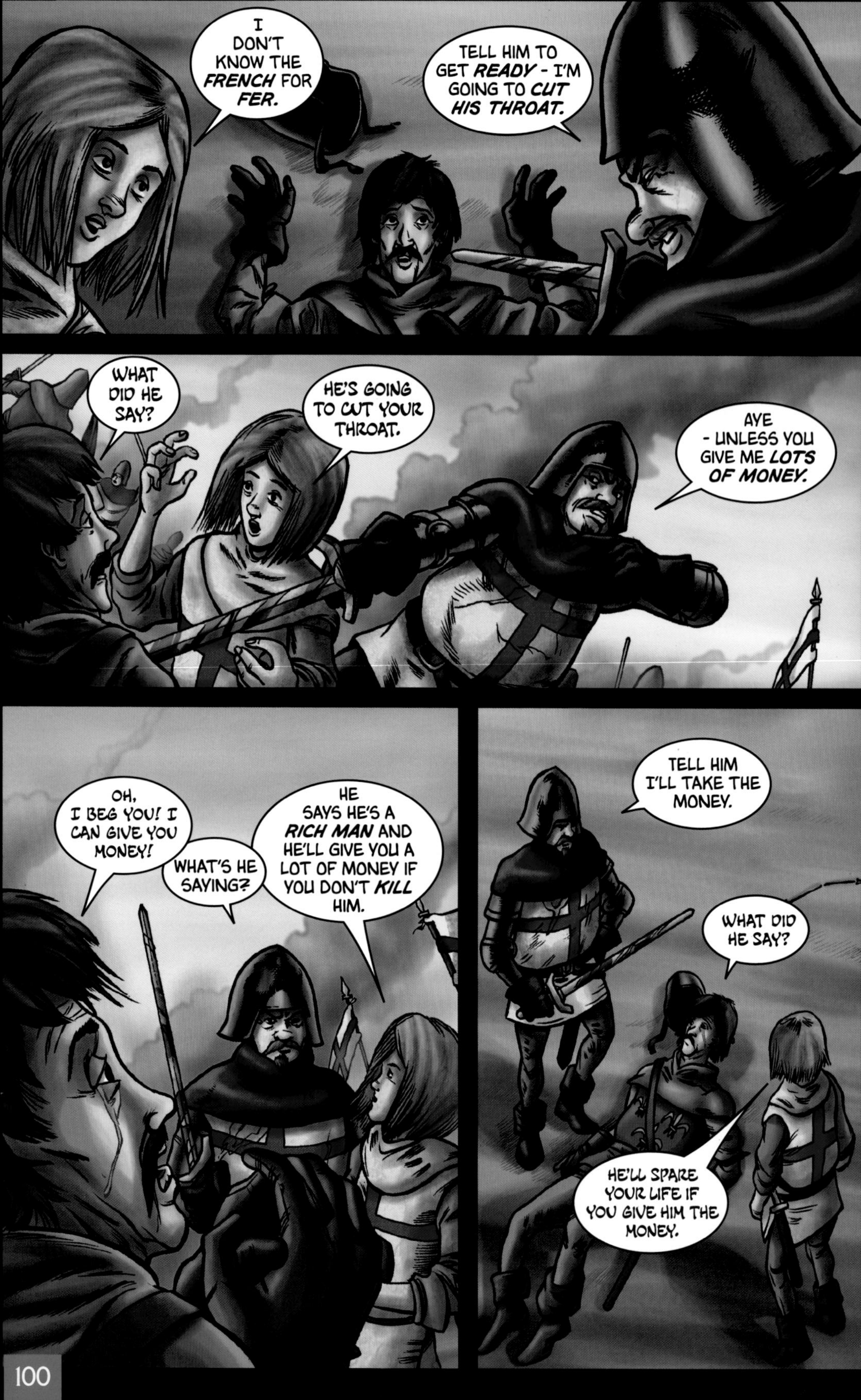
I DON'T KNOW THE FRENCH FOR FER.
TELL HIM TO GET READY - I'M GOING TO CUT HIS THROAT.
WHAT DID HE SAY?
HE'S GOING TO CUT YOUR THROAT.
AYE - UNLESS YOU GIVE ME LOTS OF MONEY.
OH, I BEG YOU! I CAN GIVE YOU MONEY!
WHAT'S HE SAYING?
HE SAYS HE'S A RICH MAN AND HE'LL GIVE YOU A LOT OF MONEY IF YOU DON'T KILL HIM.
TELL HIM I'LL TAKE THE MONEY.
WHAT DID HE SAY?
HE'LL SPARE YOUR LIFE IF YOU GIVE HIM THE MONEY.

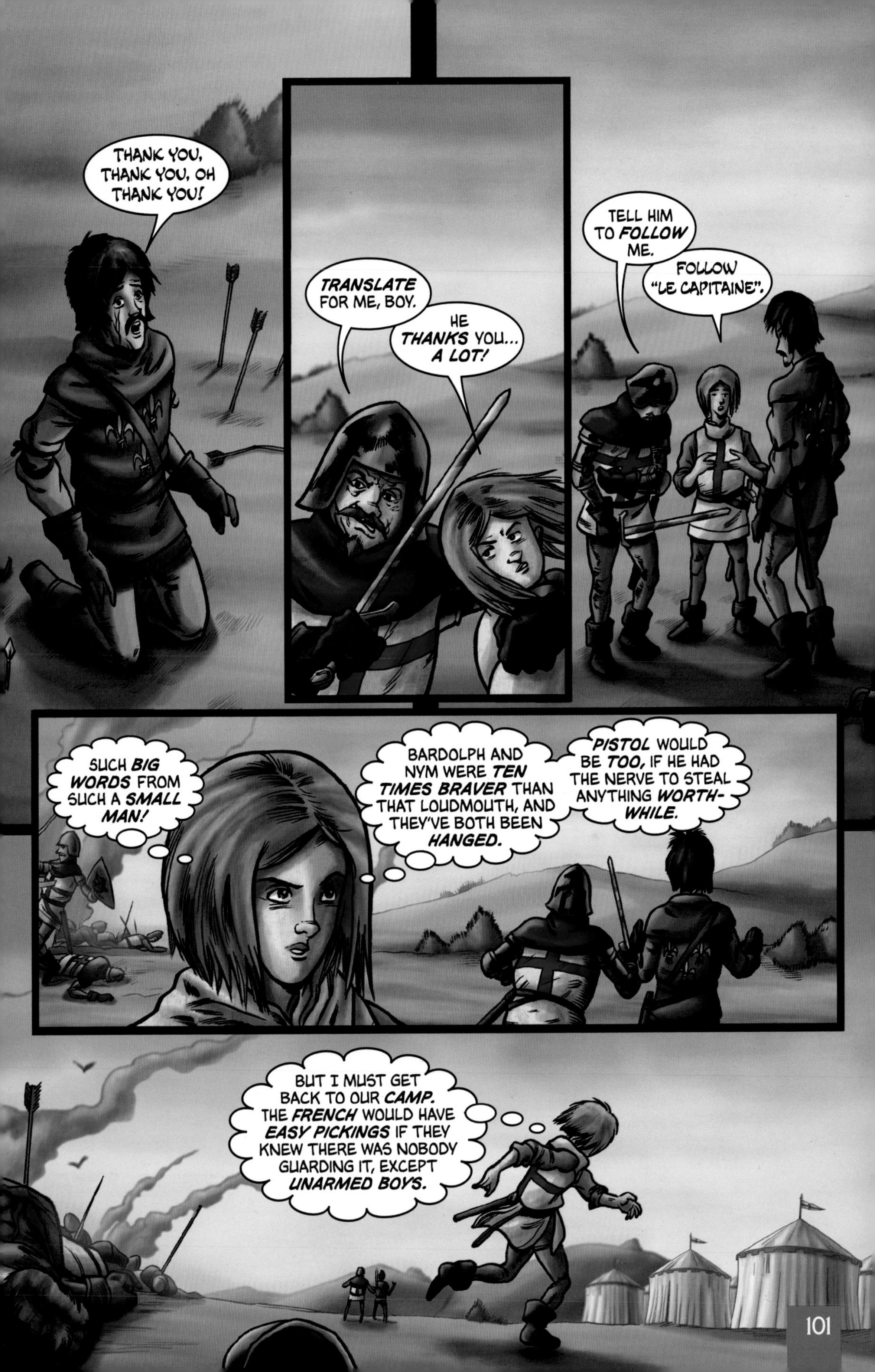
THANK YOU, THANK YOU, OH THANK YOU!
TRANSLATE FOR ME, BOY.
HE THANKS YOU... A LOT!
TELL HIM TO FOLLOW ME.
FOLLOW "LE CAPITAINE".
SUCH BIG WORDS FROM SUCH A SMALL MAN!
BARDOLPH AND NYM WERE TEN TIMES BRAVER THAN THAT LOUDMOUTH, AND THEY'VE BOTH BEEN HANGED.
PISTOL WOULD BE TOO, IF HE HAD THE NERVE TO STEAL ANYTHING WORTH-WHILE.
BUT I MUST GET BACK TO OUR CAMP. THE FRENCH WOULD HAVE EASY PICKINGS IF THEY KNEW THERE WAS NOBODY GUARDING IT, EXCEPT UNARMED BOYS.

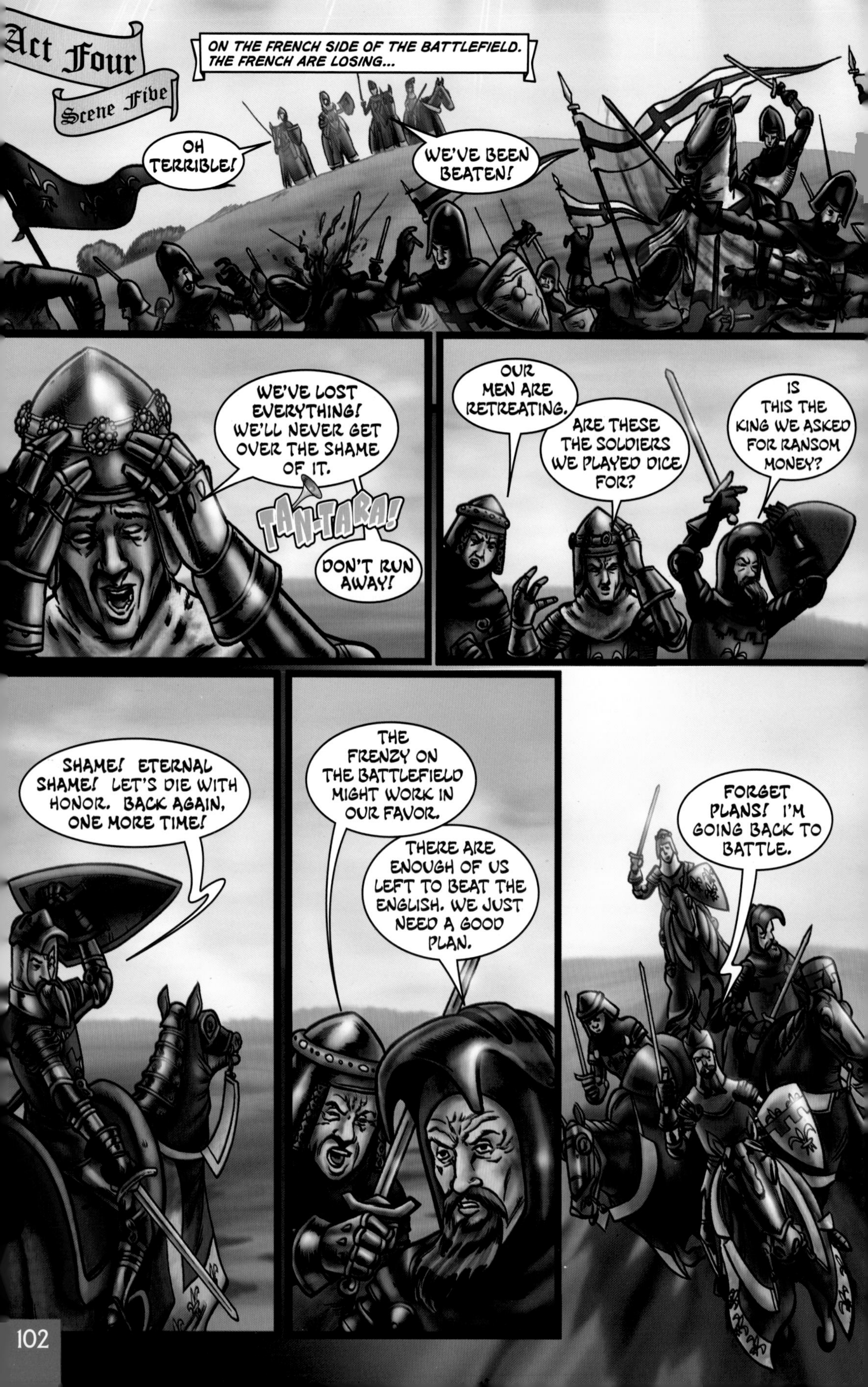
Act Four
Scene Five
ON THE FRENCH SIDE OF THE BATTLEFIELD. THE FRENCH ARE LOSING...
OH TERRIBLE!
WE'VE BEEN BEATEN!
WE'VE LOST EVERYTHING! WE'LL NEVER GET OVER THE SHAME OF IT.
TAN-TARA!
DON'T RUN AWAY!
OUR MEN ARE RETREATING.
ARE THESE THE SOLDIERS WE PLAYED DICE FOR?
IS THIS THE KING WE ASKED FOR RANSOM MONEY?
SHAME! ETERNAL SHAME! LET'S DIE WITH HONOR. BACK AGAIN, ONE MORE TIME!
THE FRENZY ON THE BATTLEFIELD MIGHT WORK IN OUR FAVOR.
THERE ARE ENOUGH OF US LEFT TO BEAT THE ENGLISH. WE JUST NEED A GOOD PLAN.
FORGET PLANS! I'M GOING BACK TO BATTLE.

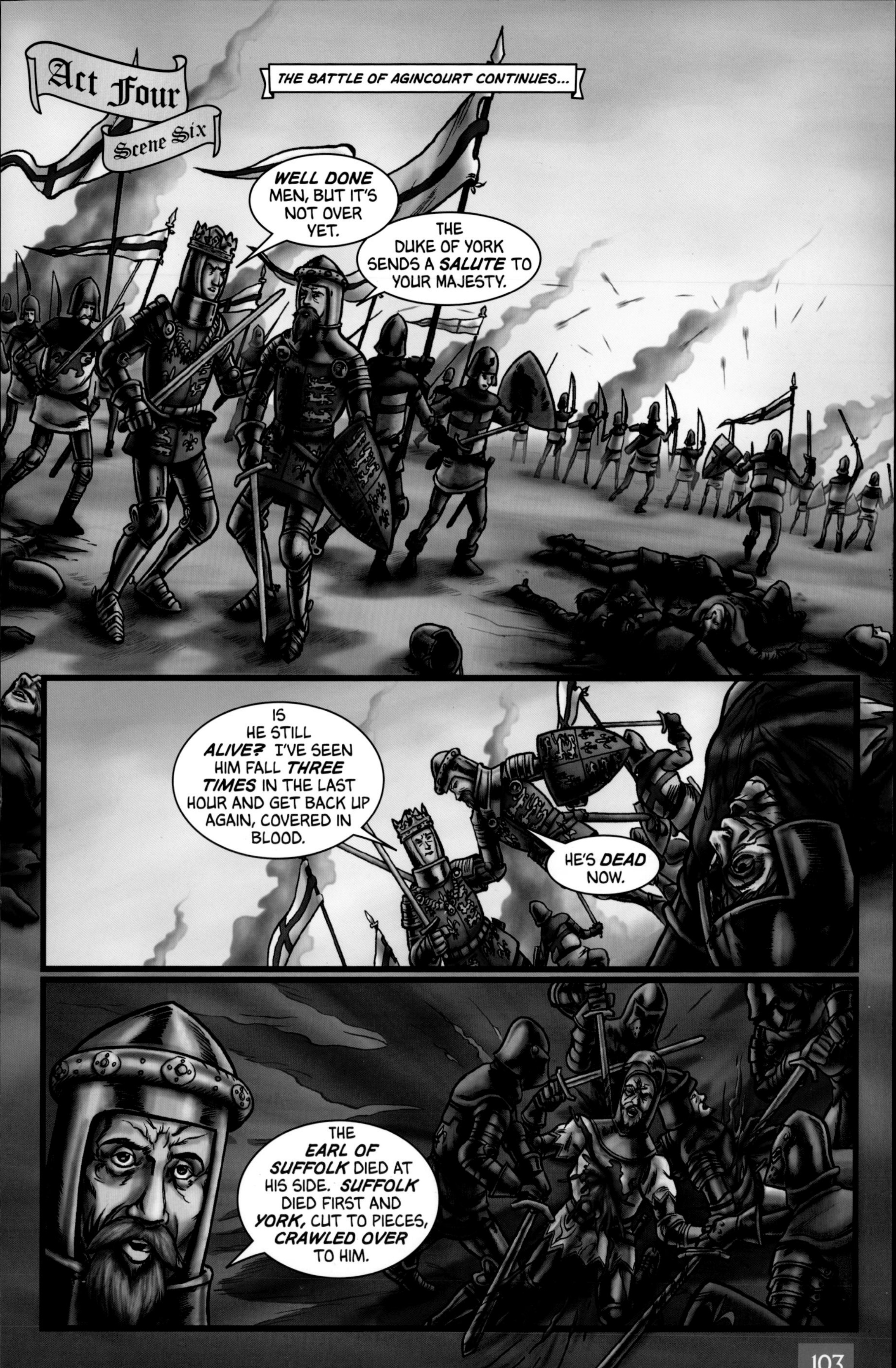
Act Four
Scene Six
THE BATTLE OF AGINCOURT CONTINUES...
WELL DONE MEN, BUT IT'S NOT OVER YET.
THE DUKE OF YORK SENDS A SALUTE TO YOUR MAJESTY.
IS HE STILL ALIVE? I'VE SEEN HIM FALL THREE TIMES IN THE LAST HOUR AND GET BACK UP AGAIN, COVERED IN BLOOD.
HE'S DEAD NOW.
THE EARL OF SUFFOLK DIED AT HIS SIDE. SUFFOLK DIED FIRST AND YORK, CUT TO PIECES, CRAWLED OVER TO HIM.

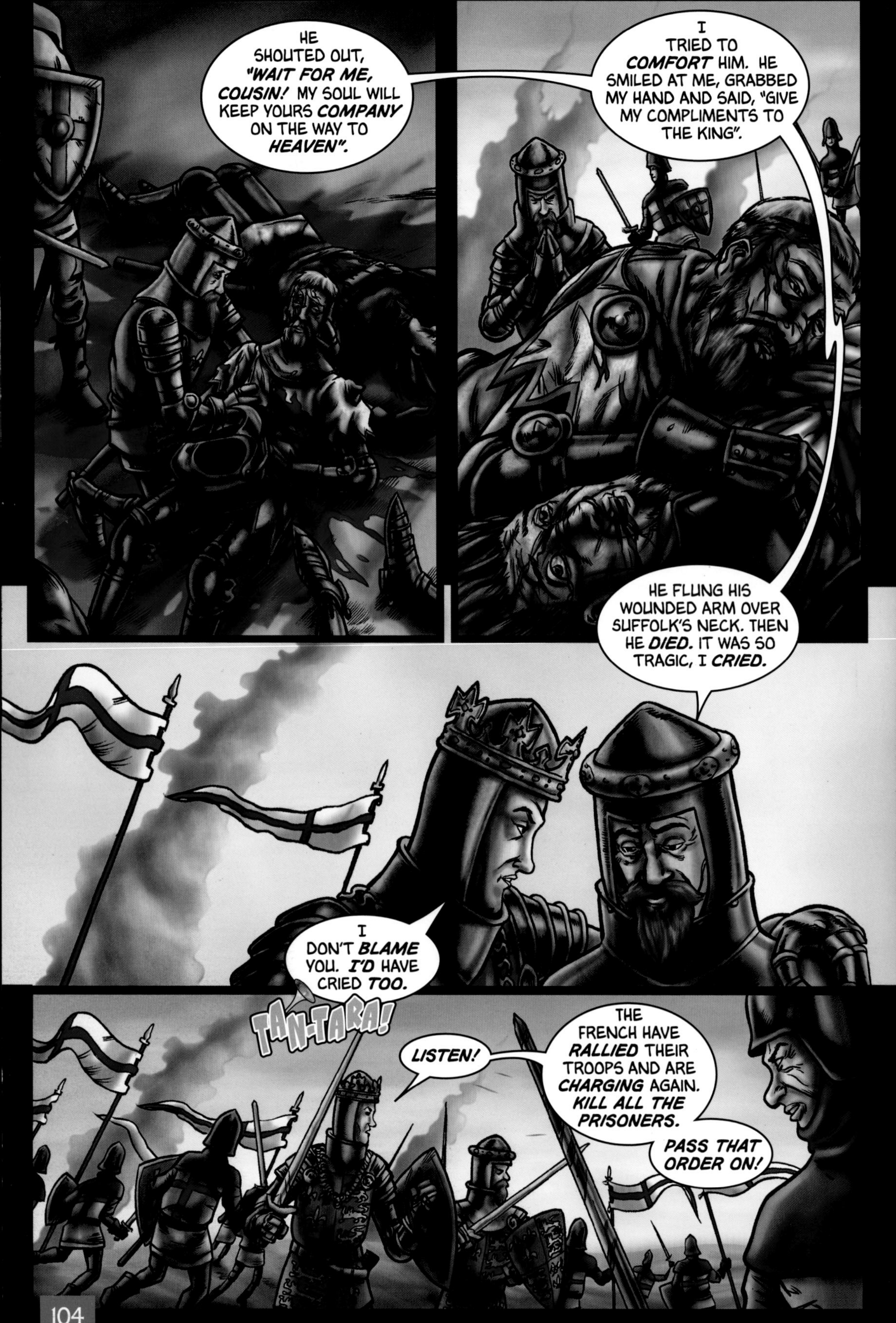
HE SHOUTED OUT, "WAIT FOR ME, COUSIN! MY SOUL WILL KEEP YOURS COMPANY ON THE WAY TO HEAVEN".
I TRIED TO COMFORT HIM. HE SMILED AT ME, GRABBED MY HAND AND SAID, "GIVE MY COMPLIMENTS TO THE KING".
HE FLUNG HIS WOUNDED ARM OVER SUFFOLK'S NECK. THEN HE DIED. IT WAS SO TRAGIC, I CRIED.
I DON'T BLAME YOU. I'D HAVE CRIED TOO.
TAN-TARA!
LISTEN!
THE FRENCH HAVE RALLIED THEIR TROOPS AND ARE CHARGING AGAIN. KILL ALL THE PRISONERS.
PASS THAT ORDER ON!

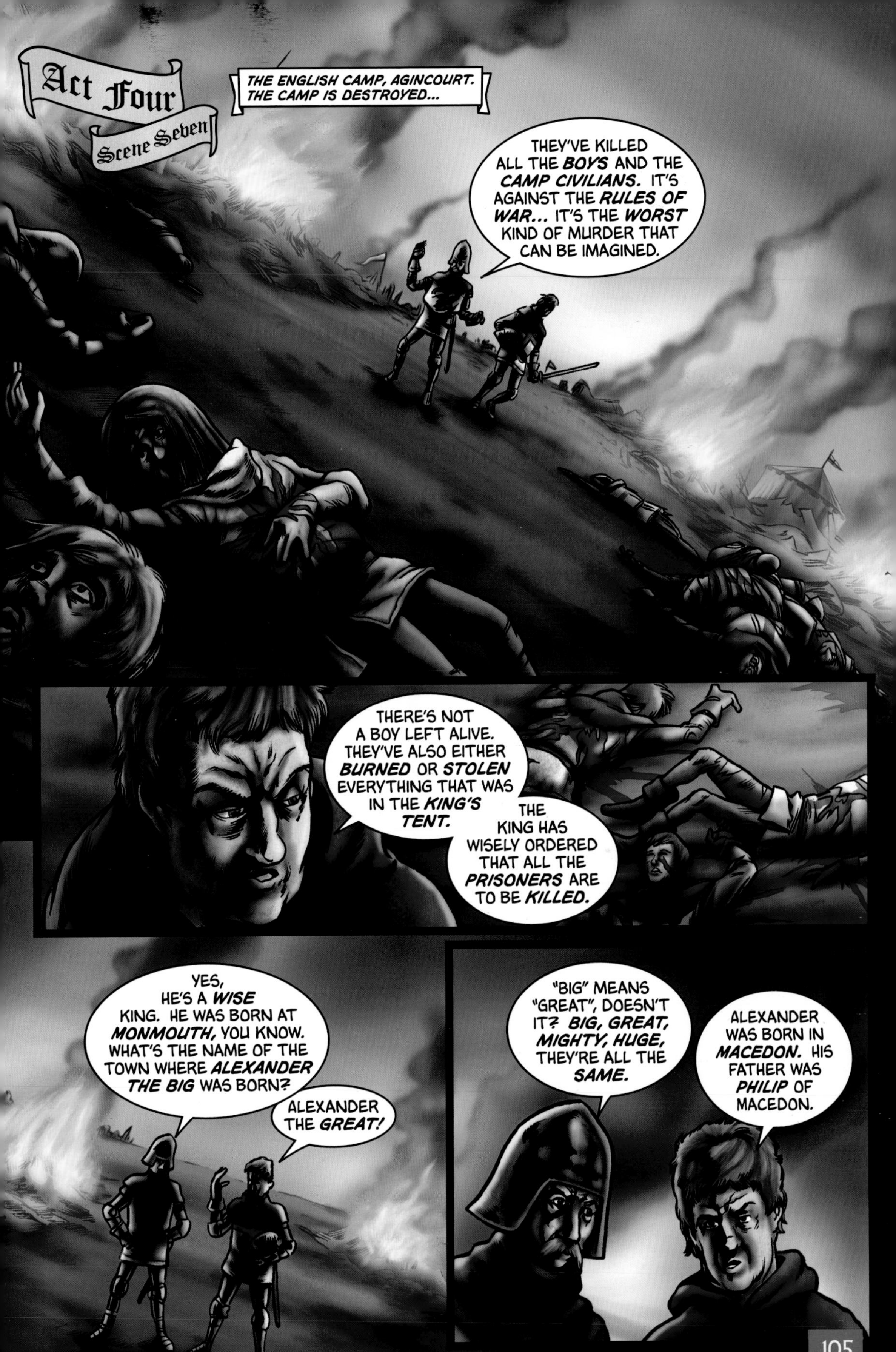
Act Four
Scene Seven
THE ENGLISH CAMP, AGINCOURT. THE CAMP IS DESTROYED...
THEY'VE KILLED ALL THE BOYS AND THE CAMP CIVILIANS. IT'S AGAINST THE RULES OF WAR... IT'S THE WORST KIND OF MURDER THAT CAN BE IMAGINED.
THERE'S NOT A BOY LEFT ALIVE. THEY'VE ALSO EITHER BURNED OR STOLEN EVERYTHING THAT WAS IN THE KING'S TENT.
THE KING HAS WISELY ORDERED THAT ALL THE PRISONERS ARE TO BE KILLED.
YES, HE'S A WISE KING. HE WAS BORN AT MONMOUTH, YOU KNOW. WHAT'S THE NAME OF THE TOWN WHERE ALEXANDER THE BIG WAS BORN?
ALEXANDER THE GREAT!
"BIG" MEANS "GREAT", DOESN'T IT? BIG, GREAT, MIGHTY, HUGE, THEY'RE ALL THE SAME.
ALEXANDER WAS BORN IN MACEDON. HIS FATHER WAS PHILIP OF MACEDON.

YOU'RE RIGHT. MACEDON AND MONMOUTH, THEY'RE BOTH *ALIKE* YOU KNOW. THERE'S A RIVER IN *MACEDON* AND THERE'S A RIVER AT *MONMOUTH*, IT'S CALLED THE *WYE* AT MONMOUTH...

BUT I CAN'T REMEMBER THE NAME OF THE *OTHER* RIVER. IT DOESN'T MATTER, THEY'RE *ALIKE* AND *HARRY OF MONMOUTH'S* LIFE RESEMBLES THAT OF *ALEXANDER THE GREAT.*

ALEXANDER *KILLED* HIS *FRIEND* WHILE IN A *RAGE,* OR WHILE *DRUNK...* I'M NOT SURE WHICH.

OUR KING'S NOT LIKE THAT! HE NEVER KILLED ANY OF HIS FRIENDS.

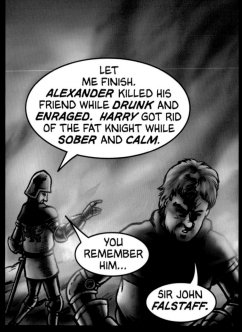

LET ME FINISH. *ALEXANDER* KILLED HIS FRIEND WHILE *DRUNK* AND *ENRAGED. HARRY* GOT RID OF THE FAT KNIGHT WHILE *SOBER* AND *CALM.*

YOU REMEMBER HIM...

SIR JOHN *FALSTAFF.*

THAT'S HIM. LET ME TELL YOU, THERE ARE *GOOD MEN* BORN AT MONMOUTH.

HERE COMES *HIS MAJESTY.*

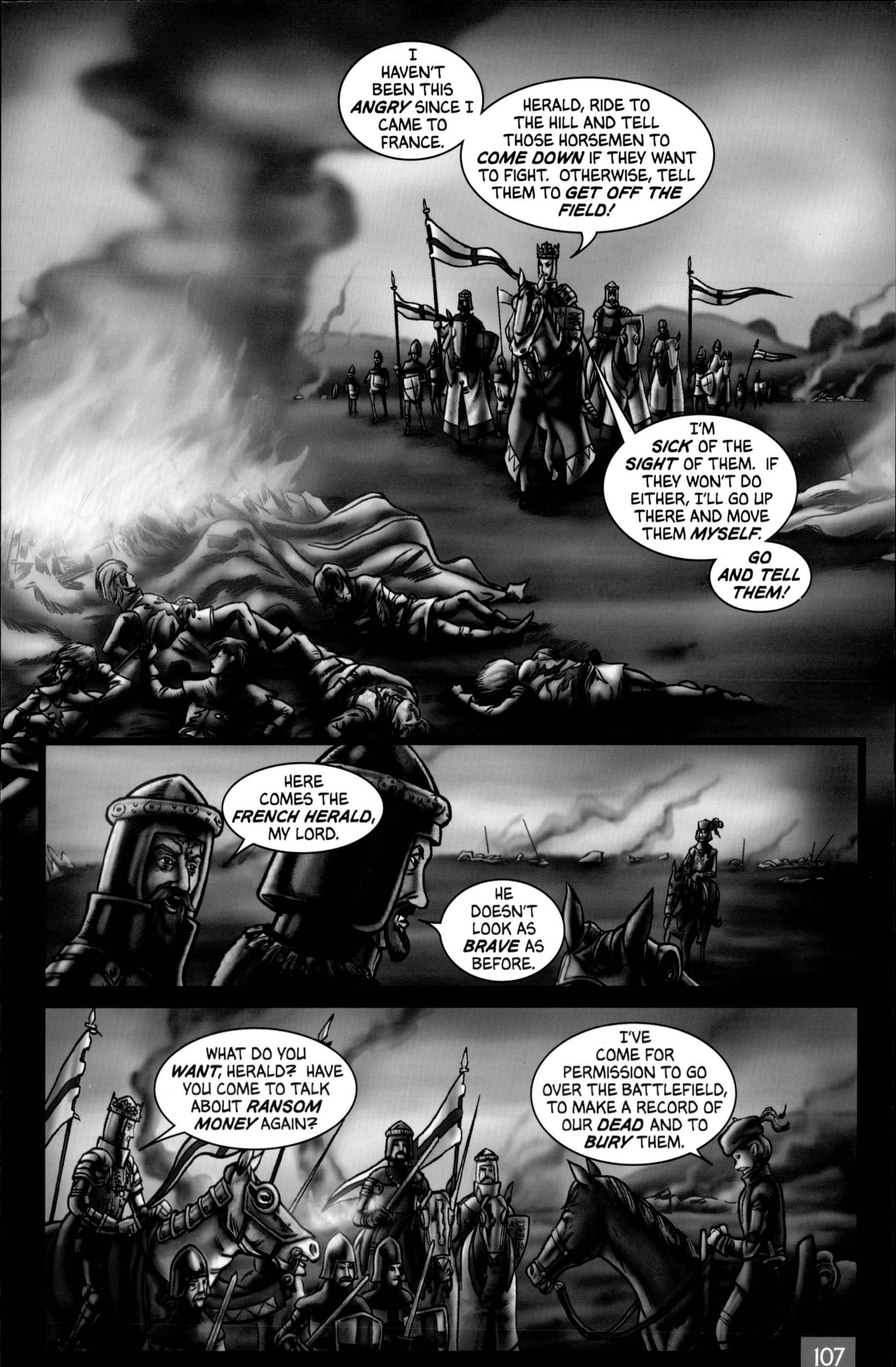
I HAVEN'T BEEN THIS ANGRY SINCE I CAME TO FRANCE.
HERALD, RIDE TO THE HILL AND TELL THOSE HORSEMEN TO COME DOWN IF THEY WANT TO FIGHT. OTHERWISE, TELL THEM TO GET OFF THE FIELD!
I'M SICK OF THE SIGHT OF THEM. IF THEY WON'T DO EITHER, I'LL GO UP THERE AND MOVE THEM MYSELF.
GO AND TELL THEM!
HERE COMES THE FRENCH HERALD, MY LORD.
HE DOESN'T LOOK AS BRAVE AS BEFORE.
WHAT DO YOU WANT, HERALD? HAVE YOU COME TO TALK ABOUT RANSOM MONEY AGAIN?
I'VE COME FOR PERMISSION TO GO OVER THE BATTLEFIELD, TO MAKE A RECORD OF OUR DEAD AND TO BURY THEM.

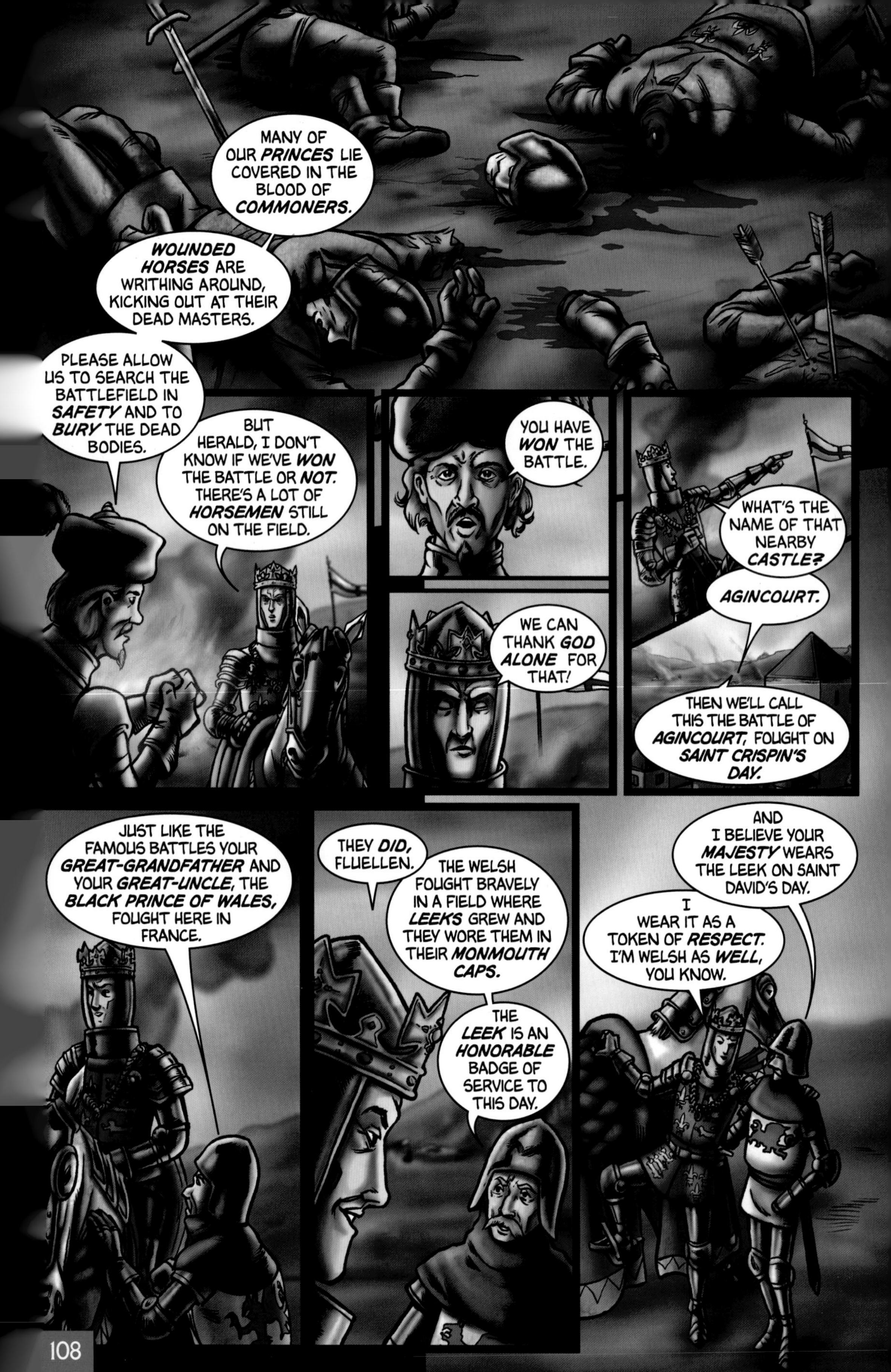

MANY OF OUR PRINCES LIE COVERED IN THE BLOOD OF COMMONERS.
WOUNDED HORSES ARE WRITHING AROUND, KICKING OUT AT THEIR DEAD MASTERS.
PLEASE ALLOW US TO SEARCH THE BATTLEFIELD IN SAFETY AND TO BURY THE DEAD BODIES.
BUT HERALD, I DON'T KNOW IF WE'VE WON THE BATTLE OR NOT. THERE'S A LOT OF HORSEMEN STILL ON THE FIELD.
YOU HAVE WON THE BATTLE.
WE CAN THANK GOD ALONE FOR THAT!
WHAT'S THE NAME OF THAT NEARBY CASTLE?
AGINCOURT.
THEN WE'LL CALL THIS THE BATTLE OF AGINCOURT, FOUGHT ON SAINT CRISPIN'S DAY.
JUST LIKE THE FAMOUS BATTLES YOUR GREAT-GRANDFATHER AND YOUR GREAT-UNCLE, THE BLACK PRINCE OF WALES, FOUGHT HERE IN FRANCE.
THEY DID, FLUELLEN.
THE WELSH FOUGHT BRAVELY IN A FIELD WHERE LEEKS GREW AND THEY WORE THEM IN THEIR MONMOUTH CAPS.
THE LEEK IS AN HONORABLE BADGE OF SERVICE TO THIS DAY.
AND I BELIEVE YOUR MAJESTY WEARS THE LEEK ON SAINT DAVID'S DAY.
I WEAR IT AS A TOKEN OF RESPECT. I'M WELSH AS WELL, YOU KNOW.

ALL THE WATER OF THE *WYE* COULDN'T WASH THE *WELSH BLOOD* OUT OF YOUR BODY. GOD BLESS AND PRESERVE IT.

THANKS, MY GOOD COUNTRY-MAN.

I *AM* YOUR MAJESTY'S COUNTRYMAN, *AND I DON'T CARE WHO KNOWS IT!*

MAY THAT *ALWAYS* BE SO!

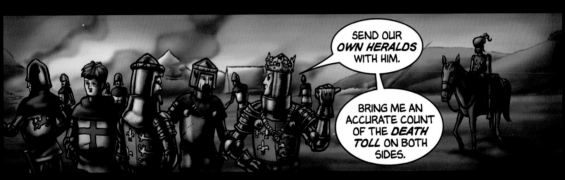

SEND OUR *OWN HERALDS* WITH HIM.

BRING ME AN ACCURATE COUNT OF THE *DEATH TOLL* ON BOTH SIDES.

CALL THAT MAN OVER.

SOLDIER, YOU MUST COME TO THE *KING.*

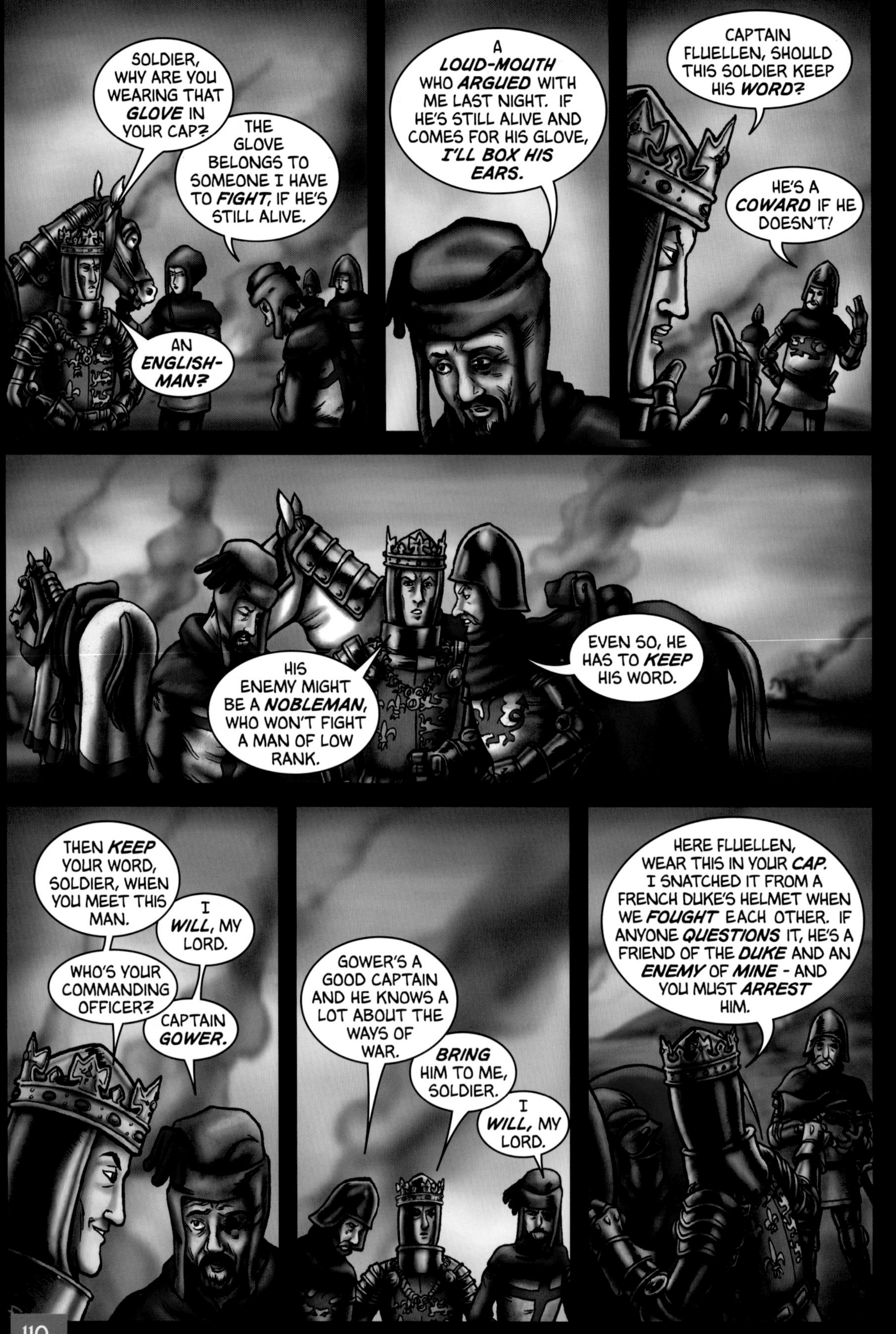
SOLDIER, WHY ARE YOU WEARING THAT **GLOVE** IN YOUR CAP?
THE GLOVE BELONGS TO SOMEONE I HAVE TO **FIGHT**, IF HE'S STILL ALIVE.
AN **ENGLISHMAN?**
A **LOUD-MOUTH** WHO **ARGUED** WITH ME LAST NIGHT. IF HE'S STILL ALIVE AND COMES FOR HIS GLOVE, **I'LL BOX HIS EARS.**
CAPTAIN FLUELLEN, SHOULD THIS SOLDIER KEEP HIS **WORD?**
HE'S A **COWARD** IF HE DOESN'T!
HIS ENEMY MIGHT BE A **NOBLEMAN,** WHO WON'T FIGHT A MAN OF LOW RANK.
EVEN SO, HE HAS TO **KEEP** HIS WORD.
THEN **KEEP** YOUR WORD, SOLDIER, WHEN YOU MEET THIS MAN.
I **WILL**, MY LORD.
WHO'S YOUR COMMANDING OFFICER?
CAPTAIN **GOWER.**
GOWER'S A GOOD CAPTAIN AND HE KNOWS A LOT ABOUT THE WAYS OF WAR.
BRING HIM TO ME, SOLDIER.
I **WILL,** MY LORD.
HERE FLUELLEN, WEAR THIS IN YOUR **CAP.** I SNATCHED IT FROM A FRENCH DUKE'S HELMET WHEN WE **FOUGHT** EACH OTHER. IF ANYONE **QUESTIONS** IT, HE'S A FRIEND OF THE **DUKE** AND AN **ENEMY** OF **MINE** - AND YOU MUST **ARREST** HIM.

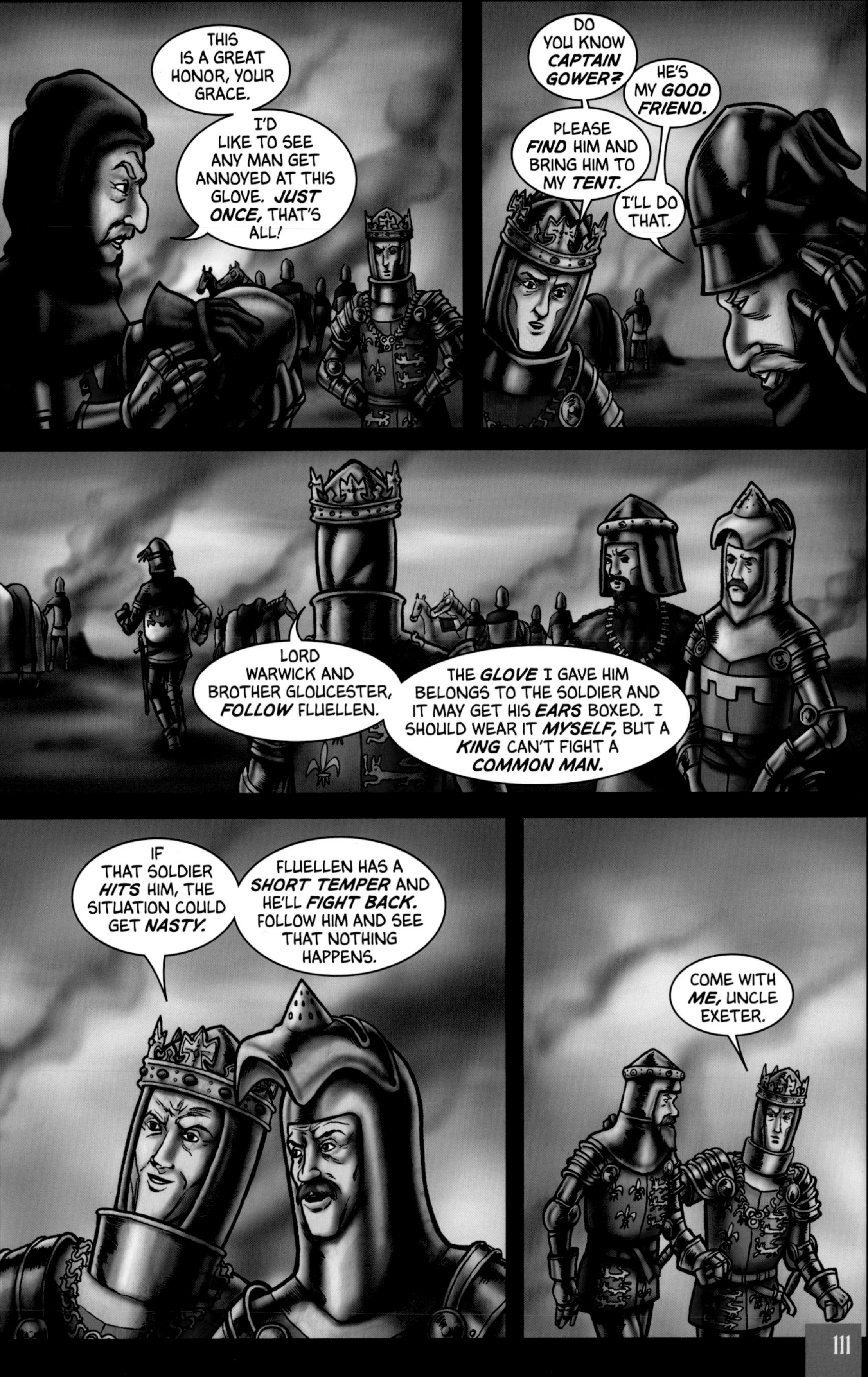
THIS IS A GREAT HONOR, YOUR GRACE.
I'D LIKE TO SEE ANY MAN GET ANNOYED AT THIS GLOVE. JUST ONCE, THAT'S ALL!
DO YOU KNOW CAPTAIN GOWER?
HE'S MY GOOD FRIEND.
PLEASE FIND HIM AND BRING HIM TO MY TENT.
I'LL DO THAT.
LORD WARWICK AND BROTHER GLOUCESTER, FOLLOW FLUELLEN.
THE GLOVE I GAVE HIM BELONGS TO THE SOLDIER AND IT MAY GET HIS EARS BOXED. I SHOULD WEAR IT MYSELF, BUT A KING CAN'T FIGHT A COMMON MAN.
IF THAT SOLDIER HITS HIM, THE SITUATION COULD GET NASTY.
FLUELLEN HAS A SHORT TEMPER AND HE'LL FIGHT BACK. FOLLOW HIM AND SEE THAT NOTHING HAPPENS.
COME WITH ME, UNCLE EXETER.

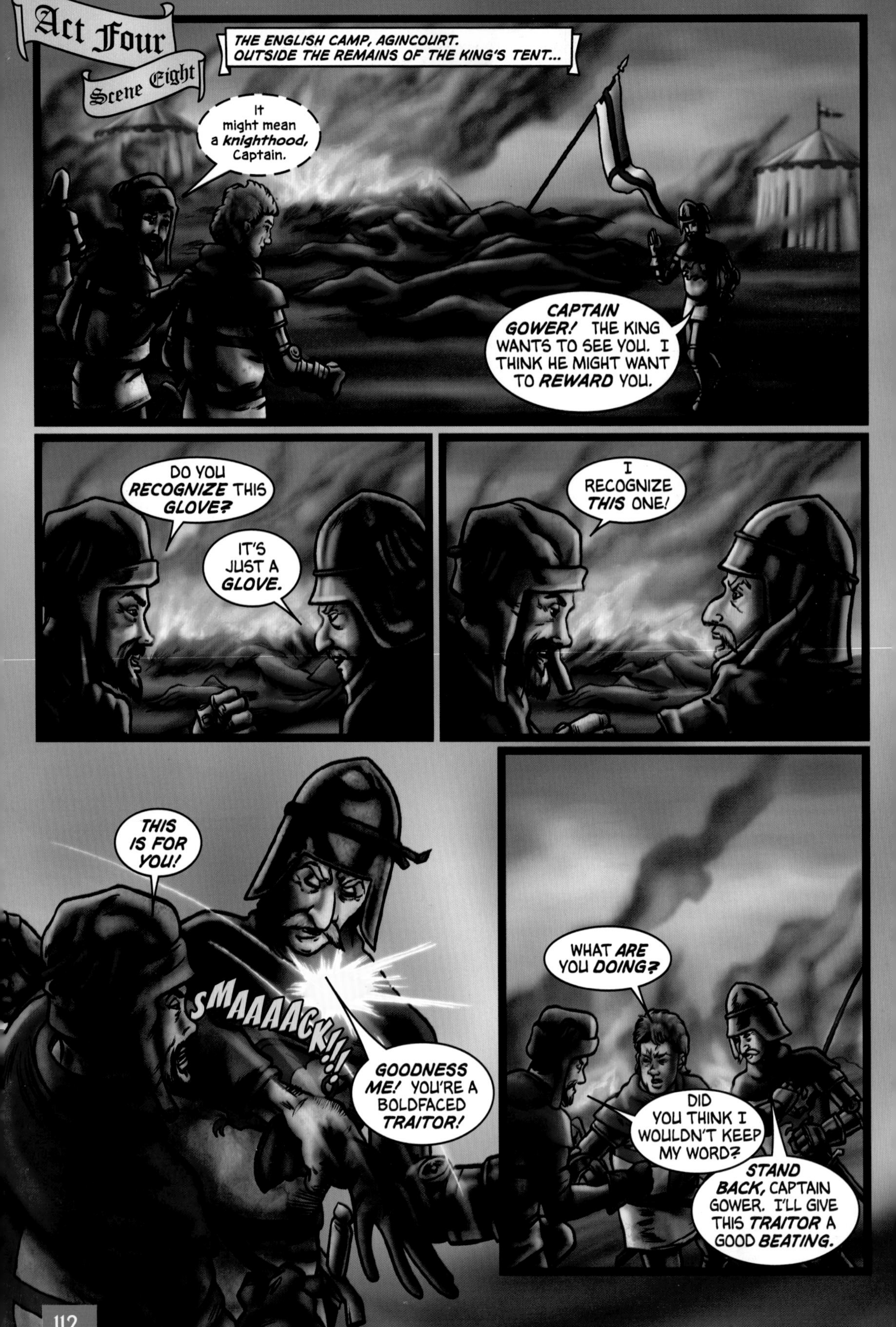
Act Four
Scene Eight
THE ENGLISH CAMP, AGINCOURT. OUTSIDE THE REMAINS OF THE KING'S TENT...
It might mean a knighthood, Captain.
CAPTAIN GOWER! THE KING WANTS TO SEE YOU. I THINK HE MIGHT WANT TO REWARD YOU.
DO YOU RECOGNIZE THIS GLOVE?
IT'S JUST A GLOVE.
I RECOGNIZE THIS ONE!
THIS IS FOR YOU!
SMAAAACK!!!
GOODNESS ME! YOU'RE A BOLDFACED TRAITOR!
WHAT ARE YOU DOING?
DID YOU THINK I WOULDN'T KEEP MY WORD?
STAND BACK, CAPTAIN GOWER. I'LL GIVE THIS TRAITOR A GOOD BEATING.

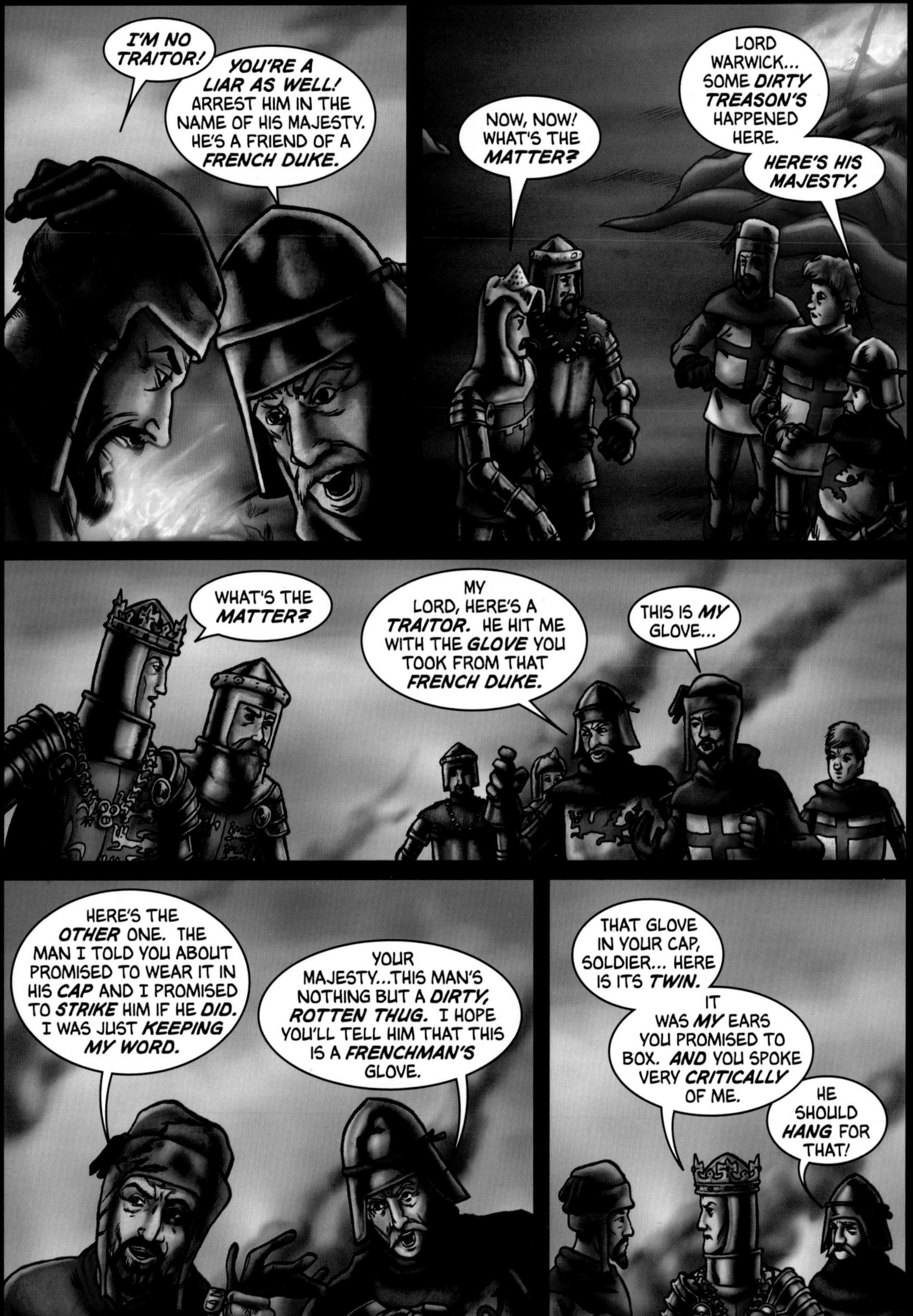
I'M NO TRAITOR!
YOU'RE A LIAR AS WELL! ARREST HIM IN THE NAME OF HIS MAJESTY. HE'S A FRIEND OF A FRENCH DUKE.
NOW, NOW! WHAT'S THE MATTER?
LORD WARWICK... SOME DIRTY TREASON'S HAPPENED HERE.
HERE'S HIS MAJESTY.
WHAT'S THE MATTER?
MY LORD, HERE'S A TRAITOR. HE HIT ME WITH THE GLOVE YOU TOOK FROM THAT FRENCH DUKE.
THIS IS MY GLOVE...
HERE'S THE OTHER ONE. THE MAN I TOLD YOU ABOUT PROMISED TO WEAR IT IN HIS CAP AND I PROMISED TO STRIKE HIM IF HE DID. I WAS JUST KEEPING MY WORD.
YOUR MAJESTY...THIS MAN'S NOTHING BUT A DIRTY, ROTTEN THUG. I HOPE YOU'LL TELL HIM THAT THIS IS A FRENCHMAN'S GLOVE.
THAT GLOVE IN YOUR CAP, SOLDIER... HERE IS ITS TWIN.
IT WAS MY EARS YOU PROMISED TO BOX. AND YOU SPOKE VERY CRITICALLY OF ME.
HE SHOULD HANG FOR THAT!

HOW CAN YOU *MAKE IT UP* TO ME?

I DIDN'T MEAN TO *OFFEND* YOUR MAJESTY.

BUT IT WAS *ME, PERSONALLY,* WHO YOU CRITICIZED.

YOU WERE *DISGUISED.* I THOUGHT YOU WERE AN *ORDINARY MAN.* IT WAS *DARK...* YOUR *CLOTHES,* YOUR *MANNER...*

WHATEVER *CRITICISM* YOUR HIGHNESS GOT, IT WAS YOUR *OWN FAULT.*

UNCLE EXETER, FILL THIS GLOVE WITH *MONEY* AND GIVE IT TO HIM.

KEEP THE GLOVE AND WEAR IT AS A *TROPHY,* SOLDIER. I MIGHT *COME* FOR IT ONE DAY. *CAPTAIN,* MAKE *FRIENDS* WITH THIS MAN.

HE HAS *GUTS,* I'LL SAY THAT!

WAIT! HERE'S A *PENNY* FOR YOU. I HOPE YOU'LL STAY OUT OF *FIGHTS* AND *ARGUMENTS* IN THE FUTURE.

I DON'T WANT *YOUR* MONEY!

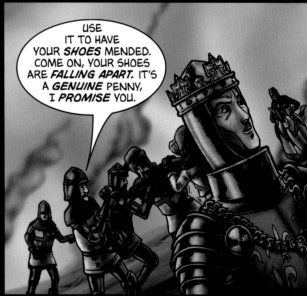

USE IT TO HAVE YOUR *SHOES* MENDED. COME ON, YOUR SHOES ARE *FALLING APART.* IT'S A *GENUINE* PENNY, I *PROMISE* YOU.

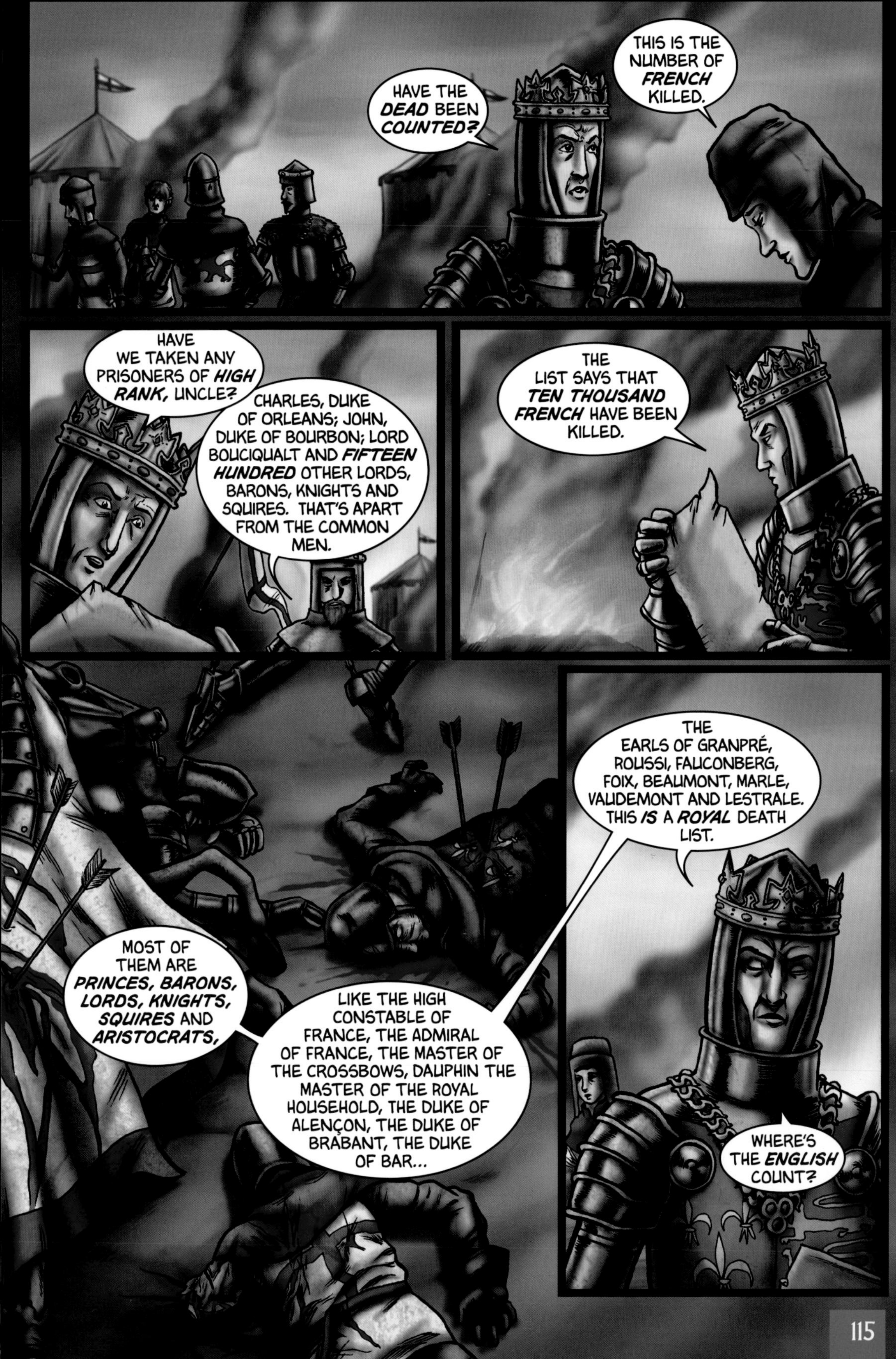
HAVE THE DEAD BEEN COUNTED?
THIS IS THE NUMBER OF FRENCH KILLED.
HAVE WE TAKEN ANY PRISONERS OF HIGH RANK, UNCLE?
CHARLES, DUKE OF ORLEANS; JOHN, DUKE OF BOURBON; LORD BOUCIQUALT AND FIFTEEN HUNDRED OTHER LORDS, BARONS, KNIGHTS AND SQUIRES. THAT'S APART FROM THE COMMON MEN.
THE LIST SAYS THAT TEN THOUSAND FRENCH HAVE BEEN KILLED.
MOST OF THEM ARE PRINCES, BARONS, LORDS, KNIGHTS, SQUIRES AND ARISTOCRATS,
LIKE THE HIGH CONSTABLE OF FRANCE, THE ADMIRAL OF FRANCE, THE MASTER OF THE CROSSBOWS, DAUPHIN THE MASTER OF THE ROYAL HOUSEHOLD, THE DUKE OF ALENÇON, THE DUKE OF BRABANT, THE DUKE OF BAR...
THE EARLS OF GRANPRÉ, ROUSSI, FAUCONBERG, FOIX, BEAUMONT, MARLE, VAUDEMONT AND LESTRALE. THIS IS A ROYAL DEATH LIST.
WHERE'S THE ENGLISH COUNT?

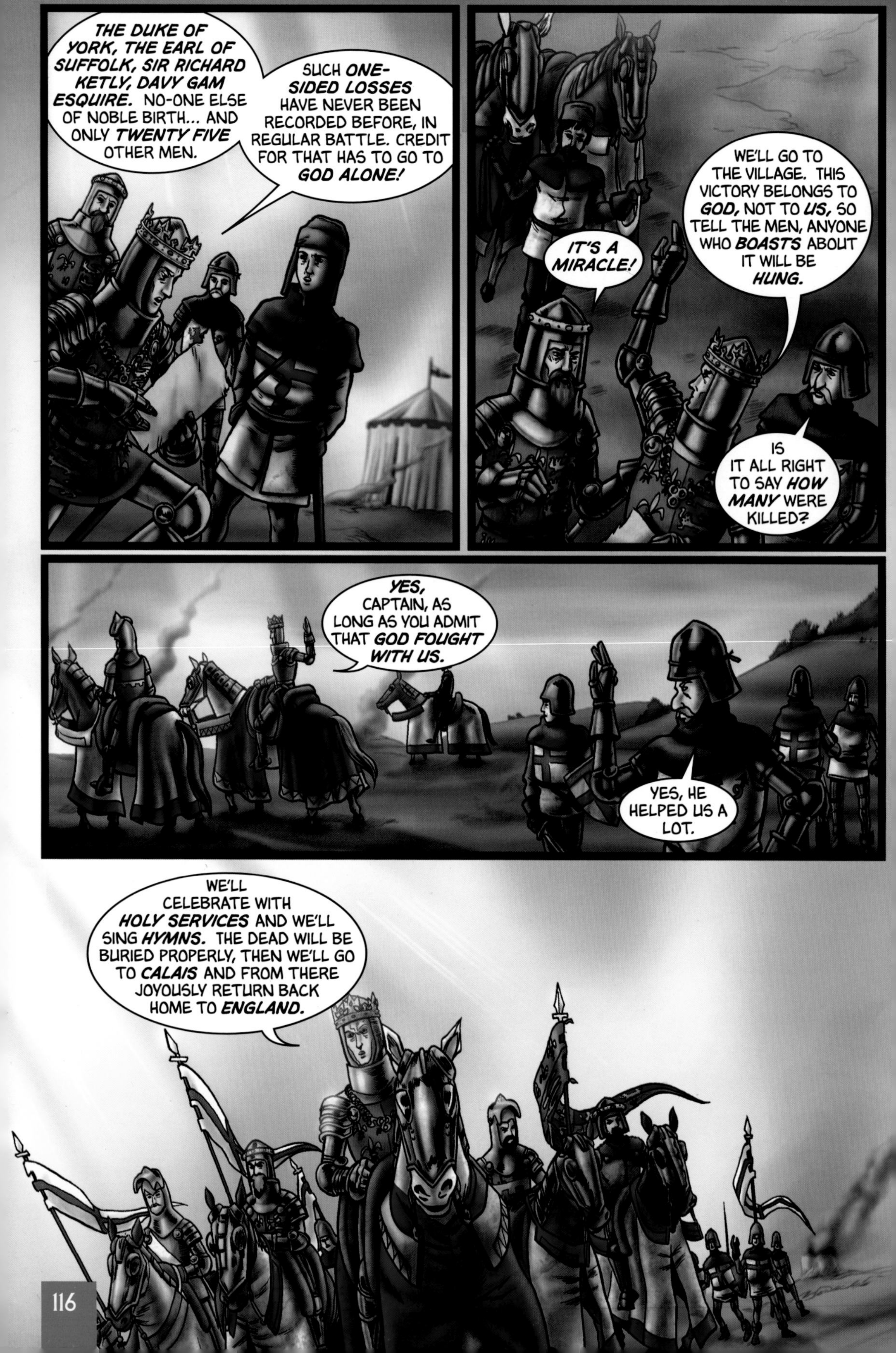
THE DUKE OF YORK, THE EARL OF SUFFOLK, SIR RICHARD KETLY, DAVY GAM ESQUIRE. NO-ONE ELSE OF NOBLE BIRTH... AND ONLY TWENTY FIVE OTHER MEN.
SUCH ONE-SIDED LOSSES HAVE NEVER BEEN RECORDED BEFORE, IN REGULAR BATTLE. CREDIT FOR THAT HAS TO GO TO GOD ALONE!
IT'S A MIRACLE!
WE'LL GO TO THE VILLAGE. THIS VICTORY BELONGS TO GOD, NOT TO US, SO TELL THE MEN, ANYONE WHO BOASTS ABOUT IT WILL BE HUNG.
IS IT ALL RIGHT TO SAY HOW MANY WERE KILLED?
YES, CAPTAIN, AS LONG AS YOU ADMIT THAT GOD FOUGHT WITH US.
YES, HE HELPED US A LOT.
WE'LL CELEBRATE WITH HOLY SERVICES AND WE'LL SING HYMNS. THE DEAD WILL BE BURIED PROPERLY, THEN WE'LL GO TO CALAIS AND FROM THERE JOYOUSLY RETURN BACK HOME TO ENGLAND.

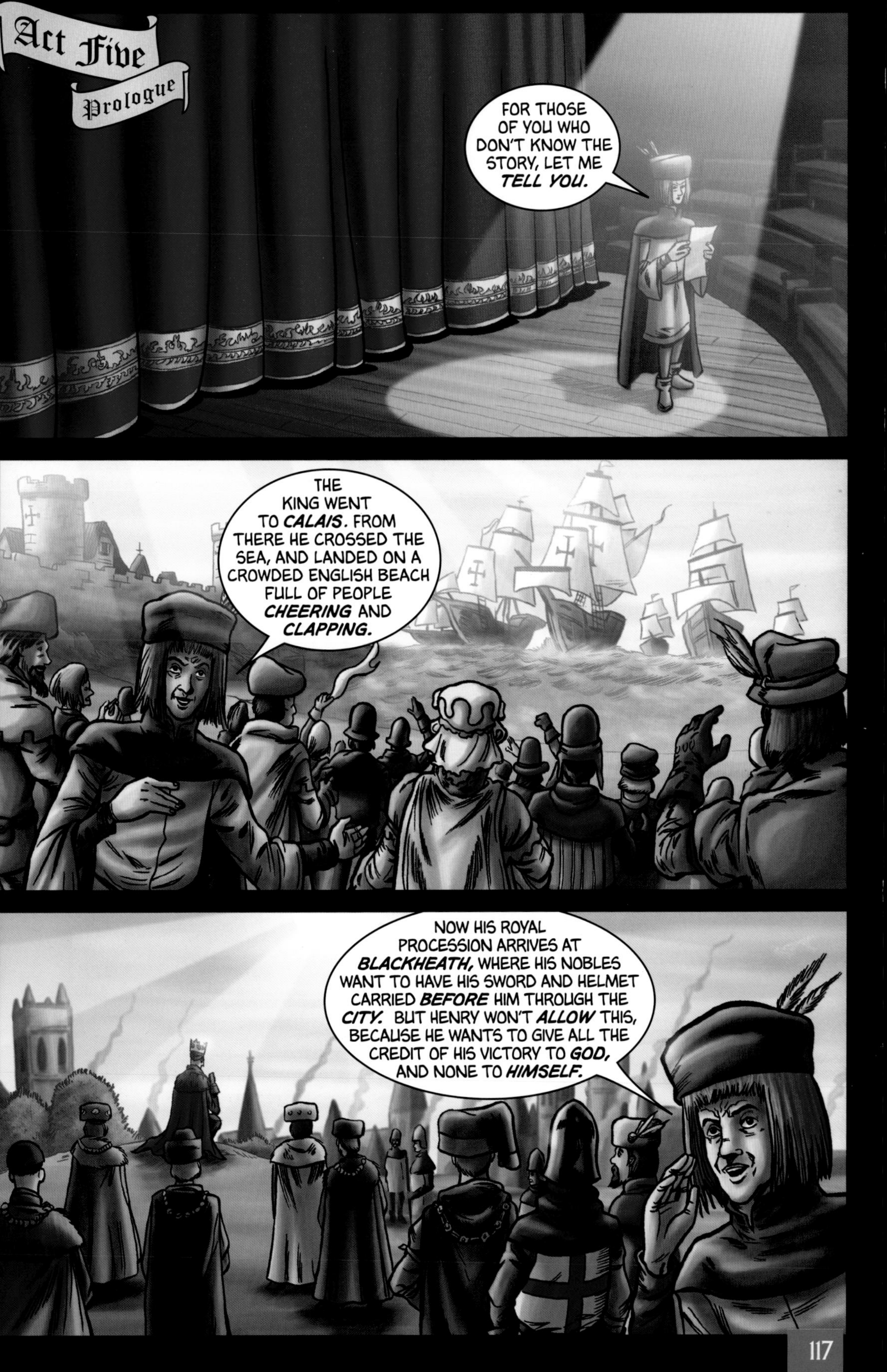
Act Five
Prologue
FOR THOSE OF YOU WHO DON'T KNOW THE STORY, LET ME *TELL YOU.*
THE KING WENT TO *CALAIS*. FROM THERE HE CROSSED THE SEA, AND LANDED ON A CROWDED ENGLISH BEACH FULL OF PEOPLE *CHEERING* AND *CLAPPING.*
NOW HIS ROYAL PROCESSION ARRIVES AT *BLACKHEATH,* WHERE HIS NOBLES WANT TO HAVE HIS SWORD AND HELMET CARRIED *BEFORE* HIM THROUGH THE *CITY.* BUT HENRY WON'T *ALLOW* THIS, BECAUSE HE WANTS TO GIVE ALL THE CREDIT OF HIS VICTORY TO *GOD,* AND NONE TO *HIMSELF.*

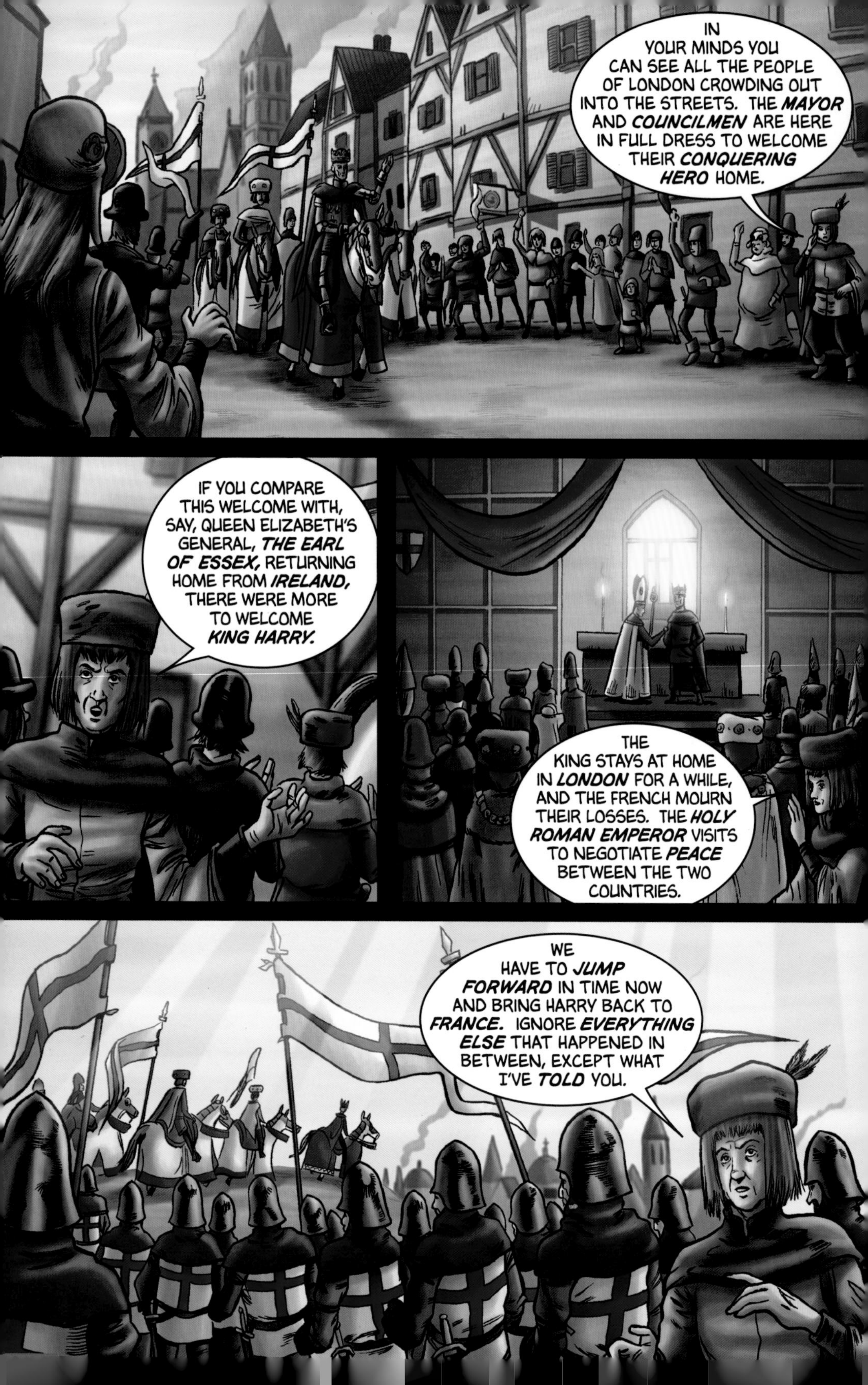
IN YOUR MINDS YOU CAN SEE ALL THE PEOPLE OF LONDON CROWDING OUT INTO THE STREETS. THE MAYOR AND COUNCILMEN ARE HERE IN FULL DRESS TO WELCOME THEIR CONQUERING HERO HOME.
IF YOU COMPARE THIS WELCOME WITH, SAY, QUEEN ELIZABETH'S GENERAL, THE EARL OF ESSEX, RETURNING HOME FROM IRELAND, THERE WERE MORE TO WELCOME KING HARRY.
THE KING STAYS AT HOME IN LONDON FOR A WHILE, AND THE FRENCH MOURN THEIR LOSSES. THE HOLY ROMAN EMPEROR VISITS TO NEGOTIATE PEACE BETWEEN THE TWO COUNTRIES.
WE HAVE TO JUMP FORWARD IN TIME NOW AND BRING HARRY BACK TO FRANCE. IGNORE EVERYTHING ELSE THAT HAPPENED IN BETWEEN, EXCEPT WHAT I'VE TOLD YOU.

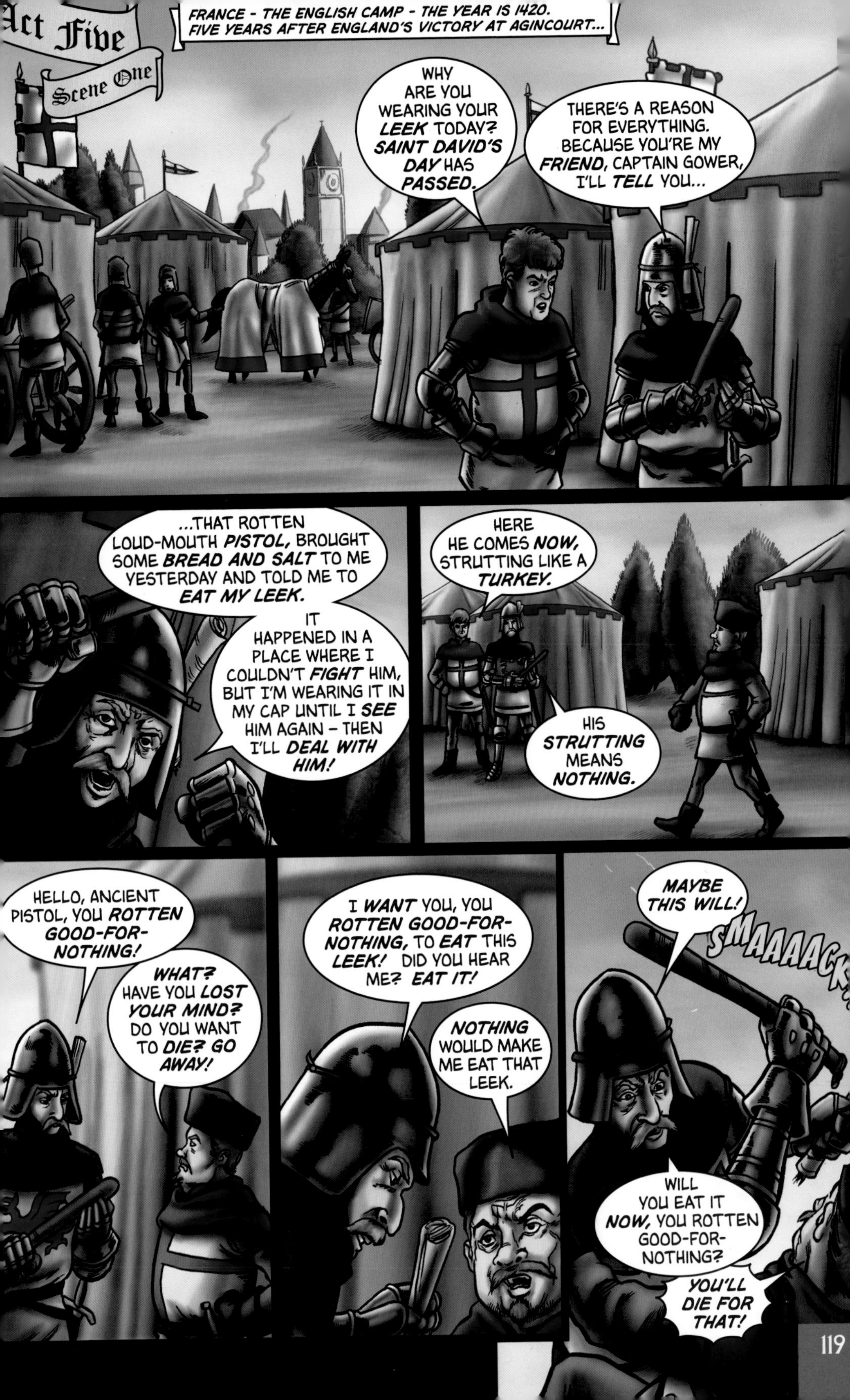
Act Five
Scene One
FRANCE - THE ENGLISH CAMP - THE YEAR IS 1420. FIVE YEARS AFTER ENGLAND'S VICTORY AT AGINCOURT...
WHY ARE YOU WEARING YOUR LEEK TODAY? SAINT DAVID'S DAY HAS PASSED.
THERE'S A REASON FOR EVERYTHING. BECAUSE YOU'RE MY FRIEND, CAPTAIN GOWER, I'LL TELL YOU...
...THAT ROTTEN LOUD-MOUTH PISTOL, BROUGHT SOME BREAD AND SALT TO ME YESTERDAY AND TOLD ME TO EAT MY LEEK.
IT HAPPENED IN A PLACE WHERE I COULDN'T FIGHT HIM, BUT I'M WEARING IT IN MY CAP UNTIL I SEE HIM AGAIN – THEN I'LL DEAL WITH HIM!
HERE HE COMES NOW, STRUTTING LIKE A TURKEY.
HIS STRUTTING MEANS NOTHING.
HELLO, ANCIENT PISTOL, YOU ROTTEN GOOD-FOR-NOTHING!
WHAT? HAVE YOU LOST YOUR MIND? DO YOU WANT TO DIE? GO AWAY!
I WANT YOU, YOU ROTTEN GOOD-FOR-NOTHING, TO EAT THIS LEEK! DID YOU HEAR ME? EAT IT!
NOTHING WOULD MAKE ME EAT THAT LEEK.
MAYBE THIS WILL!
SMAAAACK
WILL YOU EAT IT NOW, YOU ROTTEN GOOD-FOR-NOTHING?
YOU'LL DIE FOR THAT!

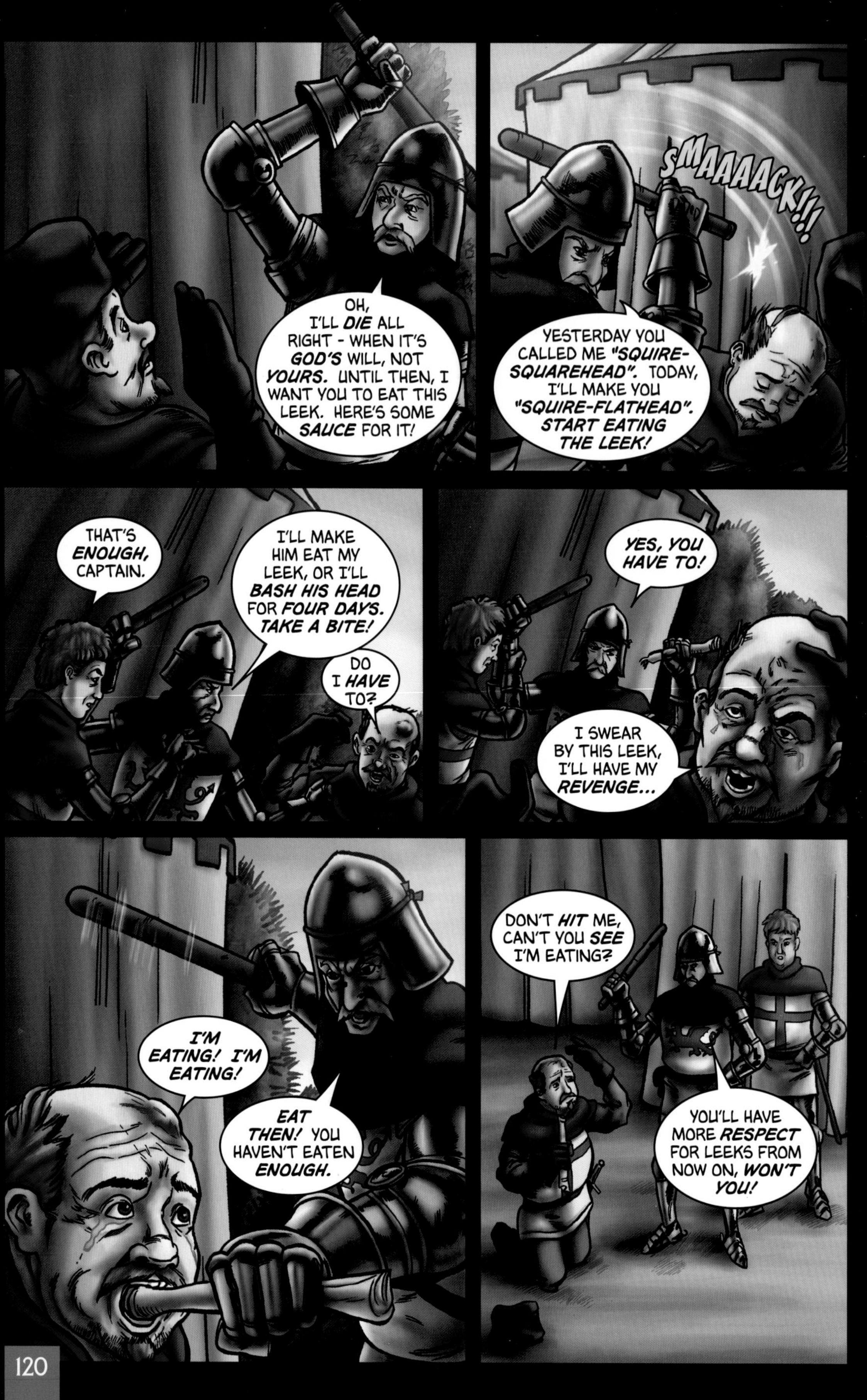
OH, I'LL DIE ALL RIGHT - WHEN IT'S GOD'S WILL, NOT YOURS. UNTIL THEN, I WANT YOU TO EAT THIS LEEK. HERE'S SOME SAUCE FOR IT!
SMAAAACK!!!
YESTERDAY YOU CALLED ME "SQUIRE-SQUAREHEAD". TODAY, I'LL MAKE YOU "SQUIRE-FLATHEAD". START EATING THE LEEK!
THAT'S ENOUGH, CAPTAIN.
I'LL MAKE HIM EAT MY LEEK, OR I'LL BASH HIS HEAD FOR FOUR DAYS. TAKE A BITE!
DO I HAVE TO?
YES, YOU HAVE TO!
I SWEAR BY THIS LEEK, I'LL HAVE MY REVENGE...
I'M EATING! I'M EATING!
EAT THEN! YOU HAVEN'T EATEN ENOUGH.
DON'T HIT ME, CAN'T YOU SEE I'M EATING?
YOU'LL HAVE MORE RESPECT FOR LEEKS FROM NOW ON, WON'T YOU!

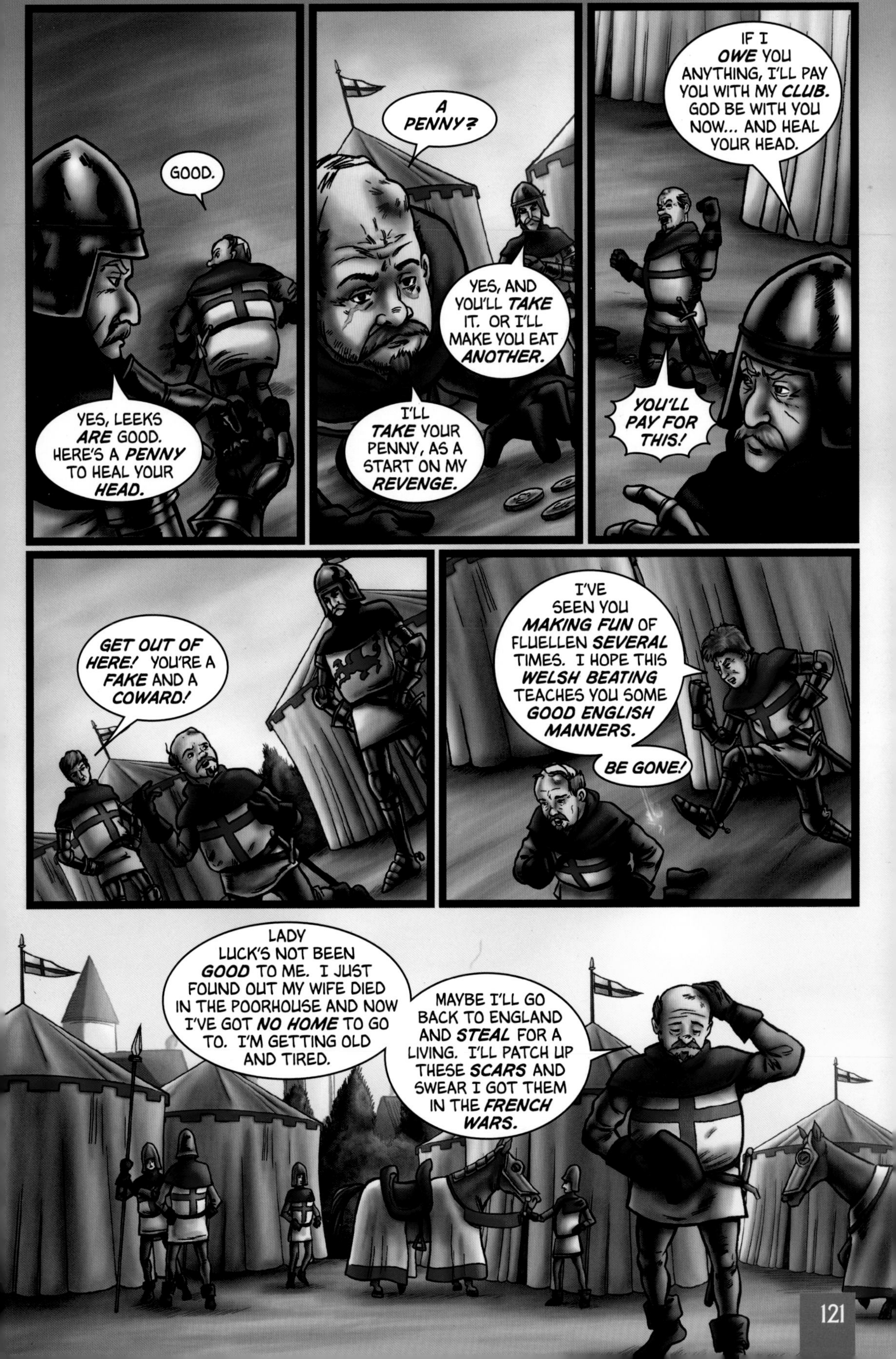
GOOD.
YES, LEEKS ARE GOOD. HERE'S A PENNY TO HEAL YOUR HEAD.
A PENNY?
YES, AND YOU'LL TAKE IT. OR I'LL MAKE YOU EAT ANOTHER.
I'LL TAKE YOUR PENNY, AS A START ON MY REVENGE.
IF I OWE YOU ANYTHING, I'LL PAY YOU WITH MY CLUB. GOD BE WITH YOU NOW... AND HEAL YOUR HEAD.
YOU'LL PAY FOR THIS!
GET OUT OF HERE! YOU'RE A FAKE AND A COWARD!
I'VE SEEN YOU MAKING FUN OF FLUELLEN SEVERAL TIMES. I HOPE THIS WELSH BEATING TEACHES YOU SOME GOOD ENGLISH MANNERS.
BE GONE!
LADY LUCK'S NOT BEEN GOOD TO ME. I JUST FOUND OUT MY WIFE DIED IN THE POORHOUSE AND NOW I'VE GOT NO HOME TO GO TO. I'M GETTING OLD AND TIRED.
MAYBE I'LL GO BACK TO ENGLAND AND STEAL FOR A LIVING. I'LL PATCH UP THESE SCARS AND SWEAR I GOT THEM IN THE FRENCH WARS.

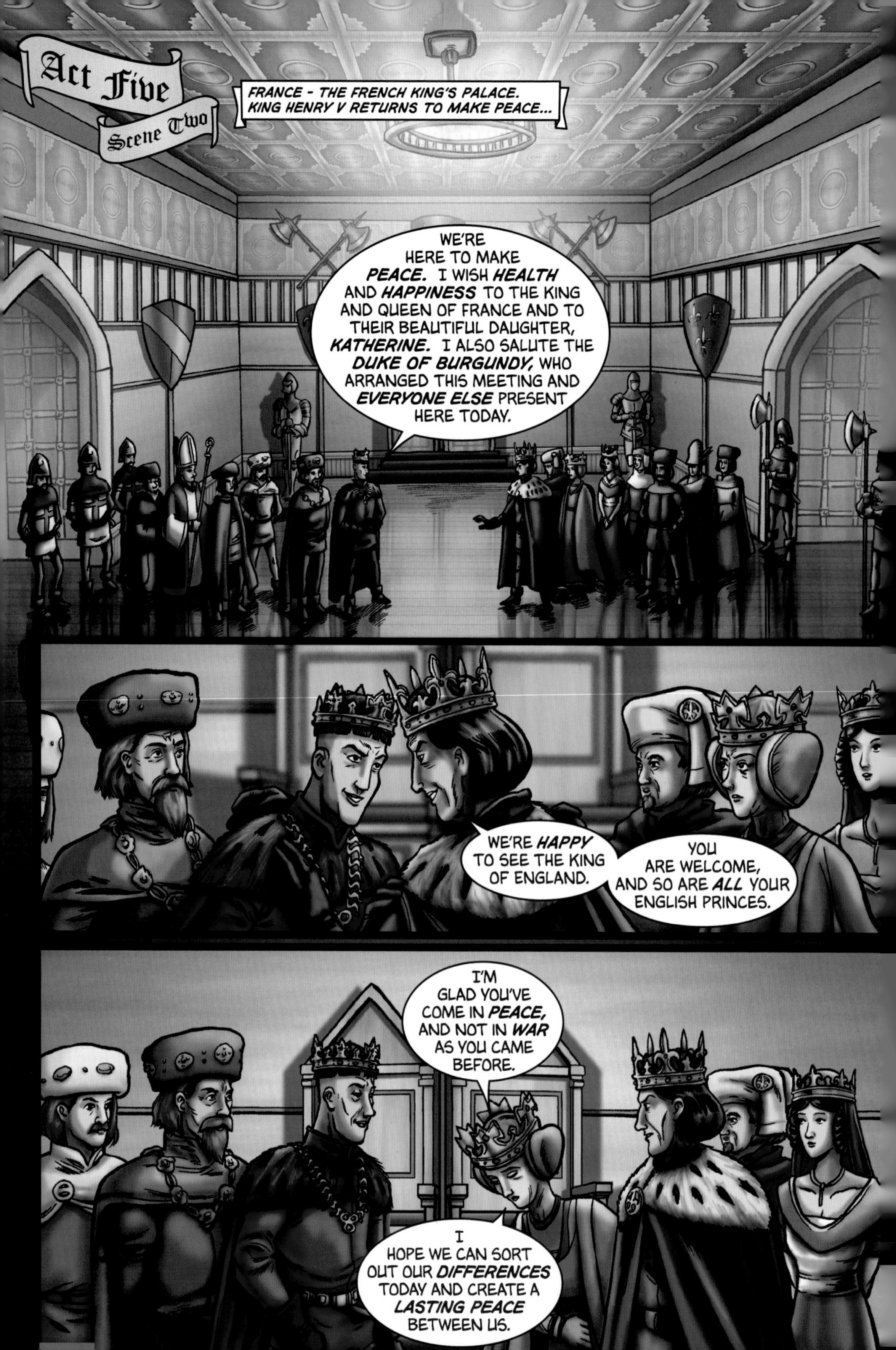
Act Five
Scene Two
FRANCE - THE FRENCH KING'S PALACE. KING HENRY V RETURNS TO MAKE PEACE...
WE'RE HERE TO MAKE PEACE. I WISH HEALTH AND HAPPINESS TO THE KING AND QUEEN OF FRANCE AND TO THEIR BEAUTIFUL DAUGHTER, KATHERINE. I ALSO SALUTE THE DUKE OF BURGUNDY, WHO ARRANGED THIS MEETING AND EVERYONE ELSE PRESENT HERE TODAY.
WE'RE HAPPY TO SEE THE KING OF ENGLAND.
YOU ARE WELCOME, AND SO ARE ALL YOUR ENGLISH PRINCES.
I'M GLAD YOU'VE COME IN PEACE, AND NOT IN WAR AS YOU CAME BEFORE.
I HOPE WE CAN SORT OUT OUR DIFFERENCES TODAY AND CREATE A LASTING PEACE BETWEEN US.

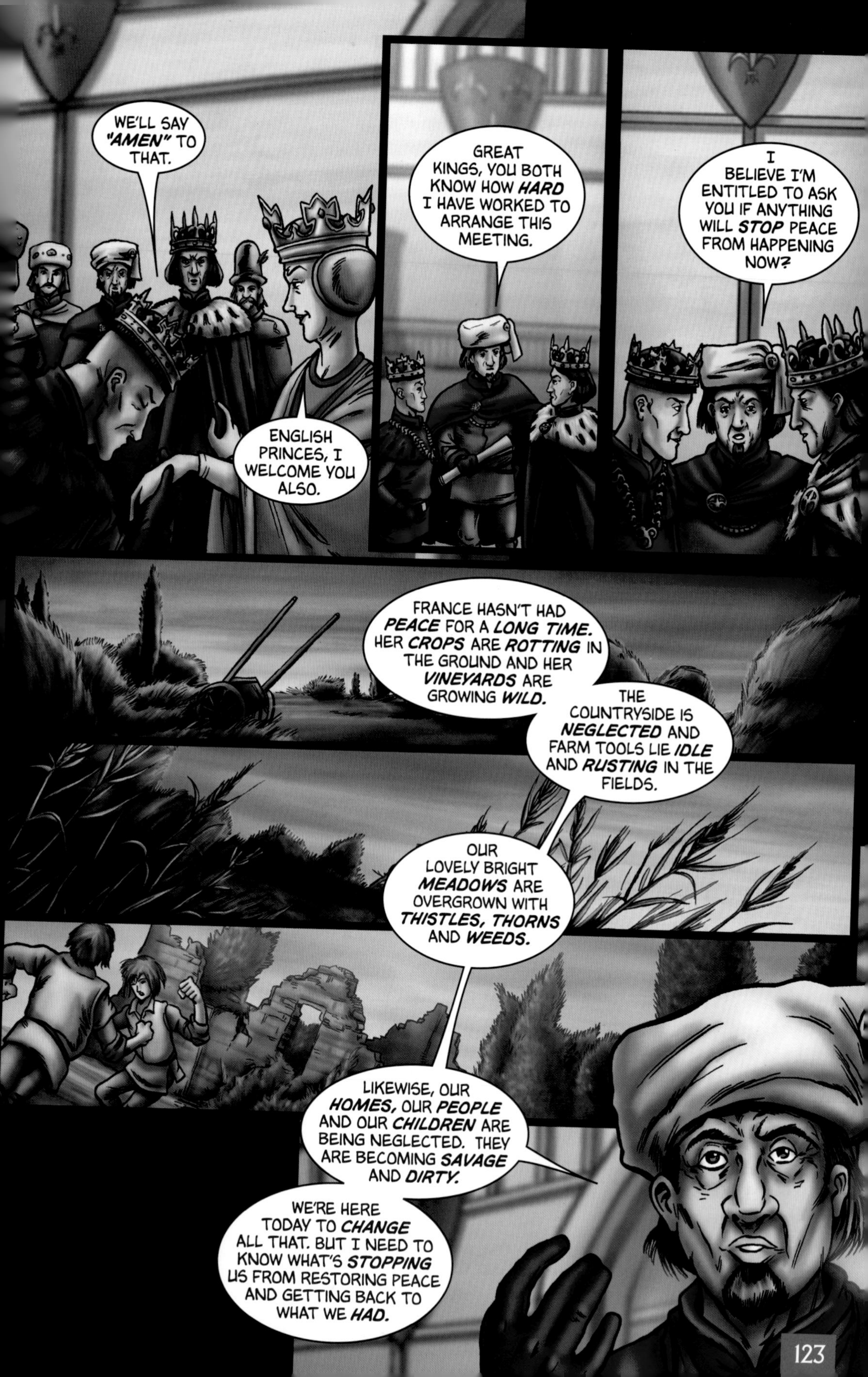
WE'LL SAY "AMEN" TO THAT.
ENGLISH PRINCES, I WELCOME YOU ALSO.
GREAT KINGS, YOU BOTH KNOW HOW HARD I HAVE WORKED TO ARRANGE THIS MEETING.
I BELIEVE I'M ENTITLED TO ASK YOU IF ANYTHING WILL STOP PEACE FROM HAPPENING NOW?
FRANCE HASN'T HAD PEACE FOR A LONG TIME. HER CROPS ARE ROTTING IN THE GROUND AND HER VINEYARDS ARE GROWING WILD.
THE COUNTRYSIDE IS NEGLECTED AND FARM TOOLS LIE IDLE AND RUSTING IN THE FIELDS.
OUR LOVELY BRIGHT MEADOWS ARE OVERGROWN WITH THISTLES, THORNS AND WEEDS.
LIKEWISE, OUR HOMES, OUR PEOPLE AND OUR CHILDREN ARE BEING NEGLECTED. THEY ARE BECOMING SAVAGE AND DIRTY.
WE'RE HERE TODAY TO CHANGE ALL THAT. BUT I NEED TO KNOW WHAT'S STOPPING US FROM RESTORING PEACE AND GETTING BACK TO WHAT WE HAD.

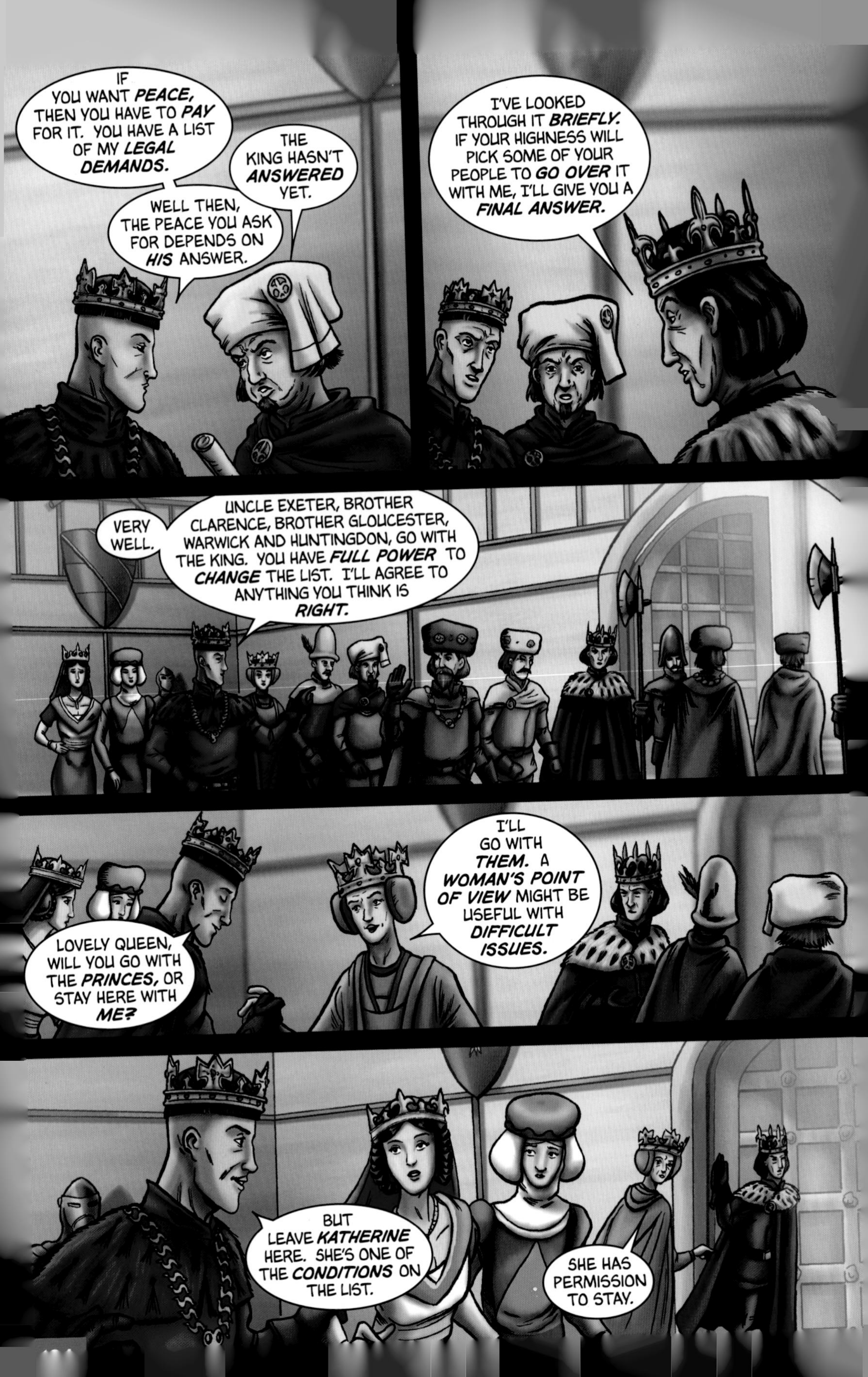
IF YOU WANT PEACE, THEN YOU HAVE TO PAY FOR IT. YOU HAVE A LIST OF MY LEGAL DEMANDS.
THE KING HASN'T ANSWERED YET.
WELL THEN, THE PEACE YOU ASK FOR DEPENDS ON HIS ANSWER.
I'VE LOOKED THROUGH IT BRIEFLY. IF YOUR HIGHNESS WILL PICK SOME OF YOUR PEOPLE TO GO OVER IT WITH ME, I'LL GIVE YOU A FINAL ANSWER.
VERY WELL.
UNCLE EXETER, BROTHER CLARENCE, BROTHER GLOUCESTER, WARWICK AND HUNTINGDON, GO WITH THE KING. YOU HAVE FULL POWER TO CHANGE THE LIST. I'LL AGREE TO ANYTHING YOU THINK IS RIGHT.
LOVELY QUEEN, WILL YOU GO WITH THE PRINCES, OR STAY HERE WITH ME?
I'LL GO WITH THEM. A WOMAN'S POINT OF VIEW MIGHT BE USEFUL WITH DIFFICULT ISSUES.
BUT LEAVE KATHERINE HERE. SHE'S ONE OF THE CONDITIONS ON THE LIST.
SHE HAS PERMISSION TO STAY.

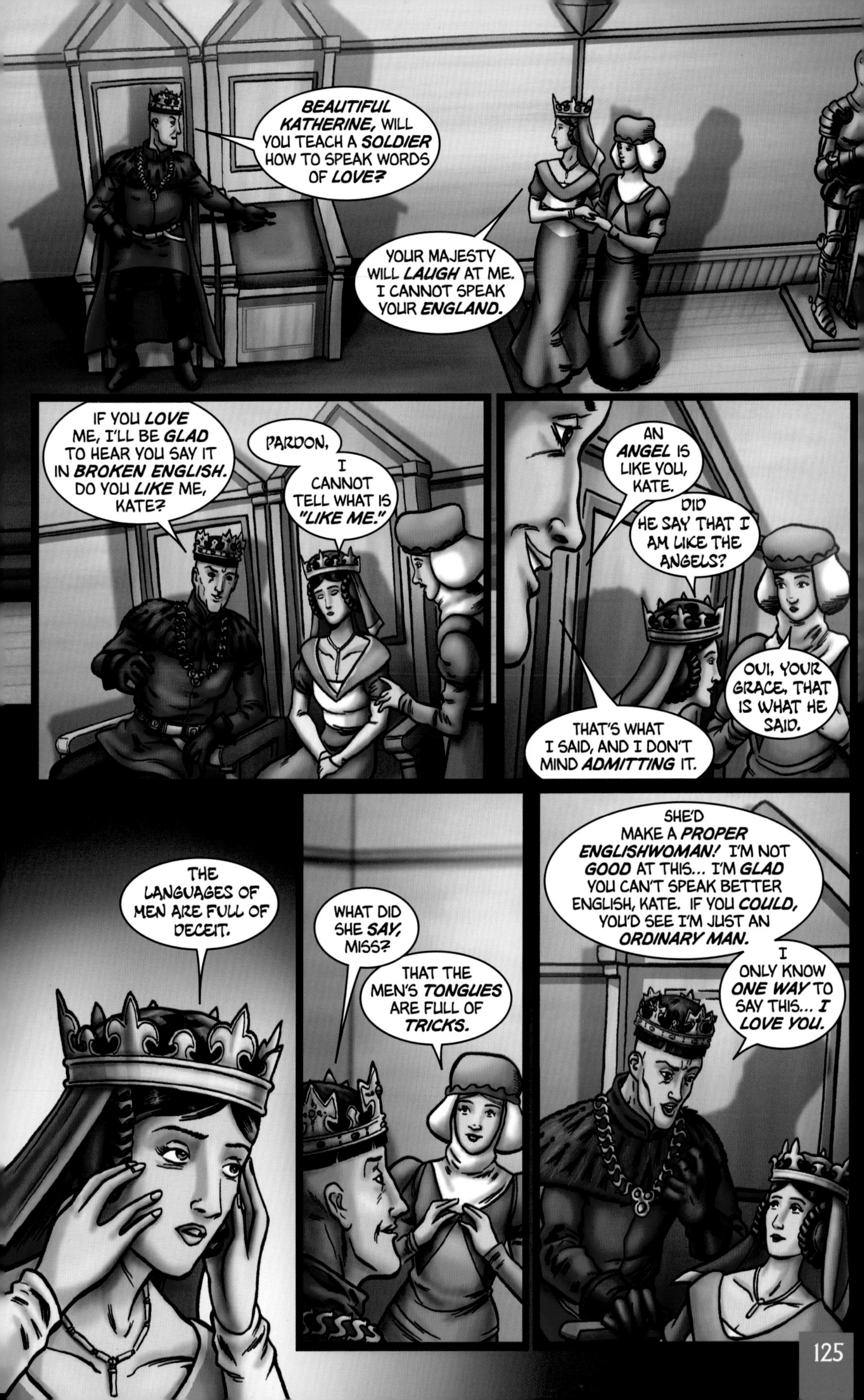
BEAUTIFUL KATHERINE, WILL YOU TEACH A SOLDIER HOW TO SPEAK WORDS OF LOVE?
YOUR MAJESTY WILL LAUGH AT ME. I CANNOT SPEAK YOUR ENGLAND.
IF YOU LOVE ME, I'LL BE GLAD TO HEAR YOU SAY IT IN BROKEN ENGLISH. DO YOU LIKE ME, KATE?
PARDON,
I CANNOT TELL WHAT IS "LIKE ME."
AN ANGEL IS LIKE YOU, KATE.
DID HE SAY THAT I AM LIKE THE ANGELS?
OUI, YOUR GRACE, THAT IS WHAT HE SAID.
THAT'S WHAT I SAID, AND I DON'T MIND ADMITTING IT.
THE LANGUAGES OF MEN ARE FULL OF DECEIT.
WHAT DID SHE SAY, MISS?
THAT THE MEN'S TONGUES ARE FULL OF TRICKS.
SHE'D MAKE A PROPER ENGLISHWOMAN! I'M NOT GOOD AT THIS... I'M GLAD YOU CAN'T SPEAK BETTER ENGLISH, KATE. IF YOU COULD, YOU'D SEE I'M JUST AN ORDINARY MAN.
I ONLY KNOW ONE WAY TO SAY THIS... I LOVE YOU.

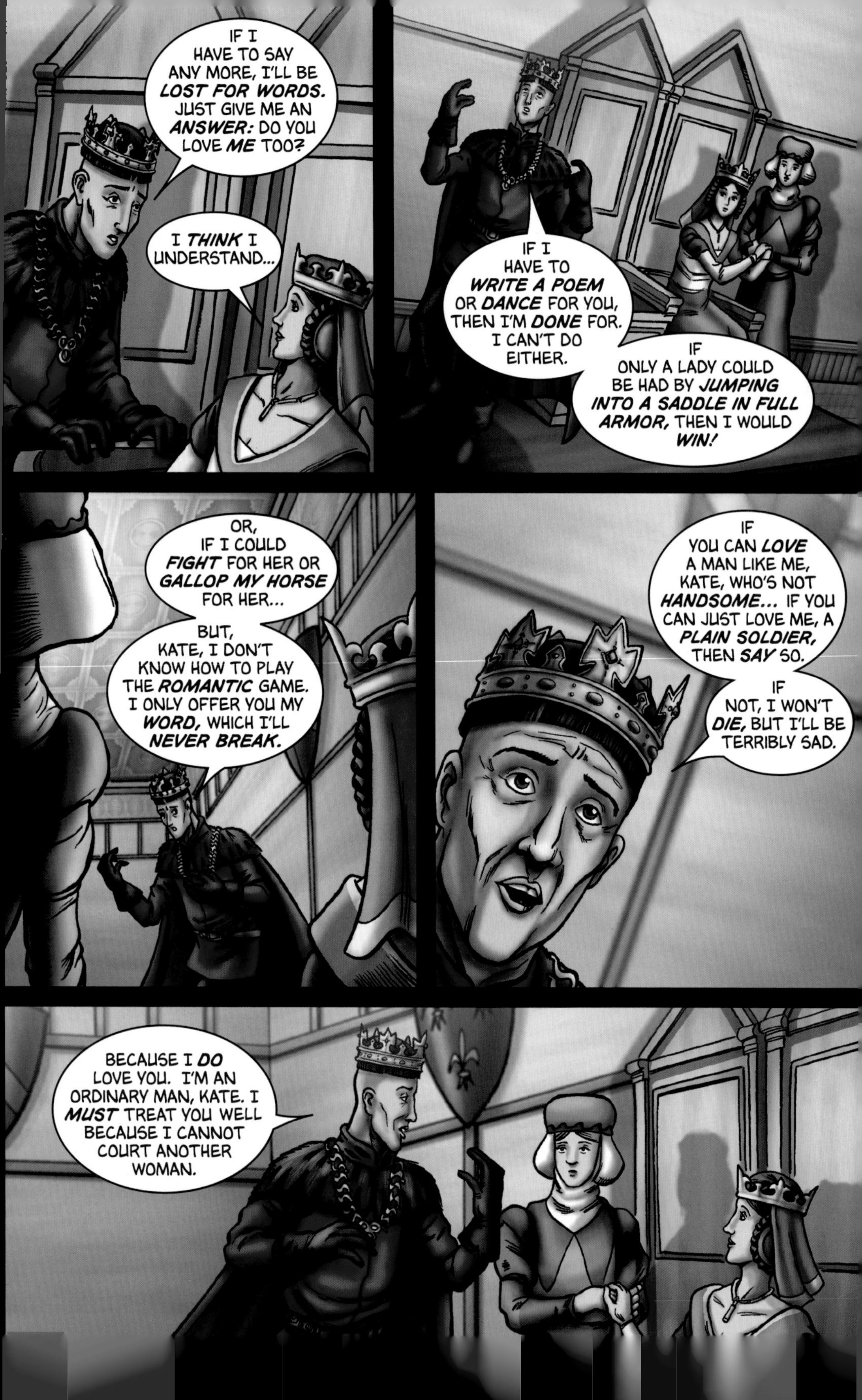
IF I HAVE TO SAY ANY MORE, I'LL BE LOST FOR WORDS. JUST GIVE ME AN ANSWER: DO YOU LOVE ME TOO?
I THINK I UNDERSTAND...
IF I HAVE TO WRITE A POEM OR DANCE FOR YOU, THEN I'M DONE FOR. I CAN'T DO EITHER.
IF ONLY A LADY COULD BE HAD BY JUMPING INTO A SADDLE IN FULL ARMOR, THEN I WOULD WIN!
OR, IF I COULD FIGHT FOR HER OR GALLOP MY HORSE FOR HER...
BUT, KATE, I DON'T KNOW HOW TO PLAY THE ROMANTIC GAME. I ONLY OFFER YOU MY WORD, WHICH I'LL NEVER BREAK.
IF YOU CAN LOVE A MAN LIKE ME, KATE, WHO'S NOT HANDSOME... IF YOU CAN JUST LOVE ME, A PLAIN SOLDIER, THEN SAY SO.
IF NOT, I WON'T DIE, BUT I'LL BE TERRIBLY SAD.
BECAUSE I DO LOVE YOU. I'M AN ORDINARY MAN, KATE. I MUST TREAT YOU WELL BECAUSE I CANNOT COURT ANOTHER WOMAN.

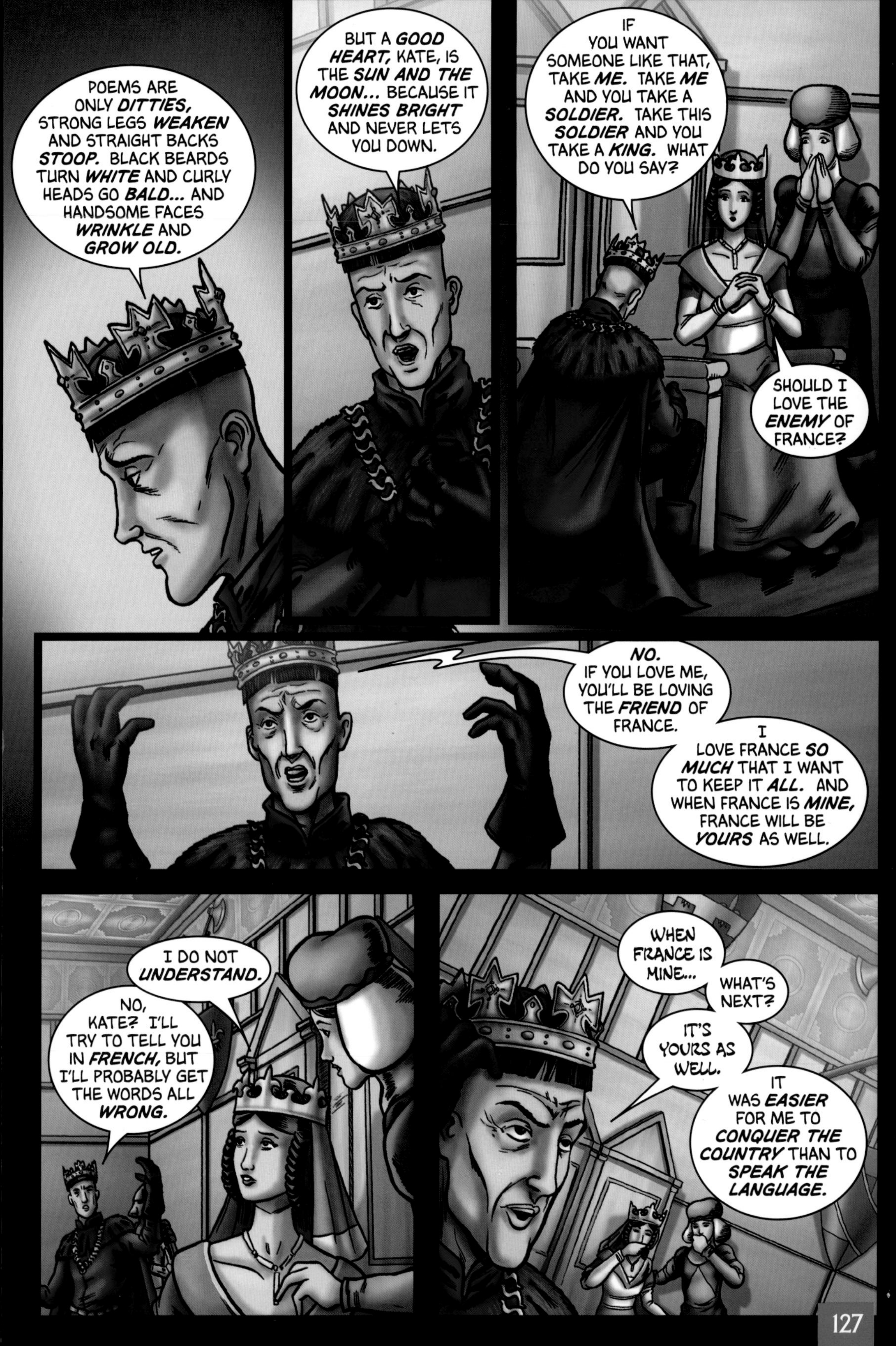
POEMS ARE ONLY DITTIES, STRONG LEGS WEAKEN AND STRAIGHT BACKS STOOP. BLACK BEARDS TURN WHITE AND CURLY HEADS GO BALD... AND HANDSOME FACES WRINKLE AND GROW OLD.
BUT A GOOD HEART, KATE, IS THE SUN AND THE MOON... BECAUSE IT SHINES BRIGHT AND NEVER LETS YOU DOWN.
IF YOU WANT SOMEONE LIKE THAT, TAKE ME. TAKE ME AND YOU TAKE A SOLDIER. TAKE THIS SOLDIER AND YOU TAKE A KING. WHAT DO YOU SAY?
SHOULD I LOVE THE ENEMY OF FRANCE?
NO. IF YOU LOVE ME, YOU'LL BE LOVING THE FRIEND OF FRANCE.
I LOVE FRANCE SO MUCH THAT I WANT TO KEEP IT ALL. AND WHEN FRANCE IS MINE, FRANCE WILL BE YOURS AS WELL.
I DO NOT UNDERSTAND.
NO, KATE? I'LL TRY TO TELL YOU IN FRENCH, BUT I'LL PROBABLY GET THE WORDS ALL WRONG.
WHEN FRANCE IS MINE...
WHAT'S NEXT?
IT'S YOURS AS WELL.
IT WAS EASIER FOR ME TO CONQUER THE COUNTRY THAN TO SPEAK THE LANGUAGE.

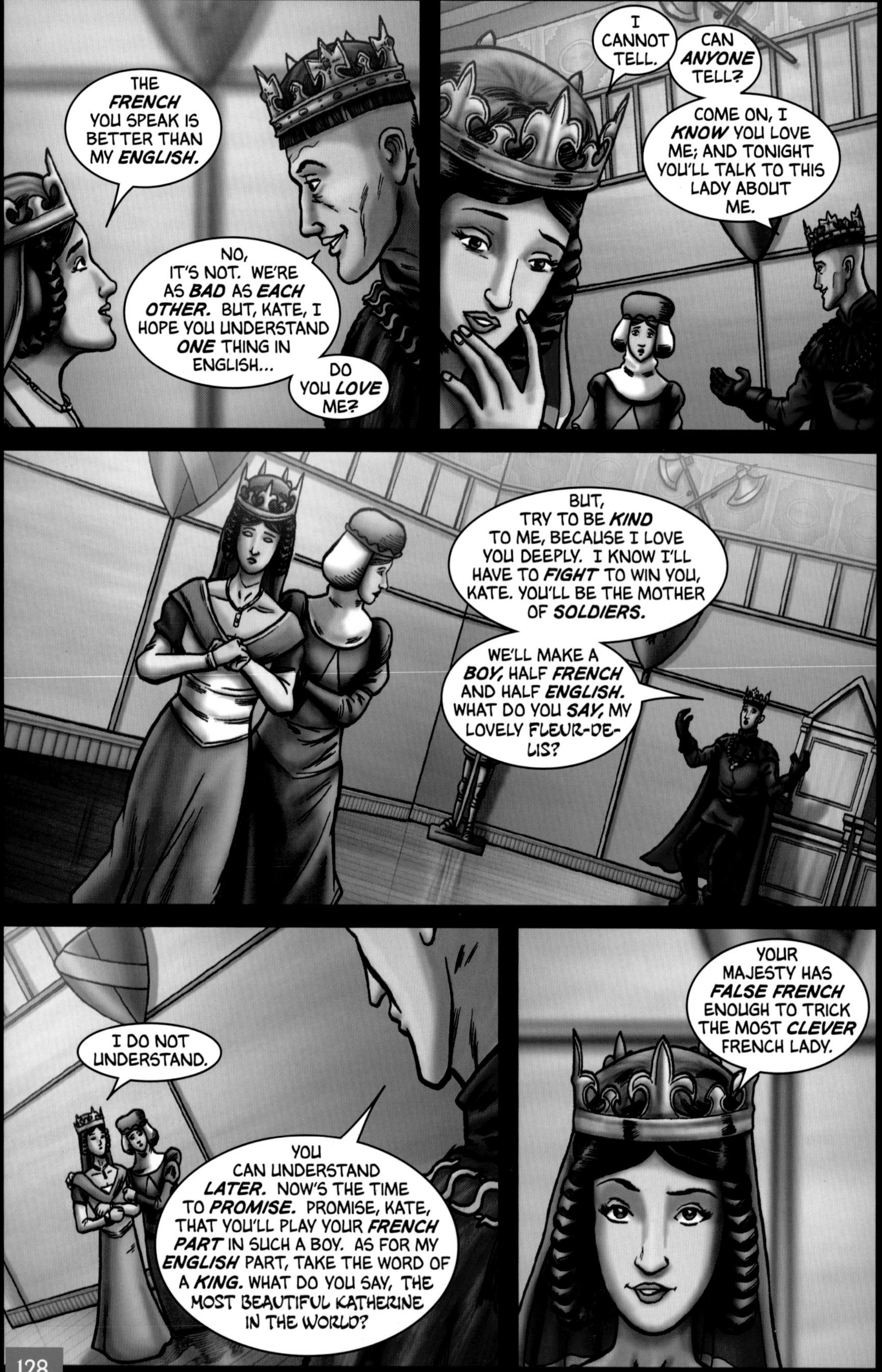
THE FRENCH YOU SPEAK IS BETTER THAN MY ENGLISH.
NO, IT'S NOT. WE'RE AS BAD AS EACH OTHER. BUT, KATE, I HOPE YOU UNDERSTAND ONE THING IN ENGLISH...
DO YOU LOVE ME?
I CANNOT TELL.
CAN ANYONE TELL?
COME ON, I KNOW YOU LOVE ME; AND TONIGHT YOU'LL TALK TO THIS LADY ABOUT ME.
BUT, TRY TO BE KIND TO ME, BECAUSE I LOVE YOU DEEPLY. I KNOW I'LL HAVE TO FIGHT TO WIN YOU, KATE. YOU'LL BE THE MOTHER OF SOLDIERS.
WE'LL MAKE A BOY, HALF FRENCH AND HALF ENGLISH. WHAT DO YOU SAY, MY LOVELY FLEUR-DE-LIS?
I DO NOT UNDERSTAND.
YOU CAN UNDERSTAND LATER. NOW'S THE TIME TO PROMISE. PROMISE, KATE, THAT YOU'LL PLAY YOUR FRENCH PART IN SUCH A BOY. AS FOR MY ENGLISH PART, TAKE THE WORD OF A KING. WHAT DO YOU SAY, THE MOST BEAUTIFUL KATHERINE IN THE WORLD?
YOUR MAJESTY HAS FALSE FRENCH ENOUGH TO TRICK THE MOST CLEVER FRENCH LADY.

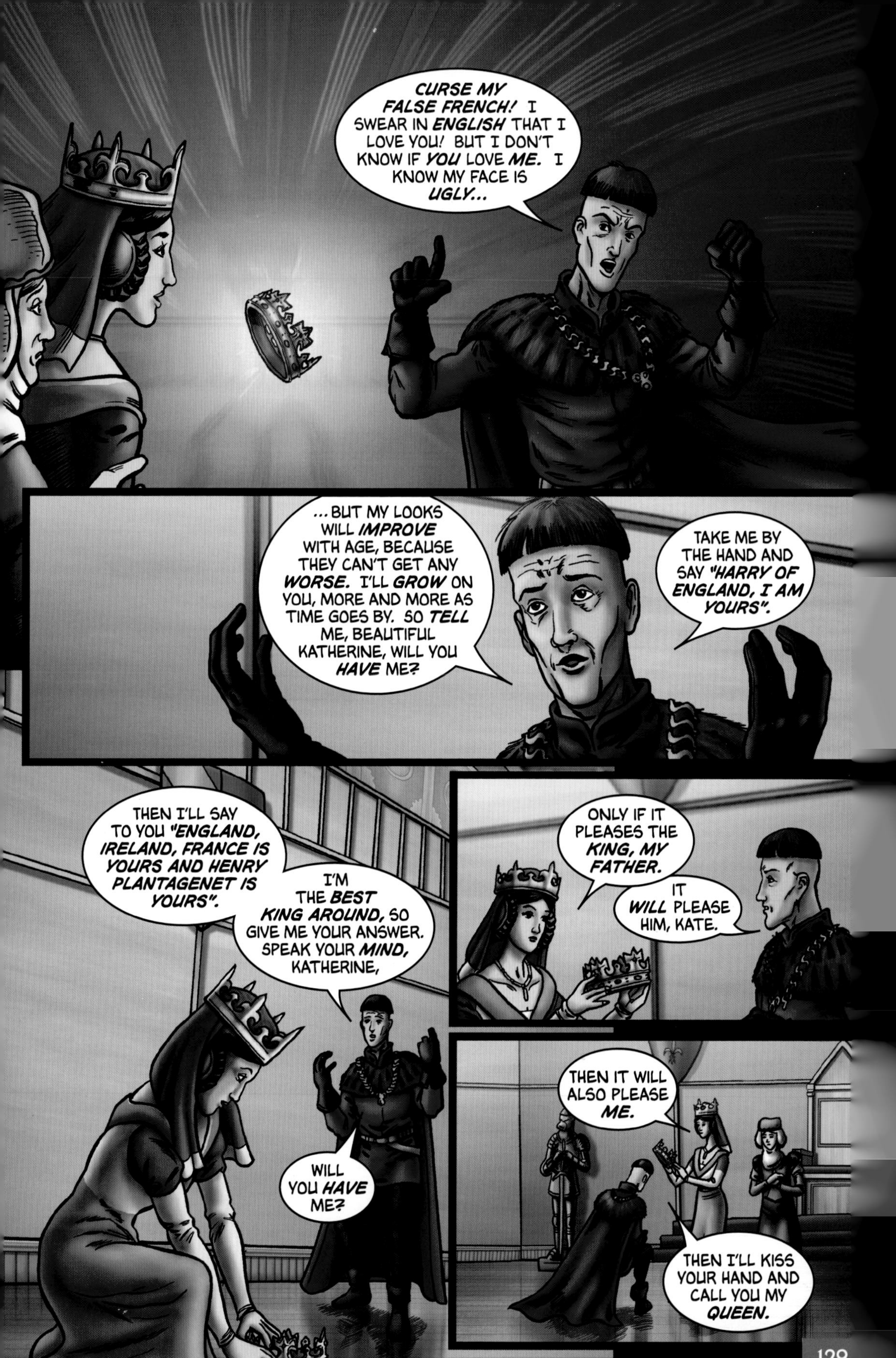
CURSE MY FALSE FRENCH! I SWEAR IN ENGLISH THAT I LOVE YOU! BUT I DON'T KNOW IF YOU LOVE ME. I KNOW MY FACE IS UGLY...
...BUT MY LOOKS WILL IMPROVE WITH AGE, BECAUSE THEY CAN'T GET ANY WORSE. I'LL GROW ON YOU, MORE AND MORE AS TIME GOES BY. SO TELL ME, BEAUTIFUL KATHERINE, WILL YOU HAVE ME?
TAKE ME BY THE HAND AND SAY "HARRY OF ENGLAND, I AM YOURS".
THEN I'LL SAY TO YOU "ENGLAND, IRELAND, FRANCE IS YOURS AND HENRY PLANTAGENET IS YOURS".
I'M THE BEST KING AROUND, SO GIVE ME YOUR ANSWER. SPEAK YOUR MIND, KATHERINE,
WILL YOU HAVE ME?
ONLY IF IT PLEASES THE KING, MY FATHER.
IT WILL PLEASE HIM, KATE.
THEN IT WILL ALSO PLEASE ME.
THEN I'LL KISS YOUR HAND AND CALL YOU MY QUEEN.

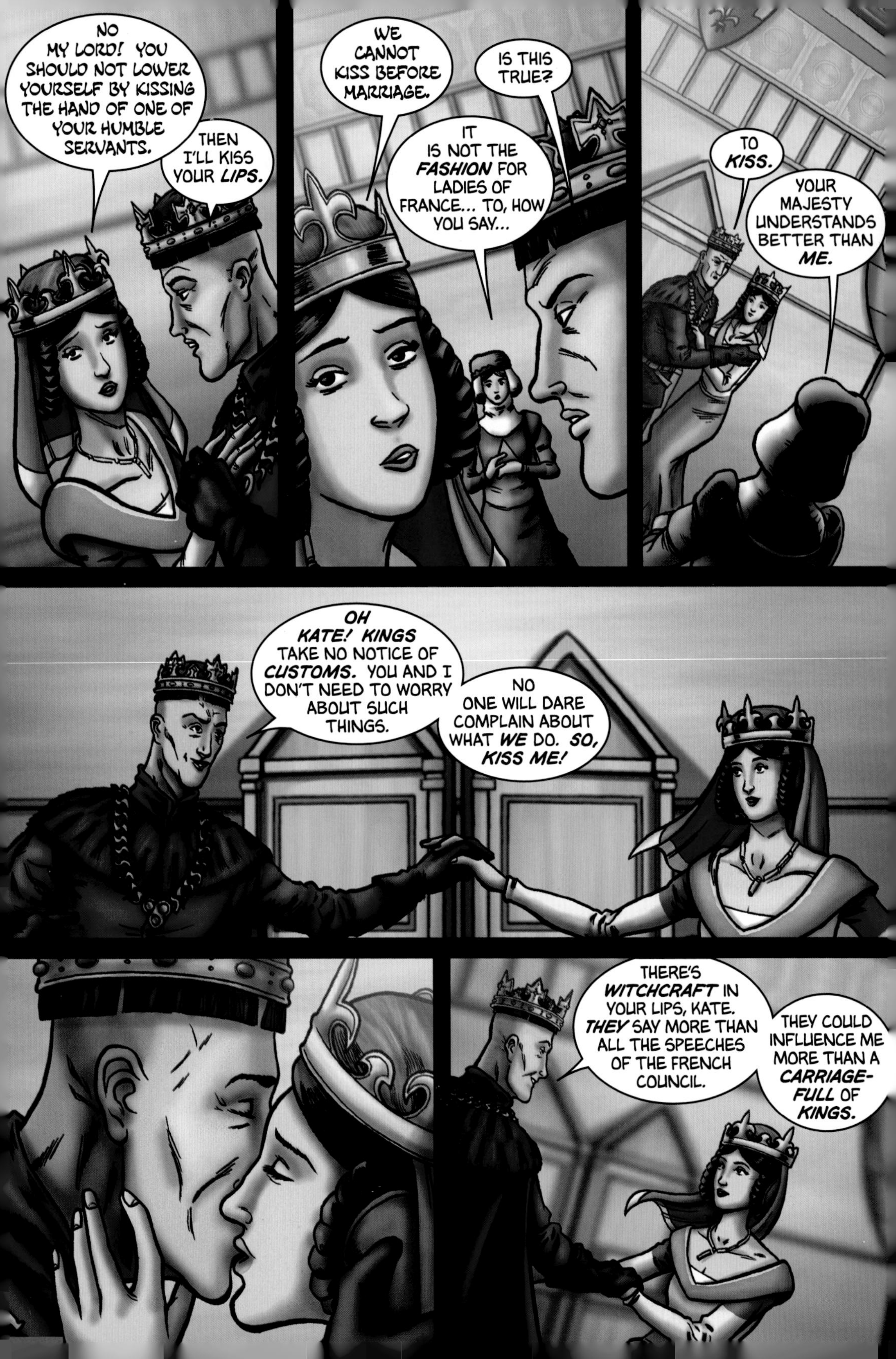
NO MY LORD! YOU SHOULD NOT LOWER YOURSELF BY KISSING THE HAND OF ONE OF YOUR HUMBLE SERVANTS.
THEN I'LL KISS YOUR LIPS.
WE CANNOT KISS BEFORE MARRIAGE.
IS THIS TRUE?
IT IS NOT THE FASHION FOR LADIES OF FRANCE... TO, HOW YOU SAY...
TO KISS.
YOUR MAJESTY UNDERSTANDS BETTER THAN ME.
OH KATE! KINGS TAKE NO NOTICE OF CUSTOMS. YOU AND I DON'T NEED TO WORRY ABOUT SUCH THINGS.
NO ONE WILL DARE COMPLAIN ABOUT WHAT WE DO. SO, KISS ME!
THERE'S WITCHCRAFT IN YOUR LIPS, KATE. THEY SAY MORE THAN ALL THE SPEECHES OF THE FRENCH COUNCIL.
THEY COULD INFLUENCE ME MORE THAN A CARRIAGE-FULL OF KINGS.

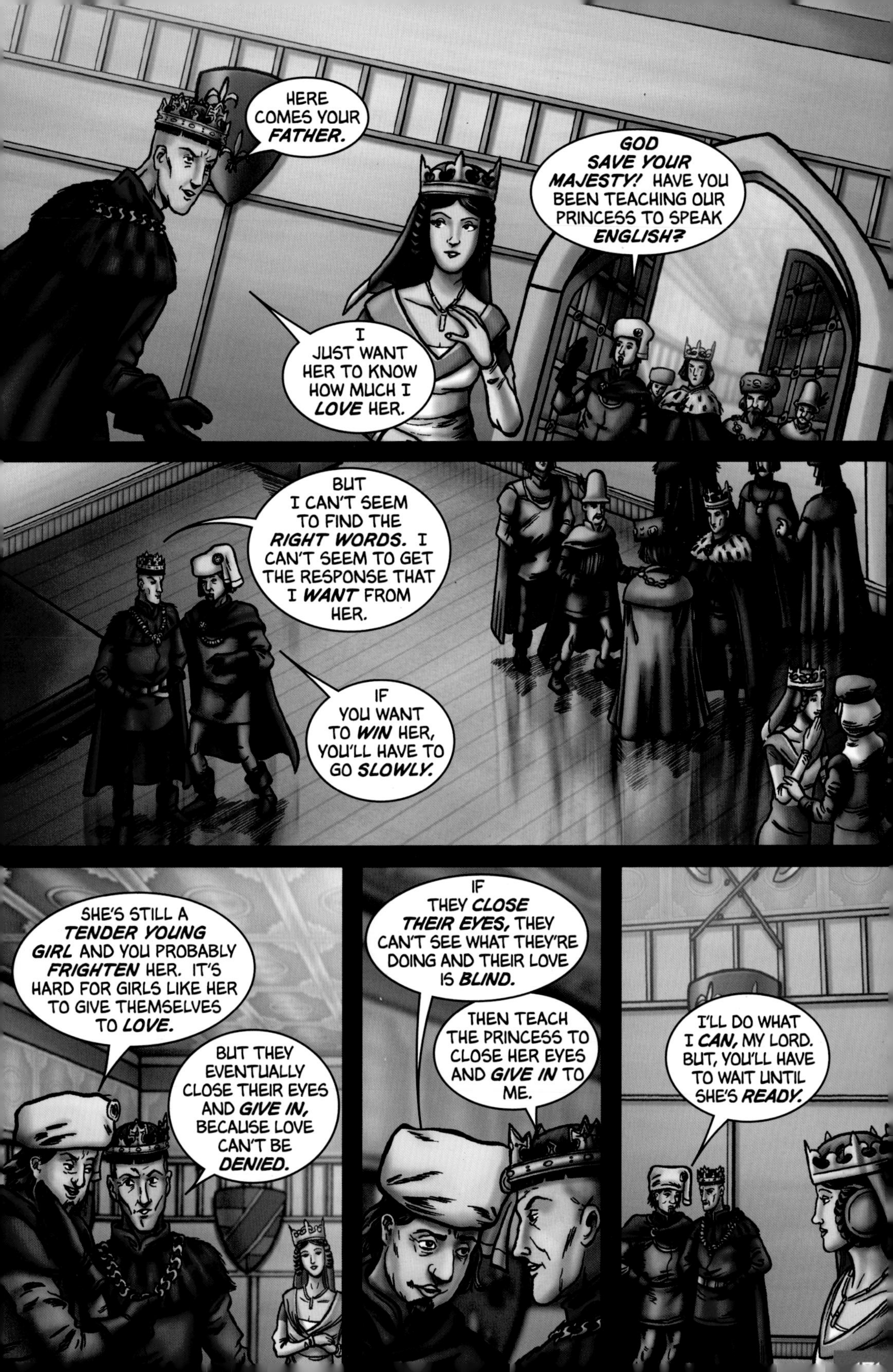
HERE COMES YOUR FATHER.
GOD SAVE YOUR MAJESTY! HAVE YOU BEEN TEACHING OUR PRINCESS TO SPEAK ENGLISH?
I JUST WANT HER TO KNOW HOW MUCH I LOVE HER.
BUT I CAN'T SEEM TO FIND THE RIGHT WORDS. I CAN'T SEEM TO GET THE RESPONSE THAT I WANT FROM HER.
IF YOU WANT TO WIN HER, YOU'LL HAVE TO GO SLOWLY.
SHE'S STILL A TENDER YOUNG GIRL AND YOU PROBABLY FRIGHTEN HER. IT'S HARD FOR GIRLS LIKE HER TO GIVE THEMSELVES TO LOVE.
BUT THEY EVENTUALLY CLOSE THEIR EYES AND GIVE IN, BECAUSE LOVE CAN'T BE DENIED.
IF THEY CLOSE THEIR EYES, THEY CAN'T SEE WHAT THEY'RE DOING AND THEIR LOVE IS BLIND.
THEN TEACH THE PRINCESS TO CLOSE HER EYES AND GIVE IN TO ME.
I'LL DO WHAT I CAN, MY LORD. BUT, YOU'LL HAVE TO WAIT UNTIL SHE'S READY.

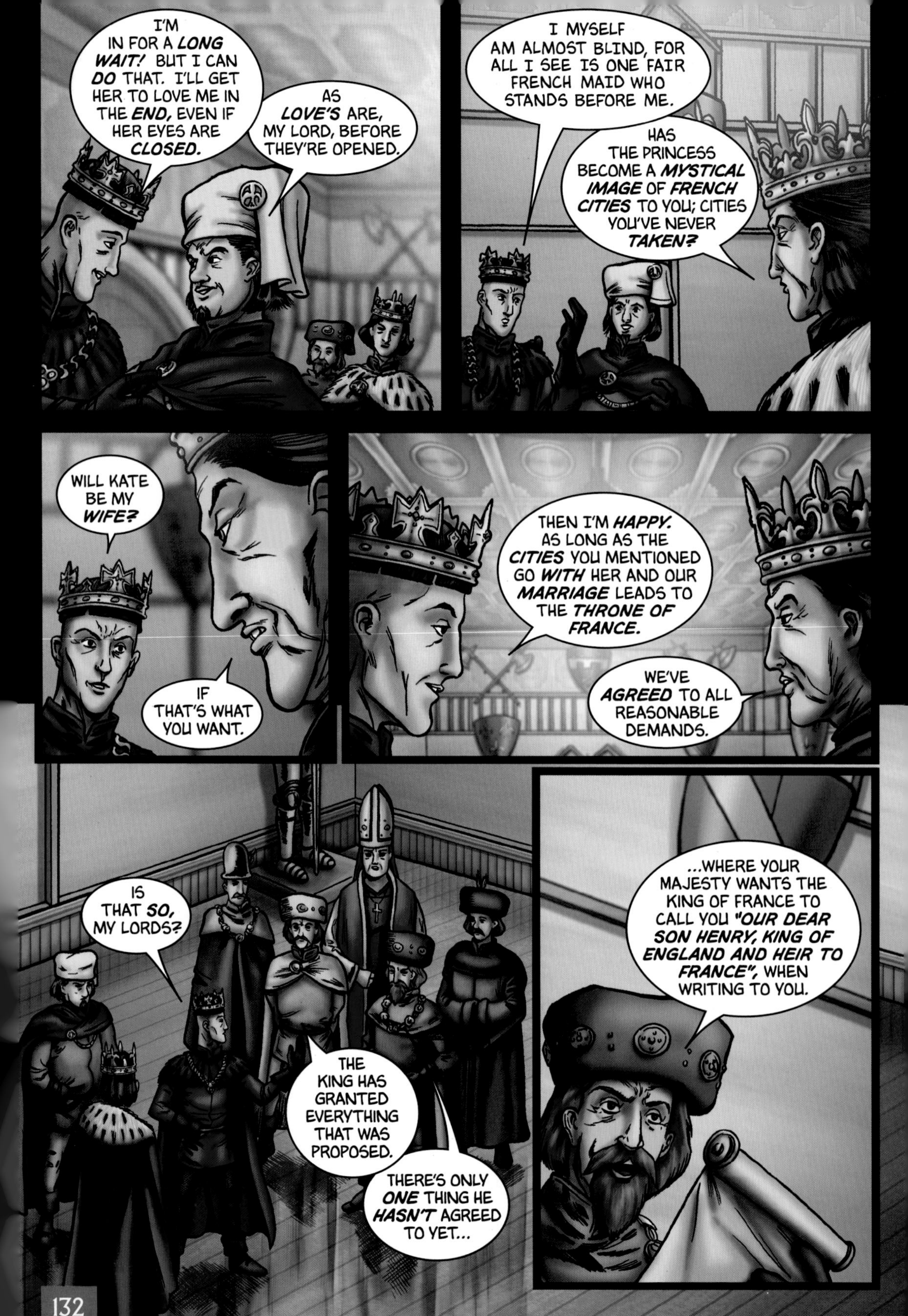
I'M IN FOR A LONG WAIT! BUT I CAN DO THAT. I'LL GET HER TO LOVE ME IN THE END, EVEN IF HER EYES ARE CLOSED.
AS LOVE'S ARE, MY LORD, BEFORE THEY'RE OPENED.
I MYSELF AM ALMOST BLIND, FOR ALL I SEE IS ONE FAIR FRENCH MAID WHO STANDS BEFORE ME.
HAS THE PRINCESS BECOME A MYSTICAL IMAGE OF FRENCH CITIES TO YOU; CITIES YOU'VE NEVER TAKEN?
WILL KATE BE MY WIFE?
IF THAT'S WHAT YOU WANT.
THEN I'M HAPPY. AS LONG AS THE CITIES YOU MENTIONED GO WITH HER AND OUR MARRIAGE LEADS TO THE THRONE OF FRANCE.
WE'VE AGREED TO ALL REASONABLE DEMANDS.
IS THAT SO, MY LORDS?
THE KING HAS GRANTED EVERYTHING THAT WAS PROPOSED.
THERE'S ONLY ONE THING HE HASN'T AGREED TO YET...
...WHERE YOUR MAJESTY WANTS THE KING OF FRANCE TO CALL YOU "OUR DEAR SON HENRY, KING OF ENGLAND AND HEIR TO FRANCE", WHEN WRITING TO YOU.

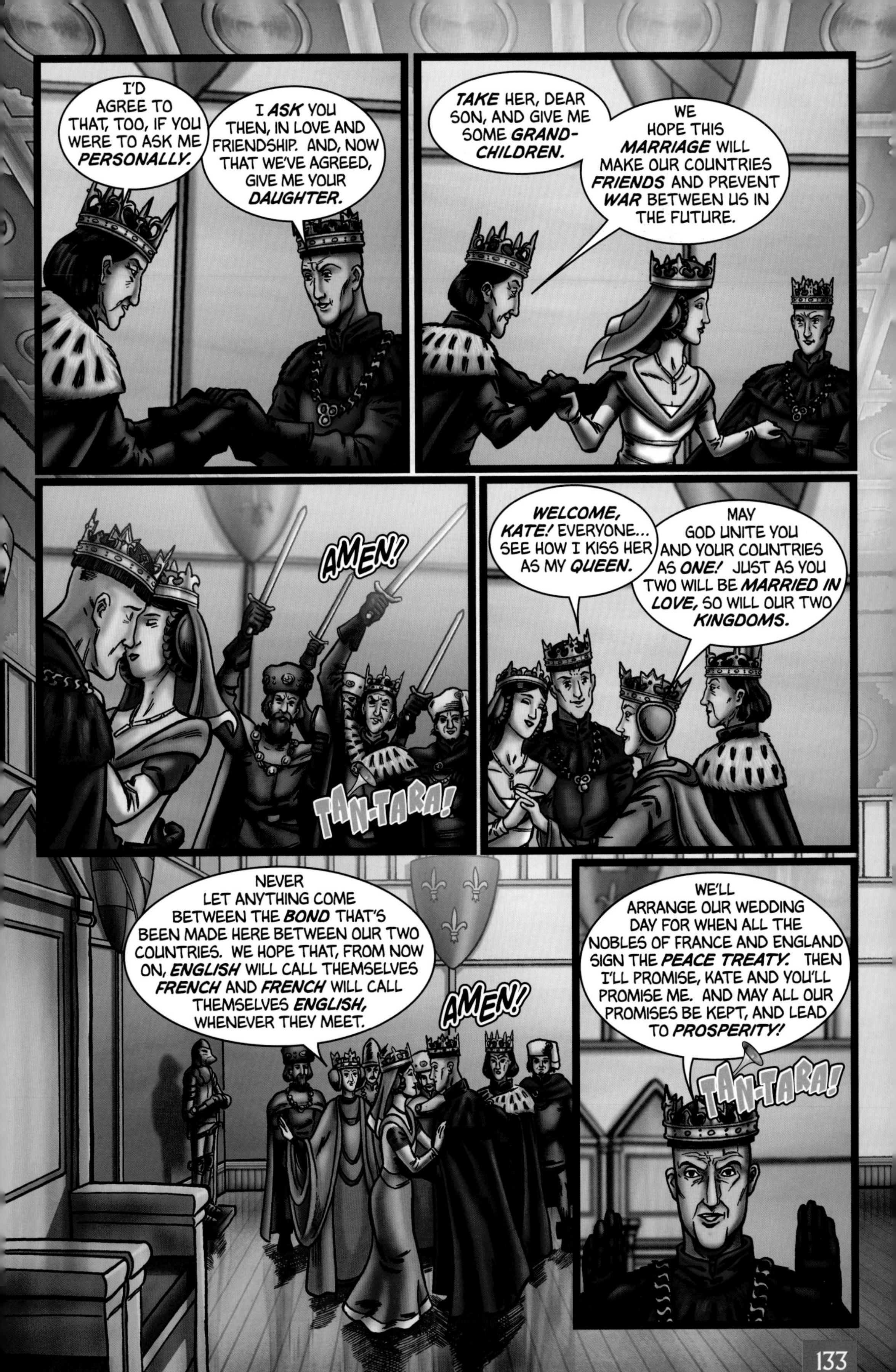
I'D AGREE TO THAT, TOO, IF YOU WERE TO ASK ME PERSONALLY.
I ASK YOU THEN, IN LOVE AND FRIENDSHIP. AND, NOW THAT WE'VE AGREED, GIVE ME YOUR DAUGHTER.
TAKE HER, DEAR SON, AND GIVE ME SOME GRAND-CHILDREN.
WE HOPE THIS MARRIAGE WILL MAKE OUR COUNTRIES FRIENDS AND PREVENT WAR BETWEEN US IN THE FUTURE.
AMEN!
TAN-TARA!
WELCOME, KATE! EVERYONE... SEE HOW I KISS HER AS MY QUEEN.
MAY GOD UNITE YOU AND YOUR COUNTRIES AS ONE! JUST AS YOU TWO WILL BE MARRIED IN LOVE, SO WILL OUR TWO KINGDOMS.
NEVER LET ANYTHING COME BETWEEN THE BOND THAT'S BEEN MADE HERE BETWEEN OUR TWO COUNTRIES. WE HOPE THAT, FROM NOW ON, ENGLISH WILL CALL THEMSELVES FRENCH AND FRENCH WILL CALL THEMSELVES ENGLISH, WHENEVER THEY MEET.
AMEN!
WE'LL ARRANGE OUR WEDDING DAY FOR WHEN ALL THE NOBLES OF FRANCE AND ENGLAND SIGN THE PEACE TREATY. THEN I'LL PROMISE, KATE AND YOU'LL PROMISE ME. AND MAY ALL OUR PROMISES BE KEPT, AND LEAD TO PROSPERITY!
TAN-TARA!

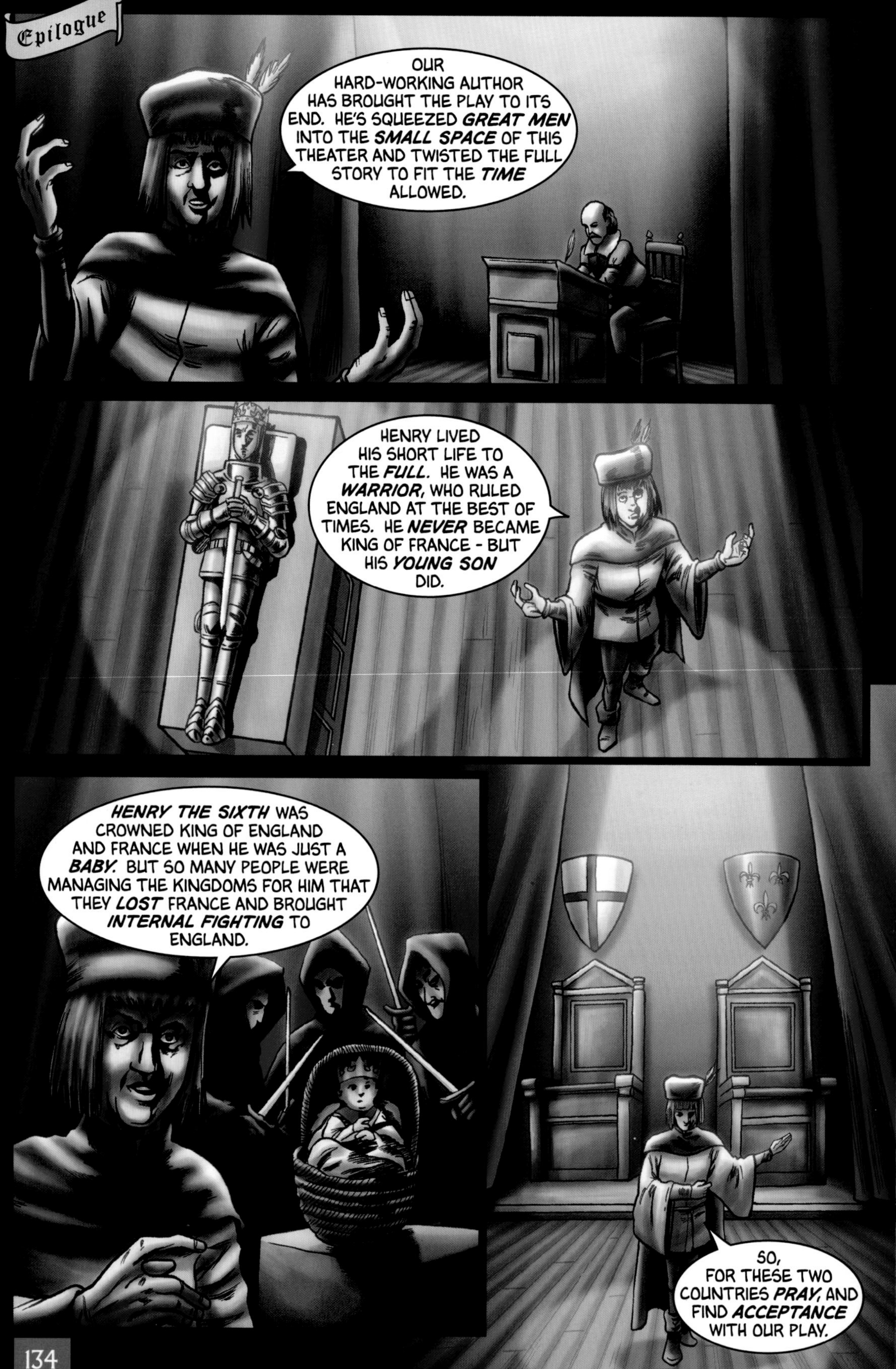
Epilogue
OUR HARD-WORKING AUTHOR HAS BROUGHT THE PLAY TO ITS END. HE'S SQUEEZED GREAT MEN INTO THE SMALL SPACE OF THIS THEATER AND TWISTED THE FULL STORY TO FIT THE TIME ALLOWED.
HENRY LIVED HIS SHORT LIFE TO THE FULL. HE WAS A WARRIOR, WHO RULED ENGLAND AT THE BEST OF TIMES. HE NEVER BECAME KING OF FRANCE - BUT HIS YOUNG SON DID.
HENRY THE SIXTH WAS CROWNED KING OF ENGLAND AND FRANCE WHEN HE WAS JUST A BABY. BUT SO MANY PEOPLE WERE MANAGING THE KINGDOMS FOR HIM THAT THEY LOST FRANCE AND BROUGHT INTERNAL FIGHTING TO ENGLAND.
SO, FOR THESE TWO COUNTRIES PRAY, AND FIND ACCEPTANCE WITH OUR PLAY.

Henry V

End

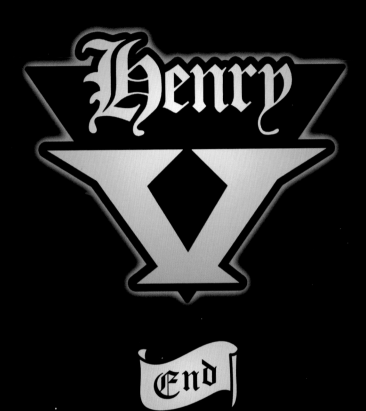

William Shakespeare

(c.1564 - 1616 AD)

National Portrait Gallery, London

William Shakespeare is one of the most widely read authors and possibly the best dramatist ever to live. The actual date of his birth is not known, but April 23rd 1564 (St George's Day) has traditionally been his accepted birthday, as this was three days before his baptism. He died on the same date in 1616, at the age of fifty-two.

The life of William Shakespeare can be divided into three acts. The first twenty years of his life were spent in Stratford-upon-Avon, where he grew up, went to school, got married and became a father. The next twenty-five years he spent as an actor and playwright in London. He spent his last few years back in Stratford-upon-Avon, where he enjoyed his retirement in moderate wealth gained from his successful years in the theater.

William, the third of eight children, was the eldest son of tradesman John Shakespeare and Mary Arden. His father was later elected mayor of Stratford, which was the highest post a man in civic politics could attain. In sixteenth-century England, William was lucky to survive into adulthood: syphilis, scurvy, smallpox, tuberculosis, typhus and dysentery shortened life expectancy at the time to approximately thirty-five years. The Bubonic Plague took the lives of many and was believed to have been the cause of death for three of William's seven siblings.

Little is known of William's childhood, but he is thought to have attended the local grammar school, where he studied Latin and English Literature. In 1582, at the age of eighteen, William married a local farmer's daughter, Anne Hathaway, who was eight years his senior and three months pregnant. During their marriage they had three children: Susanna, born on May 26th 1583, and twins, Hamnet and Judith, born on February 2nd 1585. Hamnet, William's only son, caught Bubonic Plague and died at the age of eleven.

Five years into his marriage, William moved to London and appeared in many small parts at The Globe Theatre, then one of the biggest theaters in England. His first appearance in public as a poet was in 1593 with *Venus and Adonis* and again in the following year with *The Rape of Lucrece*. Six years later, in 1599, he became joint proprietor of The Globe Theatre.

When Queen Elizabeth died in 1603, she was succeeded by her cousin King James of Scotland. King James supported Shakespeare and his band of actors and gave them license to call themselves "The King's Men" in return for entertaining the court.

In just twenty-three years, between 1590 and 1613, William Shakespeare is attributed with writing thirty-eight plays, one-hundred-and-fifty-four sonnets and five poems. No original manuscript exists for any of his plays, so it is hard to date them accurately. However, from their contents and reports at the time, it is believed that his first play was ***The Taming of the Shrew*** and that his last complete work was ***Two Noble Kinsmen***, written two years before he died. The cause of his death remains unknown.

He was buried on April 25th 1616, two days after his death, at the Church of the Holy Trinity (the same Church where he had been baptized fifty-two years earlier). His gravestone bears these words, believed to have been written by William himself:-

"Good friend for Jesus sake forbear,
To dig the dust enclosed here!
Blest be the man that spares these stones,
And curst be he that moves my bones"

At the time of his death, William had substantial properties, which he bestowed on his family and associates from the theater.

In his will he left his wife, the former Anne Hathaway, his second best bed!

William Shakespeare's last direct descendant died in 1670. She was his granddaughter, Elizabeth.

Henry V, King of England

(c.1387 - 1422 AD)

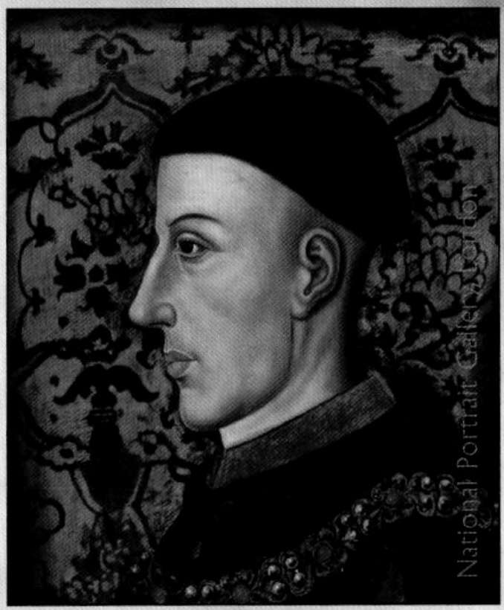
National Portrait Gallery, London

One of the great warrior kings of medieval England, Henry is most famous for his victory against the French at the Battle of Agincourt.

Henry V, the eldest son of Henry IV and Mary Bohun, was born in 1387. He became Prince of Wales at his father's coronation in 1399. Henry was an accomplished soldier: at fourteen he fought the Welsh forces of Owain Glyndwr; in 1403, aged sixteen, he commanded his father's forces at the battle of Shrewsbury. He was also keen to have a role in government, leading to many disagreements with his father. Henry became king in 1413.

In 1415, he successfully crushed an uprising designed to put Edmund Mortimer, Earl of March, on the throne. Shortly afterwards he sailed for France, which was to be the focus of his attentions for most of his reign. Henry was determined to regain the lands in France previously held by his ancestors and so laid his claim to the French throne. The French war served two purposes - to gain lands lost in previous battles and to focus attention away from any of his cousins' royal ambitions.

He first captured the port of Harfleur and then on October 25th 1415 defeated the French at the Battle of Agincourt. Between 1417 and 1419 Henry followed up this success with the conquest of Normandy. Rouen surrendered in January 1419 and his successes forced the French to agree to the Treaty of Troyes in May 1420.

Henry was recognized as heir to the French throne and married Katherine, the daughter of the French king. In February 1421, Henry returned to England for the first time in three-and-a-half years, and he and Katherine undertook a royal progress around the country. In June, he returned to France and died suddenly, probably of dysentery, on August 31st 1422. His nine-month-old son succeeded him as King of England (Henry never saw his child). Had Henry lived a mere two months longer, he would have been king of both England and France.

The Elizabethan historian Rafael Holinshed, in his ***Chronicles of England***, summed up Henry's reign as such: "This Henry was a king, of life without spot, a prince whom all men loved, and of none disdained, a captain against whom fortune never frowned, nor mischance once spurned, whose people him so severe a justicer both loved and obeyed (and so humane withal) that he left no offence unpunished, nor friendship unrewarded; a terror to rebels, and suppressor of sedition, his virtues notable, his qualities most praiseworthy."

The Battle of Agincourt October 25th, 1415 (St. Crispin's Day)

"From the thirteenth until the sixteenth century, the national weapon of the English army was the longbow. It was this weapon which conquered Wales and Scotland, gave the English their victories in the Hundred Years War, and permitted England to replace France as the foremost military power in Medieval Europe. The longbow was the machine gun of the Middle Ages: accurate, deadly, possessed of a long-range and rapid rate of fire, the flight of its missiles was liken to a storm. Cheap and simple enough for the yeoman to own and master, it made him superior to a knight on the field of battle."

The Medieval English Longbow
by Robert E. Kaiser, M.A.

Henry V, King of England, and (according to him and his advisors), parts of France, invaded France on August 13th, 1415 to claim by force his French Kingdom. He first laid siege to the port of Harfleur, in the classic medieval style using primitive cannons (bombards), trenches and ramparts encircling the town's walls. Harfleur finally fell on September 22nd and on October 8th Henry's by now smaller, starving and weary army of some 5,000 archers and 1,000 men-at-arms began a 260-mile march to Calais, hoping to reach England before winter set in.

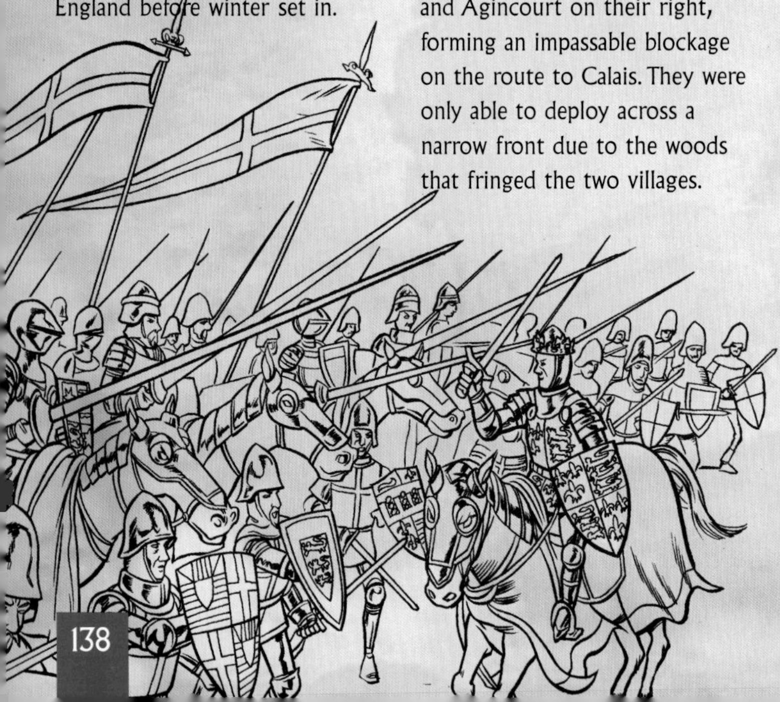

The main French army started from Rouen in pursuit of the English. On October 24th Henry's scouts spotted the French army near the little river of Ternoise, completely blocking the path to Calais. Henry now had no choice but to give battle to the far larger French army of some 15,000-36,000 men (as accurate an estimate as can be given!)

October 25th dawned cold and wet, with the French army drawn up between the villages of Tramecourt on their left flank and Agincourt on their right, forming an impassable blockage on the route to Calais. They were only able to deploy across a narrow front due to the woods that fringed the two villages.

The English army was gathered in between the woods at the other end of the field, roughly a mile from the French.

This meant that the battle took place on recently plowed fields between the woods - a decisive factor in the final outcome.

The French formed three massive divisions (called "battles"), with the first two consisting of dismounted men-at-arms with cavalry on their flanks, and a third division consisting entirely of cavalry. Crossbowmen and archers were to take up position at the front of the divisions.

The French planned to shower the English with arrows, then move in with the flanking cavalry to take out the bowmen of the English army, as the French men-at-arms moved in to dispatch the English infantry.

By 11am the English could wait no longer for a French advance. Henry's troops were tired and weak from hunger, dysentery and the long, wet march; so they advanced to within 250 yards of the French troops. At this point the English archers halted and pounded in pointed wooden stakes (palings) in front of their positions to keep the French cavalry at bay.

Charles d'Albret
Agincourt
Tramecourt
Archers
Archers
Camoys
Henry V
York

The English advance threw the French into confusion and forced the premature charge of the French heavy cavalry. The cavalry advanced slowly in the mud and under a hail of arrows. They tried to outflank the English but were hemmed in by the woods and forced to continue with a frontal assault. They quickly found themselves and their horses impaled upon the stakes and under unremitting fire from the English archers. The English line held and what was left of the French cavalry was forced to withdraw.

The first French division of men-at-arms lumbered forward after the failure of the cavalry assault. The English arrows took their toll but the French finally closed with the English men-at-arms. Many French nobles had already been killed by arrows and, as the line pushed forward, many more men fell and were trampled to death, hampered by their heavy armor.

Initially the impact of the French advance drove the English line back, but they quickly recovered; and the English men-at-arms and archers joined the fray with mallets, axes and swords, easily dispatching the tightly packed and heavily armored columns of French knights. As the first French division was being decimated, the remaining English archers kept up a heavy hail of arrows on the advancing second French division of men-at-arms. The knights in this second division saw what was happening to their comrades and began leaving the field without engaging the English. This left the mounted French third division as the last hope for the French to gain victory from defeat. However attacking the English longbowmen was more than those troops wished to contemplate and they too began drifting away through the Tramecourt Woods.

The English interpreted this movement as a potential threat, with the French moving through the woods and possibly threatening the English from the rear. This news, coupled with reports that the English baggage train had been attacked, led Henry to order the deaths of all the prisoners, as there were not enough soldiers left to guard the prisoners and fend off a further attack.

Many prisoners were killed but some English knights who were horrified by this order saved their prisoners. It is believed that more French deaths took place during this slaughter, than during the battle itself.

By the end of the day it is estimated that between 7,000 and 10,000 French had perished but only 500 English. Henry and his army went on to Calais and then back to England, with a number of French nobles held to ransom.

It was an incredible English victory that would go down in the annals of warfare.

Arguably, the deciding factor for the outcome was the terrain. The narrow field of battle, of recently plowed land hemmed in by dense woodland, favored the English.

However, Shakespeare appears to have exploited a rather different rationale, basing the victory on the will of God, given that Henry's cause was just.

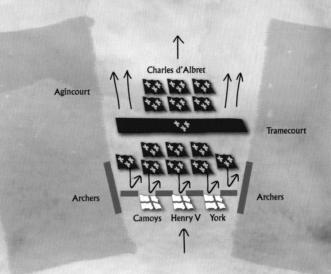

Page Creation

In order to create three versions of the same book, the play is first adapted into three scripts: Original Text, Plain Text and Quick Text. While the degree of complexity changes for each script, the artwork remains the same for all three books.

Above is a rough thumbnail sketch of pages 86 and 87 created from the script. Once the rough sketch is approved it is redrawn as a clean finished pencil sketch (left).

318.	Henry kneels inside his tent. He joins his hands in prayer.		
	QUICK TEXT	**PLAIN ENGLISH TEXT**	**ORIGINAL TEXT**
HENRY (TH)	And don't let the way my father took the crown from Richard II go against me now. I've re-buried Richard's body in Westminster Abbey. I've cried with regret and I've given 500 pensions to the holy poor to pray for my father's pardon.	Not today, Oh Lord. Don't think today about my father's fault in taking the crown! I've re-buried Richard II's body in Westminster Abbey and I've cried more remorseful tears on it than the drops of blood it spilled. I've given pensions to 500 paupers to pray twice daily to heaven for my father's pardon...	Not to-day, O Lord! O! not to-day, think not upon the fault My father made in compassing the crown. I Richard's body have interred new; And on it have bestow'd more contrite tears Than from it issued forced drops of blood. Five hundred poor I have in yearly pay, Who twice a day their wither'd hands hold up Toward heaven, to pardon blood;
319.	The Duke of Gloucester (Henry's brother) enters the tent and watches the King in prayer.		
HENRY (TH)	I've built two chapels where priests sing and pray for Richard's soul. And I'll do more. I'll do more, even if it's all for nothing...	...and I've built two chapels where devout priests sing and pray for Richard's soul. I'll do even more, even if everything I do means nothing, since it's all just a plea for personal pardon.	and I have built Two chantries, where the sad and solemn priests Sing still for Richard's soul. More will I do; Though all that I can do is nothing worth, Since that my penitence comes after all, Imploring pardon.
GLOUCESTER	My lord!	My liege!	My liege!
320.	Henry doesn't look up.		
HENRY	That's my brother Gloucester's voice. I know what you want. I'll go with you, because everything waits for me.	My brother Gloucester's voice? Yes, I know what you want. I'll go with you. The day, my friends, and all other things wait for me.	My brother Gloucester's voice? —Ay; I know thy errand, I will go with thee:— The day, my friends, and all things stay for me.

From the pencil sketch we can now create an inked version of the same page (below).

Inking is not simply tracing over the pencil sketch, it is the process of using black ink to fill in the shaded areas and to add clarity and cohesion to the "pencils".

The "inks" give us the final outline and the next stage is to add color to the inked image.

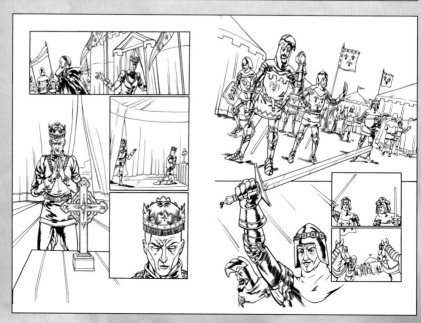

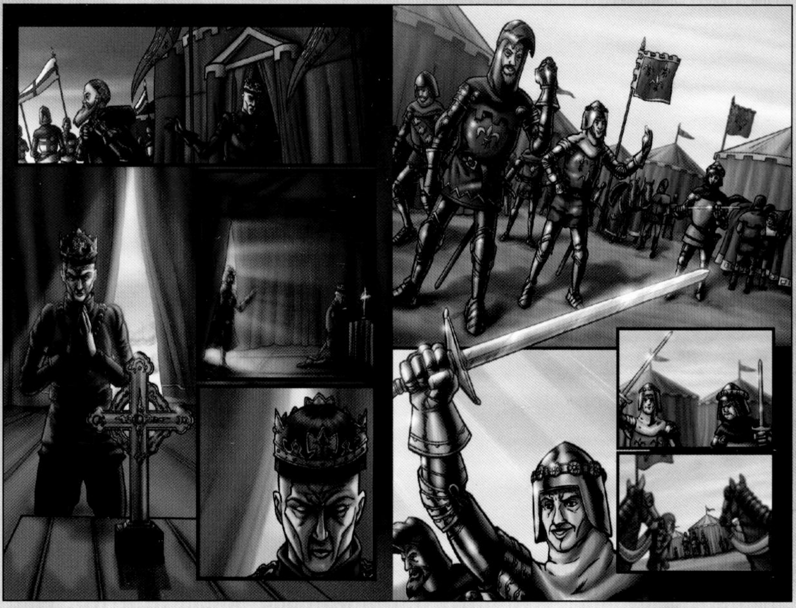

Adding color brings the page and its characters to life.

Each character has a detailed Character Study drawn. This is useful for the inkers and the colorists to refer to and ensures continuity throughout the book.

The last stage of page creation is to add the speech and any sound effects.

Speech bubbles are created from the script and are laid over the finished colored pages.

Three versions of lettered pages are produced for the three different versions of ***Henry V***. These are then saved as final artwork pages and compiled into books.

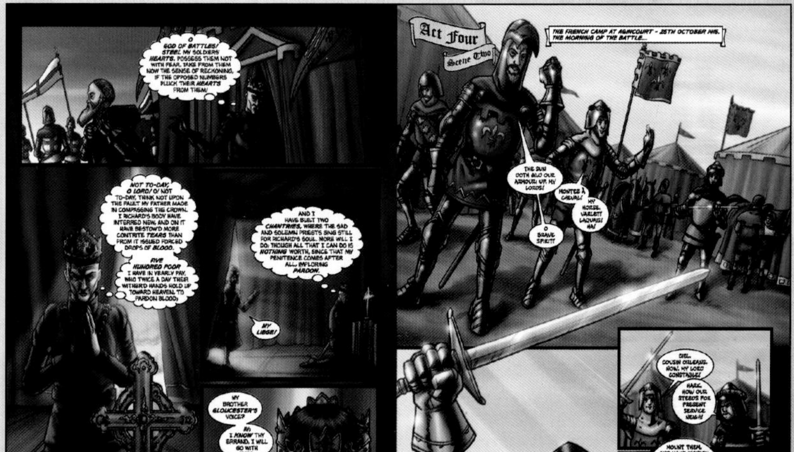

O GOD OF BATTLES! STEEL MY SOLDIERS' HEARTS. POSSESS THEM NOT WITH FEAR. TAKE FROM THEM NOW THE SENSE OF RECKONING, IF THE OPPOSED NUMBERS PLUCK THEIR HEARTS FROM THEM!
NOT TO-DAY, O LORD! O! NOT TO-DAY, THINK NOT UPON THE FAULT MY FATHER MADE IN COMPASSING THE CROWN. I RICHARD'S BODY HAVE INTERRED NEW, AND ON IT HAVE BESTOW'D MORE CONTRITE TEARS THAN FROM IT ISSUED FORCED DROPS OF BLOOD.
FIVE HUNDRED POOR I HAVE IN YEARLY PAY, WHO TWICE A DAY THEIR WITHER'D HANDS HOLD UP TOWARD HEAVEN, TO PARDON BLOOD;
AND I HAVE BUILT TWO CHANTRIES, WHERE THE SAD AND SOLEMN PRIESTS SING STILL FOR RICHARD'S SOUL. MORE WILL I DO; THOUGH ALL THAT I CAN DO IS NOTHING WORTH, SINCE THAT MY PENITENCE COMES AFTER ALL, IMPLORING PARDON.
MY LIEGE!
MY BROTHER GLOUCESTER'S VOICE?
AY; I KNOW THY ERRAND, I WILL GO WITH THEE:
THE DAY, MY FRIENDS, AND ALL THINGS STAY FOR ME.
86
Act Four
Scene Two
THE FRENCH CAMP AT AGINCOURT - 25TH OCTOBER 1415. THE MORNING OF THE BATTLE...
THE SUN DOTH GILD OUR ARMOUR; UP, MY LORDS!
MONTEZ À CHEVAL!
MY HORSE, VARLET! LAQUAIS! HA!
O BRAVE SPIRIT!
CIEL, COUSIN ORLEANS. NOW, MY LORD CONSTABLE!
HARK, HOW OUR STEEDS FOR PRESENT SERVICE NEIGH!
MOUNT THEM, AND MAKE INCISION IN THEIR HIDES, THAT THEIR HOT BLOOD MAY SPIN IN ENGLISH EYES, AND DOUT THEM WITH SUPERFLUOUS COURAGE. HA!
VIA! — LES EAUX ET LA TERRE.
87

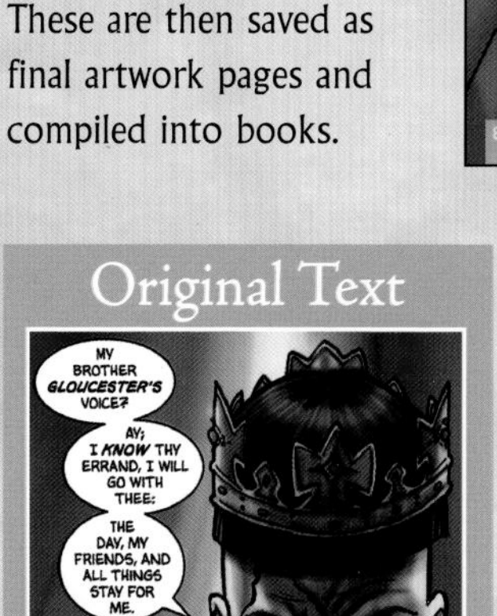

Original Text
MY BROTHER GLOUCESTER'S VOICE?
AY; I KNOW THY ERRAND, I WILL GO WITH THEE:
THE DAY, MY FRIENDS, AND ALL THINGS STAY FOR ME.

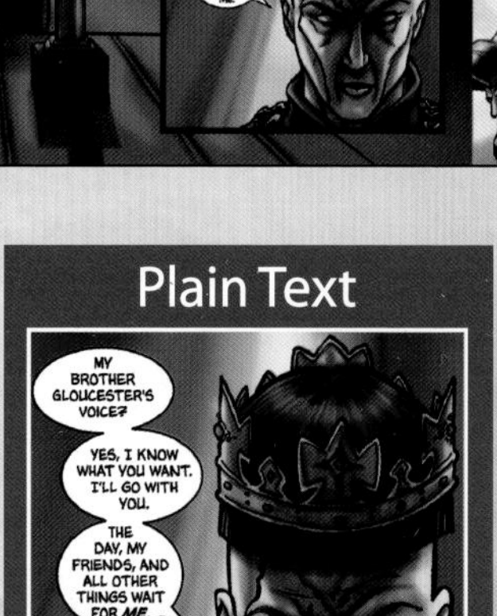

Plain Text
MY BROTHER GLOUCESTER'S VOICE?
YES, I KNOW WHAT YOU WANT. I'LL GO WITH YOU.
THE DAY, MY FRIENDS, AND ALL OTHER THINGS WAIT FOR ME.

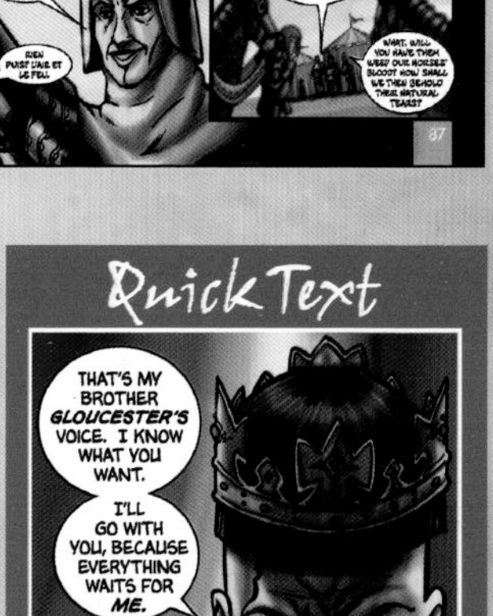

Quick Text
THAT'S MY BROTHER GLOUCESTER'S VOICE. I KNOW WHAT YOU WANT.
I'LL GO WITH YOU, BECAUSE EVERYTHING WAITS FOR ME.

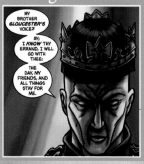

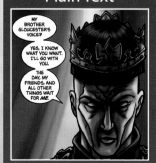

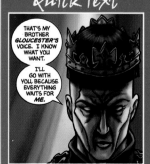

Shakespeare Around the Globe

The Globe Theatre and Shakespeare

It is hard to appreciate today how theaters were actually a new idea in William Shakespeare's time. The very first theater in Elizabethan London to show only plays, aptly called "The Theatre", was introduced by an entrepreneur by the name of James Burbage. In fact, "The Globe Theatre", possibly the most famous theater of that era, was built from the timbers of "The Theatre". The landlord of "The Theatre" was Giles Allen, a Puritan who disapproved of theatrical entertainment. When he decided to enforce a huge rent increase in the winter of 1598, the theater members dismantled the building piece by piece and shipped it across the Thames to Southwark for reassembly. Allen was powerless to do anything, as the company owned the wood - although he spent three years in court trying to sue the perpetrators!

The report of the dismantling party (written by Schoenbaum) says: **"ryotous... armed... with divers and manye unlawfull and offensive weapons... in verye ryotous outragious and forcyble manner and contrarye to the lawes of your highnes Realme... and there pulling breaking and throwing downe the sayd Theater in verye outragious violent and riotous sort to the great disturbance and terrefyeing not onlye of your subjectes... but of divers others of your majesties loving subjectes there neere inhabitinge."**

William Shakespeare became a part owner of this new Globe Theatre in 1599. It was one of four major theaters in the area, along with the Swan, the Rose, and the Hope. The exact physical structure of the Globe is unknown, although scholars are fairly sure of some details through drawings from the period. The theater itself was a closed structure with an open courtyard where the stage stood. Tiered galleries around the open area accommodated the wealthier patrons who could afford seats, and those of the lower classes - the "groundlings" - stood around the platform or "thrust" stage during the performance of a play. The space under and behind the stage was used for special effects, storage and costume changes. Surprisingly, although the entire structure was not very big by modern standards, it is known to have accommodated fairly large crowds - as many as 3,000 people - during a single performance.

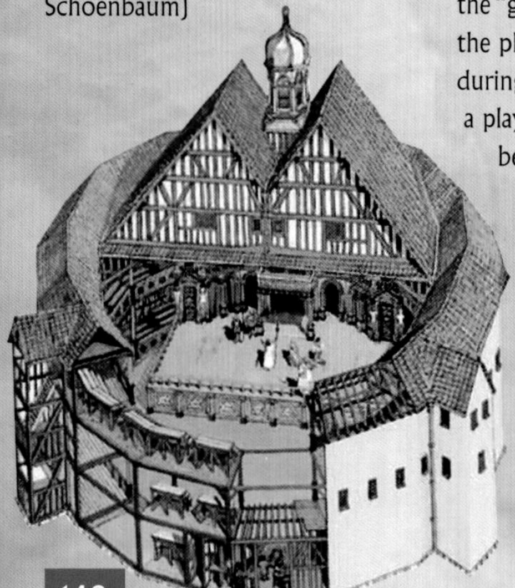

The Globe II

In 1613, the original Globe Theatre burned to the ground when a cannon shot during a performance of ***Henry VIII*** set fire to the thatched roof of the gallery. Undeterred, the company completed a new Globe (this time with a tiled roof) on the foundations of its predecessor. Shakespeare didn't write any new plays for this theater. He retired to Stratford-Upon-Avon that year, and died two years later. Performances continued until 1642, when the Puritans closed down all theaters and places of entertainment. Two years later, the Puritans razed the building to the ground in order to build tenements upon the site. No more was to be seen of the Globe for 352 years.

Shakespeare's Globe

Led by the vision of the late Sam Wanamaker, work began on the construction of a new Globe in 1993, close to the site of the original theater. It was completed three years later, and Queen Elizabeth II officially opened the New Globe Theatre on June 12th 1997 with a production of ***Henry V.***

The New Globe Theatre is as faithful a reproduction as possible to the Elizabethan theater, given that the details of the original are only known from sketches of the time. The building can accommodate 1,500 people between the galleries and the "groundlings".

www.shakespeares-globe.org

There are also replica Globe theaters in Rome and Berlin and The Old Globe in San Diego. In New York, ambitious plans are underway to convert a decaying military fortification, built to defend America against the British in the War of 1812, into a New Globe – and amazingly, the existing structure has an identical footprint to Shakespeare's Globe Theatre in London.

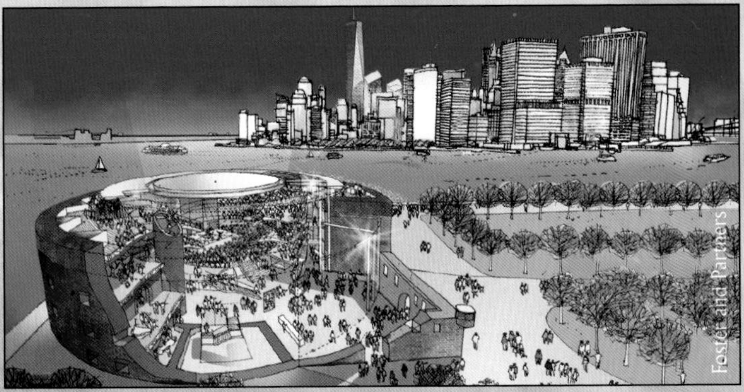
Foster and Partners

New Globe Theater, New York

Shakespeare Today

Our fascination with William Shakespeare has not diminished over the centuries. Despite being written over 400 years ago, his plays are still read in schools, adapted into graphic novels(!), made into films, performed in theaters the world over, and are still taken to the public by acting troupes, such as **the British Shakespeare Company**. The tradition of open-air theater is deeply rooted in British culture. For over a thousand years companies have created theaters in the center of towns, erecting a pageant wagon or scaffolding stage from which to perform great historical and classical drama for a mass audience. These open-air acting troupes, which weathered the theatrical shifts from medieval Mystery and Morality plays to the sophisticated characterization of Elizabethan drama, were the inspiration behind the British Shakespeare Company (BSC). The pageant wagons, and later inn-yards and amphitheaters outside London, were for centuries the only means by which Shakespeare and others could communicate with audiences beyond the capital. Today, more than 100,000 people watch BSC performances each year. With a full company of players and performances that feature original live music and songs, beautiful period costumes and the magic of a summer's evening, the BSC is fulfilling that primary aim of all performers throughout the years: to enchant and delight audiences of all classes and ages. **www.britishshakespearecompany.com**

The Lord Chamberlain's Men are another open-air performance troupe, with the interesting, but authentic twist that all the parts are played by men (as was the case in Shakespeare's day). **www.tcm.co.uk**

In America, New York has Shakespeare in the Park. Since 1962, The Public Theater has staged productions of Shakespeare at The Delacorte Theater in Central Park. These performances are seen by approximately 80,000 New Yorkers and visitors each summer. In fact, since its inception, any of today's most acclaimed actors have taken part, including Patrick Stewart, Morgan Freeman, Meryl Streep, Denzel Washington, Kevin Kline and Jeff Goldblum. **www.publictheater.org**

Since 1997, Shakespeare 4 Kidz have been successfully providing an education in Shakespeare to children and young people all over the UK, and across the globe. Their unique approach has proved a hit with kids and adults alike. Their musicals have brought The Bard's work to life for thousands of people, and their creative education package is used extensively by teachers and education authorities throughout the UK. **www.shakespeare4kidz.com**

It seems that whatever time brings to our global society, and whatever developments take place within our cultures, William Shakespeare continues to have a place in our hearts and in our lives.

A UK publisher creating graphic novel adaptations of literary classics.
True to the original vision of the authors, our books have been further enhanced by using only the finest artists - giving you a truly wonderful reading experience that you'll return to again and again.

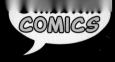

Henry V is available in three text formats, all using the same high quality artwork:

Henry
V
THE GRAPHIC NOVEL

Original Text
WE DOUBT NOT OF A FAIR AND LUCKY WAR, SINCE GOD SO GRACIOUSLY HATH BROUGHT TO LIGHT THIS DANGEROUS TREASON LURKING IN OUR WAY TO HINDER OUR BEGINNINGS: WE DOUBT NOT NOW BUT EVERY RUB IS SMOOTHED ON OUR WAY.
THEN FORTH, DEAR COUNTRYMEN! LET US DELIVER OUR PUISSANCE INTO THE HAND OF GOD, PUTTING IT STRAIGHT IN EXPEDITION. CHEERLY TO SEA! THE SIGNS OF WAR ADVANCE!
NO KING OF ENGLAND, IF NOT KING OF FRANCE!

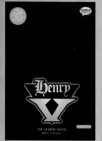

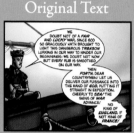

Original Text

This is the full, original script - just as The Bard intended. This version is ideal for purists, students and for readers who want to experience the unaltered text; but unlike a cold script, our beautiful artwork turns reading the play into a much more fulfilling experience. All of the text, all of the excitement!

Henry
V
THE GRAPHIC NOVEL
Plain Text

Plain Text
THERE'S NO DOUBT NOW THAT ALL OBSTACLES HAVE BEEN REMOVED. SO, MY COUNTRYMEN, LET'S GO!
LET'S DELIVER OUR ARMY INTO THE HAND OF GOD AND BEGIN OUR EXPEDITION IMMEDIATELY. AWAY TO SEA, WITH OUR WARLIKE ADVANCE!
I WON'T BE KING OF ENGLAND, IF I'M NOT ALSO KING OF FRANCE!

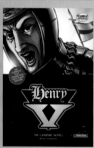

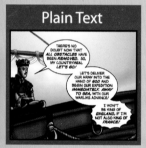

Plain Text

We take the original script and "convert" it into modern English, verse-for-verse. If you've ever wanted to fully appreciate the works of Shakespeare, but find the original language rather cryptic, then this is the version for you! This adaptation is ideal to help you fully understand the original text.

Henry
V
THE GRAPHIC NOVEL
Quick Text

Quick Text
THERE'S NOTHING ELSE IN OUR WAY, SO LET'S ADVANCE.
I WON'T BE KING OF ENGLAND, IF I'M NOT ALSO KING OF FRANCE!

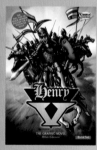

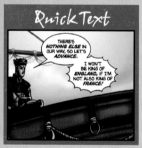

Quick Text

A revolution in graphic novels! We take the dialogue and reduce it to as few words as possible, but still retain the full essence of the story. This version allows readers to enter into and enjoy the stories quickly; and because the word balloons are smaller than in the other text versions, it also allows the fullest appreciation of our stunning artwork.

Classical Comics – Bringing Classics to Life!

OTHER CLASSICAL COMICS TITLES:

Macbeth

Macbeth
THE GRAPHIC NOVEL

Published November 2008

A Christmas Carol

A Christmas Carol

Published November 2008

Jane Eyre

Jane Eyre

Published December 2008

Frankenstein

Frankenstein
THE GRAPHIC NOVEL

Published December 2008

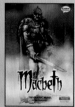

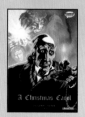

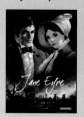

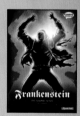